Other Earths

Other Titles in the Leonaur Collected Science Fiction & Fantasy of Stanley G. Weinbaum Series

Volume 1: Interplanetary Odysseys
Volume 3: Strange Genius
Volume 4: The Black Heart

THE COLLECTED SCIENCE FICTION & FANTASY OF STANLEY G. WEINBAUM: VOLUME 2

Other Earths

Classic Futuristic Tales Including:
Dawn of Flame and its Sequel *The Black Flame,*
Plus *The Revolution of 1960* and Others

Stanley G. Weinbaum

LEONAUR

Other Earths: Classic Futuristic Tales Including: Dawn of Flame and its Sequel The Black Flame, Plus The Revolution of 1960 and Others
by Stanley G. Weinbaum

FIRST EDITION

Published by Leonaur Ltd

ISBN (10 digit): 1-84677-072-6 (hardcover)
ISBN (13 digit): 978-1-84677-072-2 (hardcover)

ISBN (10 digit): 1-84677-062-9 (softcover)
ISBN (13 digit): 978-1-84677-062-3 (softcover)

http://www.leonaur.com

Publisher's Notes

In the interests of authenticity, the spellings, grammar and place names used by the author have been retained.

The views expressed in this book are not necessarily those of the publisher.

Contents

Dawn of Flame	7
The Black Flame	77
Revolution of 1960	225
Smothered Seas	275
Shifting Seas	306

Dawn of Flame

1. The World

Hull Tarvish looked backward but once, and that only as he reached the elbow of the road. The sprawling little stone cottage that had been home was visible as he had seen it a thousand times, framed under the cedars. His mother still watched him, and two of his younger brothers stood staring down the Mountainside at him. He raised his hand in farewell, then dropped it as he realized that none of them saw him now; his mother had turned indifferently to the door, and the two youngsters had spied a rabbit. He faced about and strode away, down the slope out of Ozarky.

He passed the place where the great steel road of the Ancients had been, now only two rusty streaks and a row of decayed logs. Beside it was the mossy heap of stones that had been an ancient structure in the days before the Dark Centuries, when Ozarky had been a part of the old state of M'souri. The mountain people still sought out the place for squared stones to use in building, but the tough metal of the steel road itself was too stubborn for their use, and the rails had rusted quietly these three hundred years.

That much Hull Tarvish knew, for they were things still spoken of at night around the fireplace. They had been mighty sorcerers, those Ancients; their steel roads went everywhere, and everywhere were the ruins of their towns, built, it was said, by a magic that lifted weights. Down in the valley, he knew, men were still seeking that magic; once a rider had stayed by night at the Tarvish home, a little man who said that in the far south the secret had been found, but nobody ever heard any more of it.

So Hull whistled to himself, shifted the rag bag on his shoulder, set his bow more comfortably on his mighty back, and trudged on. That was why he himself was seeking the valley; he wanted to see what the world was like. He had been always a restless sort, not at all like the other six Tarvish sons, nor like the three Tarvish daughters. They were true mountainies, the sons great hunters, and the daughters stolid and industrious. Not Hull, however; he was neither lazy like his brothers nor stolid like his sisters, but restless, curious, dreamy. So he whistled his way into the world, and was happy.

At evening he stopped at the Hobel cottage on the edge of the mountains. Away before him stretched the plain, and in the darkening distance was visible the church spire of Norse. That was a village; Hull had never seen a village, or no more of it than this same distant steeple, shaped like a straight white pine. But he had heard all about Norse, because the mountainies occasionally went down there to buy powder and ball for their rifles, those of them who had rifles.

Hull had only a bow. He didn't see the use of guns; powder and ball cost money, but an arrow did the same work for nothing, and that without scaring all the game a mile away.

Morning he bade goodbye to the Hobels, who thought him, as they always had, a little crazy, and set off. His powerful, brown bare legs flashed under his ragged trousers, his bare feet made a pleasant soosh in the dust of the road, the June sun beat warm on his right cheek. He was happy; there never was a pleasanter world than this, so he grinned and whistled, and spat carefully into the dust, remembering that it was bad luck to spit toward the sun. He was bound for adventure.

Adventure came. Hull had come down to the plain now, where the trees were taller than the scrub of the hill country, and where the occasional farms were broader, well tilled, more prosperous. The trail had become a wagon road, and here it cut and angled between two lines of forest. And unexpectedly a man—no, two men—rose from a log at the roadside and approached Hull. He watched them; one was tall and light-haired as himself, but without his mighty frame, and the other was a head shorter, and dark. Valley people, surely, for the dark one had a stubby pistol at his belt, wooden-stocked like those of the Ancients, and the tall man's bow was of glittering spring steel.

"Ho, mountainy!" said the dark one. "Where going?"

"Norse," answered Hull shortly,

"What's in the bag?"

"My tongue,"* snapped the youth.

"Easy, there," grunted the light man. "No offense, mountainy. We're just curious. That's a good knife you got. I'll trade it."

---

* Idiom of the of the second century of the Enlightement. To "have one's tongue in the bag" was to refuse to answer questions.

"For what?"

"For lead in your craw," growled the dark one. Suddenly the blunt pistol was in his hand. "Pass it over, and the bag too."

Hull scowled from one to the other. At last he shrugged, and moved as if to lift his bag from his shoulders. And then, swift as the thrust of a striking diamondback, his left foot shot forward, catching the dark one squarely in the pit of his stomach, with the might of Hull's muscles and weight behind it.

The man had breath for a low grunt; he doubled and fell, while his weapon spun a dozen feet away into the dust. The light one sprang for it, but Hull caught him with a great arm about his throat, wrenched twice, and the brief fight was over. He swung placidly on toward Norse with a blunt revolver primed and capped at his hip, a glistening spring-steel bow on his shoulder, and twenty-two bright tubular steel arrows in his quiver.

He topped a little rise and the town lay before him. He stared. A hundred houses at least. Must be five hundred people in the town, more people than he'd ever seen in his life all together. He strode eagerly on, goggling at the church that towered high as a tall tree, at the windows of bits of glass salvaged from ancient ruins and carefully pieced together, at the tavern with its swinging emblem of an unbelievably fat man holding a mammoth mug. He stared at the houses, some of them with shops before them, and at the people, most of them shod in leather.

He himself attracted little attention. Norse was used to the mountainies, and only a girl or two turned appraising eyes toward his mighty figure. That made him uncomfortable, however; the girls of the mountains giggled and blushed, but never at that age did they stare at a man. So he gazed defiantly back, letting his eyes wander from their bonnets to the billowing skirts above their leather strap-sandals, and they laughed and passed on.

Hull didn't care for Norse, he decided. As the sun set, the houses loomed too close, as if they'd stifle him, so he set out into the countryside to sleep. The remains of an ancient town bordered the village, with its spectral walls crumbling against the west. There were ghosts there, of course, so he walked farther, found a wooded spot, and lay down, putting his bow and the steel arrows into his bag against the rusting effect of night-dew. Then he tied the bag about his bare feet and legs, sprawled comfortably, and slept with his hand on the pistol grip. Of course there were no animals to fear in these woods save wolves, and they never attacked humans during the warm parts of the year, but there were men, and they *bound* themselves by no such seasonal laws.

He awoke dewy wet. The sun shot golden lances through the trees, and he was ravenously hungry. He ate the last of his mother's brown bread from his bag, now crumbled by his feet, and then strode out to the road. There was a wagon creaking there, plodding northward; the bearded, kindly man in it was glad enough to have him ride for company.

"Mountainy?" he asked.

"Yes."

"Bound where?"

"The world," said Bull.

"Well," observed the other, "it's a big place, and all I've seen of it much like this. All except Selui. That's a city. Yes, that's a city. Been there?"

"No."

"It's got," said the farmer impressively, "twenty thousand people in it. Maybe more. And they got ruins there the biggest you ever saw. Bridges. Buildings. Four—five times as high as the Norse church, and at that they're fallen down. The Devil knows how high they used to be in the old days."

"Who lived in 'em?" asked Hull.

"Don't know. Who'd want to live so high up it'd take a full morning to climb there? Unless it was magic. I don't hold much with magic, but they do say the Old People knew how to fly."

Hull tried to imagine this. For a while there was silence save for the slow clump of the horses' hooves. "I don't believe it," he said at last.

"Nor I. But did you hear what they're saying in Norse?"

"I didn't hear anything."

"They say," said the farmer, "that Joaquin Smith is going to march again."

"Joaquin Smith!"

"Yeah. Even the mountainies know about him, eh?"

"Who doesn't?" returned Hull. "Then there'll be fighting in the south, I guess. I have a notion to go south."

"Why?"

"I like fighting," said Hull simply.

"Fair answer," said the farmer, "but from what folks say, there's not much fighting when the Master marches. He has a spell; there's great sorcery in N'Orleans, from the merest warlock up to Martin Sair, who's blood-son of the Devil himself, or so they say."

"I'd like to see his sorcery against the mountainy's arrow and ball," said Hull grimly. "There's none of us can't spot either eye at a thousand paces, using rifle. Or two hundred with arrow."

"No doubt; but what if powder flames, and guns fire themselves before he's even across the horizon? They say he has a spell for that, he or Black Margot."

"Black Margot?"

"The Princess, his half-sister. The dark witch who rides beside him, the Princess Margaret."

"Oh—but why Black Margot?"

The farmer shrugged. "Who knows? It's what her enemies call her."

"Then so I call her," said Hull.

"Well, I don't know," said the other. "It makes small difference to me whether I pay taxes to N'Orleans or to gruff old Marcus Ormiston, who's eldarch of Ormiston village there." He flicked his whip toward the distance ahead, where Hull now descried houses and the flash of a little river. "I've sold produce in towns within the Empire, and the people of them seemed as happy as ourselves, no more, no less."

"There is a difference, though. It's freedom."

"Merely a word, my friend. They plow, they sow, they reap, just as we do. They hunt, they fish, they fight. And as for freedom, are they less free with a warlock to rule them than I with a wizened fool?"

"The mountainies pay taxes to no one."

"And no one builds them roads, nor digs them public wells. Where you pay little you get less, and I will say that the roads within the Empire are better than ours."

"Better than this?" asked Hull, staring at the dusty width of the highway.

"Far better. Near Memphis town is a road of solid rock, which they spread soft through some magic, and let harden, so there is neither mud nor dust."

Hull mused over this. "The Master," he burst out suddenly, "is he really immortal?"

The other shrugged. "How can I say? There are great sorcerers in the southlands, and the greatest of them is Martin Sair. But I do know this, that I have seen sixty-two years, and as far back as memory goes here was always Joaquin Smith in the south, and always an Empire gobbling cities as a hare gobbles carrots. When I was young it was far away, now it reaches close at hand; that is all the difference. Men talked of the beauty of Black Margot then as they do now, and of the wizardry of Martin Sair.

Hull made no answer, for Ormiston was at hand. The village was much like Norse save that it huddled among low hills, on the crest of some of which loomed ancient ruins. At the near side his companion halted, and Hull thanked him as he leaped to the ground.

"Where to?" asked the farmer.

Hull thought a moment. "Selui," he said.

"Well, it's a hundred miles, but there'll be many to ride you."

"I have my own feet," said the youth. He spun suddenly about at a voice across the road: "Hi! Mountainy!"

It was a girl. A very pretty girl, slim waisted, copper haired, blue eyed, standing at the gate before a large stone house. "Hi!" she called. "Will you work for your dinner?"

Hull was ravenous again. "Gladly!" he cried.

The voice of the farmer sounded behind him. "It's Vail Ormiston, the dotard eldarch's daughter. Hold her for a full meal, mountainy. My taxes are paying for it."

But Vail Ormiston was above much converse with a wandering mountain-man. She surveyed his mighty form approvingly, showed him the logs he was to quarter, and then disappeared into the house. If, perchance, she peeped out through the clearest of the ancient glass fragments that formed the window, and if she watched the flexing muscles of his great bare arms as he swung the axe—well, he was unaware of it.

So it happened that afternoon found him trudging toward Selui with a hearty meal inside him and three silver dimes in his pocket, ancient money, with the striding figure of the woman all but worn away. He was richer than when he had set out by those coins, by the blunt pistol at his hip, by the shiny steel bow and arrows, and by the memory of the copper hair and blue eyes of Vail Ormiston.

2. Old Einar

Three weeks in Selui had served to give Hull Tarvish a sort of speaking acquaintancy with the place. He no longer gaped at the sky-piercing ruins of the ancient city, or the vast fallen bridges, and he was quite at home in the town that lay beside it. He had found work easily enough in a baker's establishment, where his great muscles served well; the hours were long, but his pay was munificent—five silver quarters a week. He paid two for lodging, and food—what he needed beyond the burnt loaves at hand from his employment cost him another quarter, but that left two to put by. He never gambled other than a wager now and then on his own marksmanship, and that was more profitable than otherwise.

Ordinarily Hull was quick to make friends, but his long hours hindered him. He had but one, an incredibly old man who sat at evening on the step beyond his lodging, Old Einar. So this evening Hull wandered out as usual to join him, staring at the crumbling towers of the Ancients glowing in the sunset. Trees sprung on many, and all were green with vine and tussock and the growth of wind-carried seeds. No one dared build among the ruins, for none could guess when a great tower might come crashing down.

"I wonder," he said to Old Einar, "what the Ancients were like. Were they men like us? Then how could they fly?"

"They were men like us, Hull. As for flying—well, it's my belief that flying is a legend. See here; there was a man supposed to have flown over the cold lands to the north and those to the south, and also across the great sea. But this flying man is called in some accounts Lindbird and in others Bird and surely one can see the origin of such a legend. The migrations of birds, who cross land and seas each year, that is all."

"Or perhaps magic," suggested Hull.

"There is no magic. The Ancients themselves denied it and I have struggled through many a moldy book in a curious, archaic tongue."

Old Einar was the first scholar Hull had ever encountered. Though there were many during the dawn of that brilliant age called the Second Enlightenment, most of them were still within the Empire. John Holland was dead, but Olin was yet alive in the world, and Kohlmar, and Jorgensen, and Teran, and Martin Sair, and Joaquin Smith the Master. Great names—the names of demigods.

But Hull knew little of them. "You can read!" he exclaimed. "That in itself is a sort of magic. And you have been within the Empire, even in N'Orleans. Tell me, what is the Great City like? Have they really learned the secrets of the Ancients? Are the Immortals truly immortal? How did they gain their knowledge?"

Old Einar settled himself on the step and puffed blue smoke from his pipe filled with the harsh tobacco of the region. "Too many questions breed answers to none," he observed. "Shall I tell you the true story of the world, Hull—the story called History?"

"Yes. In Ozarky we spoke little of such things."

"Well," said the old man comfortably, "I will begin then, at what to us is the beginning, but to the Ancients was the end. I do not know what factors, what wars, what struggles, led up to the mighty world that died during the Dark Centuries, but I do know that three hundred years ago the world reached its climax. You cannot imagine such a place, Hull. It was a time of vast cities, too—fifty times as large as N'Orleans with its hundred thousand people."

He puffed slowly. "Great steel wagons roared over the iron roads of the Ancients. Men crossed the oceans to east and west. The cities were full of whirring wheels, and instead of the many little city-states of our time, there were giant nations with thousands of cities and a hundred million—a hundred and fifty million people."

Hull stared. "I do not believe there are so many people in the world," he said.

Old Einar shrugged. "Who knows?" he returned. "The ancient books—all too few—tell us that the world is round, and that beyond the seas lie one, or several continents, but what races are there today not even Joaquin Smith can say." He puffed smoke again. "Well, such was the ancient world. These were warlike nations, so fond of battle that they had to write many books about the horrors of war to keep themselves at peace, but they always failed. During the time they called their twentieth century there was a whole series of wars, not such little quarrels as we have so often between our city states, nor even such as that between the Memphis League and the Empire, five years ago.

Their wars spread like storm clouds around the world, and were fought between millions of men with unimaginable weapons that flung destruction a hundred miles, and with ships on the seas, and with gases."

"What's gases?" asked Hull.

Old Einar waved his hand so that the wind of it brushed the youth's brown cheek. "Air is a gas," he said. "They knew how to poison the air so that all who breathed it died. And they fought with diseases, and legend says that they fought also in the air with wings, but that is only legend."

"Diseases!" said Hull. "Diseases are the breath of Devils, and if they controlled Devils they used sorcery, and therefore they knew magic."

"There is no magic," reiterated the old man. "I do not know how they fought each other with diseases, but Martin Sair of N'Orleans knows. That was his study, not mine, but I know there was no magic in it." He resumed his tale. "So these great fierce nations flung themselves against each other, for war meant more to them than to us. With us it is something of a rough, joyous, dangerous game, but to them it was a passion. They fought for any reason, or for none at all save the love of fighting."

"I love fighting," said Hull.

"Yes, but would you love it if it meant simply the destroying of thousands of men beyond the horizon? Men you were never to see?"

"No. War should be man to man, or at least no farther than the carry of a rifle ball."

"True. Well, some time near the end of their twentieth century, the ancient world exploded into war like a powder horn in a fire. They say every nation fought, and battles surged back and forth across seas and continents. It was not only nation against nation, but race against race, black and white and yellow and red, all embroiled in a titanic struggle."

"Yellow and red?" echoed Hull. "There are a few black men called Nigs in Ozarky, but I never heard of yellow or red men."

"I have seen yellow men," said Old Einar. "There are some towns of yellow men on the edge of the western ocean, in the region called Friscia. The red race, they say, is gone, wiped out by the plague called the Grey Death, to which they yielded more readily than the other races."

"I have heard of the Grey Death," said Hull. "When I was very young, there was an old, old man who used to say that his grandfather had lived in the days of the Death."

Old Einar smiled. "I doubt it, Hull. It was something over two and a half centuries ago. However," he resumed, "the great ancient nations were at war, and as I say, they fought with diseases. Whether some nation learned the secret of the Grey Death, or whether it grew up as a sort of cross between two or more other diseases, I do not know. Martin Sair says that diseases are living things, so it may be so. At any rate, the Grey Death leaped suddenly across the world, striking alike at all people. Everywhere it blasted the armies, the cities, the countryside, and of those it struck, six out of every ten died. There must have been chaos in the world; we have not a single book printed during that time, and only legend tells the story.

"But the war collapsed. Armies suddenly found themselves unopposed, and then were blasted before they could move. Ships in mid-ocean were stricken, and drifted unmanned to pile in wreckage, or to destroy others. In the cities the dead were piled in the streets, and after a while, were simply left where they fell, while those who survived fled away into the country. What remained of the armies became little better than roving robber bands, and by the third year of the plague there were few if any stable governments in the world."

"What stopped it?" asked Hull.

"I do not know. They end, these pestilences. Those who take it and live cannot take it a second time, and those who are somehow immune do not take it at all, and the rest—die. The Grey Death swept the world for three years; when it ended, according to Martin Sair, one person in four had died. But the plague came back in lessening waves for many years; only a pestilence in the Ancient's fourteenth century, called the Black Death, seems ever to have equaled it.

"Yet its effects were only beginning. The ancient transport system had simply collapsed, and the cities were starving. Hungry gangs began raiding the countryside, and instead of one vast war there were now a million little battles. The weapons of the Ancients were everywhere, and these battles were fierce enough, in all truth, though nothing like the colossal encounters of the great war. Year by year the cities decayed until by the fiftieth year after the Grey Death, the world's population had fallen by three-fourths, and civilization was ended. It was barbarism now that ruled the world, but only barbarism, not savagery. People still remembered the mighty ancient civilization, and everywhere there were attempts to combine into the old nations, but these failed for lack of great leaders."

"As they should fail," said Hull. "We have freedom now."

"Perhaps. By the first century after the Plague, there was little left of the Ancients save their ruined cities where lurked robber bands that scoured the country by night. They had little interest in anything save food or the coined money of the old nations, and they did incalculable damage. Few could read, and on cold nights it was usual to raid the ancient libraries for books to burn and to make things worse, fire gutted the ruins of all cities, and there was no organized resistance to it. The flames simply burned themselves out, and priceless books vanished."

"Yet in N'Orleans they study, don't they?" asked Hull.

"Yes, I'm coming to that. About two centuries after the Plague—a hundred years ago, that is—the world had stabilized itself. It was much as it is here today, with little farming towns and vast stretches of deserted country. Gunpowder had been rediscovered, rifles were used, and most of the robber bands had been destroyed. And then, into the town of N'Orleans, built beside the ancient city, came young John Holland.

"Holland was a rare specimen, anxious for learning. He found the remains of an ancient library and began slowly to decipher the archaic words in the few books that had survived. Little by little others joined him, and as the word spread slowly, men from other sections wandered in with books, and the Academy was born. No one taught, of course; it was just a group of studious men living a sort of communistic, monastic life. There was no attempt at practical use of the ancient knowledge until a youth named Teran had a dream—no less a dream than to recondition the centuries-old power machines of N'Orleans, to give the city the power that travels on wires!"

"What's that?" asked Hull. "What's that, Old Einar?"

"You wouldn't understand, Hull. Teran was an enthusiast; it didn't stop him to realize that there was no coal or oil to run his machines. He believed that when power was needed, it would be there, so he and his followers scrubbed and filed and welded away, and Teran was right. When he needed power, it was there.

"This was the gift of a man named Olin, who had unearthed the last, the crowning secret of the Ancients, the power called atomic energy. He gave it to Teran, and N'Orleans became a miracle city where lights glowed and wheels turned. Men came from every part of the continent to see, and among these were two called Martin Sair and Joaquin Smith, come out of Mexico with the half-sister of Joaquin, the Satanically beautiful being sometimes called Black Margot.

"Martin Sair was a genius. He found his field in the study of medicine, and it was less than ten years before he had uncovered the secret of the hard rays. He was studying sterility but he found—immortality!"

"Then the Immortals are immortal !" murmured Hull.

"It may be, Hull. At least they do not seem to age, but— Well, Joaquin Smith was also a genius, but of a different sort. He dreamed of the re-uniting of the peoples of the country. I think he dreams of even more, Hull; people say he will stop when he rules a hundred cities, but I think he dreams of an American Empire, or"—Old Einar's voice dropped—"a world Empire. At least, he took Martin Sair's immortality and traded it for power. The Second Enlightenment was dawning and there was genius in N'Orleans. He traded immortality to Kohlmar for a weapon, he offered it to Olin for atomic power, but Olin was already past youth, and refused, partly because he didn't want it, and partly because he was not entirely in sympathy with Joaquin Smith. So the Master seized the secret of the atom despite Olin, and the Conquest began.

"N'Orleans, directly under the influence of the Master's magnetic personality, was ready to yield, and yielded to him cheering. He raised his army and marched north, and everywhere cities fell or yielded willingly. Joaquin Smith is magnificent, and men flock to him, cities cheer him, even the wives and children of the slain swear allegiance when he forgives them in that noble manner of his. Only here and there men hate him bitterly, and speak such words as tyrant, and talk of freedom."

"Such are the mountainies," said Hull.

"Not even the mountainies can stand the ionic beams that Kohlmar dug out of ancient books, nor the Erden resonator that explodes gunpowder miles away. I think that Joaquin Smith will succeed, Hull. Moreover, I do not think it entirely bad that he should, for he is a great ruler, and a bringer of civilization."

"What are they like, the Immortals?"

"Well, Martin Sair is as cold as mountain rock, and the Princess Margaret is like black fire. Even my old bones feel younger only to look at her, and it is wise for young men not to look at her at all, because she is quite heartless, ruthless, and pitiless. As for Joaquin Smith, the Master—I do not know the words to describe so complex a character, and I know him well. He is mild, perhaps, but enormously strong, kind or cruel as suits his purpose, glitteringly intelligent, and dangerously charming."

"You know him!" echoed Hull, and added curiously, "What is your other name, Old Einar, you who know the Immortals?"

The old man smiled. "When I was born," he said, "my parents called me Einar Olin."

3. The Master Marches

Joaquin Smith was marching. Hull Tarvish leaned against the door of File Ormson's iron worker's shop in Ormiston, and stared across the fields and across the woodlands, and across to the blue mountains of Ozarky in the south. There is where he should have been, there with the mountainy men, but by the time the tired rider had brought the news to Selui, and by the time Hull had reached Ormiston, it was already too late, and Ozarky was but an outlying province of the expanding Empire, while the Master camped there above Norse, and sent representations to Selui.

Selui wasn't going to yield. Already the towns of the three months old Selui Confederation were sending in their men, from Bloom'ton, from Cairo, even from distant Ch'cago on the shores of the saltless sea Mitchin. The men of the Confederation hated the little, slender, dark Ch'cagoans, for they had not yet forgotten the disastrous battle at Starved Rock, but any allies were welcome against Joaquin Smith. The Ch'cagoans were good enough fighters, too, and heart and soul in the cause, for if the Master took Selui, his Empire would reach dangerously close to the saltless seas, spreading from the ocean on the cast to the mountains on the west, and north as far as the great confluence of the M'sippi and M'souri.

Hull knew there was fighting ahead, and he relished it. It was too bad that he couldn't have fought in Ozarky for his own people, but Ormiston would do. That was his home for the present, since he'd found work here with File Ormson, the squat iron-worker, broad-shouldered as Hull himself and a head shorter. Pleasant work for his mighty muscles, though at the moment there was nothing to do.

He stared at the peaceful countryside. Joaquin Smith was marching, and beyond the village, the farmers were still working in their fields. Hull listened to the slow Sowing Song:

"*This is what the ground needs:*
First the plow and then the seeds,
Then the harrow and then the hoe,
And rain to make the harvest grow.

"This is what the man, needs:
First the promises, then the deeds,
Then the arrow and then the blade,
And last the digger with his black spade.

"This is what his wife needs:
First a garden free of weeds,
Then the daughter, and then the son,
And a fireplace warm when the work is done.

"This is what his son needs—"

Hull ceased to listen. They were singing, but Joaquin Smith was marching, marching with the men of a hundred cities, with his black banner and its golden serpent fluttering. That serpent, Old Einar had said, was the Midgard Serpent, which ancient legend related had encircled the earth. It was the symbol of the Master's dream, and for a moment Hull had a stirring of sympathy for that dream.

"No!" he growled to himself. "Freedom's better, and it's for us to blow the head from the Midgard Serpent."

A voice sounded at his side. "Hull! Big Hull Tarvish! Are you too proud to notice humble folk?"

It was Vail Ormiston, her violet eyes whimsical below her smooth copper hair. He flushed; he was not used to the ways of these valley girls, who flirted frankly and openly in a manner impossible to the shy girls of the mountains. Yet he—well, in a way, he liked it, and he liked Vail Ormiston, and he remembered pleasantly an evening two days ago when he had sat and talked a full three hours with her on the bench by the tree that shaded Ormiston well. And he remembered the walk through the fields when she had shown him the mouth of the great ancient storm sewer that had run under the dead city, and that still stretched crumbling for miles underground toward the hills, and he recalled her story of how, when a child, she had lost herself in it, so that her father had planted the tangle of blackberry bushes that still concealed the opening.

He grinned, "Is it the eldarch's daughter speaking of humble folk? Your father will be taxing me double if he hears of this."

She tossed her helmet of metallic hair. "He will if he sees you in that Selui finery of yours." Her eyes twinkled. "For whose eyes was it bought, Hull? For you'd be better saving your money."

"Save silver, lose luck," he retorted. After all, it wasn't so difficult a task to talk to her. "Anyway, better a smile from you than the glitter of money."

She laughed. "But how quickly you learn, mountainy! Still, what if I say I liked you better in tatters, with your powerful brown muscles quivering through the rips?"

"Do you say it, Vail?"

"Yes, then!"

He chuckled, raising his great hands to his shoulders. There was the rasp of tearing cloth, and a long rent gleamed in the back of his Selui shirt. "There, Vail!"

"Oh!" she gasped. "Hull, you wastrel! But it's only a seam." She fumbled in the bag at her belt. "Let me stitch it back for you."

She bent behind him, and he could feel her breath on his skin, warm as spring sunshine. He set his jaw, scowled, and then plunged determinedly into what he had to say. "I'd like to talk to you again this evening, Vail."

He sensed her smile at his back. "Would you?" she murmured demurely.

"Yes, if Enoch Ormiston hasn't spoken first for your time."

"But he has, Hull."

He knew she was teasing him deliberately. "I'm sorry," he said shortly.

"But—I told him I was busy," she finished.

"And are you?"

Her voice was a whisper behind him. "No. Not unless you tell me I am."

His great roar of a laugh sounded. "Then I tell you so, Vail."

He felt her tug at the seam, then she leaned very close to his neck, but it was only to bite the thread with her white teeth. "So!" she said gaily. "Once mended, twice new."

Before Hull could answer there came the clang of File Ormson's sledge, and the measured bellow of his Forge Song. They listened as his resounding strokes beat time to the song.

"*Then it's ho—oh—ho—oh—ho!*
While I'm singing to the ringing
Of each blow—blow—blow!
Till the metal's soft as butter

Let my forge and bellows sputter
Like the revels of the devils down below—low—LOW!
Like the revels of the devils down below!"

"I must go," said Hull, smiling reluctantly. "There's work for me now."

"What does File make?" asked Vail.

Instantly Hull's smile faded. "He forges—a sword!"

Vail too was no longer the joyous one of a moment ago. Over both of them had come a shadow, the shadow of the Empire. Out in the blue hills of Ozarky Joaquin Smith was marching.

* * *

Evening. Hull watched the glint of a copper moon on Vail's copper hair, and leaned back on the bench. Not the one near the pump this time; that had been already occupied by two laughing couples, and though they had been welcomed eagerly enough, Hull had preferred to be alone. It wasn't mountain shyness any more, for his great, good-natured presence had found ready friendship in Ormiston village; it was merely the projection of that moodiness that had settled over both of them at parting, and so they sat now on the bench near Vail Ormiston's gate at the edge of town. Behind them the stone house loomed dark, for her father was scurrying about in town on Confederation business, and the help had availed themselves of the evening of freedom to join the crowd in the village square. But the yellow daylight of the oil lamp showed across the road in the house of Hue Helm, the farmer who had brought Hull from Norse to Ormiston.

It was at this light that Hull stared thoughtfully. "I like fighting," he repeated, "but somehow the joy has gone out of this. It's as if one waited an approaching thunder cloud."

"How," asked Vail in a timid, small voice, "can one fight magic?"

"There is no magic," said the youth, echoing Old Einar's words. "There is no such thing—"

"Hull! How can you say such stupid words?"

"I say what was told me by one who knows."

"No magic!" echoed Vail. "Then tell me what gives the wizards of the south their power. Why is it that Jaoquin Smith has never lost a battle? What stole away the courage of the men of the Memphis League, who are good fighting men? And what—for this I have seen with my own eyes—pushes the horseless wagons of N'Orleans through the streets, and what lights that city by night? If not magic, then what?"

"Knowledge," said Hull. "The knowledge of the Ancients."

"The knowledge of the Ancients was magic," said the girl. "Everyone knows that the Ancients were wizards, warlocks, and sorcerers. If Holland, Olin, and Martin Sair are not sorcerers, then what are they? If Black Margot is no witch, then my eyes never looked on one."

"Have you seen them?" queried Hull.

"Of course, all but Holland, who is dead. Three years ago during the Peace of Memphis my father and I traveled into the Empire. I saw all of them about the city of N'Orleans."

"And is she—what they say she is?"

"The Princess?" Vail's eyes dropped. "Men say she is beautiful."

"But you think not?"

"What if she is?" snapped the girl almost defiantly. "Her beauty is like her youth, like her very life—artificial, preserved after its allotted time, frozen. That's it—frozen by sorcery. And as for the rest of her—" Vail's voice lowered, hesitated, for not even the plain-spoken valley girls discussed such things with men. "They say she has outworn a dozen lovers," she whispered.

Hull was startled, shocked. "Vail!" he muttered.

She swung the subject back to safer ground, but he saw her flush red. "Don't tell me there's no magic!" she said sharply.

"At least," he returned, "there's no magic will stop a bullet save flesh and bone. Yes, and the wizard who stops one with his skull lies just as dead as an honest man."

"I hope you're right," she breathed timidly. "Hull, he must be stopped! He must!"

"But why feel so strongly, Vail? I like a fight—but men say that life in the Empire is much like life without, and who cares to whom he pays his taxes if only—" He broke off suddenly, remembering. "Your father!" he exclaimed. "The eldarch!"

"Yes, my father, Hull. If Joaquin Smith takes Ormison, my father is the one to suffer. His taxes will be gone, his lands parceled out, and he's old, Hull—old. What will become of him then? I know many people feel the way you—the way you said, and so they fight halfheartedly, and the Master takes town after town without killing a single man. And then they think there is magic in the very name of Joaquin Smith, and he marches through armies that outnumber him ten to one." She paused. "But not Ormiston!" she cried fiercely. "Not if the women have to bear arms!"

"Not Ormiston," he agreed gently.

"You'll fight, Hull, won't you? Even though you're not Ormiston born?"

"Of course. I have bow and sword, and a good pistol. I'll fight."

"But no rifle? Wait, Hull." She rose and slipped away in the darkness.

In a moment she was back again. "Here. Here is rifle and horn and ball. Do you know its use?"

He smiled proudly. "What I can see I can hit," he said, "like any mountain man."

"Then," she whispered with fire in her voice, "send me a bullet through the Master's skull. And one besides between the eyes of Black Margot—for me!"

"I do not fight women," he said.

"Not woman but witch!"

"None the less, Vail, it must be two bullets for the Master and only the captive's chains for Princess Margaret, at least so far as Hull Tarvish is concerned. But wouldn't it please you fully as well to watch her draw water from your pump, or shine pots in your kitchen?" He was jollying her, trying to paint fanciful pictures to lift her spirit from the somber depths.

But she read it otherwise. "Yes!" she blazed. "Oh, yes, Hull, that's better. If I could ever hope to see that—" She rose suddenly, and he followed her to the gate. "You must go," she murmured, "but before you leave, you can—if you wish it, Hull—kiss me."

Of a sudden he was all shy mountainy again. He set the rifle against the fence with its horn swinging from the trigger guard. He faced her flushing a furious red, but only half from embarrassment, for the rest was happiness. He circled her with his great arms and very hastily, fire touched his lips to her soft ones.

"Now," he said exultantly, "now I will fight if I have to charge the men of the Empire alone."

4. The Battle of Eaglefoot Flow

The men of the Confederation were pouring into Ormiston all night long, the little dark men of Ch'cago and Selui, the tall blond ones from the regions of Iowa, where Dutch blood still survived, mingled now with a Scandinavian infusion from the upper rivers. All night there was a rumble of wagons, bringing powder and ball from Selui, and food as well for Ormiston couldn't even attempt to feed so many ravenous mouths. A magnificent army, ten thousand strong, and all of them seasoned fighting men, trained in a dozen little wars and in the bloody War of the Lakes and Rivers, when Ch'cago had bitten so large a piece from Selui territories.

The stand was to be at Ormiston, and Norse, the only settlement now between Joaquin Smith and the Confederation, was left to its fate. Experienced leaders had examined the territory, and had agreed on a plan. Three miles south of the town, the road followed an ancient railroad cut, with fifty-foot embankments on either side, heavily wooded for a mile north and south of the bridge across Eaglefoot Flow.

Along this course they were to distribute their men, a single line where the bluffs were high and steep, massed forces where the terrain permitted. Joaquin Smith must follow the road; there was no other. An ideal situation for ambush, and a magnificently simple plan. So magnificent and so simple that it could not fail, they said, and forgot completely that they were facing the supreme military genius of the entire Age of the Enlightenment.

It was mid-morning when the woods runners that had been sent into Ozarky returned with breath-taking news. Joaquin Smith had received the Selui defiance of his representations, and was marching. The Master was marching, and though they had come swiftly and had ridden horseback from Norse, he could not now be far distant. His forces? The runners estimated them at four thousand men, all mounted, with perhaps another thousand auxiliaries. Outnumbered two to one! But Hull Tarvish remembered tales of other encounters where Joaquin Smith had overcome greater odds than these.

The time was at hand. In the little room beside File Ormson's workshop, Hull was going over his weapons while Vail Ormiston, pale and nervous and very lovely, watched him. He drew a bit of oiled rag through the bore of the rifle she had given him, rubbed a spot of rust from the hammer, blew a speck of dust from the pan. Beside him on the table lay powder horn and ball, and his steel bow leaned against his chair.

"A sweet weapon!" he said admiringly, sighting down the long barrel.

"I—I hope it serves you well," murmured Vail tremulously. "Hull, he must be stopped. He must!"

"We'll try, Vail." He rose. "It's time I started."

She was facing him. "Then, before you go, will you—kiss me, Hull?"

He strode toward her, then recoiled in sudden alarm, for it was at that instant that the thing happened. There was a series of the faintest possible clicks, and Hull fancied that he saw for an instant a glistening of tiny blue sparks on candle-sticks and metal objects about the room, and that he felt for a brief moment a curious tingling. Then he forgot all of these strange trifles as the powder horn on the table roared into terrific flame, and flaming wads of powder shot meteor-like around him.

For an instant he froze rigid. Vail was screaming; her dress was burning. He moved into sudden action, sweeping her from her feet, crashing her sideways to the floor, where his great hands beat out the fire. Then he slapped table and floor; he brought his ample sandals down on flaming spots, and finally there were no more flames.

He turned coughing and choking in the black smoke, and bent over Vail, who gasped half overcome. Her skirt had burned to her knees, and for the moment she was too distraught to cover them, though there was no modesty in the world in those days like that of the women of the middle river regions. But as Hull leaned above her she huddled back.

"Are you hurt?" he cried. "Vail, are you burned?"

"No—no!" she panted.

"Then outside!" he snapped, reaching down to lift her.

"Not—not like this!"

He understood. He snatched his leather smith's apron from the wall, whipped it around her, and bore her into the clearer air of the street.

Outside there was chaos. He set Vail gently on the step and surveyed a scene of turmoil. Men ran shouting, and from windows along the street black smoke poured. A dozen yards away a powder wagon had blasted itself into a vast mushroom of smoke, incinerating horses and driver alike. On the porch across the way lay a writhing man, torn by the rifle that had burst in his hands.

He comprehended suddenly. "The sparkers!"* he roared. "Joaquin Smith's sparkers! Old Einar told me about them." He groaned. "There goes our ammunition." The girl made a great effort to control herself. "Joaquin Smith's sorcery," she said dully. "And there goes hope as well."

He started. "Hope? No! Wait, Vail."

He rushed toward the milling group that surrounded bearded old Marcus Ormiston and the Confederation leaders. He plowed his way fiercely through, and seized the panic-stricken greybeard. "What now?" he roared. "What are you going to do?"

"Do? Do?" The old man was beyond comprehending.

"Yes, do! I'll tell you." He glared at the five leaders. "You'll carry through. Do you see? For powder and ball there's bow and sword, and just as good for the range we need. Gather your men! Gather your men and march!"

And such, within the hour, was the decision. Hull marched first with the Ormiston men, and he carried with him the memory of Vail's farewell. It embarrassed him cruelly to be kissed thus in public, but there was great pleasure in the glimpse of Enoch Ormiston's sour face as he had watched her.

The Ormiston men were first on the line of the Master's approach, and they filtered to their forest-hidden places as silently as foxes. Hull let his eyes wander back along the cut and what he saw pleased him, for no eye could have detected that along the deserted road lay ten thousand fighting men. They were good woodsmen too, these fellows from the upper rivers and the saltless seas.

---

*The Erden Resonators. A device, now obsolete, that projected an inductive field sufficient to induce tiny electrical discharges in metal objects up to a distance of many miles. Thus it ignited flammables like gunpowder.

Down the way from Norse a single horseman came galloping. Old Marcus Ormiston recognized him, stood erect, and hailed him. They talked; Hull could hear the words. The Master had passed through Norse, pausing only long enough to notify the eldarch that henceforth his taxes must be transmitted to N'Orleans, and then had moved leisurely onward. No, there had been no sign of sorcery, nor had he even seen any trace of the witch Black Margot, but then, he had ridden away before the Master had well arrived.

Their informant rode on toward Ormiston, and the men fell to their quiet waiting. A half hour passed, and then, faintly drifting on the silent air, came the sound of music. Singing; men's voices in song. Hull listened intently, and his skin crept and his hair prickled as he made out the words of the Battle Song of N'Orleans:

"Queen of cities, reigning
Empress, starry pearled
See our arms sustaining
Battle flags unfurled!
Hear our song rise higher,
Fierce as battle fire,
Death our one desire
Or
The Empire of the World!"

Hull gripped his bow and set feather to cord. He knew well enough that the plan was to permit the enemy to pass unmolested until his whole line was within the span of the ambush, but the rumble of that distant song was like spark to powder. And now, far down the way beyond the cut, he saw the dust rising. Joaquin Smith was at hand.

Then—the unexpected! Ever afterward Hull told himself that it should have been the expected, that the Master's reputation should have warned them that so simple a plan as theirs must fail. There was no time now for such vain thoughts, for suddenly, through the trees to his right, brown-clothed, lithe little men were slipping like charging shadows, horns sounding, whistles shrilling. The woods runners of the Master! Joaquin Smith had anticipated just such an ambush.

Instantly Hull saw their own weakness. They were ten thousand, true enough, but here they were strung thinly over a distance of two miles, and now the woods runners were at a vast advantage in numbers, with the main body approaching. One chance! Fight it out, drive off the scouts, and retire into the woods. While the army existed, even though Ormiston fell, there was hope.

He shouted, strung his arrow, and sent it flashing through the leaves. A bad place for arrows; their arching flight was always deflected by the tangled branches. He slung bow on shoulder and gripped his sword; close quarters was the solution, the sort of fight that made blood tingle and life seem joyous.

Then—the second surprise! The woods runners had flashed their own weapons, little blunt revolvers. But they sent no bullets; only pale beams darted through leaves and branches, faint blue streaks of light. Sorcery? And to what avail?

He learned instantly. His sword grew suddenly scorching hot in his hands, and a moment later the queerest pain he had ever encountered racked his body. A violent, stinging, inward tingle that twitched his muscles and paralyzed his movements. A brief second and the shock ceased, but his sword lay smoking in the leaves, and his steel bow had seared his shoulders. Around him men were yelling in pain, writhing on the ground, running back into the forest depths. He cursed the beams; they flicked like sunlight through branched and leafy tangles where an honest arrow could find no passage.

Yet apparently no man had been killed. Hands were seared and blistered by weapons that grew hot under the blue beams, bodies were racked by the torture that Hull could not know was electric shock, but none was slain. Hope flared again, and he ran to head off a retreating group.

"To the road!" he roared. "Out where our arrows can fly free! Charge the column!"

For a moment the group halted. Hull seized a yet unheated sword from someone, and turned back. "Come on!" he bellowed. "Come on! We'll have a fight of this yet!"

Behind him he heard the trample of feet. The beams flicked out again, but he held his sword in the shadow of his own body, gritted his teeth, and bore the pain that twisted him. He rushed on; he heard his own name bellowed in the booming voice of File Ormson, but he only shouted encouragement and burst out into the full sunlight of the road.

Below in the cut was the head of the column, advancing placidly. He glimpsed a silver helmeted, black haired man on a great white mare at its head, and beside him a slighter figure on a black stallion. Joaquin Smith! Hull roared down the embankment toward him.

Four men spurred instantly between him and the figure with the silver helmet. A beam flicked; his sword scorched his skin and he flung it away. "Come on!" he bellowed. "Here's a fight!"

Strangely, in curious clarity, he saw the eyes of the Empire men, a smile in them, mysteriously amused. No anger, no fear—just amusement. Hull felt a sudden surge of trepidation, glanced quickly behind him, and knew finally the cause of that amusement. No one had followed him; he had charged the Master's army alone!

Now the fiercest anger he had ever known gripped Hull. Deserted! Abandoned by those for whom he fought. He roared his rage to the echoing bluffs, and sprang at the horseman nearest him.

The horse reared, pawing the air. Hull thrust his mighty arms below its belly and heaved with a convulsion of his great muscles. Backward toppled steed and rider, and all about the Master was a milling turmoil where a man scrambled desperately to escape the clashing hooves. But Hull glimpsed Joaquin Smith sitting statuelike and smiling on his great white mare.

He tore another rider from his saddle, and then caught from the corner of his eye, he saw the slim youth at the Master's side raise a weapon, coolly, methodically. For the barest instant Hull faced icy green eyes where cold, passionless death threatened. He flung himself aside as a beam spat smoking against the dust of the road.

"Don't!" snapped Joaquin Smith, his low voice clear through the turmoil. "The youth is splendid!"

But Hull had no mind to die uselessly. He bent, flung himself halfway up the bluff in a mighty leap, caught a dragging branch, and swung into the forest. A startled woods runner faced him; he flung the fellow behind him down the slope, and slipped into the shelter of leaves. "The wise warrior fights pride," he muttered to himself. "It's no disgrace for one man to run from an army."

He was mountain bred. He circled silently through the forest, avoiding the woods runners who were herding the Confederation army back towards Ormiston. He smiled grimly as he recalled the words he had spoken to Vail. He had justified them; he had charged the army of the Master alone.

5. Black Margot

Hull circled wide through the forest, and it took all his mountain craft to slip free through the files of woods runners. He came at last to the fields east of Ormiston, and there made the road, entering from the direction of Selui.

Everywhere were evidences of rout. Wagons lay overturned, their teams doubtless used to further the escape of their drivers. Guns and rifles, many of them burst, littered the roadside, and now and again he passed black smoking piles and charred areas that marked the resting place of an ammunition cart.

Yet Ormiston was little damaged. He saw the firegutted remains of a shed or two where powder had been stored, and down the street a house roof still smoked. But there was no sign of battle carnage, and only the crowded street gave evidence of the unusual.

He found File Ormson in the group that stared across town to where the road from Norse elbowed east to enter. Hull had outsped the leisurely march of the Master, for there at the bend was the glittering army, now halted. Not even the woods runners had come into Ormiston town, for there they were too, lined in a brown-clad rank along the edge of the wood-lots beyond the nearer fields. They had made no effort, apparently, to take prisoners but had simply herded the terrified defenders into the village. Joaquin Smith had done it again; he had taken a town without a single death, or at least no casualties other than whatever injuries had come from bursting rifles and blazing powder.

Suddenly Hull noticed something. "Where are the Confederation men?" he asked sharply.

File Ormson turned gloomy eyes on him. "Gone. Flying back to Selui like scared gophers to their holes." He scowled, then smiled. "That was a fool's gesture of yours at Eaglefoot Flow, Hull. A fool's gesture, but brave."

The youth grimaced wryly. "I thought I was followed."

"And so you should have been, but that those fiendish ticklers tickled away our courage. But they can kill as well as tickle; when there was need of it before Memphis they killed quickly enough."

Hull thought of the green-eyed youth. "I think I nearly learned that," he said smiling.

Down the way there was some sort of stir. Hull narrowed his eyes to watch, and descried the silver helmet of the Master. He dismounted and faced someone; it was—yes, old Marcus Ormiston. He left File Ormson and shouldered his way to the edge of the crowd that circled the two.

Joaquin Smith was speaking. "And," he said, "all taxes are to be forwarded to N'Orleans, including those on your own lands. Half of them I shall use to maintain my government, but half will revert to your own district, which will be under a governor I shall appoint in Selui when that city is taken. You are no longer eldarch, but for the present you may collect the taxes at the rate I prescribe."

Old Marcus was bitterly afraid; Hull could see his beard waggling like an oriole's nest in a breeze. Yet there was a shrewd, bargaining streak in him. "You are very hard," he whined. "You left Pace Helm as eldarch undisturbed in Norse. Why do you punish me because I fought to hold what was mine? Why should that anger you so?"

"I am not angry," said the Master passively. "I never blame any for fighting against me, but it is my policy to favor those eldarchs who yield peacefully." He paused. "Those are my terms, and generous enough."

They were generous, thought Hull, especially to the people of Ormiston, who received back much less than half their taxes from the eldarch as roads, bridges, or wells.

"My—my lands?" faltered the old man.

"Keep what you till," said Joaquin Smith indifferently. "The rest of them go to their tenants." He turned away, placed foot to stirrup, and swung upon his great white mare.

Hull caught his first fair glimpse of the conqueror. Black hair cropped below his ears, cool greenish grey eyes, a mouth with something faintly humorous about it. He was tall as Hull himself, more slender, but with powerful shoulders, and he seemed no older than the late twenties, or no more than thirty at most, though that was only the magic of Martin Sair, since more than eighty years had passed since his birth in the mountains of Mexico. He wore the warrior's garb of the southlands, a shirt of metallic silver scales, short thigh-length trousers of some shiny, silken material, cothurns on his feet. His bronzed body was like the ancient statues Hull had seen in Selui, and he looked hardly the fiend that most people thought him. A pleasant seeming man, save for something faintly arrogant in his face—no, not arrogant, exactly, but proud or confident, as if he felt himself a being driven by fate, as perhaps he was.

He spoke again, now to his men. "Camp there," he ordered, waving at Ormiston square, "and there," pointing at a fallow field. "Do not damage the crops." He rode forward, and a dozen officers followed. "The Church," he said.

A voice, a tense, shrieking voice behind Hull. "You! It is, Hull! It's you!" It was Vail, teary eyed and pale. "They said you were—" She broke off sobbing, clinging to him, while Enoch Ormiston watched sourly.

He held her. "It seems I failed you," he said ruefully. "But I did do my best, Vail."

"Failed? I don't care." She calmed. "I don't care, Hull, since you're here."

"And it isn't as bad as it might be," he consoled. "He wasn't as severe as I feared."

"Severe!" she echoed. "Do you believe those mild words of his, Hull? First our taxes then our lands, and next it will be our lives—or at least my father's life. Don't you understand? That was no eldarch from some enemy town, Hull—that was Joaquin Smith. Joaquin Smith! Do you trust him?"

"Vail, do you believe that?"

"Of course I believe it!" She began to sob again. "See how he has already won over half the town with—with that about the taxes. Don't you be won over, Hull. I—couldn't stand it!"

"I will not," he promised.

"He and Black Margot and their craft! I hate them, Hull. I—Look there! Look there!"

He spun around. For a moment he saw nothing save the green-eyed youth who had turned death-laden eyes on him at Eaglefoot Flow, mounted on the mighty black stallion. Youth! He saw suddenly that it was a woman—a girl rather. Eighteen—twenty-five?

He couldn't tell. Her face was averted as she scanned the crowd that lined the opposite side of the street, but the sunset fell on a flaming black mop of hair, so black that it glinted blue—an intense, unbelievable black. Like Joaquin Smith she wore only a shirt and very abbreviated shorts, but a caparison protected the slim daintiness of her legs from any contact with the mount's ribs. There was a curious grace in the way she sat the idling steed, one hand on its haunches, the other on withers, the bridle dangling loose. Her Spanish mother's blood showed only in the clear, transparent olive of her skin, and of course, in the startling ebony of her hair.

"Black Margot!" Hull whispered, "Brazen! Half naked! What's so beautiful about her?"

As if she heard his whisper, she turned suddenly, her emerald eyes sweeping the crowd about him, and he felt his question answered. Her beauty was starkly incredible—audacious, outrageous. It was more than a mere lack of flaws; it was a sultry, flaming positive beauty with a hint of sullenness in it. The humor of the Master's mouth lurked about hers as mockery; her perfect lips seemed always about to smile, but to smile cruelly and sardonically. Hers was a ruthless and pitiless perfection, but it was nevertheless perfection, even to the faintly Oriental cast given by her black hair and sea-green eyes.

Those eyes met Hull's and it was almost as if he heard an audible click. He saw recognition in her face, and she passed her glance casually over his mighty figure. He stiffened, stared defiantly back, and swept his own gaze insolently over her body from the midnight hair to the diminutive cothurns on her feet. If she acknowledged his gaze at all, it was by the faintest of all possible smiles of mockery as she rode coolly away toward Joaquin Smith.

Vail was trembling against him, and it was a great relief to look into her deep but not at all mysterious blue eyes, and to see the quite understandable loveliness of her pale features. What if she hadn't the insolent brilliance of the Princess, he thought fiercely. She was sweet and honest and loyal to her beliefs, and he loved her. Yet he could not keep his eyes from straying once more to the figure on the black stallion.

"She—she smiled at you, Hull!" gasped Vail. "I'm frightened. I'm terribly frightened."

His fascination was yielding now to a surge of hatred for Joaquin Smith, for the Princess, for the whole Empire. It was Vail he loved, and she was being crushed by these. An idea formed slowly as he stared down the street to where Joaquin Smith had dismounted and was now striding into the little church. He heard an approving murmur sweep the crowd, already half won over by the distribution of land. That was simply policy, the Master's worshipping in Ormiston church, a gesture to the crowd.

He lifted the steel bow from his back and bent it. The spring was still in it; it had been heated enough to scorch his skin but not enough to untemper it. "Wait here!" he snapped to Vail, and strode up the street toward the church.

Outside stood a dozen Empire men, and the Princess idled on her great black horse. He slipped across the churchyard, around behind where a tangle of vines stretched toward the roof. Would they support his weight? They did, and he pulled himself hand over hand to the eaves, and thence to the peak. The spire hid him from the Master's men, and not one of the Ormiston folk glanced his way.

He crept forward to the base of the steeple. Now he must leave the peak and creep precariously along the steep slope around it. He reached the street edge and peered cautiously over.

The Master was still within. Against his will he glanced at Black Margot, and even put cord to feather and sighted at her ivory throat. But he could not. He could not loose the shaft.

Below him there was a stir. Joaquin Smith came out and swung to his white horse. Now was the moment. Hull rose to his knees, hoping that he could remain steady on the sharp pitch of the roof. Carefully, carefully, he drew the steel arrow back.

There was a shout. He had been seen, and a blue beam sent racking pain through his body. For an instant he bore it, then loosed his arrow and went sliding down the roof edge and over.

He fell on soft loam. A dozen hands seized him, dragged him upright, thrust him out into the street. He saw Joaquin Smith still on his horse, but the glistening arrow stood upright like a plume in his silver helmet, and a trickle of blood was red on his cheek.

But he wasn't killed. He raised the helmet from his head, waved aside the cluster of officers, and with his own hands bound a white cloth about his forehead. Then he turned cool grey eyes on Hull.

"You drive a strong shaft," he said, and then recognition flickered in his eyes. "I spared your life some hours ago, did I not?"

Hull said nothing.

"Why," resumed the Master, "do you seek to kill me after your eldarch has made peace with me? You are part of the Empire now, and this is treason."

"I made no peace!" growled Hull.

"But your leader did, thereby binding you."

Hull could not keep his gaze from the emerald eyes of the Princess, who was watching him without expression save faint mockery.

"Have you nothing to say," asked Joaquin Smith.

"Nothing."

The Master's eyes slid over him. "Are you Ormiston born?" he asked. "What is your name?"

No need to bring troubles on his friends. "No," said Hull. "I am called Hull Tarvish."

The conqueror turned away. "Lock him up," he ordered coolly. "Let him make whatever preparations his religion requires, and then—execute him."

Above the murmur of the crowd Hull heard Vail Ormiston's cry of anguish. He turned to smile at her, watched her held by two Empire men as she struggled to reach him. "I'm sorry," he called gently. "I love you, Vail." Then he was being thrust away down the street.

He was pushed into Hue Helm's stonewalled tool shed. It had been cleared of everything, doubtless for some officer's quarters. Hull drew himself up and stood passively in the gathering darkness where a single shaft of sunset light angled through the door, before which stood two grim Empire men.

One of them spoke. "Keep peaceful, Weed,"* he said in his N'Orleans drawl. "Go ahead with your praying, or whatever it is you do."

"I do nothing," said Hull. "The mountainies believe that a right life is better than a right ending, and right or wrong a ghost's but a ghost anyway."

---

* Weed: The term applied by Dominists [the Master's partisans] to their opposers. It originated in Joaquin Smith's remark before the Battle of Memphis: "Even the weeds of the fields have taken arms against me."

The guard laughed. "And a ghost you'll be."

"If a ghost I'll be," retorted Hull, turning slowly toward him, "I'd sooner turn one—fighting!"

He sprang suddenly, crashed a mighty fist against the arm that bore the weapon, thrust one guard upon the other, and overleaped the tangle into the dusk. As he spun to circle the house, something very hard smashed viciously against the back of his skull, sending him sprawling half dazed against the wall.

6. The Harriers

After a brief moment Hull sprawled half stunned, then his muscles lost their paralysis and he thrust himself to his feet, whirling to face whatever assault threatened. In the doorway the guards still scrambled, but directly before him towered a rider on a black mount, and two men on foot flanked him. The rider, of course, was the Princess, her glorious green eyes luminous as a cat's in the dusk as she slapped a short sword into its scabbard. It was a blow from the flat of its blade that had felled him.

She held now the blunt weapon of the blue beam. It came to him that he had never heard her speak, but she spoke now in a voice low and liquid, yet cold, cold as the flow of an ice-crusted winter stream. "Stand quiet, Hull Tarvish," she said. "One flash will burst that stubborn heart of yours forever."

Perforce he stood quiet, his back to the wall of the shed. He had no doubt at all that the Princess would kill him if he moved; he couldn't doubt it with her icy eyes upon him. He stared sullenly back, and a phrase of Old Einar's came strangely to his memory. "Satanically beautiful," the old man had called her, and so she was. Hell or the art of Martin Sair had so fashioned her that no man could gaze unmoved on the false purity of her face, no man at least in whom flowed red blood.

She spoke again, letting her glance flicker disdainfully over the two appalled guards. "The Master will be pleased," she said contemptuously, "to learn that one unarmed Weed outmatches two men of his own cohort."

The nearer man faltered, "But your Highness, he rushed us unexpect—"

"No matter," she cut in, and turned back to Hull. For the first time now he really felt the presence of death as she said coolly, "I am minded to kill you."

"Then do it!" he snapped.

"I came here to watch you die," she observed calmly. "It interests me to see men die, boldly or cowardly or resignedly. I think you would die boldly."

It seemed to Hull that she was deliberately torturing him by this procrastination. "Try me!" he growled.

"But I think also," she resumed, "that your living might amuse me more than your death, and" for the first time there was a breath of feeling in her voice "God knows I need amusement!" Her tones chilled again. "I give you your life."

"Your Highness," muttered the cowed guard, "the Master has ordered—"

"I countermand the orders," she said shortly. And then to Hull. "You are a fighter. Are you also a man of honor?"

"If I'm not," he retorted, "the lie that says I am would mean nothing to me."

She smiled coldly. "Well, I think you are, Hull Tarvish. You go free on your word to carry no weapons, and your promise to visit me this evening in my quarters at the eldarch's home." She paused. "Well?"

"I give my word."

"And I take it." She crashed her heels against the ribs of the great stallion, and the beast reared and whirled. "Away, all of you!" she ordered. "You two, carry tub and water for my bath." She rode off toward the street.

Hull let himself relax against the wall with a low "whew!" Sweat started on his cold forehead, and his mighty muscles felt almost weak. It wasn't that he had feared death, he told himself, but the strain of facing those glorious, devilish emerald eyes, and the cold torment of the voice of Black Margot, and the sense of her taunting him, mocking him, even her last careless gesture of freeing him. He drew himself erect. After all, fear of death or none, he loved life, and let that be enough.

He walked slowly toward the street. Across the way lights glowed in Marcus Orison's home, and he wondered if Vail were there, perhaps serving the Princess Margaret as he had so lately suggested the contrary. He wanted to find Vail; he wanted to use her cool loveliness as an antidote for the dark poison of the beauty he had been facing. And then, at the gate, he drew back suddenly. A group of men in Empire garb came striding by, and among them, helmetless and with his head bound, moved the Master.

His eyes fell on Hull. He paused suddenly and frowned. "You again!" he said. "How is it that you still live, Hull Tarvish?"

"The Princess ordered it."

The frown faded. "So," said Joaquin Smith slowly, "Margaret takes it upon herself to interfere somewhat too frequently. I suppose she also freed you?"

"Yes, on my promise not to bear arms."

There was a curious expression in the face of the conqueror. "Well," he said almost gently, "it was not my intention to torture you, but merely to have you killed for your treason. It may be that you will soon wish that my orders had been left unaltered." He strode on into the eldarch's dooryard, with his silent men following.

Hull turned his steps toward the center of the village. Everywhere he passed Empire men scurrying about the tasks of encampment, and supply wagons rumbled and jolted in the streets. He saw files of the soldiers passing slowly before cook-wagons and the smell of food floated on the air, reminding him that he was ravenously hungry. He hurried toward his room beside File Ormiston's shop, and there, tragic-eyed and mist-pale, he found Vail Ormiston.

She was huddled on the doorstep with sour Enoch holding her against him. It was Enoch who first perceived Hull, and his jaw dropped and his eyes bulged, and a gurgling sound issued from his throat. And Vail looked up with uncomprehending eyes, stared for a moment without expression, and then, with a little moan, crumpled and fainted.

She was unconscious only a few moments, scarcely long enough for Hull to bear her into his room. There she lay now on his couch, clinging to his great hand, convinced at last of his living presence.

"I think," she murmured, "that you're as deathless as Joaquin Smith, Hull. I'll never believe you dead again. Tell me—tell me how it happened."

He told her. "Black Margot's to thank for it," he finished.

But the very name frightened Vail. "She means evil, Hull. She terrifies me with her witch's eyes and her hellstained hair. I haven't even dared go home for fear of her."

He laughed. "Don't worry about me, Vail. I'm safe enough."

Enoch cut in. "Here's one for the Harriers, then," he said sourly. "The pack needs him."

"The Harriers?" Hull looked up puzzled.

"Oh, Hull, yes!" said Vail. "File Ormson's been busy. The Harriers are what's left of the army—the better citizens of Ormiston. The Master's magic didn't reach beyond the ridge, and over the hills there's still powder and rifles. And the spell is no longer in the valley, either. One of the men carried a cup of powder across the ridge, and it didn't burn."

The better citizens, Hull thought smiling. She meant, of course, those who owned land and feared a division of it such as Marcus Ormiston had suffered. But aloud he said only, "How many men have you?"

"Oh, there'll be several hundred with the farmers across the hills." She looked into his eyes, "I know it's a forlorn hope, Hull, but—we've got to try. You'll help, won't you?"

"Of course. But all your Harriers can attempt is raids. They can't fight the Master's army."

"I know. I know it, Hull. It's a desperate hope."

"Desperate?" said Enoch suddenly. "Hull, didn't you say you were ordered to Black Margot's quarters this evening?"

"Yes."

"Then—see here! You'll carry a knife in your armpit. Sooner or later she'll want you alone with her, and when that happens, you'll slide the knife quietly into her ruthless heart! There's a hope for you—if you've courage!"

"Courage!" he growled. "To murder a woman "

"Black Margot's a devil!"

"Devil or not, what's the good of it? It's Joaquin Smith that's building the Empire, not the Princess."

"Yes," said Enoch, "but half his power is the art of the witch. Once she's gone the Confederation could blast his army like ducks in a frog pond."

"It's true!" gasped Vail. "What Enoch says is true!"

Hull scowled. "I swore not to bear weapons!"

"Swore to her!" snapped Enoch. "That needn't bind you."

"My word's given," said Hull firmly. "I do not lie."

Vail smiled. "You're right," she whispered, and as Enoch's face darkened, "I love you for it, Hull."

"Then," grunted Enoch, "if it's not lack of courage, do this. Lure her somehow across the west windows. We can slip two or three Harriers to the edge of the woodlot, and if she passes a window with the light behind her—well, they won't miss."

"Oh, I won't," said Hull wearily. "I won't fight women, nor betray even Black Margot to death."

But Vail's blue eyes pleaded. "That won't be breaking your word, Hull. Please. It isn't betraying a woman. She's a sorceress. She's evil. Please, Hull."

Bitterly he yielded. "I'll try, then." He frowned gloomily. "She saved my life, and— Well, which room is hers?"

"My father's. Mine is the western chamber, which she took for her—her maid," Vail's eyes misted at the indignity of it. "We," she said, "are left to sleep in the kitchen."

An hour later, having eaten, he walked somberly home with Vail while Enoch slipped away toward the hills. There were tents in the dooryard, and lights glowed in every window, and before the door stood two dark Empire men who passed the girl readily enough, but halted Hull with small ceremony. Vail cast him a wistful backward glance as she disappeared toward the rear, and he submitted grimly to the questioning of the guards.

"On what business?"

"To see the Princess Margaret."

"Are you Hull Tarvish?"

"Yes."

One of the men stepped to his side and ran exploratory hands about his body. "Orders of Her Highness," he explained gruffly.

Hull smiled. The Princess had not trusted his word too implicitly. In a moment the fellow had finished his search and swung the door open.

Hull entered. He had never seen the interior of the house, and for a moment its splendor dazzled him. Carved ancient furniture, woven carpets, intricately worked standards for the oil lamps, and even—for an instant he failed to comprehend it—a full-length mirror of ancient workmanship wherein his own image faced him. Until now he had seen only bits and fragments of mirrors.

To his left a guard blocked an open door whence voices issued. Old Marcus Ormiston's voice. "But I'll pay for it. I'll buy it with all I have." His tones were wheedling.

"No." Cool finality in the voice of Joaquin Smith. "Long ago I swore to Martin Sair never to grant immortality to any who have not proved themselves worthy." A note of sarcasm edged his voice. "Go prove yourself deserving of it, old man, in the few years left to you."

Hull sniffed contemptuously. There seemed something debased in the old man's whining before his conqueror. "The Princess Margaret?" he asked, and followed the guard's gesture.

Upstairs was a dimly lit hall where another guard stood silently. Hull repeated his query, but in place of an answer came the liquid tones of Margaret herself. "Let him come in, Corlin."

A screen within the door blocked sight of the room. Hull circled it, steeling himself against the memory of that soul-burning loveliness he remembered. But his defense was shattered by the shock that awaited him.

The screen, indeed, shielded the Princess from the sight of the guard in the hall, but not from Hull's eyes. He stared utterly appalled at the sight of her lying in complete indifference in a great tub of water, while a fat woman scrubbed assiduously at her bare body. He could not avoid a single glimpse of her exquisite form, then he turned and stared deliberately from the east windows, knowing that he was furiously crimson even to his shoulders.

"Oh, sit down!" she said contemptuously. "This will be over in a moment."

He kept his eyes averted while water splashed and a towel whisked sibilantly. When he heard her footsteps beside him he glanced up tentatively, still fearful of what he might see, but she was covered now in a full robe of shiny black and gold that made her seem taller, though its filmy delicacy by no means concealed what was beneath. Instead of the cothurns she wore when on the march, she had slipped her feet into tiny high-heeled sandals that were reminiscent of the footgear he had seen in ancient pictures. The black robe and her demure coif of short ebony hair gave her an appearance of almost nunlike purity, save for the green hell-fires that danced in her eyes.

In his heart Hull cursed that false aura of innocence, for he felt again the fascination against which he had steeled himself.

"So," she said. "You may sit down again. I do not demand court etiquette in the field." She sat opposite, and produced a black cigarette, lighting it at the chimney of the lamp on the table. Hull stared; not that he was unaccustomed to seeing women smoke, for every mountainy woman had her pipe, and every cottage its tobacco patch, but cigarettes were new to him.

"Now," she said with a faintly ironic smile, "tell me what they say of me here."

"They call you witch."

"And do they hate me?"

"Hate you?" he echoed thoughtfully. "At least they will fight you and the Master to the last feather on the last arrow."

"Of course. The young men will fight—except those that Joaquin has bought with the eldarch's lands—because they know that once within the Empire, fighting is no more to be had. No more joyous, thrilling little wars between the cities, no more boasting and parading before the pretty provincial girls." She paused. "And you, Hull Tarvish—what do you think of me?"

"I call you witch for other reasons."

"Other reasons?"

"There is no magic," said Hull, echoing the words of old Einar in Selui. "There is only knowledge."

The Princess looked narrowly at him. "A wise thought for one of you," she murmured, and then, "You came weaponless."

"I keep my word."

"You owe me that. I spared your life."

"And I," declared Hull defiantly, "spared yours. I could have sped an arrow through that white throat of yours, there on the church roof. I aimed one."

She smiled. "What held you?"

"I do not fight women." He winced as he thought of what mission he was on, for it belied his words.

"Tell me," she said, "was that the eldarch's pretty daughter who cried so piteously after you there before the church?"

"Yes."

"And do you love her?"

"Yes." This was the opening he had sought, but it came bitterly now, facing her. He took the opportunity grimly. "I should like to ask one favor."

"Ask it."

"I should like to see"—lies were not in him but this was no lie—"the chamber that was to have been our bridal room. The west chamber." That might be—should be—truth.

The Princess laughed disdainfully. "Go see it then."

For a moment he feared, or hoped, perhaps, that she was going to let him go alone. Then she rose and followed him to the hall, and to the door of the west chamber.

7. Betrayal

Hull paused at the door of the west chamber to permit the Princess to enter. For the merest fraction of a second her glorious green eyes flashed speculatively to his face, then she stepped back. "You first, Weed," she commanded.

He did not hesitate. He turned and strode into the room, hoping that the Harrier riflemen, if indeed they lurked in the copse, might recognize his mighty figure in time to stay their eager trigger fingers. His scalp prickled as he moved steadily across the window, but nothing happened.

Behind him the Princess laughed softly. "I have lived too long in the aura of plot and counterplot in N'Orleans," she said. "I mistrust you without cause, honest Hull Tarvish."

Her words tortured him. He turned to see her black robe mold itself to her body as she moved, and, as sometimes happens in moments of stress, he caught an instantaneous picture of her with his senses so quickened that it seemed as if she, himself, and the world were frozen into immobility. He remembered her forever as she was then, with her limbs in the act of striding, her green eyes soft in the lamplight, and her perfect lips in a smile that had a coloring of wistfulness. Witch and devil she might be, but she looked like a dark-haired angel, and in that moment his spirit revolted.

"No!" he bellowed, and sprang toward her, striking her slim shoulders with both hands in a thrust that sent her staggering back into the hallway, there to sit hard and suddenly on the floor beside the amazed guard.

She sprang up instantly, and there was nothing angelic now in her face. "You—hurt me!" she hissed. "Me! Now, I'll—" She snatched the guard's weapon from his belt, thrust it full at Hull's chest, and sent the blue beam humming upon him.

It was pain far worse than that at Eaglefoot Flow. He bore it stolidly, grinding into silence the groan that rose in his throat, and in a moment she flicked it off and slapped it angrily into the guard's holster. "Treachery again!" she said. "I won't kill you, Hull Tarvish.

I know a better way." She whirled toward the stair-well. "Lebeau!" she called. "Lebeau! There's—" She glanced sharply at Hull, and continued, *"Il y a des tirailleurs dans le bois. Je vais les tireer en avant!"** It was the French of N'Orleans, as incomprehensible to Hull as Aramaic.

She spun back. "Sora!" she snapped, and then, as the fat woman appeared, "Never mind. You're far too heavy." Then back to Hull. "I've a mind," she blazed, "to strip the Weed clothes from the eldarch's daughter and send her marching across the window!"

He was utterly appalled. "She—she was in town!" he gasped, then fell silent at the sound of feet below.

"Well, there's no time," she retorted. "So, if I must—" She strode steadily into the west chamber, paused a moment, and then stepped deliberately in front of the window!

Hull was aghast. He watched her stand so that the lamplight must have cast her perfect silhouette full on the pane, stand tense and motionless for the fraction of a breath, and then leap back so sharply that her robe billowed away from her body.

She had timed it to perfection. Two shots crashed almost together, and the glass shattered. And then, out in the night, a dozen beams crisscrossed, and, thin and clear in the silence after the shots, a yell of mortal anguish drifted up, and another, and a third.

The Princess Margaret smiled in malice, and licked a crimson drop from a finger gashed by flying glass. "Your treachery reacts," she said in the tones of a sneer. "Instead of my betrayal, you have betrayed your own men."

"I need no accusation from you," he said gloomily. "I am my own accuser, and my own judge. Yes, and my own executioner as well. I will not live a traitor."

She raised her dainty eyebrows, and blew a puff of grey smoke from the cigarette still in her hand. "So strong Hull Tarvish will die a suicide," she remarked indifferently. "I had intended to kill you now. Should I leave you to be your own victim?"

He shrugged. "What matter to me?"

"Well," she said musingly, "you're rather more entertaining than I had expected. You're strong, you're stubborn, and you're dangerous. I give you the right to do what you wish with your own

*"There are snipers in the copse. I'll draw them out!"

life, but"—her green eyes flickered mockingly—"if I were Hull Tarvish, I should live on the chance of justifying myself. You can wipe out the disgrace of your weakness by an equal courage. You can sell your life in your own cause, and who knows?—perhaps for Joaquin's—or mine!"

He chose to ignore the mockery in her voice. "Perhaps," he said grimly, "I will."

"Why, then, did you weaken, Hull Tarvish? You might have had my life."

"I do not fight women," he said despondently. "I looked at you—and turned weak." A question formed in his mind. "But why did you risk your life before the window? You could have had fifty woods runners scour the copse. That was brave, but unnecessary."

She smiled, but there was a shrewd narrowness in her eyes. "Because so many of these villages are built above the underground ways of the Ancients—the subways, the sewers. How did I know but that your assassins might slip into some burrow and escape? It was necessary to lure them into disclosure."

Hull shadowed the gleam that shot into his own eyes. He remembered suddenly the ancient sewer in which the child Vail had wandered, whose entrance was hidden by blackberry bushes. Then the Empire men were unaware of it! He visioned the Harriers creeping through it with bow and sword—yes, and rifle, now that the spell was off the valley—springing suddenly into the center of the camp, finding the Master's army, sleeping, disorganized, unwary. What a plan for a surprise attack!

"Your Highness," he said grimly, "I think of suicide no more, and unless you kill me now, I will be a bitter enemy to your Empire army."

"Perhaps less bitter than you think," she said softly. "See, Hull, the only three that know of your weakness are dead. No one can name you traitor or weakling."

"But I can," he returned somberly. "And you."

"Not I, Hull," she murmured. "I never blame a man who weakens because of me—there have been many. Men as strong as you, Hull, and some that the world still calls great." She turned toward her own chamber. "Come in here," she said in altered tones. "I will have some wine. Sora!" As the fat woman padded off, she took another cigarette and lit it above the lamp, wrinkling her dainty nose distastefully at the night-flying insects that circled it.

"What a place!" she snapped impatiently.

"It is the finest house I have ever seen," said Hull stolidly.

She laughed. "It's a hovel. I sigh for the day we return to N'Orleans, where windows are screened, where water flows hot at will, where lights do not flicker as yellow oil lamps nor send heat to stifle one. Would you like to see the Great City, Hull?"

"You know I would."

"What if I say you may?"

"What could keep me from it if I go in peace?"

She shrugged. "Oh, you can visit N'Orleans, of course, but suppose I offered you the chance to go as the—the guest, we'll say, of the Princess Margaret. What would you give for that privilege?"

Was she mocking him again? "What would you ask for it?" he rejoined guardedly.

"Oh, your allegiance, perhaps. Or perhaps the betrayal of your little band of Harriers, who will be the devil's own nuisance to stamp out of these hills."

He looked up startled that she knew the name. "The Harriers? How?"

She smiled. "We have friends among the Ormiston men. Friends bought with land," she added contemptuously. "But what of my offer, Hull?"

He scowled. "You say as your guest. What am I to understand by that?"

She leaned across the table, her exquisite green eyes on his, her hair flaming blue-black, her perfect lips in a faint smile. "What you please, Hull. Whatever you please."

Anger was rising. "Do you mean," he asked huskily, "that you'd do that for so small a thing as the destruction of a little enemy band? You, with the whole Empire at your back?"

She nodded. "It saves trouble, doesn't it?"

"And honesty, virtue, honor, mean as little to you as that? Is this one of your usual means of conquest? Do you ordinarily sell your—your favors for—?"

"Not ordinarily," she interrupted coolly. "First I must like my co-partner in the trade. You, Hull—I like those vast muscles of yours, and your stubborn courage, and your slow, clear mind. You are not a great man, Hull, for your mind has not the cold fire of genius, but you are a strong one, and I like you for it."

"Like me!" he roared, starting up in his chair. "Yet you think I'll trade what honor's left me for—that! You think I'll betray my cause! You think— Well, you're wrong, that's all. You're wrong!"

She shook her head, smiling. "No. I wasn't wrong, for I thought you wouldn't."

"Oh, you did!" he snarled. "Then what if I'd accepted? What would you have done then?"

"What I promised." She laughed at his angry, incredulous face. "Don't look so shocked, Hull. I'm not little Vail Ormiston. I'm the Princess Margaret of N'Orleans, called Margaret the Divine by those who love me, and by those who hate me called— Well, you must know what my enemies call me."

"I do!" he blazed. "Black Margot, I do!"

"Black Margot!" she echoed smiling. "Yes, so called because a poet once amused me, and because there was once a very ancient, very great French poet named Francois Villon, who loved a harlot called Black Margot." She sighed. "But my poet was no Villon; already his works are nearly forgotten."

"A good name!" he rasped. "A good name for you!"

"Doubtless. But you fail to understand, Hull. I'm an Immortal. My years are three times yours. Would you have me follow the standards of death-bound Vail Ormiston?"

"Yes! By what right are you superior to all standards?"

Her lips had ceased to smile, and her deep green eyes turned wistful. "By the right that I can act in no other way, Hull," she said softly. A tinge of emotion quavered in her voice. "Immortality!" she whispered. "Year after year after year of sameness, tramping up and down the world on conquest! What do I care for conquest? I have no sense of destiny like Joaquin, who sees before him Empire—Empire—Empire, ever larger, ever growing. What's Empire to me? And year by year I grow bored until fighting, killing, danger, and love are all that keep me breathing!"

His anger had drained away. He was staring at her aghast, appalled.

"And then they fail me!" she murmured. "When killing palls and love grows stale, what's left? Did I say love? How can there be love for me when I know that if I love a man, it will be only to watch him age and turn wrinkled, weak, and flabby? And when I beg Joaquin for immortality for him, he flaunts before me that promise of his to Martin Sair, to grant it only to those already proved worthy. By the time a man's worthy he's old." She went on tensely, "I tell you, Hull, that I'm so friendless and alone that I envy you death-bound ones! Yes, and one of these days I'll join you!"

He gulped. "My God!" he muttered. "Better for you if you'd stayed in your native mountains with friends, home, husband, and children."

"Children!" she echoed, her eyes misting with tears. "Immortals can't have children. They're sterile; they should be nothing but brains like Joaquin and Martin Sair, not beings with feelings—like me. Sometimes I curse Martin Sair and his hard rays. I don't want immortality; I want life!"

Hull found his mind in a whirl. The impossible beauty of the girl he faced, her green eyes now soft and moist and unhappy, her lips quivering, the glisten of a tear on her cheek—these things tore at him so powerfully that he scarcely knew his own allegiance. "God!" he whispered. "I'm sorry!"

"And you, Hull—will you help me—a little?"

"But we're enemies—enemies!"

"Can't we be—something else?" A sob shook her.

"How can we be?" he groaned.

Suddenly some quirk to her dainty lips caught his attention. He stared incredulously into the green depths of her eyes. It was true. There was laughter there. She had been mocking him! And as she perceived his realization, her soft laughter rippled like rain on water.

"You—devil!" he choked. "You black witch! I wish I'd let you be killed!"

"Oh, no," she said demurely. "Look at me, Hull."

The command was needless. He couldn't take his fascinated gaze from her exquisite face.

"Do you love me, Hull?"

"I love Vail Ormiston," he rasped.

"But do you love me?"

"I hate you!"

"But do you love me as well?"

He groaned. "This is bitterly unfair," he muttered.

She knew what he meant. He was crying out against the circumstances that had brought the Princess Margaret—the most brilliant woman of all that brilliant age, and one of the most brilliant of any age—to flash all her fascination on a simple mountainy from Ozarky. It wasn't fair; her smile admitted it, but there was triumph there, too.

"May I go?" he asked stonily.

She nodded. "But you will be a little less my enemy, won't you, Hull?"

He rose. "Whatever harm I can do your cause," he said, "that harm will I do. I will not be twice a traitor." But he fancied a puzzling gleam of satisfaction in her green eyes at his words.

8. Torment

Hull looked Down at noon over Ormiston valley, where Joaquin Smith was marching. At his side Vail paused, and together they gazed silently over Selui road, now black with riding men and rumbling wagons on their way to attack the remnant of the Confederation army in Selui. But Ormiston was not entirely abandoned, for three hundred soldiers and two hundred horsemen remained to deal with the Harriers, under Black Margot herself. It was not the policy of the Master to permit so large a rebel band to gather unopposed in conquered territory; within the Empire, despite the mutual hatred among rival cities, there existed a sort of enforced peace.

"Our moment comes tonight," Hull said soberly. "We'll never have a better chance than now, with our numbers all but equal to theirs, and surprise on our side."

Vail nodded. "The ancient tunnel was a bold thought, Hull. The Harriers are shoring up the crumbled places. Father is with them."

"He shouldn't be. The aged have no place in the field."

"But this is his hope, Hull. He lives for this."

"Small enough hope! Suppose we're successful, Vail. What will it mean save the return of Joaquin Smith and his army? Common sense tells me this is a fool's hunt, and if it were not for you and the chance of fairer fighting than we've had until now—well, I'd be tempted to concede the Master his victory."

"Oh, no!" cried Vail. "If our success means the end of Black Margot, isn't that enough? Besides, you know that half the Master's powers are the work of the witch. Enoch—poor Enoch—said so."

Hull winced. Enoch had been one of the three marksmen slain outside the west windows, and the girl's words brought memory of his own part in that. But her words pricked painfully in yet another direction, for the vision of the Princess that had plagued him all night long still rose powerfully in his mind, nor could he face the mention of her death unmoved.

But Vail read only distress for Enoch in his face. "Enoch," she repeated softly. "He loved me in his sour way, Hull, but once I had known you, I had no thoughts for him."

Hull slipped his arm about her, cursing himself that he could not steal his thought away from Margaret of N'Orleans, because it was Vail he loved, and Vail he wanted to love. Whatever spell the Princess had cast about him, he knew her to be evil, ruthless, and inhumanly cold—a sorceress, a devil. But he could not blot her Satanic loveliness from his inward gaze.

"Well," he sighed, "let it be tonight, then. Was it four hours past sunset? Good. The Empire men should be sleeping or gaming in Tigh's tavern by that time. It's for us to pray for our gunpowder."

"Gunpowder? Oh, but didn't you hear what I told File Ormson and the Harriers, back there on the ridge? The casters of the spell are gone; Joaquin Smith has taken them to Selui. I watched and listened from the kitchen this morning."

"The sparkers? They're gone?"

"Yes. They called them reson—resators—"

"Resonators," said Hull, recalling Old Einar's words.

"Something like that. There were two of them, great iron barrels on swivels, full of some humming and clicking magic, and they swept the valley north and south, and east and west, and over toward Norse there was the sound of shots and the smoke of a burning building. They loaded them on wagons and dragged them away toward Selui."

"They didn't cross the ridge with their spell," said Hull.* "The Harriers still have powder."

"Yes," murmured Vail, drawing his arm closer about her. "Tell me," she said suddenly, "what did she want of you last night?"

Hull grimaced. He had told Vail little enough of that discreditable evening, and he had been fearing her question. "Treason," he said finally. "She wanted me to betray the Harriers."

"You? She asked that of you?"

"Do you think I would?" countered Hull.

"I know you never would. But what did she offer you for betrayal?"

---

* The field of the Erden resonators passes readily through structures and walls, but it is blocked by any considerable natural obstructions, hills, and for some reason, fog-banks or low clouds.

Again he hesitated. "A great reward," he answered at last. "A reward out of all proportion to the task."

"Tell me, Hull, what is she like face to face?"

"A demon. She isn't exactly human."

"But in what way? Men say so much of her beauty, of her deadly charm. Hull—did you feel it?"

"I love you, Vail."

She sighed, and drew yet closer. "I think you're the strongest man in the world, Hull. The very strongest."

"I'll need to be," he muttered, staring gloomily over the valley. Then he smiled faintly as he saw men plowing, for it was late in the season for such occupation. Old Marcus Ormiston was playing safe; remembering the Master's words, he was tilling every acre across which a horse could drag a blade.

Vail left him in Ormiston village and took her way hesitantly homeward. Hull did what he could about the idle shop, and when the sun slanted low, bought himself a square loaf of brown bread, a great slice of cheese, and a bottle of the still, clear wine of the region. It was just as he finished his meal in his room that a pounding on the door of the shop summoned him.

It was an Empire man. "Hull Tarvish?" he asked shortly. At Hull's nod he continued, "From Her Highness," and handed him a folded slip of black paper.

The mountain youth stared at it. On one side, in raised gold, was the form of a serpent circling a globe, its tail in its mouth—the Midgard Serpent. He slipped a finger through the fold, opened the message, and squinted helplessly at the characters written in gold on the black inner surface.

"This scratching means nothing to me," he said.

The Empire man sniffed contemptuously. "I'll read it," he said, taking the missive. "It says, 'Follow the messenger to our quarters,' and it's signed *Margarita Imperii Regina*, which means Margaret, Princess of the Empire. Is that plain?" He handed back the note. "I've been looking an hour for you."

"Suppose I won't go," growled Hull.

"This isn't an invitation, Weed. It's a command."

Hull shrugged. He had small inclination to face Black Margot again, especially with his knowledge of the Harriers' plans. Her complex personality baffled and fascinated him, and he could not help fearing that somehow, by some subtle art, she might wring that secret from him. Torture wouldn't force it out of him, but those green eyes might read it. Yet—better to go quietly than be dragged or driven; he grunted assent and followed the messenger.

He found the house quiet. The lower room where Joaquin Smith had rested was empty now, and he mounted the stairs again steeling himself against the expected shock of Black Margot's presence. This time, however, he found her clothed, or half clothed by Ormiston standards, for she wore only the diminutive shorts and shirt that were her riding costume, and her dainty feet were bare. She sat in a deep chair beside the table, a flagon of wine at hand and a black cigarette in her fingers. Her jet hair was like a helmet of ebony against the ivory of her forehead and throat, and her green eyes like twin emeralds.

"Sit down," she said as he stood before her. "The delay is your loss, Hull. I would have dined with you."

"I grow strong enough on bread and cheese," he growled.

"You seem to." Fire danced in her eyes. "Hull, I am as strong as most men, but I believe those vast muscles of yours could overpower me as if I were some shrinking provincial girl. And yet—"

"And yet what?"

"And yet you are much like my black stallion Eblis. Your muscles are nearly as strong, but like him, I can goad you, drive you, lash you, and set you galloping in whatever direction I choose."

"Can you?" he snapped. "Don't try it." But the spell of her unearthly beauty was hard to face.

"But I think I shall try it," she cooed gently. "Hull, do you ever lie?"

"I do not."

"Shall I make you lie, then, Hull? Shall I make you swear such falsehoods that you will redden forever afterward at the thought of them? Shall I?"

"You can't!"

She smiled, then in altered tones, "Do you love me, Hull?"

"Love you? I hate—" He broke off suddenly.

"Do you hate me, Hull?" she asked gently.

"No," he groaned at last. "No, I don't hate you."

"But do you love me?" Her face was saint-like, earnest, pure, even the green eyes were soft now as the green of spring. "Tell me, do you love me?"

"No!" he ground out savagely, then flushed crimson at the smile on her lips. "That isn't a lie!" he blazed. "This sorcery of yours isn't love. I don't love your beauty. It's unnatural, hellish, and the gift of Martin Sair. It's a false beauty, like your whole life!"

"Martin Sair had little to do with my appearance," she said gently. "What do you feel for me, Hull, if not love?"

"I—don't know. I don't want to think of it!" He clenched a great fist. "Love? Call it love if you wish, but it's a hell's love that would find satisfaction in killing you!" But here his heart revolted again. "That isn't so," he ended miserably. "I couldn't kill you."

"Suppose," she proceeded gently, "I were to promise to abandon Joaquin, to be no longer Black Margot and Princess of the Empire, but to be only—Hull Tarvish's wife. Between Vail and me, which would you choose?"

He said nothing for a moment. "You're unfair," he said bitterly at last. "Is it fair to compare Vail and yourself? She's sweet and loyal and innocent, but you—you are Black Margot!"

"Nevertheless," she said calmly, "I think I shall compare us. Sora!" The fat woman appeared. "Sora, the wine is gone. Send the eldarch's daughter here with another bottle and a second goblet."

Hull stared appalled. "What are you going to do?"

"No harm to your little Weed. I promise no harm."

"But—" He paused. Vail's footsteps sounded on the stairs, and she entered timidly, bearing a tray with a bottle and a metal goblet. He saw her start as she perceived him, but she only advanced quietly, set the tray on the table, and backed toward the door.

"Wait a moment," said the Princess. She rose and moved to Vail's side as if to force the comparison on Hull. He could not avoid it; he hated himself for the thought, but it came regardless. Barefooted, the Princess Margaret was exactly the height of Vail in her lowheeled sandals, and she was the merest shade slimmer. But her startling black hair and her glorious green eyes seemed almost to fade the unhappy Ormiston girl to a colorless dun, and the coppery hair and blue eyes seemed water pale. It wasn't fair; Hull realized that it was like comparing candlelight to sunbeam, and he despised himself even for gazing.

"Hull," said the Princess, "which of us is the more beautiful?"

He saw Vail's lips twitch fearfully, and he remained stubbornly silent.

"Hull," resumed the Princess, "which of us do you love?"

"I love Vail!" he muttered.

"But do you love her more than you love me?"

Once again he had recourse to silence.

"I take it," said the Princess, smiling, "that your silence means you love me the more. Am I right?"

He said nothing.

"Or am I wrong, Hull? Surely you can give little Vail the satisfaction of answering this question! For unless you answer I shall take the liberty of assuming that you love me the more. Now do you?"

He was in utter torment. His white lips twisted in anguish as he muttered finally, "Oh, God! Then yes!"

She smiled softly. "You may go," she said to the pallid and frightened Vail.

But for a moment the girl hesitated. "Hull," she whispered, "Hull, I know you said that to save me. I don't believe it, Hull, and I love you. I blame—her!"

"Don't!" he groaned. "Don't insult her."

The Princess laughed, "Insult me! Do you think I could be insulted by a bit of creeping dust as it crawls its way from cradle to grave?" She turned contemptuous green eyes on Vail as the terrified girl backed through the door.

"Why do you delight in torture?" cried Hull. "You're cruel as a cat. You're no less than a demon."

"That wasn't cruelty," said the Princess gently. "It was but a means of proving what I said, that your mighty muscles are well-broken to my saddle."

"If that needed proof," he muttered.

"It needed none. There's proof enough, Hull, in what's happening even now, if I judge the time rightly. I mean your Harriers slipping through their ancient sewer right into my trap behind the barn."

He was thunderstruck. "You—are you—you must be a witch!" he gasped.

"Perhaps. But it wasn't witchcraft that led me to put the thought of that sewer into your head, Hull. Do you remember now that it was my suggestion, given last evening there in the hallway? I knew quite well that you'd put the bait before the Harriers."

His brain was reeling. "But why— Why—?"

"Oh," she said indifferently, "it amuses me to see you play the traitor twice, Hull Tarvish."

9. The Trap

The Princess stepped close to him, her magnificent eyes gentle as an angel's, the sweet curve of her lips in the ghost of a pouting smile. "Poor, strong, weak Hull Tarvish!" she breathed. "Now you shall have a lesson in the cost of weakness. I am not Joaquin, who fights benignly with his men's slides in the third notch. When I go to battle, my beams flash full, and there is burning flesh and bursting heart. Death rides with me."

He scarcely heard her. His gyrating mind struggled with an idea. The Harriers were creeping singly into the trap, but they could not all be through the tunnel. If he could warn them—His eyes shifted to the bell-pull in the hall beside the guard, the rope that tolled the bronze bell in the belfry to summon public gatherings, or to call aid to fight fires. Death, beyond doubt, if he rang it, but that was only a fair price to pay for expiation.

His great arm flashed suddenly, sweeping the Princess from her feet and crashing her dainty figure violently against the wall. He heard her faint "O—o—oh" of pain as breath left her and she dropped slowly to her knees, but he was already upon the startled guard, thrusting him up and over the rail of the stair-well to drop with a sullen thumb below. And then he threw his weight on the bellrope, and the great voice of bronze boomed out, again, and again.

But Black Margot was on her feet, with the green hell-sparks flickering in her eyes and her face a lovely mask of fury. Men came rushing up the stairs with drawn weapons, and Hull gave a last tug on the rope and turned to face death. Half a dozen weapons were on him.

"No—no!" gasped the Princess, struggling for the breath he had knocked out of her. "Hold him—for me! Take him—to the barn!"

She darted down the stairway, her graceful legs flashing bare, her bare feet padding softly. After her six grim Empire men thrust Hull past the dazed guard sitting on the lower steps and out into a night where blue beams flashed and shots and yells sounded.

Behind the barn was comparative quiet, however, by the time

Hull's captors had marched him there. A closepacked mass of dark figures huddled near the mouth of the ancient tunnel, where the bushes were trampled away, and a brown-clad file of Empire woods runners surrounded them. A few figures lay sprawled on the turf, and Hull smiled a little as he saw that some were Empire men. Then his eyes strayed to the Princess where she faced a dark-haired officer.

"How many, Lebeau?"

"A hundred and forty or fifty, Your Highness."

"Not half! Why are you not pursuing the rest through the tunnel?"

"Because, Your Highness, one of them pulled the shoring and the roof down upon himself, and blocked us off. We're digging him out now."

"By then they'll have left their burrow. Where does this tunnel end?" She strode over to Hull. "Hull, where does this tunnel end?" At his silence, she added. "No matter. They'd be through it before we could reach it." She spun back. "Lebeau! Burn down what we have and the rest we'll stamp out as we can." A murmur ran through the crowd of villagers that was collecting, and her eyes, silvery green in the moonlight, flickered over them. "And any sympathizers," she added coldly. "Except this man, Hull Tarvish."

File Ornison's great voice rumbled out of the mass of prisoners. "Hull! Hull! Was this trap your doing?"

Hull made no answer, but Black Margot herself replied. "No," she snapped, "but the warning bell was."

"Then why do you spare him?"

Her eyes glittered icy green. "To kill in my own way, Weed," she said in tones so cold that it was as if a winter wind had sent a shivering breath across the spring night. "I have my own account to collect from him."

Her eyes blazed chill emerald fire into Hull's. He met her glance squarely, and said in a low voice, "Do you grant any favors to a man about to die?"

"Not by custom," she replied indifferently. "Is it the safety of the eldarch's daughter? I plan no harm to her."

"It isn't that."

"Then ask it—though I am not disposed to grant favors to you, Hull Tarvish, who have twice laid hands of violence on me."

His voice dropped almost to a whisper. "It is the lives of my companions I ask."

She raised here eyebrows in surprise, then shook her ebony flame of hair. "How can I? I remained here purposely to wipe them out. Shall I release the half I have, only to destroy them with the rest?"

"I ask their lives," he repeated.

A curious, whimsical fire danced green in her eves. "I will try," she promised, and turned to the officer, who was ranging his men so that the cross-fire of execution could not mow down his own ranks. "Lebeau!" she snapped. "Hold back a while."

She strode into the gap between the prisoners and her own men. Hand on hip she surveyed the Harriers, while moonlight lent her beauty an aura that was incredible, unearthly. There in the dusk of night she seemed no demon at all, but a girl, almost a child, and even Hull, who had learned well enough what she was, could not but sweep fascinated eyes from her jet hair to her tiny white feet.

"Now," she said, passing her glance over the group, on my promise of amnesty, how many of you would join me?"

A stir ran through the mass. For a moment there was utter immobility, then, very slowly, two figures moved forward, and the stir became an angry murmur. Hull recognized the men; they were stragglers of the Confederation army, Ch'cago men, good fighters but merely mercenaries, changing sides as mood or advantage moved them. The murmur of the Harriers became an angry growl.

"You two," said the Princess, "are you Ormiston men?"

"No," said one. "Both of us come from the shores of Mitchin."

"Very well," she proceeded calmly. With a movement swift as arrow flight she snatched the weapon from her belt, the blue beam spat twice, and the men crumpled, one with face burned carbon-black, and both sending forth an odorous wisp of flesh-seared smoke.

She faced the aghast group. "Now," she said, "Who is your leader?"

File Ormson stepped forth, scowling and grim. "What do you want of me?"

"Will you treat with me? Will your men follow your agreements?"

File nodded. "They have small choice."

"Good. Now that I have sifted the traitors from your ranks—for I will not deal with traitors—I shall make my offer." She smiled at the squat ironsmith. "I think I've served both of us by so doing," she said softly, and Hull gasped as he perceived the sweetness of the glance she bent on the scowling File. "Would you, with your great muscles and warrior's heart, follow a woman?"

The scowl vanished in surprise. "Follow you? You?"

"Yes." Hull watched her in fascination as she used her voice, her eyes, her unearthly beauty intensified by the moonlight, all on hulking File Ormson, behind whom the Harrier prisoners stood tense and silent. "Yes, I mean to follow me," she repeated softly. "You are brave men, all of you, now that I have weeded out the two cowards." She smiled wistfully, almost tenderly at the squat figure before her. "And you—you are a warrior."

"But—" File gulped, "our others—"

"I promise you need not fight against your companions. I will release any of you who will not follow me. And your lands—it is your lands you fight for, is it not? I will not touch, not one acre save the eldarch's." She paused. "Well?"

Suddenly File's booming laugh roared out. "By God!" he swore. "If you mean what you say, there's nothing to fight about! For my part, I'm with you!" He turned on his men. "Who follows me?"

The group stirred. A few stepped forward, then a few more, and then, with a shout, the whole mass. "Good!" roared File. He raised his great hard hand to his heart in the Empire salute. "To Black—to the Princess Margaret!" he bellowed. "To a warrior!"

She smiled and dropped her eyes as if in modesty. When the cheer had passed, she addressed File Ormson again. "You will send men to your others?" she asked. "Let them come in on the same terms."

"They'll come!" growled File.

The Princess nodded. "Lebeau," she called, "order off your men. These are our allies."

The Harriers began to separate, drifting away with the crowd of villagers. The Princess stepped close to Hull, smiling maliciously up into his perplexed face. He scarcely knew whether to be glad or bitter, for indeed, though she had granted his request to spare his companions, she had granted it only at the cost of the destruction of the cause for which he had sacrificed everything. There were no Harriers any more, but he was still to die for them.

"Will you die happy now?" she cooed softly.

"No man dies happy," he growled.

"I granted your wish, Hull."

"If your promises can be trusted," he retorted bitterly. "You lied coolly enough to the Ch'cago men, and you made certain they were not loved by the Harriers before you killed them."

She shrugged. "I lie, I cheat, I swindle by whatever means comes to hand," she said indifferently, "but I do not break my given word. The Harriers are safe."

Beyond her, men came suddenly from the tunnel mouth, dragging something dark behind them.

"The Weed who pulled down the roof, Your Highness," said Lebeau.

She glanced behind her, and pursed her dainty lips in surprise. "The eldarch! The dotard died bravely enough." Then she shrugged. "He had but a few more years anyway."

But Vail slipped by with a low moan of anguish, and Hull watched her kneel desolately by her father's body. A spasm of pity shook him as he realized that now she was utterly, completely alone. Enoch had died in the ambush of the previous night, old Marcus lay dead here before her, and he was condemned to death. The three who loved her and the man she loved—all slain in two nights passing. He bent a slow, helpless, pitying smile on her, but there was nothing he could do or say.

And Black Margot, after the merest glance, turned back to Hull, "Now," she said, the ice in her voice again, "I deal with you!"

He faced her dumbly. "Will you have the mercy to deal quickly, then?" he muttered at last.

"Mercy? I do not know the word where you're concerned, Hull. Or rather I have been already too merciful. I spared your life three times—once at Joaquin's request at Eaglefoot Flow, once before the guardhouse, and once up there in the hallway." She moved closer. "I cannot bear the touch of violence, Hull, and you have laid violent hands on me twice. Twice!"

"Once was to save your life," he said, "and the other to rectify my own unwitting treason. And I spared your life three times too,

Black Margot—once when I aimed from the church roof, once from the ambush in the west chamber, and once but a half hour ago, for I could have killed you with this fist of mine, had I wished to strike hard enough. I owe you nothing."

She smiled coldly. "Well argued, Hull, but you die none the less in the way I wish." She turned. "Back to the house!" she commanded, and he strode away between the six guards who still flanked him.

She led them into the lower room that had been the Master's. There she sat idly in a deep chair of ancient craftsmanship, lit a black cigarette at the lamp, and thrust her slim legs carelessly before her, gazing at Hull. But he, staring through the window behind her, could see the dark blot that was Vail Ormiston weeping beside the body of her father.

"Now," said the Princess, "how would you like to die, Hull.

"Of old age!" he snapped. "And if you will not permit that, then as quickly as possible."

"I might grant the second," she observed. "I might."

The thought of Vail was still torturing him. At last he said, "Your Highness, is your courage equal to the ordeal of facing me alone? I want to ask something that I will not ask in others' ears."

She laughed contemptuously. "Get out," she snapped at the silent guards. "Hull, do you think I fear you? I tell you your great muscles and stubborn heart are no more than those of Eblis, the black stallion. Must I prove it again to you?"

"No," he muttered. "God help me, but I know it's true. I'm not the match for Black Margot."

"Nor is any other man," she countered. Then, more softly, "But if ever I do meet the man who can conquer me, if ever he exists, he will have something of you in him, Hull. Your great, slow strength, and your stubborn honesty, and your courage. I promise that." She paused, her face now pure as a marble saint's. "So say what you have to say, Hull. What do you ask?"

"My life," he said bluntly.

Her green eyes widened in surprise. "You, Hull? You beg your life? You?"

"Not for myself," he muttered. "There's Vail Ormiston weeping over her father. Enoch, who would have married her and loved her, is dead in last night's ambush, and if I die, she's left alone. I ask my life for her."

"Her troubles mean nothing to me," said Margaret of N'Orleans coldly.

"She'll die without someone—someone to help her through this time of torment."

"Let her die, then. Why do you death-bound cling so desperately to life, only to age and die anyway? Sometimes I myself would welcome death, and I have infinitely more to live for than you. Let her die, Hull, as I think you'll die in the next moment or so!"

Her hand rested on the stock of the weapon at her belt. "I grant your second choice," she said coolly. "The quick death."

10. Old Einar Again

Black Margot ground out her cigarette with her left hand against the polished wood of the table top, but her right rested inexorably on her weapon. Hull knew beyond doubt or question that he was about to die, and for a moment he considered the thought of dying fighting, of being blasted by the beam as he flung himself at her. Then he shook his head; he revolted at the idea of again trying violence on the exquisite figure he faced, who, though witch or demon, had the passionless purity and loveliness of divinity. It was easier to die passively, simply losing his thoughts in the glare of her unearthly beauty.

She spoke. "So die, Hull Tarvish," she said gently, and drew the blunt weapon.

A voice spoke behind him, a familiar, pleasant voice. "Do I intrude, Margaret?"

He whirled. It was Old Einar, thrusting his goodhumored, wrinkled visage through the opening he had made in the doorway. He grinned at Hull, flung the door wider, and slipped into the room.

"Einar!" cried the Princess, springing from her chair. "Einar Olin! Are you still in the world?" Her tones took on suddenly the note of deep pity. "But so old—so old!"

The old man took her free hand. "it is forty years since last I saw you, Margaret—and I was fifty then,"

"But so old!" she repeated. "Einar, have I changed?"

He peered at her. "Not physically, my dear. But from the stories that go up and down the continent, you are hardly the gay madcap that N'Orleans worshipped as the Princess Peggy, nor even the valiant little warrior they used to call the Maid of Orleans."

She had forgotten Hull, but the guards visible through the half open door still blocked escape. He listened fascinated, for it was almost as if he saw a new Black Margot.

"Was I ever the Princess Peggy?" she murmured. "I had forgotten—Well, Martin Sair can stave off age but he cannot halt the flow of time. But Einar—Einar, you were wrong to refuse him!"

"Seeing you, Margaret, I wonder instead if I were not very wise. Youth is too great a restlessness to bear for so long a time, and you have borne it less than a century. What will you be in another fifty years? In another hundred, if Martin Sair's art keeps its power? What will you be?"

She shook her head; her green eyes grew deep and sorrowful. "I don't know, Einar. I don't know."

"Well," he said placidly, "I am old, but I am contented. I wonder if you can say as much."

"I might have been different, Einar, had you joined us. I could have loved you, Einar."

"Yes," he agreed wryly. "I was afraid of that, and it was one of the reasons for my refusal. You see, I did love you, Margaret, and I chose to outgrow the torture rather than perpetuate it. That was a painful malady, loving you, and it took all of us at one time or another. 'Flame-struck', we used to call it." He smiled reflectively. "Are any left save me of all those who loved you?"

"Just Jorgensen," she answered sadly. "That is if he has not yet killed himself in his quest for the secret of the Ancient's wings. But he will."

"Well," said Olin dryly, "my years will yet make a mock of their immortality." He pointed a gnarled finger at Hull. "What do you want of my young friend here?"

Her eyes flashed emerald, and she drew her hand from that of Old Einar. "I plan to kill him."

"Indeed? And why?"

"Why?" Her voice chilled. "Because he struck me with his hands. Twice."

The old man smiled. "I shouldn't wonder if he had cause enough, Margaret. Memory tells me that I myself have had the same impulse."

"Then it's well you never yielded, Einar. Even you."

"Doubtless. But I think I shall ask you to forgive young Hull Tarvish."

"You know his name! Is he really your friend?"

Old Einar nodded. "I ask you to forgive him."

"Why should I?" asked the Princess. "Why do you think a word from you can save him?"

"I am still Olin," said the aged one, meeting her green eyes steadily with his watery blue ones. "I still carry Joaquin's seal."

"As if that could stop me!" But the cold fire died slowly in her gaze, and again her eyes were sad. "But you are still Olin, the Father of Power," she murmured. With a sudden gesture she thrust her weapon back into her belt. "I spare him again," she said, and then, in tones gone strangely dull, "I suppose I wouldn't have killed him anyway. It is a weakness of mine that I cannot kill those who love me in a certain way—a weakness that will cost me dear some day."

Olin twisted his lips in that skull-like smile, turning to the silent youth. "Hull," he said kindly, "you must have been born under fortunate stars. But if you're curious enough to tempt your luck further, listen to this old man's advice." His smile became a grin. "Beyond the western mountains there are some very powerful, very rare hunting cats called lions, which Martin Sair says are not native to this continent, but were brought here by the Ancients to be caged and gazed at, and occasionally trained. As to that I know nothing, but I do say this, Hull—go twist the tail of a lion before you again try the wrath of Black Margot. And now get out of here."

"Not yet, Hull," snapped the Princess. "I have still my score to settle with you." She turned back to Olin. "Where do you wander now, Einar?"

"To N'Orleans. I have some knowledge to give Jorgensen, and I am homesick besides for the Great City."

He paused. "I have seen Joaquin. Selui has fallen."

"I know. I ride to meet him tonight."

"He has sent representations to Ch'cago."

"Good!" she flashed. "Then there will be fighting." Then her eyes turned dreamy. "I have never seen the saltless seas," she added wistfully, "but I wonder if they can be as beautiful as the blue Gulf beyond N'Orleans."

But Old Einar shook his thin white hair. "What will be the end of this, Margaret?" he asked gently. "After Ch'cago is taken—for you will take it—what then?"

"Then the land north of the saltless seas, and east of them. N'York, and all the cities on the ocean shore."

"And then?"

"Then South America, I suppose."

"And then, Margaret?"

"Then? There is still Europe veiled in mystery, and Asia, Africa—all the lands known to the Ancients."

"And after all of them?"

"Afterwards," she replied wearily, "we can rest. The fierce destiny that drives Joaquin surely cannot drive him beyond the boundaries of the world."

"And so," said Olin, "you fight your way around the world so you can rest at the end of the journey. Then why not rest now, Margaret? Must you pillow your head on the globe of the planet?"

Fury flamed green in her eyes. She raised her hand and struck the old man across his lips, but it must have been lightly, for he still smiled.

"Fool!" she cried. "Then I will see to it that there is always war! Between me and Joaquin, if need be—or between me and anyone—anyone—so that I fight!" She paused panting. "Leave me, Einar," she said tensely. "I do not like the things you bring to mind."

Still smiling, the old man backed away. At the door he paused. "I will see you before I die, Margaret," he promised, and was gone.

She followed him to the doorway. "Sora!" she called. "Sora! I ride!"

Hull heard the heavy tread of the fat Sora, and in a moment she entered bearing the diminutive cothurns and a pair of glistening silver gauntlets on her hands, and then she too was gone.

Slowly, almost wearily, the Princess turned to face Hull, who had as yet permitted no gleam of hope to enter his soul, for he had experienced too much of her mockery to trust the promise of safety Old Einar had won for him. He felt only the fascination that she always bound about him, the spell of her unbelievable black hair and her glorious sea-green eyes, and all her unearthly beauty.

"Hull," she said gently, "what do you think of me now?"

"I think you are a black flame blowing cold across the world. I think a demon drives you."

"And do you hate me so bitterly?"

"I pray every second to hate you."

"Then see, Hull." With her little gauntleted fingers she took his great hands and placed them about the perfect curve of her throat. "Here I give you my life for the taking. You have only to twist once with these mighty hands of yours and Black Margot will be out of the world forever." She paused. "Must I beg you?"

Hull felt as if molten metal flowed upward through his arms from the touch of her white skin. His fingers were rigid as metal bars, and all the great strength of them could not put one feather's weight of pressure on the soft throat they circled. And deep in the lambent emerald flames that burned in her eyes he saw again the fire of mockery—jeering, taunting.

"You will not?" she said, lifting away his hands, but holding them in hers. "Then you do not hate me?"

"You know I don't," he groaned.

"And you do love me?"

"Please," he muttered. "Is it necessary again to torture me? I need no proof of your mastery."

"Then say you love me."

"Heaven forgive me for it;" he whispered, "but I do!"

She dropped his hands and smiled. "Then listen to me, Hull. You love little Vail with a truer love, and month by month memory fades before reality. After a while there will be nothing left in you of Black Margot, but there will be always Vail. I go now hoping never to see you again, but"—and her eyes chilled to green ice—"before I go I settle my score with you."

She raised her gauntleted hand. "This for your treachery!" she said, and struck him savagely across his right check. Blood spouted, there would be scars, but he stood stolid. "This for your violence!" she said, and the silver gauntlet tore his left check. Then her eyes softened. "And this," she murmured, "for your love!"

Her arms circled him, her body was warm against him, and her exquisite lips burned against his. He felt as if he embraced a flame for a moment, and then she was gone, and a part of his soul went with her. When he heard the hooves of the stallion Eblis pounding beyond the window, he turned and walked slowly out of the house to where Vail still crouched beside her father's body. She clung to him, wiped the blood from his cheeks, and strangely, her words were not of her father, nor of the sparing of Hull's life, but of Black Margot.

"I knew you lied to save me," she murmured. "I knew you never loved her."

And Hull, in whom there was no falsehood, drew her close to him and said nothing.

But Black Margot rode north from Selui through the night. In the sky before her were thin shadows leading phantom armies, Alexander the Great, Attila, Genghis Khan, Tamerlane, Napoleon, and clearer than all, the battle queen Semiramis. All the mighty conquerors of the past, and where were they, where were their empires, and where, even, were their bones? Far in the south were the graves of men who had loved her, all except Old Einar, who tottered like a feeble grey ghost across the world to find his.

At her side Joaquin Smith turned as if to speak stared, and remained silent. He was not accustomed to the sight of tears in the eyes and on the cheeks of Black Margot.*

* All conversation ascribed to the Princess Margaret in this story is taken verbatim from an anonymous volume published in Urbs in the year 186, called "Loves of the Black Flame." It is credited to Jacques Lebeau, officer in command of the Black Flame's personal guard.

The Black Flame

1. Penalty – and Aftermath

Thomas Marshall Connor was about to die. The droning voice of the prison chaplain gradually dulled his perception instead of stimulating his mind. Everything was hazy and indistinct to the condemned man. He was going to the electric chair in just ten minutes to pay the supreme penalty because he had accidentally killed a man with his bare fists.

Connor, vibrantly alive, vigorous and healthy, only twenty-six, a brilliant young engineer, was going to die. And, knowing, he did not care. But there was nothing at all nebulous about the gray stone and cold iron bars of the death cell. There was nothing uncertain about the split down his trouser leg and the shaven spot on his head.

The condemned man was acutely aware of the solidarity of material things about him. The world he was leaving was concrete and substantial. The approaching footsteps of the death guard sounded heavily in the distance.

The cell door opened, and the chaplain ceased his murmuring. Passively Thomas Marshall Connor accepted his blessings, and calmly took his position between his guards for his last voluntary walk.

He remained in his state of detachment as they seated him in the chair, strapped his body and fastened the electrodes. He heard the faint rustling of the witnesses and the nervous, rapid scratching of reporters' pencils. He could imagine their adjectives—*Calloused murderer—Brazenly indifferent to his fate.*

But it was as if the matter concerned a third party.

He simply relaxed and waited. To die so quickly and painlessly was more a relief than anything. He was not even aware when the warden gave his signal. There was a sudden silent flash of blue light. And then—nothing at all.

***

So this was death. The slow and majestic drifting through the Stygian void, borne on the ageless tides of eternity.

Peace, at last—peace, and quiet, and rest.

But what was this sensation like the glimpse of a faint, faraway light which winked on and off like a star? After an interminable period the light became fixed and steady, a thing of annoyance. Thomas Marshall Connor slowly became aware of the fact of his existence as an entity, in some unknown state. The senses and memories that were his personality struggled weakly to reassemble themselves into a thinking unity of being—and he became conscious of pain and physical torture.

There was a sound of shrill voices, and a stir of fresh air. He became aware of his body again. He lay quiet, inert, exhausted. But not as lifeless as he had lain for—how long?

When the shrill voices sounded again, Connor opened unseeing eyes and stared at the blackness just above him. After a space he began to see, but not to comprehend. The blackness became a jagged, pebbled roof no more than twelve inches from his eyes—rough and unfinished like the under side of a concrete walk.

The light became a glimmer of daylight from a point near his right shoulder.

Another sensation crept into his awareness. He was horribly, bitterly cold. Not with the chill of winter air, but with the terrible frigidity of inter-galactic space. Yet he was on—no, in, earth of some sort. It was as if icy water flowed in his veins instead of blood. Yet he felt completely dehydrated. His body was as inert as though detached from his brain, but he was cruelly imprisoned within it. He became conscious of a growing resentment of this fact.

Then, stimulated by the shrilling, piping voices and the patter of tiny feet out there somewhere to the right, he made a tremendous effort to move. There was a dry, withered crackling sound—like the crumpling of old parchment—but indubitably his right arm had lifted!

The exertion left him weak and nauseated. For a time he lay as in a stupor. Then a second effort proved easier. After another timeless interval of struggling torment his legs yielded reluctant obedience to his brain. Again he lay quietly, exhausted, but gathering strength for the supreme effort of bursting from his crypt.

For he knew now where he was. He lay in what remained of his grave. How or why, he did not know. That was to be determined.

With all his weak strength he thrust against the left side of his queer tomb, moving his body against the crevice at his right. Only a thin veil of loose gravel and rubble blocked the way to the open. As his shoulder struck the pile, it gave and slid away, outward and downward, in a miniature avalanche.

Blinding daylight smote Connor like an agony. The shrill voices screamed.

"'S moom!" A child's voice cried tremulously. "'S moom!".

Connor panted from exertion, and struggled to emerge from his hole, each movement producing another noise like rattling paper. And suddenly he was free! The last of the gravel tinkled away and he rolled abruptly down a small declivity to rest limply at the bottom of the little hillside.

He saw now that erosion had cut through this burial ground—wherever it was—and had opened a way for him through the side of his grave. His sight was strangely dim, but he became aware of half a dozen little figures in a frightened semicircle beyond him.

Children! Children in strange modernistic garb of bright colors, but nevertheless human children who stared at him with wide-open mouths and popping eyes. Their curiously cherubic faces were set in masks of horrified terror.

Suddenly recalling the terrors he had sometimes known in his own childhood, Connor was surprised they did not flee. He stretched forth an imploring hand and made a desperate effort to speak. This was his first attempt to use his voice, and he found that he could not.

The spell of dread that held the children frozen was instantly broken. One of them gave a dismayed cry:

"A-a-a-h! 'S a specker!"

In panic, shrieking that cry, the entire group turned and fled. They disappeared around the shoulder of the eroded hill, and Connor was left horribly alone. He groaned from the depths of his despair and was conscious of a faint rasping noise through his cracked and parched lips.

He realized suddenly that he was quite naked—his shroud had long since moldered to dust. At the same moment that full comprehension of what this meant came to him, he was gazing in horror at his body. Bones! Nothing but bones, covered with a dirty, parchment-like skin!

So tightly did his skin cover his skeletal framework that the very structure of the bones showed through. He could see the articulation at knuckles, knees, and toes. And the parchment skin was cracked like an ancient Chinese vase, checked like aged varnish. He was a horror from the tomb, and he nearly fainted at the realization.

After a swooning space, he endeavored to arise. Finding that he could not, he began crawling painfully and laboriously toward a puddle of water from the last rain. Reaching it, he leaned over to place his lips against its surface, reckless of its potability, and sucked in the liquid until a vast roaring filled his ears.

The moment of dizziness passed. He felt somewhat better, and his breathing rasped a bit less painfully in his moistened throat. His eyesight was slowly clearing and as he leaned above the little pool, he glimpsed the specter reflected there. It looked like a skull—a face with lips shrunken away from the teeth, so fleshless that it might have been a death's head.

"Oh, God!" he called out aloud, and his voice croaked like that of a sick raven. "What and where am I!"

In the back of his mind all through this weird experience, there had been a sense of something strange aside from his emergence from a tomb in the form of a living scarecrow. He stared up at the sky.

The vault of heaven was blue and fleecy with the whitest of clouds. The sun was shining as he had never thought to see it shine again. The grass was green. The ground was normally earthy. Everything was as it should be—but there was a strangeness about it that frightened him. Instinctively he knew that something was direfully amiss.

It was not the fact that he failed to recognize his surroundings. He had not had the strength to explore; neither did he know where he had been buried. It was that indefinable homing instinct possessed in varying degree by all animate things. That instinct was out of gear. His time sense had stopped with the throwing of that electric switch—how long ago? Somehow, lying there under the warming rays of the sun, he felt like an alien presence in a strange country.

"Lost!" he whimpered like a child.

After a long space in which he remained in a sort of stupor, he became aware of the sound of footsteps. Dully he looked up. A group of men, led by one of the children, was advancing slowly toward him. They wore brightly colored shirts—red, blue, violet—and queer baggy trousers gathered at the ankles in an exotic style.

With a desperate burst of energy, Connor gained his knees. He extended a pleading skeleton like claw.

"Help me!" he croaked in his hoarse whisper.

The beardless, queerly effeminate-looking men halted and stared at him in horror.

"'Assim!" shrilled the child's voice. "'S a specker. 'S dead."

One of the men stepped forward, looking from Connor to the gaping hole in the hillside.

"Wassup?" he questioned.

Connor could only repeat his croaking plea for aid.

"'Esick," spoke another man gravely. "Sleeper, eh?"

There was a murmur of consultation among the men with the bright clothes and oddly soft, womanlike voices.

"T' Evanie!" decided one. "T' Evanie, the Sorc'ess."

They closed quickly around the half reclining Connor and lifted him gently. He was conscious of being borne along the curving cut to a yellow country road, and then black oblivion descended once more to claim him.

When he regained consciousness the next time, he found that he was within walls, reclining on a soft bed of some kind. He had a vague dreamy impression of a girlish face with bronze hair and features like Raphael's angels bending over him. Something warm and sweetish, like glycerin, trickled down his throat.

Then, to the whispered accompaniment of that queerly slurred English speech, he sank into the blissful repose of deep sleep.

2. Evanie the Sorceress

There were successive intervals of dream and oblivion, of racking pain and terrible nauseating weakness; of voices murmuring queer, unintelligible words that yet were elusively familiar.

Then one day he awoke to the consciousness of a summer morning. Birds twittered; in the distance children shouted. Clear of mind at last, he lay on a cushioned couch puzzling over his whereabouts, even his identity, for nothing within his vision indicated where or who he was.

The first thing that caught his attention was his own right hand. Paper-thin, incredibly bony, it lay like the hand of death on the rosy coverlet, so transparent that the very color shone through. He could not raise it; only a twitching of the horrible fingers attested its union with his body.

The room itself was utterly unfamiliar in its almost magnificently simple furnishings. There were neither pictures nor ornaments. Only several chairs of aluminum-like metal, a gleaming silvery table holding a few ragged old volumes, a massive cabinet against the opposite wall, and a chandelier pendant by a chain from the ceiling.

He tried to call out. A faint croak issued.

The response was startlingly immediate. A soft voice said, "Hahya?" in his ear and he turned his head painfully to face the girl of the bronze hair, seated at his side. She smiled gently.

She was dressed in curious green baggy trousers gathered at the ankle, and a brilliant green shirt. She had rolled the full sleeves to her shoulders. Hers was like the costume of the men who had brought him here.

"Whahya?" she said softly.

He understood.

"Oh ! I'm—uh—Thomas Connor, of course."

"F'm 'ere?"

"From St. Louis."

"Selui? 'Sfar off."

Far off? Then where was he? Suddenly a fragment of memory

returned. The trial—Ruth—that catastrophic episode of the grim chair. Ruth! The yellow-haired girl he had once adored, who was to have been his wife—the girl who had coldly sworn his life away because he had killed the man she loved.

Dimly memory came back of how he had found her in that other man's arms on the very eve of their wedding; of his bitter realization that the man he had called friend had stolen Ruth from him. His outraged passions had flamed, the fire had blinded him, and when the ensuing battle had ended, the man had been crumpled on the green sward of the terrace, with a broken neck.

He had been electrocuted for that. He had been strapped in that chair!

Then—then the niche on the hill. But how—how? Had he by some miracle survived the burning current? He must have—and he still had the penalty to pay!

He tried desperately to rise.

"Must leave here!" he muttered. "Get away—must get away." A new thought. "No! I'm legally dead. They can't touch me now; no double jeopardy in this country. I'm safe!"

Voices sounded in the next room, discussing him.

"F'm Selui, he say," said a man's voice. "Longo, too."

"Eah," said another. "'S lucky to live—lucky! 'L be rich."

That meant nothing to him. He raised his hand with a great effort; it glistened in the light with an oil of some sort. It was no longer cracked, and the ghost of a layer of tissue softened the bones. His flesh was growing back.

His throat felt dry. He drew a breath that ended in a tickling cough.

"Could I have some water?" he asked the girl.

"N-n-n!" She shook her head. "N' water. S'm licket?"

"Licket?" Must be liquid, he reflected. He nodded, and drank the mug of thick fluid she held to his lips.

He grinned his thanks, and she sat beside him. He wondered what sort of colony was this into which he had fallen—with their exotic dress and queer, clipped English.

His eyes wandered appreciatively over his companion; even if she were some sort of foreigner, she was gloriously beautiful, with her bronze hair gleaming above the emerald costume.

"C'n talk," she said finally as if in permission.

He accepted. "What's your name?"

"'M Evanie Sair. Evanie the Sorc'ess."

"Evanie the Sorceress!" he echoed. "Pretty name—Evanie. Why the Sorceress, though? Do you tell fortunes?"

The question puzzled her.

"N'onstan," she murmured.

"I mean—what do you do?"

"Sorc'y." At his mystified look, she amplified it. "To give strength—to make well." She touched his flesh-less arm.

"But that's medicine—a science. Not sorcery."

"Eah. Science—sorc'y. 'S all one. My father, Evan Sair the Wizard, taught me." Her face shadowed. "'S dead now." Then abruptly: "Whe's your money?" she asked.

He stared. "Why—in St. Louis. In a bank."

"Oh!" she exclaimed. "N-n-n! Selui! N'safe!"

"Why not?" He started. "Has there been another flood of bank-bustings?"

The girl looked puzzled.

"N'safe," she reiterated. "Urbs is better. For very long, Urbs is better." She paused. "When'd you sleep?"

"Why, last night."

"N-n-n. The long sleep."

The long sleep! It struck him with stunning force that his last memories before that terrible awakening had been of a September world—and this was mid-summer! A horror gripped him. How long—how long—had he lain in his—grave? Weeks? No—months, at least.

He shuddered as the girl repeated gently, "When?"

"In September," he muttered.

"What year?"

Surprise strengthened him. "Year? Nineteen thirty-eight, of course!"

She rose suddenly. "'S no Nineteen thirty-eight. 'S only Eight forty-six now!"

Then she was gone, nor on her return would she permit him to talk. The day vanished; he slept, and another day dawned and passed. Still Evanie Sair refused to allow him to talk again, and the succeeding days found him fuming and puzzled. Little by little, however, her strange clipped English became familiar.

So he lay thinking of his situation, his remarkable escape, the miracle that had somehow softened the discharge of Missouri's generators. And he strengthened. A day came when Evanie again permitted speech, while he watched her preparing his food.

"Y'onger, Tom?" she asked gently. "'L bea soon." He understood; she was saying, "Are you hungry, Tom? I'll be there soon."

He answered with her own affirmative "Eah," and watched her place the meal in a miraculous cook stove that could be trusted to prepare it without burning.

"Evanie," he began, "how long have I been here?"

"Three months," said Evanie. "You were very sick."

"But how long was I asleep?"

"You ought to know," retorted Evanie. "I told you this was Eight forty-six."

He frowned.

"The year Eight forty-six of what?"

"Just Eight forty-six," Evanie said matter-of-factly. "Of the Enlightenment, of course. What year did you sleep?"

"I told you—Nineteen thirty-eight," insisted Connor, perplexed. "Nineteen thirty-eight, A.D."

"Oh," said Evanie, as if humoring a child.

Then, "A.D.?" she repeated. "Anno Domini, that means. Year of the Master. But the Master is nowhere near nineteen hundred years old."

Connor was nonplussed. He and Evanie seemed to be talking at cross-purposes. He calmly started again.

"Listen to me," he said grimly. "Suppose you tell me exactly what you think I am—all about it, just as if I were a—oh, a Martian. In simple words."

"I know what you are," said Evanie. "You're a Sleeper. Often they wake with muddled minds."

"And what," he pursued doggedly, "is a Sleeper?"

Surprisingly Evanie answered that, in a clear, understandable—but most astonishing—way. Almost as astonished herself that Connor should not know the answer to his question.

"A Sleeper," she said simply, and Connor was now able to understand her peculiar clipped speech—the speech of all these people—with comparative ease, "is one of those who undertake electrolepsis. That is, have themselves put to sleep for a long term of years to make money."

"How? By exhibiting themselves?"

"No," she said. "I mean that those who want wealth badly enough, but won't spend years working for it, undertake the Sleep. You must remember that—if you have forgotten so much else. They put their money in the banks organized for the Sleepers. You will remember. They guarantee six percent. You see, don't you? At that rate a Sleeper's money increases three hundred times a century—three hundred units for each one deposited. Six percent doubles their money every twelve years. A thousand becomes a fortune of three hundred thousand, if the Sleeper outlasts a century—and if he lives."

"Fairy tales!" Connor said contemptuously, but now he understood her question about the whereabouts of his money, when he had first awakened. "What institution can guarantee six percent with safety? What could they invest in?"

"They invest in one percent Urban bonds."

"And run at a loss, I suppose!"

"No. Their profits are enormous—from the funds of the nine out of every ten Sleepers who fail to waken!"

"So I'm a Sleeper!" Connor said sharply. "Now tell me the truth."

Evanie gazed anxiously down at him.

"Electrolepsis often muddles one."

"I'm not muddled!" he yelled. "I want truth, that's all. I want to know the date."

"It's the middle of July, Eight hundred and forty-six," Evanie said patiently.

"The devil it is! Perhaps I slept backward then! I want to know what happened to me."

"Then suppose you tell," Evanie said gently.

"I will!" he cried frantically. "I'm the Thomas Marshall Connor of the newspapers—or don't you read 'em? I'm the man who was tried for murder, and electrocuted. Tom Connor of St. Louis—St. Louis! Understand?"

Evanie's gentle features went suddenly pale.

"St. Louis!" she whispered. "St. Louis—the ancient name of Selui! Before the Dark Centuries—impossible!"

"Not impossible—true," Connor said grimly. "Too painfully true."

"Electrocution!" Evanie whispered in awe. "The Ancients' punishment!" She stared as if fascinated, then cried excitedly: "Could electrolepsis happen by accident? Could it? But no! A milliampere too much and the brain's destroyed; a millivolt too little and asepsis fails. Either way's death—but it has happened if what you are telling is the truth, Tom Connor! You must have experienced the impossible!"

"And what is electrolepsis?" Connor asked, desperately calm.

"It—it's the Sleep!" whispered the tense girl. "Electrical paralysis of the part of the brain before Rolando's Fissure. It's what the Sleepers use, but only for a century, or a very little more. This—this is fantastic! You have slept since before the Dark Centuries! Not less than a thousand years!"

3. Forest Meeting

A week—the third since Connor's awakening to sane thought, had passed. He sat on a carved stone bench before Evanie's cottage and reveled in the burning canopy of stars and copper moon. He was living, if what he had been told was true—and he was forced to believe it now—after untold billions had passed into eternity.

Evanie must have been right. He was convinced by her gentle insistence, by the queer English on every tongue, by a subtle difference in the very world about him. It wasn't the same world—quite.

He sighed contentedly, breathing the cool night air. He had learned much of the new age from Evanie, though much was still mysteriously veiled. Evanie had spoken of the city of Urbs and the Master, but only vaguely. One day he asked her why.

"Because"—she hesitated—"well, because it's best for you to form your own judgments. We—the people around here—are not fond of Urbs and the Immortals, and I would not like to influence you, Tom, for in all truth it's the partisans of the Master who have the best of it, not his enemies. Urbs is in power; it will probably remain in power long after our lifetimes, since it has ruled for seven centuries."

Abruptly she withdrew something from her pocket and passed it to him. He bent over it—a golden disc, a coin. He made out the lettering "10 Units," and the figure of a snake circling a globe, its tail in its mouth.

"The Midgard Serpent," said Evanie. "I don't know why, but that's what it's called."

Connor reversed the coin. There was revealed the embossed portrait of a man's head, whose features, even in miniature, looked cold, austere, powerful. Connor read:

"*Orbis Terrarum Imperator Dominusque Urbis.*"

"Emperor of the World and Master of the City," he translated.

"Yes. That is the Master." Evanie's voice was serious as she took the coin. "This is the money of Urbs. To understand Urbs and the Master you must of course know something of history since your—sleep."

"History?" he repeated.

She nodded. "Since the Dark Centuries. Some day one of our patriarchs will tell you more than I know. For I know little of your mighty ancient world. It seems to us an incredible age, with its vast cities, its fierce nations, its inconceivable teeming populations, its terrific energies and its flaming genius. Great wars, great industries, great art—and then great wars again."

"But you can tell me—" Connor began, a little impatiently. Evanie shook her head.

"Not now," she said quickly. "For now I must hasten to friends who will discuss with me a matter of great moment. Perhaps some day you may learn of that, too."

And she was gone before Tom Connor could say a word to detain her. He was left alone with his thoughts—clashing, devastating thoughts sometimes, for there was so much to be learned in this strange world into which he had been plunged.

In so many ways it was a strange, new world, Connor thought, as he watched the girl disappear down the road that slanted from her hilltop home to the village. From where he sat on that bench of hewn stone he could glimpse the village at the foot of the hill—a group of buildings, low, of some white stone. All of the structures were classical, with pure Doric columns. Ormon was the name of the village, Evanie had said.

All strange to him. Not only were the people so vastly at variance with those he had known, but the physical world was bewilderingly different.

Gazing beyond the village, and bringing his attention back to the hills and the forests about him, Tom Connor wondered if they, too, would be different.

He had to know.

The springtime landscape beckoned. Connor's strength had returned to such an extent that he arose from his bench in the sun and headed toward the green of the forest stretching away behind Evanie's home. It was an enchanting prospect he viewed. The trees had the glistening new green of young foliage, and emerald green grass waved in the fields that stretched away down the hillsides and carpeted the plains.

Birds were twittering in the trees as he entered the forest—birds of all varieties, in profusion, with gaily-colored plumage. Their numbers and fearlessness would have surprised Connor had he not remembered something Evanie had told him. Urbs, she had said, had wiped out objectionable stinging insects, flies, corn-worms and the like, centuries ago, and the birds had helped. As had certain parasites that had been bred for the purpose.

"They only had to let the birds increase," Evanie had said, "by destroying their chief enemy—the Egyptian cat; the house-cat. It was acclimatized here and running wild in the woods, so they bred a parasite—the Feliphage—which destroyed it. Since then there have been many birds, and fewer insects."

It was pleasant to stroll through that green forest, to that bird orchestral accompaniment. The spring breeze touched Tom Connor's face lightly, and for the first time in his life he knew what it was to stroll in freedom, untouched by the pestiferous annoyance of mosquitoes, swarming gnats and midges, or other stinging insects that once had made the greenwood sometimes akin to purgatory.

What a boon to humanity! Honey bees buzzed in the dandelions in the carpeting grass, and drank the sweetness from spring flowers, but no mites or flies buzzed about Connor's uncovered, upflung head as he swung along briskly.

Connor did not know how far he had penetrated into the depths of the newly green woods when he found himself following the course of a small stream. Its silvery waters sparkled in the sunlight filtering through the trees as it moved along, lazily somnolent.

Now and then he passed mossy and viney heaps of stones, interesting to him, since he knew, from what he had been told, that they were the sole reminders of ancient structures erected before the Dark Centuries. Those heaps of stones had once formed buildings in another, and long-gone age—his own age.

Idly following the little stream, he came at last to a wide bend where the stream came down from higher ground to spill in a little splashing falls.

He had just rounded the bend, his gaze on a clear, still pool beyond, when he stopped stock still, his eyes widening incredulously.

It was as if he were seeing spread before him a picture, well known in his memory, and now brought to animate life. Connor had thought himself alone in that wood, but he was not. Sharing it with him, there within short yards of where he stood, was the most beautiful creature on which he had ever looked.

It was hard to believe she was a living, breathing being and not a figment of his imagination. No sound had warned her of his approach and, sublimely unaware that she was not alone, she held the pose in which Connor had first seen her, like some lovely wood sprite—which she might be, in this increasingly astonishing new world.

She was on her knees beside the darkly mirrored pool, supported by the slender arms and hands that looked alabaster white against the mossy bank on which she pressed. She was smiling down at her own reflection in the water—the famous Psyche painting which Connor so well remembered, come to life!

He was afraid to breathe, much less to speak, for fear of startling her. But when she turned her head and saw him, she showed no signs of being startled. Slowly she smiled and got gracefully to her feet, the clinging white Grecian draperies that swathed her, gently swaying in the breeze to outline a figure too perfect to be flesh and blood. It was accentuated by the silver cord that crossed beneath her breasts, as sparkling as her ink-black hair.

But as she smiled at Connor, instantly in the depths of her sea-green eyes he saw no fear of him; but mockery.

"I did not know," she said, in a voice that held the resonance of a silvery bell, "that any Weeds ever cared enough about the beauties of Nature to penetrate so far into the forest."

"I am not a Weed," Connor promptly disclaimed, as unconsciously he moved a step or two nearer her. He hoped that she would not vanish at the sound of his voice, or at his approach. "I am—"

She stared at him a moment, then laughed. And the laughter, too, was mocking.

"No need to tell me," she said airily. "I know. You are the Sleeper who was recently revived—with the great tale of having slept a thousand years. As if you were an Immortal!"

In her laughter, her voice, was the lofty intimation that she, at least, believed nothing of the sort. Connor made no attempt to convince her—not then. He was too enthralled, merely gazing at her.

"Are you one of the Immortals?" he asked, his own voice awed. "I have heard much of them."

"There are many things more immortal," she said, half cryptically, half mockingly, "than the human to whom has been given immortality. Such Immortals know nothing of all that was known, or guessed, by the Greeks of long, long ages past."

Again Connor stared at her. She spoke so confidently. And she looked. . . Could it be possible that the gods and goddesses, the sprites, of that long-dead Greek age were not legends, after all, but living entities? Could it be possible that he was gazing at one now—and that she might vanish at a touch, at a word?

She seemed real enough, though, and there was a certain imperiousness in her manner that was not his idea of what should be the reaction of any lovely sprite straight out of the pages of mythology. None of it seemed real—except her extravagant, pulse-warming beauty.

4. A Bit of Ancient History

The girl's words snapped him out of his reverie, with the confused knowledge that he was staring at her inanely as she stood there, swaying slightly, like a slender reed, while the gentle breeze whipped her white, gauzy draperies.

"Come," she said peremptorily. "Come sit beside me here. I have come to the forest to find adventure that I cannot find elsewhere in a boring world. I have not found it. Come, you shall amuse me. Sit here and tell me this story I have been hearing about your—sleep."

Half-hypnotically, Connor obeyed. Nor did he question why. It was all in a line with the rest, that he should find himself here above the sparkling dark pool, beside this woman—or girl, rather, since she could be no more than eighteen—whose beauty was starkly incredible.

The sun, filtering through the leaves, touched her mass of hair, so black that it glinted blue as it fell in waving cascades below her slender waist. Her skin, magnolia-tinted, was all the clearer because of the startling ebony of her hair. Her beauty was more than a lack of flaws; it was, in true fact, goddess like. But sultry, flaming. Her perfect lips seemed constantly smiling, but like the smile in her emerald eyes, it was sardonic, mocking.

For one moment the beauty of this wood sprite, come upon so unexpectedly, swept all other thoughts from Connor's mind; even memory of Evanie. But the next moment Evanie was back, filling his thoughts as she had from the first with her cool, understandable, coppery-haired loveliness. But even in that moment he knew that the radiant creature beside him, so different from Evanie and other Weed girls he had seen, would forever haunt him. Whoever, whatever she might be—human being or wood goddess.

The girl grew impatient at his silence.

"Tell me!" she said imperiously. "I have said to you, I would be amused. Tell me—Sleeper."

"I am no Sleeper—of the type of which you probably have customarily heard," Connor said, obedient to her command. "Whatever has come to me has been none of my doing; nor by my wishes. It was like this—"

Briefly he recited his experience, all that he knew of it, making no dramatic effort. He must have been impressive, for as he talked, he could see the incredulity and mockery pass from her sea-green eyes, to be replaced by reluctant belief, then astonishment.

"It is almost unbelievable," she said softly, when he had finished. "But I do believe you." Her marvelous eyes held a far-away expression. "If in your memory you have retained knowledge of your own ancient times, great things await you in this age to which you have come."

"But I know nothing about this age!" Connor quickly complained. "I glean snatches of this and that, of some mysterious Immortals who seem to reign supreme, of many things alien to me and my understanding. But so far, I have not been able to learn much about this age. No! Nor do I even know anything of the history of the ages that have passed while I was—sleeping!"

Connor's wood sprite looked hard at him a moment, admiration for him plain in her low-lidded glance. The mockery flickered a moment in her eyes; then died.

"Shall I tell you?" she asked. "We of the woods and valleys know many things. We learn as the cycles of years go by. But not always do we pass our knowledge along."

"Please!" begged Connor. "Please tell me—everything. I am lost!"

She seemed a little uncertain where to begin, then suddenly started to talk as if giving an all-inclusive lesson in history from the beginning of time.

"You of the ancient world had great cities," she said. "Today there are mighty cities, too. N'York had eight millions of people; Urbs, the great metropolis of this age, has thirty millions. But where there is now one metropolis, your world had a hundred. A marvelous age, that time of yours, but it ended. Some time in your Twentieth Century, it went out in a blaze of war."

"The Twentieth Century, so near my time!"

"Yes. Your fierce, warlike nations sated their lust for battle at last in one gigantic war that spread like a cloud around the planet. They fought by sea, by land, by air, and beneath sea and land. They fought with weapons whose secrets are still lost, with strange chemistries, with diseases. Every nation was caught in the struggle; all their vast knowledge went into it, and city after giant city was destroyed by atomic bombs or annihilated by infected water supplies. Famine stalked the world, and after it swept swift pestilence.

"But, by the fiftieth year after the war, the world had reached a sort of stability. Then came barbarism. The old nations had fallen, and in their place came numberless little city-states, little farming communities each sufficient to itself, weaving its own cloth, raising its own food. And then the language began to change."

"Why?" asked Connor. "Children speak like their parents."

"Not exactly," said the wood sprite, with a slow smile. "Language evolves by laws. Here's one: Consonants tend to move forward in the mouth as languages age. Take the word 'mother.' In the ancient Tokhar, it was *makar*. Then the Latin, *mater*. Then *madre*, then mother and now our modern word muvver. Do you see? K—T—D—Th—V—each sound a little advanced in the throat. The ultimate of course, is mama—pure labial sounds, which proves only that it's the oldest word in the world."

"I see," said Connor.

"Well, once it was released from the bonds of printing, language changed. It became difficult to read the old books, and then books began to vanish. Fire gutted the abandoned cities; the robber bands that lurked there burned books by winter for warmth. Worms and decay ruined them. Precious knowledge vanished, some of it forever."

She paused a moment, watching Connor keenly. "Do you see now," she asked, "why I said greatness awaits you if you retain any of your ancient knowledge?"

"Possibly," said Connor. "But go on, please."

"Other factors, too, were at work," she said, nodding. "In the first place, a group of small city-states seems to be the best environment for genius. That was the situation in Greece during the Golden Age, in Italy during the Renaissance, and all over the world before the Second Enlightenment.

"Then too, a period of barbarism seems to act as a time of rest for humanity before a charge to new heights. The Stone Age flared suddenly into the light of Egypt, Persia decayed and Greece flowered, and the Middle Ages awoke to the glory of the Renaissance. So the Dark Centuries began to flame into the brilliant age of the

Second Enlightenment, the fourth great dawn in human history.

"It began quietly enough, about two centuries after the war. A young man named John Holland drifted into the village of N'Orleans that sprawled beside the ancient city's ruins. He found the remnants of a library, and—unusual in his day—he could read. He studied alone at first, but soon others joined him, and the Academy came into being.

"The townspeople thought the students wizards and sorcerers, but as knowledge grew the words wizard and sorcerer became synonyms for what your age called scientists."

"I see!" muttered Connor, and he was thinking of Evanie the Sorceress. "I see!"

"N'Orleans," said his charming enlightener, "became the center of the Enlightenment. Holland died, but the Academy lived, and one day a young student named Teran had a vision. Some of the ancient knowledge had by now yielded its secrets, and Teran's vision was to restore the ancient N'Orleans power plants and water systems—to give the city its utilities!

"Although there was no apparent source of fuel, he and his group labored diligently on the centuries-old machines, confident that power would be at hand when they needed it.

"And it was. A man named Einar Olin, had wandered over the continent seeking—and finding—the last and greatest achievement of the Ancients; he rediscovered atomic energy. N'Orleans wakened anew to its ancient life. Across plains and mountains came hundreds just to see the Great City, and among these were three on whom history turned.

"These were sandy-haired Martin Sair, and black-haired Joaquin Smith, and his sister. Some have called her Satanically beautiful. The Black Flame, they call her now—have you heard?"

Connor shook his head, his eyes drinking in the beauty of this woman of the woods, who fascinated him in a manner he would never have believed possible. For a moment the mocking glint came back in the girl's eyes, then instantly it was gone as she shrugged her white shoulders and went on.

"Those three changed the whole course of history. Martin Sair turned to biology and medicine when he joined the half-monastic Academy, and his genius made the first new discovery to add to the knowledge of the Ancients. Studying evolution, experimenting with hard radiations, he found sterility then—immortality!

"Joaquin Smith found his field in the neglected social sciences, government, economics, psychology. He too had a dream—of rebuilding the old world. He was—or is—a colossal genius. He took Martin Sair's immortality and traded it for power. He traded immortality to Jorgensen for a rocket that flew on the atomic blast, to Kohlmar for a weapon, to Erden for the Erden resonator that explodes gunpowder miles away. And then he gathered his army and marched."

"War again!" Connor said tightly. "I should have thought they would have had enough."

But the girl did not heed him. In her emerald eyes was a light as if she were seeing visions herself—visions of glorious conquest.

"N'Orleans," she said, "directly in the light of Joaquin Smith's magnetic personality, yielded gladly. Other cities yielded almost as if fascinated, while those who fought were overcome. What chance had rifle and arrow against the flying Triangles of Jorgensen, or Kohlmar's ionic beams? And Joaquin Smith himself was—well, magnificent. Even the wives of the slain cheered him when he comforted them in that noble manner of his.

"America was conquered within sixty years. Immortality gave Smith, the Master, power, and no one save Martin Sair and those he taught has ever been able to learn its secret. Thousands have tried, many have claimed success, but the results of their failures still haunt the world.

"And—well, Joaquin Smith has his World Empire now; not America alone. He has bred out criminals and the feeble-minded, he has impressed his native English on every tongue, he has built Urbs, the vast, glittering, brilliant, wicked world capital, and there he rules with his sister, Margaret of Urbs, beside him. Yet—"

"I should think this world he conquered would worship him!" exclaimed Connor.

"Worship him! Too many hate him, in spite of all he has done, not only for this age, but for ages gone—since the Enlightenment. He—"

But Tom Connor was no longer listening. All his thoughts, his attention, his eyes that drank in her beauty, were on the girl. So lovely—and to have so much wisdom stored up in the brain beneath the sheen of that satiny-black cap that was her hair. There could only be one answer to that. She must be a goddess, come to life.

He ached to touch her, to touch only the hem of her gauzy garment, but that must not be. His heart pounded at the very nearness of her—but it was with a worship that could have thrown him prostrate at her feet.

"It's all like a dream, what you've told me," he said, his voice far-away, musing. "You're a dream."

The dancing light of mockery came back into her sea-green eyes. "Shall we leave it a dream—this meeting of ours?" she asked softly. She laid one white hand lightly on his arm and he thrilled at the touch as though an electric current had shot through him—but not a painful, annihilating one now. "Man of the Ancients," she said, "will you give me a promise?"

"Anything—anything!" Connor said eagerly.

"Then promise me you will say nothing, not even to the Weed girl who is called Evanie the Sorceress, about having seen me this morning. No slightest hint."

For a moment Connor hesitated. Would it be disloyalty to Evanie, in any way, to make that promise? He did not know. What he did know was that it fell in with his own ideas to keep this meeting a secret—like something sacred; something to hold as a memory deep within his own heart only.

"Promise?" she repeated, in that silvery-bell voice.

Connor nodded. "I promise," he said soberly. "But tell me, will I see you again? Will you—"

Suddenly the girl leaped lightly to her feet, startled, as she stood listening, like the faun she appeared to be. Her astonishing emerald eyes were wide, as she poised for flight. Dimly, the entranced Connor became aware of voices back in the woods. Men were probably coming to seek him, knowing how sick he had been.

"I must go!" the girl whispered quickly. "But Man of the Ancients, we shall meet again! That is my promise. Keep yours!"

And then, before he could speak, she had whirled like a butterfly in flight, and was speeding through the woods on noiseless feet. Connor caught one last glimpse of her fluttering white draperies against the brown and green of tree trunks and leaves, then she was gone.

He passed a hand slowly before his bewildered eyes. A dream! But she had promised they would meet again. When?

5. The Village

Days slipped imperceptibly by. Connor had almost regained his full strength. Time and again, whenever he could do so unobserved, he slipped away to the woods alone, but never again did he catch sight of the wood nymph who had so deeply fascinated him. Gradually he came to persuade himself that the whole incident had been a dream. Many things as strange had happened to him since his awakening. Only one thing gave it the semblance of reality—the knowledge he had gleaned from the inky-haired girl of mystery, a knowledge later confirmed when he began to enter the peaceful life of the village.

Aside from Evanie, however, he had but one other close friend. He had taken at once to Jan Orm, engineer and operator of the village of Ormon's single factory on the hill.

The factory was a perpetual surprise to Connor. The incredibly versatile machines made nearly everything except the heavier mechanisms used in the fields, and these, he learned, could have been made. That was not necessary since the completed machines could as easily be transported as the steel necessary to construct them.

The atomic power amazed Tom Connor. The motors burned only water, or rather the hydrogen in it, and the energy was the product of synthesis rather than disintegration. Four hydrogen atoms, with their weight of 1.008, combined into one helium atom, with a weight of 4; somewhere had disappeared the difference of .032, and this was the source of that abundant energy—matter being destroyed, weight transformed to energy.

There was a whole series of atomic furnaces, too. The release of energy was a process of one degree, like radium; once started, neither temperature nor pressure could speed or slow it in the least. But the hydrogen burned steadily into helium at the uniform rate of half its mass in three hundred days.

Jan Orm was proud of the plant.

"Neat, isn't it?" he asked Connor. "One of the type called Omnifac; makes anything. There's thousands of 'em about the country; practically make each town independent, self-sustaining. We don't need your ancient cumbersome railroad system to transport coal and ore."

"How about the metal you use?"

"Nor metal either," Jan said. "Just as there was a stone age, a bronze age, and an iron age, just as history calls your time the age of steel, we're in the aluminum age. And aluminum's everywhere; it's the base of all clays, almost eight per cent of the Earth's crust."

"I know it's there," grunted Connor. "It used to cost too much to get it out of clay."

"Well, power costs nothing now. Water's free." His face darkened moodily. "If we could only control the rate, but power comes out at always the same rate—a half period of three hundred days. If we could build rockets—like the Triangles of Urbs. The natural rate is just too slow to lift its own weight; the power from a pound of water comes out too gradually to raise a one-pound mass. The Urbans know how to increase the rate, to make the water deliver half its energy in a hundred days—ten days."

"And if you could build rockets?"

"Then," said Jan, growing even moodier, "then we'd—" He paused abruptly. "We can detonate it," he said in a changed voice. "We can get all the energy in one terrific blast, but that's useless for a rocket."

"Why can't you use a firing chamber and explode say a gram of water at a time?" Connor asked. "A rapid series of little explosions should be just as effective as a continuous blast."

"My father tried that," Jan Orm said grimly. "He's buried at the bend of the river."

Later, Connor asked Evanie why Jan was so anxious to develop atom-powered rockets. The girl turned suddenly serious eyes on him, but made no direct reply.

"The Immortals guard the secret of the Triangle," was all she said. "It's a military secret."

"But what could he do with a rocket?"

She shook her glistening hair.

"Nothing, perhaps."

"Evanie," he said soberly, "I don't like to feel that you won't trust me. I know from what you've said that you're somehow opposed to the government. Well, I'll help you, if I can—but I can't if you keep me in ignorance."

The girl was silent.

"And another thing," he proceeded. "This immortality process. I've heard somebody say that the results of its failures when some tried it, still haunt the world? Why, Evanie?"

Swiftly a crimson flush spread over the girl's cheeks and throat.

"Now what the devil have I said?" he cried. "Evanie, I swear I wouldn't hurt you, for the world!"

"Don't," she only murmured, turning silently away.

He, too, was hurt, because she was. He knew he owed his life to her for her treatments and hospitality. It disturbed him to think he knew of no way in which to repay her. But he was dubious of his ability to earn much as an engineer in this world of strange devices.

"I'd have to start right at the bottom," he observed ruefully to Evanie when he spoke of that later.

"In Urbs," Evanie said, "you'd be worth your weight in radium as a source of ancient knowledge. So much has been lost; so much is gone, perhaps forever. Often we have only the record of a great man's name, and no trace of his work. Of these is a man named Einstein and another named de Sitter—men acknowledged to be supreme geniuses of science even by the supreme scientists of your age. Their work is lost."

"I'm afraid it will remain lost, then," he said whimsically. "Both Einstein and de Sitter were contemporaries of mine, but I wasn't up to understanding their theories. All I know is that they dealt with space and time, and a supposed curvature of space—Relativity, the theory was called."

"But that's exactly the clue they'd want in Urbs!" exclaimed Evanie, her eyes shining. "That's all they'd need. And think of what you could tell them of ancient literature! We haven't the artists and writers you had—not yet. The plays of a man named Shakespeare are still the most popular of all on the vision broadcasts. I always watch them." She looked up wistfully. "Was he also a contemporary of yours? And did you know a philosopher named Aristotle?"

Connor laughed.

"I missed the one by three centuries and the other by twenty-five!" he chuckled.

"I'm sorry," said the girl, flushing red. "I don't know much of history."

He smiled warmly.

"If I thought I could actually earn something—if I could pay you for all the trouble I've been, I'd go to the city of Urbs for awhile—and then come back here. I'd like to pay you."

"Pay me?" she asked in surprise. "We don't use money here, except for taxes."

"Taxes?"

"Yes. The Urban taxes. They come each year to collect, and it must be paid in money." She frowned angrily. "I hate Urbs and all it stands for! I hate it!"

"Are the taxes so oppressively high?"

"Oppressive?" she retorted. "Any tax is oppressive! It's a difference in degree, that's all! As long as a government has the right to tax, the potential injustice is there. And what of other rights the Master arrogated to himself?" She paused as if to let the full enormity of that strike in.

"Well?" he said carelessly, "That's been a privilege granted to the heads of many governments, hasn't it?"

Her eyes blazed. "I can't understand a man who's willing to surrender his natural rights!" she flared. "Our men would die for a principle!"

"But they're not doing it," observed Connor caustically.

"Because they'd be throwing their lives away uselessly—that's why! They can't fight the Master now with any chance of success. But just wait until the time comes!"

"And then, I suppose, the whole world will be just one great big beautiful state of anarchy."

"And isn't that an ideal worth fighting for?" asked the girl hotly. "To permit every single individual to attain his rightful liberty? To destroy every chance of injustice?"

"But—"

Connor paused, considering. Why should he be arguing like this with Evanie? He felt no allegiance to the government of Urbs; the Master meant nothing to him. The only government he could have fought for, died for, was lost a thousand years in the past. Whatever loyalty he owed in this topsy-turvy age belonged to

Evanie. He grinned. "Crazy or not, Evanie," he promised, "your cause is mine!"

She softened suddenly.

"Thank you, Tom." Then, in lower tones, "Now you know why Jan Orm is so anxious for the secret of the rocket blast. Do you see?" Her voice dropped to a whisper. "Revolution!"

He nodded. "I guessed that. But since you've answered one question, perhaps you'll answer my other one. What are the failures that still haunt the world, the products of the immortality treatment?"

Again that flush of unhappiness.

"He meant—the metamorphs," she murmured softly.

Quickly she rose and passed into the cottage.

6. The Metamorphs

Connor's strength swiftly approached normal, and shortly little remained of that unbelievable sojourn in the grave. His month's grizzle of beard began to be irritating, and one day he asked Jan for a razor.

Jan seemed puzzled; at Connor's explanation he laughed, and produced a jar of salve that quickly dissolved the stubble, assuring Connor that the preparation would soon destroy the growth entirely.

But Evanie's reaction surprised him. She stared for a moment without recognition.

"Tom!" she cried. "You look—you look like an ancient statue!"

He did look different from the mild-featured villagers. With the beard removed, his lean face had an aura of strength and ruggedness that was quite unlike the appearance of his neighbors.

Time slipped pleasantly away. Evenings he spent talking to newly made friends, relating stories of his dead age, explaining the state of politics, society, and science in that forgotten time. Often Evanie joined in the conversation, though at other times she amused herself at the "vision," a device of remarkable perfection, on whose two-foot screen actors in distant cities spoke and moved with the naturalness of miniature life.

Connor himself saw "Winter's Tale" and "Henry the Eighth" given in accurate portrayal, and was once surprised to discover a familiar-seeming musical comedy, complete to scantily-clad chorus. In many ways Evanie puzzled Tom Connor. There was some mystery about her that he could not understand. Life in Ormon, it seemed to him, was essentially what it had been in his old days in St. Louis. Young men still followed immemorial routine; each evening saw them walking, sitting, talking, with girls, idling through the park like arcades of trees, strolling along the quiet river.

But not Evanie. No youth ever climbed the hill to her cottage, or sat with her at evening—except when Jan Orm occasionally came.

And this seemed strange, considering the girl's loveliness. Connor couldn't remember a more attractive girl than this spirited, gentle, demure Evanie—except his girl of the woods. Not even Ruth of the buried days of the past.

He mused over the matter until a more sensational mystery effaced it. Evanie went hunting game up-river. Deer were fairly plentiful, and game-birds, wild turkeys, and pheasants had increased until they were nearly as common as crows once had been.

The trio carried glistening bows of spring steel that flung slender steel arrows with deadly accuracy, if used properly. Connor was awkward, but Evanie and Jan Orm handled them with skill. Connor bemoaned the lack of rifles; he had been a fair marksman in the old days.

"I'd show you!" he declared. "If I only had my Marlin repeater!"

"Guns aren't made any more," said Jan. "The Erden Resonator finished them; they're useless for military weapons."

"But for hunting?"

"They're banned by law. For awhile after the founding of the Urban Empire people kept 'em hidden around, but no one knew when a resonator might sweep the section, and folks got tired of having the things go off at night, smashing windows and plowing walls. They weren't safe house-pets."

"Well," grumbled Connor, "I'd like one now, even an air-rifle. Say!" he exclaimed. "Why not a water-gun?"

"A water-gun?"

"One run by atomic energy. Didn't you say you could detonate it—get all the power out at once?"

"Yes, but—" Jan Orm paused. "By God!" he roared.

"That's the answer! That's the weapon! Why didn't anybody think of that before? There's what we need to—" He broke his sentence in mid-air.

Evanie smiled. "It's all right," she said. "Tom knows."

"Yes," said Connor, "and I'm with you in your revolutionary ambitions."

"I'm glad," Jan Orm said simply. His eyes lighted. "That gun! It's a stroke of genius. The resonators can't damage an atom-powered rifle! Evanie, the time draws near!"

The three proceeded thoughtfully up the river bank. The mid-summer sun beat down upon them with withering intensity. Connor mopped his streaming brow.

"How I'd like a swim," he ejaculated. "Evanie, do you people ever swim here? That place where the river's backed up by that fallen bridge—it should be a great place for a dip!"

"Oh, no!" the girl said quickly. "Why should we swim? You can bathe every day in the pool at home."

That was true. The six-foot basin where water, warmed to a pleasant tepidity by atomic heat, bubbled steadily through, was always available. But it was a poor substitute for swimming in open water.

"That little lake looked tempting," Connor sighed.

"The lake!" cried Evanie, in horror. "Oh, no! No! You can't swim there!"

"Why not?"

"You just can't!"

And that was as much information as he could obtain. Shortly afterward, swinging the half-dozen birds that had fallen to their arrows, they started back for the village.

But Connor was determined to ferret out at least that one mystery—why he should not swim in the lake. The next time he accompanied Jan Orm on a tramp up-river, he plied Jan with questions. But it was futile. He could extract no more from Jan Orm than he had from Evanie.

As the pair approached the place of the ruined bridge that dammed the stream, they turned a little way inland. Jan's keen eyes spotted a movement in a thick copse.

"Deer in there," he whispered. "Let's separate and start him."

He bore off to the left, and Connor, creeping cautiously to the right, approached the grass-grown bank of the watercourse. Suddenly he stopped short. Ahead of him the sun had glinted on something large and brown and wet, and he heard a rustle of movement. He moved stealthily forward; with utmost care he separated a screen of brush, and gazed through it to a little open glade, and on the creature that sprawled there beside the water.

At first he saw only a five-foot strip of wet, hairless, oily skin that heaved to the thing's slow breathing. He held his bow ready lest it prove dangerous, and stared, wondering what sort of creature it could be. It was certainly nothing native to the North America of his day. And then, at some sound or movement of his, the beast rolled over and faced him.

Connor felt sick. He glimpsed short, incredibly thick limbs, great splay feet with webbed toes, broad hands with webbed fingers. But what sickened him was the smooth bulbous face with its tiny eyes and little round red-lipped mouth.

The thing was, or had been, human!

Connor let out a choking yell. The creature, with a mumble that might have been speech, flopped awkwardly to the bank and into the water, where it cleaved the element like an otter and disappeared with a long, silent wake.

He heard the crashing of Jan Orm's approach, and his cry of inquiry. But a webbed print in the mud of the bank told Jan Orm the story.

"Wh—what was it?" Connor choked.

"A metamorph," said Jan soberly.

Empty-handed as they were, he turned homeward.

Connor, too aghast to press questions, followed him. And then came the second mystery.

Connor saw it first—a face, a child's face, peering at them from a leafy covert. But this was no human child. Speechless, Connor saw the small pointed ears that twitched, the pointed teeth, the black slanting eyes squinting at him beadily. The face was that of a young satyr, a child of Pan. It was the spirit of the wilderness incarnate, not evil exactly, not even savage, but just wild—wild!

The imp vanished instantly. As Connor gasped. "What's that?" It was already far beyond arrow-shot, headed for the forest. Jan viewed it without surprise.

"It's a young metamorph," he said. "A different sort than the one at the lake." He paused and stared steadily into Connor's eyes.

"Promise me something," he muttered.

"What?"

"That you'll not tell Evanie you saw these things."

"If you wish," said Connor slowly. It was all beyond him.

7. Panate Blood

But Tom Connor was determined now to fathom these mysteries. Jan should no longer put him off. He stopped and placed a hand firmly on Jan's arm, forced the man to look into his eyes when Jan would have evaded his gaze.

"Just what," he said bluntly, "is a metamorph? You must tell me, Jan!"

There was a moment's uncomfortable silence.

"That question has been evaded long enough," Connor said firmly, "and I intend to know why. This is my world now. I've got to live in it, and I want to know what others know of it—its faults as well as its virtues. Why have you shunned the question?"

"Because—because—"

"Because of Evanie!" supplied Connor.

"Yes," Jan agreed, reluctantly. "Because of Evanie."

"What has that monster at the lake to do with her?"

"Nothing directly." Jan Orm paused. "Before I tell you more, Tom, I'm going to ask you something. Do you love Evanie?"

"I'm very fond of her."

"But do you love her?" Jan insisted.

"Yes," said Connor suddenly. "I do."

A swift thought had come to him before he had readied that decision. The vision of a smiling wood nymph was before his eyes. But only a human being could be loved by a man—a coolly lovely girl like Evanie; not a goddess.

"Why do the youths of Ormon ignore Evanie so, Jan?" Connor asked abruptly. "She's far the loveliest girl in town."

"So she is, Tom. It's her own doing that they ignore her. They have tried to be friends with her—have tried hard. But she—well, she has always discouraged them."

"Why?"

"Because, I think, she feels that in justice to everybody she can't marry."

"And again why?"

For a long moment Jan Orm hesitated. "I'll tell you," he said finally. "She's one-eighth metamorph!"

"What?"

"Yes, her mother was the daughter of Montmerci the Anadominist. A great man, but half metamorph."

"Do you mean," asked Connor, aghast, "that she has the blood of that lake monster in her?"

"No! Oh, no! There are two kinds of metamorphs. One sort, the Panate metamorph, is human; the others, the amphimorphs, are just—horrors. Evanie's blood is Panate. But she had conquered her metamorphic heredity."

"A metamorph!" Connor groaned.

The picture of that flopping horror rose in his mind, and then the vision of the wild, impish face of the woods child. There was something reminiscent of Evanie in that, the color of her bronze hair, an occasional glint in her deep eyes.

"Tell me," he said huskily, "about that heredity of hers. Might her child, for instance, turn wild? Or turn into such a horror as an—amphimorph?"

Jan Orm smiled.

"By no chance! The Panate metamorphs, I tell you, are human. They're people. They're much like us—good and bad, brilliant and stupid, and many of them surpassingly beautiful in their wild way."

"But just what are they? Where'd they come from?"

"Do you remember hearing Martin Sair mentioned? He was companion of the Master, Evanie's great-uncle thirty generations removed."

"The discoverer of immortality? I remember."

But Connor made no mention of when he had first heard of both Martin Sair and the Master—from an uncannily beautiful wood sprite who had seemed to possess all the wisdom of the ages.

"Yes," Jan told him. "And you must have heard, too, that there were other attempts at making men immortal, in the first century of the Enlightenment. And failures. Some that still haunt the world. Well the metamorphs are those failures."

"I see," said Connor slowly.

"They're a mutation, an artificial mutation," Jan explained. "When Martin Sair's discovery became known, thousands sought to imitate him. It was understood that he was working with hard radiations, but just what was a mystery—whether as hard as the cosmic rays or as soft as the harder x-rays. Nevertheless, many charlatans claimed to be able to give immortality, and there were thousands of eager victims. It was a mania, a wave of lunacy. The laboratories of the tricksters were packed.

"There were four directions of error to be made; those who had not Sair's secret, erred in all four. People who were treated with too hard radiations died; those treated with too soft rays simply became sterile. Those treated with the right rays, but for too long a time, remained themselves unchanged, but bore amphimorphs as children; those treated for too short a time bore Panate metamorphs.

"Can you imagine the turmoil? In a world just emerging from barbarism, still disorganized, of course some of the freaks survived. Near the sea coasts amphimorphs began to appear, and in lakes and rivers; while in the hills and forests the Children of Nature, the Panate type, went trouping through the wilderness."

"But why weren't they exterminated?" asked Connor tensely. "You've bred out criminals. Why let these creatures exist. Why not kill them off?"

"Would you favor such a measure?"

"No," Connor said, adding in impassioned tone: "It would be nothing less than murder, even to kill the swimmers! Are they—intelligent?"

"In a dim fashion. The amphimorphs are creatures cast back to the amphibious stage of the human embryo—just above the gilled period. The others, the Panates, are strange. Except for an odd claustrophobia, the fear of enclosed things—of houses or clothing—they're quite as intelligent as most of us. And they're comparatively harmless."

Connor heaved a sigh of relief. "Then they aren't a problem?"

"Oh, there were consequences," Jan said wryly. "Their women are often very beautiful, like the marble figures of nymphs dug up in Europe. There have been many cases like Evanie's. Many of us may have a drop or so of metamorphic blood. But it falls hardest on the first offspring, the hybrids, miserable creatures unable to endure civilized life, and often most unhappy in the wilds. Yet even these occasionally produce a genius. Evanie's grandfather is one."

"What did he do?"

"He was known as Montmerci the Anodominist, half human, half metamorph. Yet his was a powerful personality. He was strong enough to lead an abortive revolution against the Master. Both humans and metamorphs followed him. He even managed to direct a group of amphimorphs, who got into the city's water supply and erupted into the sewers by hundreds."

"But what happened to the revolution?"

"It was quickly suppressed," Jan said bitterly. "What could a horde armed with bows and knives do against the Rings and ionic beams of Urbs?"

"And Montmerci?"

"He was executed—a rare punishment. But the Master realized the danger from this wild metamorph. A second attempt might have been successful. That's why Evanie hates Urbs so intensely."

"Evanie!" Connor said musingly. "Tell me, what was it that led to her father's marrying a—a—"

"A cross? Well, Evan Sair was like Evanie, a doctor. He came upon Meria, the daughter of Montmerci, down in the mountain region called Ozarky. He found her there sick just after the collapse of the uprising. So Evan Sair cared for her and fell in love with her. He brought her here to his home, and married her, but she soon began to weaken again from lack of the open woods and sunlight.

"She died when Evanie was born, but she would have died anyway."

Jan Orm paused and drew a long breath. "Now do you see why Evanie fears her own blood? Why she has driven away the youths who tried to arouse even friendship? She's afraid of the sleeping metamorphic nature in her, and needlessly afraid, since she's safely human. She has even tried to drive me away, but I refuse to be so driven. I understand."

"So do I," said Connor soberly. "And I'm going to marry her."

Jan Orm smiled dryly. "And if she thinks otherwise?"

"Then I must convince her."

Jan shook his head in mild wonderment. "Perhaps you can," he said, with the barest hint of reluctance. "There's something dynamic about you. In some ways you're like the Immortals of Urbs."

When they reached the village Connor left Jan Orm and

trudged in a deep reverie up Evanie's hill, musing on the curious revelations he had heard, analyzing his own feelings. Did he really love the bronze-haired Evanie? The query had never presented itself until Jan had put it to him, so bluntly, yet now he was certain he did. Admitting that, then—had he the right to ask her to marry a survival of the past, a revivified mummy, a sort of living fossil?

What damage might that millennium of sleep have done him? Might he not awake some morning to find the weight of his years suddenly upon him? Might he not disintegrate like a veritable mummy when its wrappings were removed? Still he had never felt stronger or healthier in his life. And was he such a freak, after all, in this world of Immortals, satyrs, and half-human swimmers?

He paused at the door of the cottage, peering within. The miraculous cook-stove hissed quietly, and Evanie was humming to herself as she stood before a mirror, brushing the shining metal of her hair. She glimpsed him instantly and whirled. He strode forward and caught her hands.

"Evanie—" he began, and paused as she jerked violently to release herself.

"Please go out!" she said.

He held her wrists firmly. "Evanie, you've got to listen to me. I love you! I know those aren't the right words," he stumbled on. "It's just—the best I can do."

"I don't—permit this," she murmured.

"I know you don't, but—Evanie I mean it!"

He tried to draw her closer but she stood stiffly while he slipped his arms about her. By sheer strength he tilted her head back and kissed her.

For a moment he felt her relax against him, then she had thrust him away.

"Please!" she gasped. "You can't! You don't—understand I"

"I do," he said gently.

"Then you see how impossible it is for me to—marry!"

"Any wildness in any children of ours," he said with a smile, "might as easily come of the Connor blood."

For a long moment Evanie lay passive in his arms, and then, when she struggled away, he was startled to see tears.

"Tom," she whispered, "if I say I love you will you promise me something?"

"You know I will!"

"Then, promise you'll not mention love again, nor try to kiss me, nor even touch me—for a month. After that, I'll—I'll do as you wish. Do you promise?"

"Of course, but why, Evanie? Why?"

"Because within a month," she murmured tensely, "there'll be war!"

8. In Time of Peace

Connor held strictly to his word with Evanie. But the change in their relationship was apparent to both of them. Evanie no longer met his gaze with frank steadiness. Her eyes would drop when they met his, and she would lose the thread of her sentences in confusion.

Yet when he turned unexpectedly, he always found her watching him with a mixture of abstractedness and speculation. And once or twice he awakened in the morning to find her gazing at him from the doorway with a tender, wistful smile.

One afternoon Jan Orm hailed him from the foot of Evanie's hill.

"I've something to show you," he called, and Connor rose from his comfortable sprawl in the shade and joined him, walking toward the factory across the village.

"I've been thinking, Jan," Connor remarked. "Frankly, I can't yet understand why you consider the Master such a despicable tyrant. I've yet to hear of any really tyrannous act of his."

"He isn't a tyrant," Jan said gloomily. "I wish he were. Then our revolution would be simple. Almost everybody would be on our side. It's evidence of his ability that he avoids any misgovernment, and keeps the greater part of the people satisfied. He's just, kind, and benevolent—on the surface!"

"What makes you think he's different underneath?"

"He retains the one secret we'd all like to possess—the secret of immortality. Isn't that evidence enough that he's supremely selfish? He and his two or three million Immortals—sole rulers of the Earth!"

"Two or three million!"

"Yes. What's the difference how many? They're still ruling half a billion people—a small percentage ruling the many. If he's so benevolent, why doesn't he grant others the privilege of immortality?"

"That's a fair question," said Connor slowly, pondering. "Anyway, I'm on your side, Jan. You're my people now; I owe you all my allegiance." They entered the factory. "And now—what was it you brought me here to see?"

Jan's face brightened.

"Ah!" he exclaimed. "Have a look at this."

He brought forth an object from a desk drawer in his office, passing it pridefully to Connor. It was a blunt, thick-handled, blue steel revolver.

"Atom-powered," Jan glowed. "Here's the magazine."

He shook a dozen little leaden balls, each the size of his little fingernail, into his palm.

"No need of a cartridge, of course," commented Connor. "Water in the handle? ... I thought so. But here's one mistake. You don't want your projectiles round; you lose range and accuracy. Make 'em cylindrical and blunt-pointed." He squinted through the weapon's barrel. "And—there's no rifling."

He explained the purpose of rifling the barrel to give the bullet a rotary motion.

"I should have known enough to consult you first," Jan Orm said wryly. "Want to try it out anyway? I haven't been able to hit much with it so far."

They moved through the whirring factory. At the rear the door opened upon a slope away from the village. The ground slanted gently toward the river. Glancing about for a suitable target, Connor seized an empty can from a bench within the door and flung it as far as he could down the slope. He raised the revolver, and suddenly perceived another imperfection that had escaped his notice.

"There are no sights on it!" he ejaculated.

"Sights?" Jan was puzzled.

"To aim by." He explained the principle. "Well, let's try it as is."

He squinted down the smooth barrel, squeezed the trigger. There was a sharp report, his arm snapped back to a terrific recoil, and the can leaped spinning high into the air, to fall yards farther toward the river.

"Wow!" he exclaimed. "What a kick!"

But Jan was leaping with enthusiasm.

"You hit it! You hit it!"

"Yeah, but it hit back," Connor said ruefully. "While you're making the other changes, lighten the charge a little, else you'll have broken wrists in your army. And I'd set somebody to work on ordnance and rifles. They're a lot more useful than revolvers." At Jan's nod, he asked, "You don't expect to equip the whole revolution with the products of this one factory, do you?"

"Of course not! There are thousands like it, in villages like Ormon. I've already sent descriptions of the weapons we'll need. I'll have to correct them."

"How many men can you count on? Altogether, I mean."

"We should muster twenty-five thousand."

"Twenty-five thousand for a world revolution? An even twenty-five thousand to attack a city of thirty million?"

"Don't forget that the city is all that counts. Who holds Urbs holds the world."

"But still—a city that size! Or even just the three million Immortals. We'll be overwhelmed!"

"I don't think so," Jan said grimly. "Don't forget that in Urbs are several million Anadominists. I count on them to join us. In fact, I'm planning to smuggle arms to them, provided our weapons are successful. They won't be as effective as the ionic beam, but—we can only try. We'll have at least the advantage of surprise, since we don't plan to muster and march on Urbs. We'll infiltrate slowly, and on the given day, at the given hour, we'll strike!"

"There'll be street fighting, then," Connor said. "There's nothing like machine-guns for that."

"What are they?"

Jan's eyes glowed as Connor explained. "We can manage those," he decided. "That should put us on a par with the Urban troops, so long as we remain in the city where the air forces can't help them. If only we had aircraft!"

"There're airplanes, such as my generation used."

"Too flimsy. Useless against the fliers of Urbs. No, what we need is the secret of the rocket blast, and since that's unobtainable, we'll have to do without. We'll manage to keep our fighting in the city itself. And how we'll need you!"

Connor soon came to realize the truth of Jan's words. What little he knew of trajectories, velocities, and the science of ballistics was taxed to the uttermost. He was astounded to discover that calculus was a lost knowledge, and that Jan was even unacquainted with the use of logarithms and the slide rule.

Rather than plod through hours and hours of mathematical computation, it seemed to Connor the shorter method was to work out a table of logarithms to four places, and to construct a slide rule; in both of these operations Jan joined with growing enthusiasm as understanding increased.

As the preparations progressed, Connor began to notice other things—the vanishing of familiar faces, the lack of youthful activities. He knew what that meant. The revolutionaries were gradually filtering into Urbs, and the day of the uprising was at hand.

How close it was, however, he never dreamed until he emerged one morning to find Evanie talking to Jan Orm, with her eyes alight. She turned eagerly to Tom, led him back into the cottage.

"Kiss me!" she whispered. "The day is here! We leave for Urbs tonight!"

All day there was a hush over the village. It was bereft of youth, girls as well as men. Only the oldsters plodded about in street and field.

Jan Orm confessed to Connor that he was not entirely pleased with all details. His estimate of the number of revolutionaries who would join him had been too high. But the infiltration into the city had been successful, and twenty-two thousand villagers lay armed and hidden among their Urban sympathizers. This, Jan argued, promised a great accession to their ranks once the hour had struck.

"What are your arrangements?" Connor asked.

"Each village has chosen its leader. These leaders have again centralized their command into ten, of whom our Ormon leader happens to be one. But each variety of Weed has its own corps." He smiled. "They call us Weeds, because we're supposed to run wild."

And again there came to Connor a quick mental picture of his beautiful girl of the forest. She, too, had spoken of "Weeds," a little contemptuously, he seemed to remember now. He had not understood her allusion then, had not asked her to explain. But it was plain enough now. Her lofty attitude toward "Weeds," or the common people, must have been because she was an aristocrat herself. Who could she have been? He had seen no one hereabouts bearing any faintest resemblance to her.

He brought his mind swiftly back to Jan.

"If you win," he observed, "you'll have a general battle over the spoils. You may find yourself worse off after the revolution than before."

"We know that," Jan said grimly. "Yet we'll fight side by side until the Master's done for. Afterward—"

He spread his hands expressively.

"You mentioned 'our Ormon leader'," remarked Connor. "That's you, of course."

"Oh, no!" Jan chuckled. "That's Evanie."

"The devil!" Connor stared amazed at the gentle, shy, and quiet girl.

"Jan exaggerated," she said, smiling. "I depend on all the rest of you. Especially Jan—and you, Tom."

He shook his head, puzzled about this revolution—shadowy, vague, ill-planned. To assault a world ruler in a colossal city with untrained rabble using weapons unfamiliar to them! Surely the Master must know there was sedition and plotting among his people.

He was about to voice his doubts when a flash of iridescence down the sunny slope caught his eye. It seemed more like a disturbance in the air or a focus of light than a material body. It swept in wide circles as if hunting or seeking, and—Connor heard its high, humming buzz. The creature, if it were a creature, was no more than eighteen inches long, and featureless save for a misty beak at the forward end.

It circled closer, and suddenly he perceived an amazing phenomenon. It was circling the three of them and, he had thought, the cottage too. Then he saw that instead of circling the building it was passing through the walls!

"Look!" he cried. "What's that?"

9. The Way to Urbs

The effect on Jan and Evanie was startling. As they perceived the almost invisible thing, the girl shrieked in terror.

"Don't look at it!" Jan choked out. "Don't even think of it!"

Both of them covered their faces with their hands.

They made no attempt to flee; indeed, Connor thought confusedly, how could one hide from a thing that could pass like a phantom through rock walls? He tried to follow their example but could not resist another peep at the mystery. It was still visible, but further off down the slope towards the river, and as he gazed, it abandoned its circling, passed like a streak of mist over the water, and vanished.

"It's gone," he said mildly. "Suppose you tell me what it was."

"It—it was a Messenger of the Master," murmured Evanie fearfully. "Jan, do you think it was for one of us? If so, that means he suspects!"

"God knows!" Jan muttered. "It looked dim to me, like a stray."

"And what," Connor demanded to know, "is a Messenger of the Master?"

"It's to carry the Master's commands," said Evanie.

"You don't say!" he snapped ironically. "I could guess that from its name. But what is it?"

"It's a mechanism of force, or so we think," said Jan. "It's—did you ever see ball-lightning?"

Connor nodded.

"Well, there's nothing material, strictly speaking, in ball-lightning. It's a balance of electrical forces. And so are the Messengers—a structure of forces."

"But—was it alive?"

"We believe not. Not exactly alive."

Connor groaned. "Not material, strictly speaking, and not exactly alive! In other words, a ghost."

Jan smiled nervously.

"It does sound queer. What I mean is that the Messengers are composed of forces, like ball-lightning. They're stable as long as

Urbs supplies enough energy to offset the losses. They don't discharge all at once like ball-lightning. When their energy is cut off, they just dissipate, fade out, vanish. That one missed its mark, if it was for us."

"How do they bear the Master's commands?"

"I hope you never find out," Evanie said softly. "I was sent for once before, but that Messenger missed like this. Jan and I—can close our minds to them. It takes practice to learn how."

"Well," said Connor, "if the Master suspects, you'd better change your plans. Surprise was your one advantage."

"We can't," Jan said grimly. "Our cooperating groups would split into factions in half an hour, given any excuse."

"But—that might have been sent as a warning!"

"No matter. We've got to go ahead. What's more, we'd better leave now."

Jan rose abruptly and departed. A moment later Connor saw him back in a motor vehicle from the hill below the factory. And then, with no more preparation than that, they were jolting over the rutted red clay road, Jan driving. Evanie between the two men.

When they swung suddenly to a wide paved highway, the battered vehicle leaped swiftly to unexpected speed. A full hundred miles an hour, though that was not so greatly in excess of the speed of cars of Connor's own day.

Hour after hour they rushed down the endless way. They passed tree-grown ruins and little villages like Ormon, and as night fell, here and there the lights of some peaceful farm dwelling. Evanie relieved Jan, and then Connor, pleading his acquaintance with ancient automobiles, drove for awhile, to the expressed admiration of the other two.

"You ancients must have been amazing!" said Jan.

"What paving is this?" asked Connor as they darted along.

"Same stuff as our tires. Rubrum. Synthetic rubber."

"Paved by whom?"

"By Urbs," said Jan sourly. "Out of our taxes."

"Well isn't that one answer to your objections? No taxes, no roads."

"The road through Ormon is maintained without taxes, simply by the cooperation of the people."

Connor smiled, remembering that rutted clay road.

"Is it possible to alienate any of the Master's troops?" he asked. "Trained men would help our chances."

"No," Jan said positively. "The man has a genius for loyalty. Such an attempt would be suicide."

"Humph! Do you know—the more I hear of the Master, the more I like him? I can't see why you hate him so! Apparently, he's a good ruler."

"He is a good ruler, damn his clever soul! If he weren't, I told you everybody'd be on our side." Jan turned to Evanie. "See how dangerous the Master is? His charm strikes even through the words of his enemies!"

When they finally stopped for refreshments, Evanie described for Connor other wonders of the Master's world empire. She told him of the hot-house cities of Antarctica under their crystal domes, and especially Austropolis, of the great mining city in the shadow of the Southern Pole, and of Nyx, lying precariously on the slopes of the volcano Erebus.

She had a wealth of detail gleaned from the vision screen, but Jan Orm had traveled there, and added terse comment. All traffic and freight came in by rocket, the Triangles of Urbs, a means too expensive for general use, but the mines produced the highly prized metal, platinum.

Evanie spoke, too, of the "Urban pond," the new sea formed in the Sahara Desert by the blasting of a passage through the Atlas Mountains to the Mediterranean. That had made of Algeria and Tripoli fertile countries, and by the increased surface for evaporation, it had changed even the climate of the distant Arabian Desert.

And there was Eartheye on the summit of sky-piercing Everest, the great observatory Whose objective mirror was a spinning pool of mercury a hundred feet across, and whose images of stellar bodies were broadcast to students around the world. In this gigantic mirror, Betelgeuse showed a measurable disc, the moon was a pitted plain thirty yards away, and even Mars glowed cryptically at a distance of only two and a half miles.

Connor learned that the red planet still held its mystery. The canals had turned out to be illusion, but the seasonal changes still argued life, and a million tiny markings hinted at some sort of civilization.

"But they've been to the moon," Evanie said, continuing the discussion as they got under way again. "There's a remnant of life there, little crystalline flowers that the great ladies of Urbs sometimes wear. Moon orchids; each one worth a fortune."

"I'd like to give you one some day," murmured Connor.

"Look, Tom!" Evanie cried sharply. "A Triangle!" He saw it in the radiance of early dawn. It was in fact a triangle with three girders rising from its points to an apex, whence the blast struck down through the open center. At once he realized the logic of the construction, for it could neither tip nor fall while the blast was fed.

How large? He couldn't tell, since it hung at an unknown height. It seemed enormous, at least a hundred feet on a side. And then a lateral blast flared, and it moved rapidly ahead of them into the south.

"Were they watching us, do you suppose?" Evanie asked tensely. "But—of course not! I guess I'm just nervous. Look, Tom, there's Kaatskill, a suburb of the City."

The town was one of magnificent dwellings and vast lawns.

"Kaatskill!" mused Connor. "The home of Rip van Winkle."

Evanie did not get the meaning of that.

"If he lives in Kaatskill I never heard of him," she said. "It is a place where many wealthy Sleepers have settled to enjoy their wealth."

The road widened suddenly, then they topped the crest of a hill. Connor's eyes widened in astonishment as the scene unfolded.

A valley lay before them and, cupped in the hills as in the palm of a colossal hand, lay such a hive of mammoth buildings that for a moment reason refused to accept it. Urbs! Connor knew instantly that only the world capital could stretch in such reaches across to the distant blue hills beyond.

He stared at sky-piercing structures, at tiered streets, at the curious steel web where a monorail car sped like a spider along its silken strand.

"There! Urbs Minor!" whispered Evanie. "Lesser Urbs!"

"Lesser Urbs?"

"Yes, Urbs Major is beyond. See? Toward the hills."

He saw. He saw the incredible structures that loomed Gargantuan. He saw a fleecy cloud drift across one, while behind it twin towers struck yet higher toward the heavens.

"The spires of the Palace," murmured Evanie.

They sped along the topmost of three tiers, and the vast structures were blotted out by nearer ones. For an hour and a half they passed along that seemingly endless street. The morning life of Urbs was appearing, traffic flowed, pedestrians moved in and out of doorways.

The dress of the city had something military about it, with men and women alike garbed in metallic-scaled shirts and either kirtles or brief shorts, with sandaled feet. They were slight in build, as were the Ormon folk, but they had none of the easy-going complacency of the villagers. They were hectic and hurried, and the sight struck a familiar note across the centuries.

Urbs was city incarnate. Connor felt the brilliance, the glamour, the wickedness, that is a part of all great cities from Babylon to Chicago. Here were all of them in one, all the great cities that ever were, all in this gigantic metropolis. Babylon reborn—Imperial Rome made young again!

They crossed, suddenly, a three-tiered viaduct over brown water.

"The canal that makes Urbs a seaport," Evanie explained.

Beyond, rising clifflike from the bank, soared those structural colossi Connor had seen in the blue distance, towering unbelievably into the bright sky. He felt pygmy like, crushed, stifled, so enormous was the mass. He did not need Evanie's whisper:

"Across the water is Greater Urbs."

Those mountainous piles could be nothing less.

On the crowded sidewalks brilliantly costumed people flowed by, many smoking black cigarettes. That roused a longing in Tom Connor for his ancient pipe, now disintegrated a thousand years. He stared at the bold Urban women with their short hair and metallic garb. Now and again one stared back, either contemptuously, noting his Weed clothing, or in admiration of his strong figure.

Jan Orm guided the car down a long ramp, past the second tier and down into the dusk of the ground level. They cut into a solid line of thunderous trucks, and finally pulled up at the base of one of the giant buildings. Jan drew a deep sigh.

"We're here," he said. "Urbs !"

Connor made no reply. In his mind was only the stunning thought that this colossus called Urbs was the city they were to attempt to conquer with their Weed army—a handful of less than twenty-five thousand!

10. Revolution

With the cessation of the car's movement a blanket of humid heat closed down on them. The ground level was sultry, hot with the stagnant breath of thirty million pairs of lungs.

Then, as Connor alighted, there was a whir, and he glanced up to see a fan blower dissolve into whirling invisibility, drawing up the fetid accumulation of air. A faint coolness wafted along the tunnel-like street. For perhaps half a minute the fan hummed, then was stilled. The colossal city breathed, in thirty-second gasps!

They moved into the building, to a temperature almost chilly after the furnace heat outside. Connor heard the hiss of a cooling system, recognized the sibilance since he had heard it from a similar system in Evanie's cottage. They followed Jan to an elevator, one of a bank of fully forty, and identical to one of the automatic lifts in an ancient apartment building.

Jan pressed a button, and the cage shot into swift and silent motion. It seemed a long time before it clicked to a halt at the seventy-fourth floor. The doors swung noiselessly aside and they emerged into a carpeted hall, following Jan to a door halfway down the corridor. A faint murmur of voices within ceased as Jan pressed a bell push.

In the moment of silence a faint, bluish light outlined the faces of Jan and Evanie; Connor standing a bit to the side, was beyond it.

"Looking us over on a vision screen," whispered Jan, and instantly the door opened. Connor heard voices.

"Evanie Sair and Jan Orm! At last!"

Connor followed them into a small chamber, and was a little taken aback by the hush that greeted his appearance. He faced the group of leaders in the room, half a dozen men and an equal number of women, all garbed in Urban dress, and all frozen in immobile surprise.

"This is Tom Connor," Jan Orm said quickly. "He suggested the rifles."

"Well!" drawled a golden-haired girl, relaxing. "He looks like a cool Immortal. Lord! I thought we were in for it!"

"You'd manage, Ena," said a striking dark-haired beauty, laughing disdainfully.

"Don't mind Maris." The blonde smiled at Connor. "She's been told she looks like the Princess; hence the air of hauteur." She paused. "And what do you think of Urbs?"

"Crowded," Connor said, and grinned.

"Crowded! You should see it on a business day."

"It's their weekly holiday," explained Evanie. "Sunday. We chose it purposely. There'll be fewer guards in the Palace seeing room."

For the first time Connor realized that Sundays passed unobserved in the peaceful life of Ormon.

Jan was surveying the Urban costumes in grim disapproval.

"Let's get to business," he said shortly.

There was a chorus of, "Hush!"

The girl Maris added, "You know there's a scanner in every room in Urbs, Jan. We can be seen from the Palace, and heard too!"

She nodded toward one of the light brackets on the wall. After a moment of close inspection Connor distinguished the tiny crystal 'eye.'

"Why not cover it?" he asked in a low voice.

"That would bring a Palace officer in five minutes," responded the blonde Ena. "A blank on the screen sticks out like the Alpha Building."

She summoned the group close about her, slipping a casual arm through Connor's. In an almost inaudible whisper she began to detail the progress of the plans, replying to Jan's queries about the distribution of weapons and where they now were, to Evanie's question about the appointed time, to inquiries from each of the others.

Evanie's report of the Messenger caused some apprehension.

"Do you think he knows?" asked Ena. "He must, unless it was some stray that passed near you."

"Suppose he does," countered Evanie. "He can't know when. We're ready, aren't we? Why not strike today—now—at once?"

There was a chorus of whispered protest.

"We oughtn't to risk everything on a sudden decision—it's too reckless!"

Ena pressed Connor's arm and whispered, "What do you think?"

He caught an angry glance from Evanie. She resented the blond girl's obvious attention.

"Evanie's right," he murmured. "The only chance this half-baked revolution has is surprise. Lose that and you've lost everything."

And such, after more whispered discussion, was the decision. The blow was to be struck at one o'clock, just two hours away. The leaders departed to pass the instructions to their subordinate leaders, until only Connor and Evanie remained. Even Jan Orm had gone to warn the men of Ormon.

Evanie seemed about to speak to Connor, but suddenly turned her back on him.

"What's the matter, Evanie?" he said softly.

He was unprepared for the violence with which she swung around, her brown eyes blazing.

"Matter!" she snapped. "You dare ask! With the feel of that canary-headed Ena's fingers still warm on your arm!"

"But Evanie!" he protested. "I did nothing."

"You let her!"

"But—"

"You let her!"

Further protest was prevented by the return of the patrician Maris. Evanie dropped into a sulky silence, not broken until Jan Orm appeared.

It was a solemn group that emerged on the ground level and turned their steps in the direction of the twin-towered Palace. Evanie had apparently forgotten her grievance in the importance of the impending moment, but all were silent and thoughtful.

Not even Connor had eyes for Palace Avenue, and the tumult and turmoil of that great street boiled about him unnoticed. Through the girders above, the traffic of the second and third tiers sent rumbling thunder, but he never glanced up, trudging abstractedly beside Evanie.

A hundred feet from the street's end they paused. Through the tunnel-like opening where Palace Avenue divided to circle the broad grounds of the Palace, Connor gazed at a vista of green lawn surmounted by the flight of white steps that led to the Arch where the enormous diorite statue of Holland, the Father of Knowledge, sat peering with narrowed eyes into an ancient volume.

"Two minutes," said Jan with a nervous glance around. "We'd better move forward."

They reached the open. The grounds, surrounded by the incredible wall of mountainous buildings, glowed green as a lake in the sun, and the full vastness of the Palace burst upon Connor's eyes, towering into the heavens like a twin-peaked mountain. For a moment he gazed, awe-struck, then glanced back into the cave of the ground level, waiting for the hour to strike.

It came, booming out of the Palace tower. One o'clock! Instantly the ground level was a teeming mass of humanity, swarming out of the buildings in a torrent. Sunlight glanced, flashing from rifle barrels; shouts sounded in a wild chorus. Swiftly the Ormon men gathered around Evanie, whose brilliant costume of green and crimson formed a rallying point like a flag.

The mob became an army, each group falling into formation about its leader. Men ran shouting into the streets on the broad avenue that circled the grounds, on the second and third tiers. Instantly a traffic jam began to spread to epic proportions. And then, between the vehicles, the mass of humanity flowed across the street toward the Palace.

From other streets to right and left, other crowds were pouring. The black-haired Maris was striding bare-limbed and lithe before her forces. White, frightened faces stared from a thousand stalled cars.

Then the heterogeneous mob was sweeping up the slope of grass, a surging mass converging from every side. The Palace was surrounded, at the mercy of the mob. And then—the whole frenzied panorama froze suddenly into immobility.

From a dozen doors, and down the wide white steps came men—Urban men, with glittering metallic cuirasses and bare brown limbs. They moved deliberately, in the manner of trained troops. Quickly they formed an inner circle about the Palace, an opposing line to the menacing thousands without.

They were few compared to the revolutionary forces, yet for a tense moment the charge was halted, and the two lines glared at each other across a few hundred feet of grassy slope.

That moment was etched forever in Connor's mind. He seemed to see everything, with the strange clarity that excitement can lend.

The glint of sunlight on steel, the vast inextricable jam of traffic, the motionless thousands on the hill, the untold thousands peering from every window in every one of the gigantic buildings. And even, on a balcony of stone far up on the left tower, two tiny shining figures surveying the scene. The three Triangles hanging motionless as clouds high in the heavens. The vast brooding figure of Holland staring unperturbed into his black stone book.

"He's warned—he's ready!" Jan muttered.

"We'll have to fire," Evanie cried.

But before her command, the sharp rattle of rifles came from far to the right. Machine-guns sputtered, and all down the widespread line puffs of steam billowed like huge white chrysanthemums, and dissipated at once.

From a thousand windows in the bank of buildings burst other momentary clouds, and the medley of shouts punctuated by staccato explosions was like a chorus of wild music.

Connor stared thunderstruck. In the opposing line not a single man had fallen! Each stood motionless as the giant statue, left arm crooked across breast, right arm holding a glistening revolver like weapon. Was marksmanship responsible for that—incredibly poor marksmanship?

Impossible, with that hail of bullets! Puffs of dust spurted up before the line, splintered stone flew from the walls behind. Windows crashed. But not one Urban soldier moved.

"What's wrong?" Connor yelled.

"He knew." Jan Orm panted. "He's equipped his men with Paige deflectors. He's the devil himself!"

The girl Maris leaped forward.

"Come on!" she shouted, and led the charge.

Instantly the line of Urbans raised their weapons, laying them across their bent left arms. A faint misty radiance stabbed out, a hundred brief flashes of light. The beams swept the revolutionaries. Anguished cries broke out as men spun and writhed.

Connor leaped back as a flash caught him. Sudden pain racked him as his muscles tore against each other in violent spasmodic contractions. A moment only; then he was trembling and aching as the beam flicked out. An electric shock! None should know that better than he!

Everywhere the revolutionaries were writhing in agony. The front ranks were down, and of all those near him, only he and Evanie were standing. Her face was strained and white and agonized.

Jan Orm was struggling to his feet, his face a mask of pain. Beyond him others were crawling away. Connor was astounded. The shock had been painful, but not that painful.

Halfway up the slope before the immobile line of Urbans lay the black-haired Maris. Her nerves had been unequal to the task set them, and she had fainted from sheer pain. The whole mass of the Weed army was wavering. The revolution was failing!

11. Flight

Connor had an inspiration. The deflecting force must emanate from the glittering buttons on the Urban's left arms. Moreover, the field must be projected only before the Urban soldiers, else they'd not be able to move their own weapons. Springing to a fallen machine-gun, he righted it, spun it far to the left so as to enfilade the Urbans, to strike them from the side.

He pulled the trigger—let out a yell of fierce joy as a dozen foemen toppled. He tried to shout his discovery to the others, but none heeded, and anyhow the Urbans could counter it by a slight shift of formation. So grimly he cut as wide a gap as he could.

The beams flashed. Steeling himself to the agony of the shock, he bore it unflinchingly. When it had passed, the Weed army was in flight. He muttered a vicious curse and jerked a groaning man on the ground beside him to his feet.

"You're still alive, you sheep!" he snarled. "Get up and carry that girl!" He gestured at the prostrate Maris.

The slope was clearing. Only half a hundred Weeds lay twisting on the grass, or were staggering painfully erect. Connor glared at the slowly advancing Urbans, faced them for a moment disdainfully, then turned to follow the flying Weeds. Halfway across the grounds he paused, seized an abandoned rifle, and dropped to his knee.

In a gesture of utter defiance, he took careful aim at the two figures on the tower balcony five hundred feet above. He pressed the trigger. Ten shots spat out in quick succession. Windows splintered above the figures, below, to right and left. Tom Connor swore again as he realized that these, too, were protected. Then he gritted his teeth as the ionic beam swept him once more.

When it ceased, he fled, to mingle with the last of the retreating Weed forces. They were trickling through, over, and around that traffic jam that would take heroic efforts to untangle.

The Revolution was over. No man could now reorganize that flying mob. Connor thrust his way through the mass of panic-stricken humanity until he reached the car in which Jan and Evanie were already waiting.

Without a word Jan swung the car hastily about, for the traffic snarl was reaching even as far away as he had parked. Evanie dropped her head on Connor's shoulder, weeping quietly.

"That's a hell of a revolution!" he grunted. "Twenty minutes and it's over!"

The car swept through the semi-dusk of the ground level of Palace Avenue to the point where the ramp curved about the base of the Atlas Building. There Jan guided it into the sunlight of the upper tier. In the afternoon glare his face was worn and haggard. Evanie, her spell of weeping over, was pallid and expressionless, like a statue in ivory.

"Won't we be stopped?" Connor asked, as Jan put on speed.

"They'll try," said Jan. "They'll block all of the Hundred Bridges. I hope we get across first. We can only hope, because they can see every move we make, of course. There are scanners on every street. We may be watched from the Palace now."

The bridge over which they had come into the city loomed before them. In a moment they were over the canal and into Urbs Minor, where ten million people still moved about their occupations in utter ignorance of the revolution and its outcome.

The colossal buildings of Greater Urbs receded and took on the blue hue of distance, and Lesser Urbs slipped rapidly by them. It was not until they had surmounted the ridge and dropped into Kaatskill that Jan gave any evidence of relaxing. There he drew a deep breath.

"Respite!" he murmured gloomily. "There are no scanners here, at least."

"What's to be done now?" asked Connor.

"Heaven knows! We'll be hunted, of course—everybody who was in it. But in Montmerci's rebellion the Master punished only one—Montmerci himself; the leader."

"Evanie's grandfather."

"Yes. That may weigh against her."

"This damned revolution was doomed from the start!" declared Connor irritably. "We hadn't enough organization, nor good enough weapons, nor an effective plan—nothing! And having lost the advantage of surprise, we had no chance at all."

"Don't!" Evanie murmured wearily. "We know that now."

"I knew it the whole time," he retorted. "By the way, Jan—those Paige deflectors of theirs. Do you know how they work?"

"Of course." Jan's voice was as weary as Evanie's. "It's just an inductive field. And metal passing through it had eddy currents induced in it."

Simple enough, mused Connor. He'd seen the old experiment of the aluminum ring tossed by eddy currents from the pole of an alternating current magnet. But he asked in surprise:

"Against such velocities?"

"Yes. The greater the velocity, the stronger the eddy currents. The bullet's speed helps to deflect it."

"Did you know of these deflectors before?" snapped Connor.

"Of course. But projectile weapons haven't been used for so long—how could I dream he'd know of our rifles and resurrect the deflectors?"

"You should have anticipated the possibility. Why, we could have used—" He broke off. Recriminations were useless now. "Never mind. Tell me about the ionic beam, Jan."

"It's just two parallel beams of highly actinic light, like gamma rays. They ionize the air they pass through. The ionized air is a conductor. There's an atomic generator in the handles of the beam-pistols, and it shoots an electric charge along the beams. And when your body closes the circuit between them—Lord! They didn't use a killing potential, or we'd have been burned to a crisp. I still ache from that agony!"

"Evanie stood up to it," Connor remarked.

"Just once," murmured the girl. "A second time—Oh, I'd have died!"

It struck Connor that this delicate, small-boned, nervous race must be more sensitive, less inured to pain, than himself. He had stood the shock with little difficulty. "You're lucky you weren't touched," said Jan. Connor snorted. "I was touched three times—the third time by ten beams! If you'd listened to me we could have won the dog-fight anyway. I blew a dozen Urbans down by firing from the side."

"You what?"

"I saw that," said Evanie. "Just before the second beam. But I—I couldn't stand any more."

"It makes our position worse, I suppose," muttered Jan. "The Master will be angry at injury to his men." Connor gave it up. Jan's regret that the enemy had suffered damage simply capped a long overdue climax. He was loathe to blame Jan, or the whole Weed army, for flying from the searing touch of the ionic beams. He felt himself an unfair judge, since he couldn't feel with their nerves. More than likely what was merely painful to his more rugged body was unbearable agony to them. What did trouble him was the realization that he failed to understand these people, failed to comprehend their viewpoint. This whole mess of a revolution seemed ill-planned, futile, unnecessary, even stupid.

This set him to wondering about Evanie. Was it fair to try to bring love into her life, to rouse her from the reserve she had cast about herself? Might that not threaten unhappiness to both of them—these two strangers from different ages?

Humanity had changed during his long sleep; the only personality in this world with whom he felt the slightest sympathy was—the Master!

A man he had never even seen, unless one of the two shining figures on the tower had been he. Like himself, the Master was a survival of an earlier time. Therein, perhaps, lay the bond.

His musings were interrupted by a flash of iridescence in the air ahead. There was a long, desolate silence as the car sped onward.

"Well," Jan Orm at last said gloomily, "it's come."

But Connor already knew, instinctively, that what he had seen was the rainbow glint of one of the Master's Messengers.

"For which of us, do you suppose?" he asked soberly.

"For Evanie, I guess. But don't watch it—don't think of it. It might be for you."

Evanie was lying back in the seat, eyes shut, features blank. She had closed her mind to the unholy thing. But Connor was unable to keep either mind or eyes from the circling mystery as it swept silently about the speeding car.

"It's closing in," he whispered to Jan.

Jan reached a sudden decision. A rutted road branched ahead of them, and he swung the car into it, boring toward the hills.

"Weed village in here," he muttered. "Perhaps we can lose it there."

"How? It can pass through brick walls."

"I know, but the pneumatic freight tube goes through here. The tube's fast as a scared meteor. We can try it, and—" He paused grimly.

The sun was low in the west when they came to the village, a tiny place nestled among green hills. The ominous circling thing was glowing faintly in the dusk, now no more than twenty yards away. Evanie had kept to her resolute silence, never glancing at the threatening mystery.

In the village, Jan talked to an ancient, bearded individual, and returned to the car with a frown.

"He has only two cylinders," he announced. "You and Evanie are going."

Connor clambered out of the car.

"See here!" he whispered. "You're in more danger than I. Leave me with the car. I can find my way to Ormon."

Jan shook his head. "Listen a moment," he said firmly. "Understand what I'm saying. I love Evanie. I've always loved her, but it's you that's been given to waken her. You must go with her. And for God's sake—quickly!"

Reluctantly Connor and Evanie followed Jan into a stone building where the nervous old man stood above two seven-foot cylinders lying on a little track. Without a word the girl clambered into the first, lying flat on her face with her tiny sandals pressed against the rear.

The ancient snapped down the cover like a coffin lid. Connor's heart sank as the man shoved the metal cylinder into a round opening, closed down a door behind it, and twirled a hissing handle. Jan motioned Tom Connor to the other tube, and at that moment the flashing iridescence of the Messenger swept through the room and away. He climbed hastily in, lying as Evanie had done.

"To Ormon?" he asked.

"No. To the next Weed village, back in the mountains. Hurry!"

12. The Messenger

The old man slammed the cover. Connor lay in utter darkness, but as he felt the cylinder slide along the track, he thought he glimpsed for a bare instant the luminous Messenger in a flash through the metal sides. He heard the faint clang of the door, and there was a brief moment of quiet.

Then, with a force that bent his knees, he felt the thrust of terrific acceleration. Only a faint rumble came to his ears, but he realized that his speed must be enormous. Then the pressure shifted. He felt his hands driven against the front, and in a few more seconds, no pressure at all.

The cover was raised. He thrust himself out, to face Evanie, just clambering from her own cylinder, and a frightened nondescript man who muttered frantically:

"Don't tell on me! Don't tell!"

He turned to listen to a low-voiced inquiry from Evanie, and answered in an inaudible whisper and a gesture to the north.

Connor followed Evanie as she hurried out of the building into darkness. He caught a faint glimpse of the stone cottages of a village smaller than Ormon, then they were trudging over a dim trail toward the hills black against the stars.

"To the metamorphs of the hills," Evanie said mechanically. "They'll hide us until it's safe." She added wearily, "I'm so tired!"

That was not surprising, after such a day. She started to speak. "You've been—Oh!"

He saw it too. The luminous needle beaked shape that was the Messenger, circling them twenty yards away.

"Lord!" he whispered. "How fast can that thing travel?"

"Disembodied electric force?" she asked wearily. "As fast as light, I suppose. Well—it doesn't matter. I can fight it off if I must. But hurry!"

"God!" Connor groaned. "That persistent demon!"

His voice rose in a yell of surprise and fear. The misty thing had stopped in mid-air, poised a moment, then launched itself at his head!

There was no pain, just a brief buzzing. Connor realized that the needle beak had thrust itself into his skull, and the horror rested above his shoulder. He beat at it. His hands passed through it like mist. And then, in a squeaky little voice that clicked maddeningly within his very brain, came the words of the Messenger.

"Go back to Urbs!" it clicked. "Go back to Urbs." Over and over. "Go back to Urbs!" Just that.

He turned frantic eyes on Evanie's startled face.

"Get it off!" he cried. "Get it off!"

"It was for you!" she whispered, stricken. "Oh, if it had been for me! I can fight it. Close your mind to it, Tom. Try! Please try!"

He did try; over and over. But that maddening, clicking voice burned through his efforts; "Go back to Urbs! Go back to Urbs!"

"I can't stand it!" Connor cried frantically. "It tickles—inside my brain!" He paced back and forth in anguish. "I want to run! To walk until I'm exhausted. I can't—stand—it!"

"Yes!" Evanie said. "Walk until you're exhausted. It will give us time that way. But walk north—away from Urbs. Come."

She turned wearily to join him.

"Stay here," he said. "I'll walk alone. Not far. I'll soon return."

He rushed off into the darkness. His thoughts were turmoil as he dashed down the dim trail. I'll fight it off—*Go back to Urbs!*—I won't listen—*Go back to Urbs!*—If Evanie can, so can I. I'm a man, stronger than she—*Go back to Urbs! Go back to Urbs!*

Clicking—tickling—maddening! He rushed blindly on, tripping over branches, crashing into trees. He scrambled up the slope of a steep hill, driving himself, trying to exhaust himself until he could attain the forgetfulness of sleep.

Panting, scratched, weary, he paused from sheer necessity on the crest of the hill. The horror on his shoulder, clicking its message in his brain, gave him no surcease. He was going mad! Better death at the Master's hands than this. Better anything than this. He turned about and plunged toward the hill from which he had come. With his first step south, the maddening voice ceased.

He walked on in a relieved daze. Not even the dim mist of the Messenger on his shoulder detracted from the sheer ecstasy of stillness. He murmured meaningless words of gratitude, felt an impulse to shout a song.

Evanie, resting on a fallen log, glanced up at him as he approached.

"I'm going back to Urbs!" he cried wildly. "I can't stand this!"

"You can't! I won't let you! Please—I can rid you of it, given time. Give me a little time, Tom. Fight it!"

"I won't fight it! I'm going back!"

He turned frantically to rush on south, in any direction that would silence that clicking, tickling voice of torment.

"Go back to Urbs !" it ticked. "Go back to Urbs!"

Evanie seized his arm.

"Please—please, Tom!"

He tugged away and spun around. What he immediately saw in the darkness halted him. In a luminous arc, not three yards distant, spun a second Messenger—and in a mad moment of perversity, he was almost glad!

"Here's one for you!" he said grimly. "Now fight it!"

The girl's face turned pale and terror stricken. "Oh, no! No!" she murmured. "I'm so tired—so tired!" She turned frightened brown eyes on him. "Then stay, Tom. Don't distract me now. I need—all my strength."

It was too late. The second horror had poised itself and struck, glowing mistily against Evanie's soft bronze hair.

Connor felt a surge of sympathy that not even the insanity-breeding Messenger could overcome.

"Evanie!" he cried huskily. "Oh my God! What is it saying?"

Her eyes were wide and terrified.

"It says, 'Sleep—Sleep!' It says, 'The world grows dark—your eyes are closing.' It isn't fair! I could fight it off—I could fight both of them off, given time! The Master—the Master wants me—unable—to help you."

Her eyes grew misty.

Suddenly she collapsed at his feet.

For a long minute Connor stared down at her. Then he bent over, gathered her in his arms, and moved out into the darkness toward Urbs.

Evanie was a light burden, but that first mile down the mountain was a torment that was burned into Connor's memory forever. The Messenger was still as he began the return, and he managed well enough by the starlight to follow the trail. But a thousand feet of mountain unevenness and inequalities of footing just about exhausted him.

His breath shortened to painful gasps, and his whole body, worn out after two nights of sleeplessness, protested with aches and twinges. At last, still cradling Evanie in his arms, he sank exhausted on the moss-covered bole of a fallen tree that glowed with misty fox-fire.

Instantly the Messenger took up its distractingly irritating admonition.

"Go back to Urbs!" it clicked deep in his brain. "Go back to Urbs! Go back to Urbs!"

He bore the torment for five minutes before he rose in wild obedience and staggered south with his burden.

But another quarter mile found him reeling and dizzy with exhaustion, lurching into trees and bushes, scratched, torn, and ragged. Once Evanie's hair caught in the thorns of some shadowy shrub and when he paused to disentangle it, the Messenger took up its maddening refrain. He tore the girl loose with a desperately convulsive gesture and blundered on along the trail.

He was on the verge of collapse after a single mile, and Urbs lay—God only knew how far south! He shifted Evanie from his arms to his shoulder, but the thought of abandoning her never entered his mind.

The time came when his wearied body could go no further. Letting Evanie's limp body slide to the ground he closed his eyes in agony. As the torturing voice of the Messenger resumed, he dropped beside her.

"I can't!" he croaked as though the Messenger or its distant controller could hear him. "Do you want to kill me?"

The sublimity of relief! The voice was still, and he relaxed in an ecstasy of rest. He realized to the full the sweetness of simple silence, the absolute perfection of merely being quiet.

He slumped full length to the ground, then, and in a moment was sleeping as profoundly as Evanie herself.

When Tom Connor awoke to broad day a heap of fruit and a shallow wooden bowl of water were beside him. Connor guessed that they had been placed there by the metamorphs that roamed the hills.

They were still loyal to Evanie, watching out for her.

He ate hungrily, then lifted Evanie's bronze head, tilting the water against her lips. She choked, swallowed a mouthful or two, but moved no more than that.

The damage to his clothing from his plunge through the darkness was slight.

His shirt was torn at sleeves and shoulder, and his trousers were ripped in several places. Evanie's soft hair was tangled with twigs and burrs, and a thorn had scratched her cheek. The elastic that bound her trouser leg to her left ankle was broken, and the garment flapped loosely. The bared ankle was crossed by a reddened gash.

He poured what remained of the water over the wound to wash away any dirt or foreign substance that might be in it. That was all his surgery encompassed.

13. The Trail Back

By daylight the messenger was only a blur, visible out of the corner of his eye like a tear in the eye itself. The demon on Evanie's shoulder was a shifting iridescence no more solid than the heatwaves about a summer road. He stared compassionately down on the still, white face of the girl, and it was at that moment that the Messenger took up its inexorable, clicking chant: "Go back to Urbs! Go back to Urbs!"

He sighed, lifted the girl in arms still aching, and took up his laborious journey. Yard by yard he trudged along the uneven trail. When the blood began to pound in his ears he rested again, and the silent Messenger on his shoulder remained silent. Only when his strength had returned did its voice take up the admonition.

Connor hated the Master now, hated him for these past hours of torture, and for the pallor of Evanie's cheeks, and her body limp in his arms.

The sun rose higher, struck down burning rays on his body. The perspiration that dampened his clothes was warm and sticky while he toiled along, and clammily cold while he rested. Shiny beads of it were on the brow of the unconscious girl, while his own face was covered with trickling rivulets that stung his eyes and bore salty drops to his lips. And the air was hot—hot!

Staggering south, resting, plowing on again, it was near sunset when he approached the Weed village where they had emerged from the pneumatic tube. A man digging before a cottage stared at him and fled through the door. On the steps of the building that housed the tube, half a dozen idlers moved hastily within, and he glimpsed the panic-stricken nondescript who had released him from the freight cylinder.

Connor strode wearily to the steps and deposited Evanie. He glared at the pale faces beyond the door.

"I want food," he snapped. "And wine. Do you hear? Wine!"

Someone slipped timidly past him. In a moment he was back with coarse brown bread and cold meat, and a bottle of tart wild grape wine of the region. Connor ate silently, realizing that eyes peered at him from every window. When he had finished, he poured wine between Evanie's lips. It was the only nourishment he could give her.

"You in there!" he called. "Can any of you release us from these things?"

Evidently, that was a mistake. There was a terrified rustling within and a hurried exodus from some other door. The Messenger took up its refrain with maddening promptness. Abandoning hope of aid, once again he picked up Evanie and tramped into the darkness.

The demon on his shoulder finally let him sleep. It was just dawn when he awoke, and scarcely had he opened his eyes on this second morning of his torturous trek when the clicking voice resumed its chant. He made no attempt to resist it, but rose and struggled on with his burden. Now he followed a clay road on which he could avoid tearing thorns and branches.

No more than a mile from the village he topped a rise to view a wide black highway, perhaps the same over which he and Jan Orm and Evanie had sped to Urbs—just two days ago! He found the rubbery surface somewhat less tiring and managed a little more distance between rests. But the journey was painfully slow. Yet the Messenger never hurried him. He was permitted ample rest.

Now and again vehicles hummed past, mostly giant trucks. Occasionally a speeding machine slowed as if to stop, but one glimpse of the mistiness on his shoulder sent the driver whizzing on. No one, apparently, dared association with the bearer of that dread badge of the Master's enmity. It was with amazement, therefore, that Connor saw a truck actually stopping, and heard a cheerful invitation to "Come on in!"

He clambered laboriously into the cab, placing Evanie on the seat beside him, holding her against him. He thanked the driver, a pleasant-featured youth, and relaxed, silent.

"Weed trouble, eh?" the driver asked. He stared at Connor's shoulder.

"Say, you must be a pretty important Weed to rate a Messenger." He glanced sideward at Connor and suddenly grinned. "I know you now! You're the fellow that carried the beam when hell popped Sunday. Lord! Stood right up to the beam!" In his tone was deep admiration. Connor said nothing.

"Well, you're in for it, all right," the youth resumed cheerfully. "You blew down some of the Master's men, and that's bad!"

"What did he do with the others?" Connor asked gloomily. "They couldn't all get away."

"He only picked up the leaders. Nine of 'em. Vision didn't say what he did. Papers say he released some of 'em. Girl who thinks she looks like the Princess."

Maris, thought Connor. And Evanie was the tenth of the decemvirate. He himself was tossed in for good measure. Well, perhaps he might bargain for Evanie's release. After all, he had something to trade.

It was mid-afternoon before they looked down on Kaatskill, and Connor realized in astonishment the distance over which they must have flashed in the freight tube. Then he forgot all else as Urbs Minor appeared with its thousands of towers and, far across the valley, the misty peaks that were the colossus, Greater Urbs.

The truck kept to the ground level. The mighty buildings, shielded by the upper streets from sight, were less spectacular here, but their vast bases seemed to press upon the ground like a range of mountains, until Connor wondered why the solid earth did not sink beneath their weight. Millions upon millions of tons of metal and masonry—and all of it as if it rested on his own brain, so despondent did he feel.

Presently they were on Palace Avenue. Even the ground level of that mighty street was crowded. Connor already knew its almost legendary reputation. What the Via Appia was to Rome, or Broadway to America of yore, Palace Avenue now was to the world. Main street of the planet; highway of six—no, the seven—continents. For Antarctica was an inhabited continent now.

When the unbelievably magnificent Twin Towers came into clean view the truck came to a halt. Connor climbed out and turned to pick up Evanie.

"Thanks," he said. "You made the road to hell a lot easier."

The youth grinned.

"'S nothing. Good chances, Weed. You'll need 'em!"

Connor turned for the long ascent to the Palace. He trudged up the interminable flight of steps, passing crowds of Urbans who stared and gave him wide passageway. He moved close under the great, brooding, diorite statue of Holland, into the north doorway of the Palace, where a guard stepped hastily aside to admit him.

Through a door to his right came the clatter and rustle of voices and machines, engaged in the business of administering a world government. To his left was a closed door, and ahead the hall debouched into a room so colossal that at first it seemed an illusion.

He strode in. Along the far wall, a thousand feet away, Was a row of seats—thrones, rather—each on a dais or platform perhaps ten feet above the floor, and each apparently occupied. Perhaps fifty of them. Before the central one stood a group of people, and a few guards flanked it. Then, as he approached, he realized that all but the central throne were occupied only by images, by cleverly worked statues of bronze. No—two central thrones held living forms.

He pushed his way roughly through the knot of people, carefully deposited Evanie on the steps ascending to the seat, and glared defiantly at the Master.

For a moment, so intent was his gaze at the man he had come bitterly to hate, through all the torture of his forced trip, that he did not shift his eyes to the figure who sat beside the Master. The Princess of whom he had heard, he supposed—the beautiful cruel Margaret of Urbs who, with her brother, ruled with an iron hand.

But he was not interested in her now. Her immortal brother claimed all his attention, all his defiance. Just for a breath, though, Connor's eyes did flicker in her direction—and instantly he stood stock still, frozen, wondering if at last he had lost his mind. For here, before his staring eyes, was the most incredible thing he had come upon in all this incredible new world! And what held him spellbound was not so much the utter, unbelievable, fantastic beauty of the woman—or girl—who sat upon the throne of Urbs, as was the fact that he knew her! Gazing at her, frozen in utter surprise and fascination, Tom Connor knew in that moment that the cruel Margaret of Urbs and the inky-haired, white-robed girl with whom he had spent those unforgettable moments in the wildwood outside the village of Ormon were one and the same!

There could be no possible doubt of that, though in her emerald green eyes now was no friendly light as she looked down at him haughtily. In that same manner she might show her distaste for some crawling thing that had annoyed her. But not even her changed expression, not even her rich garb that had replaced her white robe of sylvan simplicity, could alter the fact that here before Tom Connor was his woman of the woods, his girl of mystery, the girl who had unfolded to him the history of this more and more astonishing age into which Fate had drawn him.

Not by the slightest flicker of a long, black, curling eyelash did she show that she had even seen Connor before. But even in his own quick resentment that swiftly followed his frozen moment of surprise, the man from another age uncomfortably realized that her fascination for him, the sway of her bewildering beauty, was as great as it had been the first moment he had gazed upon her.

His own predicament—Evanie—everything—was forgotten, as if he were hypnotized.

Instead of a gauzy, white robe that was in itself revealing, but with a touch of poetry and mysticism, she now wore the typical revealing costume of Urbs—rose bodice, and short kirtle of golden scales. And that hair of hers—never would Connor forget it—so black that it glinted blue in the light. Nor would he ever forget her skin, so transparently clear, with its tint like the patina over ancient silver bronze.

Looking at her now, Connor could see how Maris might claim a resemblance, but it was no more than the resemblance of a candle to the sun. Evanie was beautiful, too, but her loveliness was that of a human being, while the beauty of this girl who sat upon a throne was unearthly, unbelievable, immortal.

She sat with her slim legs thrust carelessly before her, her elbow on the arm of her chair, her chin in her cupped hand, and gazed indifferently from strange sea-green eyes into the vastness of the giant chamber. Never once did she glance at Connor after her first swift distasteful survey.

Her exquisite features were expressionless, or expressive only of complete boredom. Though there did seem to Connor that there was the faintest trace of that unforgettable mockery in the set of her perfect lips. Before he could tear his gaze away from her she moved slightly. With the movement something flamed on her breast—a great flower of seven petals that flashed and glistened in a dozen colors, as if made of jewels.

It took all of Connor's will power to keep his eyes from her, even though in that moment of long silence that had fallen in the throne room with his entry, he was resenting her, loathing her for what she was—instead of what he had thought her to be.

Deliberately he faced the Master, head up, defiant. Let the Master—let his Princess sister—do what they pleased. He was ready for them!

14. The Master

The man at whom Connor stared, the man whose features he had seen before on Evanie's coin, seemed no older than the middle twenties. He was dark-eyed, and his black hair fell in a smooth helmet below his ears.

The eyes were strange, piercing, shrewd, as if they alone had aged, as if they were the receptacles of these centuries of experience. The mouth was set in a thin, cold line and yet, strangely enough, there was a faintly humorous quirk to its corners. Or not so strangely, either, decided Connor. A man must have a sense of humor to survive seven centuries.

And then a deep, resonant voice sounded as the Master spoke.

"I see, Thomas Connor," he said ironically, "that you received my Messenger hospitably. And this is little Evanie!" His voice changed. "Good blood," he mused. "The mingling of the blood of Martin Sair with that of Montmerci."

Connor glared belligerently. "Release us from these vicious Messengers of yours, will you?" he demanded angrily. "We're here."

The Master nodded mildly, and spoke briefly into a mouthpiece on a black table beside him. There was a moment's pause, then a tingling shock as the unbound energies of the Messenger grounded through Connor's body. Evanie quivered and moaned as the thing on her shoulder vanished, but she lay as quiet as ever.

Connor shook himself. Free! He flashed an angry frown at the impassive Master, but his eyes kept straying back to the Princess, who still had not even glanced at him after that one first instant.

"Well," said the Master quietly, "your revolution was a trifle abortive, wasn't it?"

"Up to now!" snapped Connor.

His hatred suddenly overwhelmed him. The impulse for revenge shook him bodily. Swiftly stooping, he snatched Evanie's revolver from her belt, and held the trigger while twelve shots spat full at the Master's face in a continuous steaming roar.

The steam moved lazily away. The Master sat without change of expression, uninjured, while from far above a few splinters of glass from a shattered skylight tinkled about him. Of course, Connor reflected bitterly, the man would be protected by an inductive field. Glass had been able to pass through that inductive field, where Connor's bullets could not, but their glass was a dielectric.

He cast the empty gun aside and stared sullenly at the man on the throne. Then, despite his efforts, his gaze was again drawn to the Princess.

She was no longer looking abstractedly into vacancy. At the crash of the shots she had shifted slightly, without raising her chin from her hand, and was watching him. Their glances crossed. It was like the tingle of the Messenger's discharge to him as he met the cool green eyes, inscrutable and expressionless and utterly disinterested. And in them was no slightest hint of recognition! For reasons of her own she did not mean to recognize him. Well, two could play at that game.

"Your impulses take violent form," said the Master coldly. "Why do you, who claim to be a newcomer to this age, hate me so?"

"Hate you?" Connor echoed fiercely. "Why shouldn't I? Didn't you put me through two days and nights of hell with your damned Messenger?"

"But there would have been no torment had you obeyed immediately."

"But Evanie!" Connor snapped. "See what you've done to her!"

"She was interfering. I didn't want her here, particularly, but she might have released you from the Messenger. If you'd left her to herself, I would have freed her within a few hours."

"Kind, aren't you?" sneered Connor. "You're so confident in your own powers that you don't even punish revolt. Well, you're a tyrant, nevertheless, and some day you'll get more than you bargain for. *I* could have done it myself!"

He glanced again at the Princess. Was there the faintest flicker of interest in her imperious eyes?

"And what would you have done," queried the Master amiably, "if you had been running the revolution?"

"Plenty!" retorted Connor. "In the first place, I'd never have shipped weapons into Urbs through the public tubes. You were bound to discover that, and surprise was our greatest ally. I'd have had 'em made right here, or near here. There must be Weed factories around, and if not, I'd have bought one."

"Go on," said the Master interestedly. "What else?"

"I'd have had a real organization—not this cumbersome leader upon leader pyramid. I'd have laid real plans, planted spies in the Palace. And finally, your deflectors. I didn't know of them, or we could have won even as things were. My—associates—forgot, rather carelessly, to mention them."

The Master smiled. "That was an error. If you had known of them, what would you have done?"

"I'd have used wooden bullets instead of metal ones," said Connor boldly. "Your induction field won't stop wood. And your ionic beams—why the devil couldn't we have used metal screen armor? We could have closed the circuit with that instead of with our bodies!"

He was aware, though he steadfastly refused to look at her, that the Princess was watching him now with undisguised mockery, her lovely lips parted in the ghost of a smile.

"True," said the Master with a curious expression. "You could have." He frowned. "I did not believe the stories I first heard of you—that you were a Sleeper who had awakened after a sleep of a thousand years. They were too fantastic for belief. I thought you were meaning to capitalize on the Sleep in some way known only to yourself—since I understand you had no bank deposit to draw interest for you and make you a wealthy man. Now I am inclined to believe you have come from another age an—age of wisdom—and you're a dangerous man, Thomas Connor. You're a brave man to bait me as you do, and a strong one, but dangerous; too dangerous. Yet I'm rather sorry your courage and strength has been bred out of the race."

"What are you going to do?"

"I'm going to kill you," said the Master softly. "I'm sorry. Were it not for Evanie, I might be tempted to ask for your oath of allegiance and release you, but I can't trust a man who loves a Weed woman. It's a chance I dare not take, though I bitterly regret losing your blood and your ancient knowledge. If it consoles you, know that I intend to free Evanie. She's harmless to me. Any trouble she might cause can be easily handled. But you—you're different."

"Thanks," retorted Connor.

Like a compass needle his eyes did return to the face of the Princess, then. Even now, condemned to die for the second time in his strange life, he gazed fascinated at her, smiling at her with an echo of her own mockery.

"I don't suppose," said the Master hopefully, "that you'd consent to—say, marry Evanie and perpetuate your blood before you die. I need that ancient strain of yours. Our race has grown weak."

"I would not!" Connor said.

"Tell me!" said the other in sudden eagerness. "Is it true, as an Ormon prisoner told us, and which I scorned to believe, having then no faith in this thousand-year Sleep, that you understand the ancient mathematics? Calculus, logarithms, and such lost branches?"

"It's quite true," snapped Connor. "Who told you?"

"Your Ormon chemist. Would you consent to impart that knowledge? The world needs it."

"For my life, perhaps."

The Master hesitated, frowning.

"I'm sorry," he said at last. "Invaluable as the knowledge is, the danger you, personally, present, outweighs it. I could trick you out of your secrets. I could promise you life, get your information, then quietly kill you. I do not stoop to that. If you desire, your knowledge goes to the grave with you."

"Thanks again," retorted Connor. "You might remember that I could have concealed my dangerous character, too. I needn't have pointed out the weakness in your defenses."

"I already knew them. I also know the weaknesses of Weed mentality." He paused. "I'm truly sorry, but—this seems to be the end of our interview." He turned as if to gesture to the guards along the wall.

Margaret of Urbs flashed a strange, inscrutable glance at Connor, and leaned toward the Master. She spoke in low, inaudible tones, but emphatically, insistently. The Master looked up at Connor.

"I reconsider," he said coolly. "I grant you your life for the present on one condition—that you make no move against me while you are in the Palace. I do not ask your word not to escape. I only warn you that a Messenger will follow. Do you agree?"

Connor thought only a moment. "I do."

"Then you will remain within the Palace." The Master snapped an order to a guard. "I will send doctors to attend little Evanie. That's all."

The guard, as tall a man as Connor himself, stepped forward and gathered Evanie in his arms. Connor followed him, but could not resist a backward glance at the Princess, who sat once more staring idly into space. But in his mind was the thought now, exultant in spite of his resentment, that at least she had not forgotten him, or those hours together in the woods.

They moved into the hall, and into an elevator that flashed upward with sudden and sickening acceleration. He had glimpses of floor after floor through the glass doors as they mounted high into the North Tower.

The motion ceased. Connor followed the guard into a room lit by the red glow of sunset, and watched as he deposited Evanie on a white-covered bed, then turned, and threw open a door. "That is yours," the guard said briefly, and departed.

Luxury breathed through the perfumed air of the rooms, but Connor had no time for such observations. He bent anxiously over the pallid-faced Evanie, wondering miserably why the release of the Messenger had not awakened her. He was still gazing when a knock sounded, and two doctors entered.

One, the younger, set instantly to work examining the scratch on the girl's ankle, while the other pried open her eyes, parted her still lips, bent close to listen to her breathing.

"Brain-burnt," he announced. "Brain-burnt by a vitergon—the Messenger. Severe electrolepsis."

"Lord!" Connor muttered anxiously. "Is it—is it very serious?"

"Serious? Bah!" The older man spun on him. "It's exactly what happens to Sleepers—paralysis of the pre-Rolandic areas, the will, the consciousness. Like—if I'm properly informed—what happened to you! It might be serious if we let her sleep for a half a century, not otherwise." He stepped to an ebony table beside the bed, decanting a ruby liquid into a tumbler. "Here," he said. "We'll try a good stiff stimulant."

He poured the ruddy fluid between Evanie's lips, and when the last drop had vanished, stood over her watching. She moved convulsively and moaned in agony.

"Hah!" said the doctor. "That'll burn some life into her!" The girl shuddered and opened dazed and pain-racked eyes. "So! You can handle her now," he called to the younger man, and moved out through the doorway.

"Evanie!" croaked Connor tensely. "Are you all right? How do you feel?"

The dazed eyes rested on him.

"I burn! Water—oh, please—water!"

15. Two Women

Tom Connor glanced a silent question at the doctor. At his nod, Connor seized the empty tumbler and looked frantically for water. He found it beyond a door, where a silent stream gushed from the mouth of a grotesque face into a broad basin.

Evanie drank eagerly, thirstily, when he brought it to her. She stared bewilderedly about the luxurious room, and turned questioning eyes on Connor.

"Where—" she began.

"In Urbs. In the Palace."

Comprehension dawned.

"The Messengers! Oh, my God!" She shivered in fright. "How long—have I—"

"Just two days, Evanie. I carried you here."

"What is to—to be done with us?"

"I don't know, dear. But you're safe." She frowned a moment in the effort to compose her still dazed and bewildered mind.

"Well," she murmured finally, "nothing can be done about it. I'm ashamed to have been so weak. Was he—very angry?"

"He didn't seem so." The memory of the Master's impassive face rose in his mind, and with it the vision of the exquisite features of the Princess.

"I suppose the girl who sits on his right is the Princess, isn't she?" he asked. "Who is she?"

Evanie nodded. "Every one knows that. On his left sits Martin Sair, the Giver of Life, and on his right—

Why do you ask that?" She glanced up troubled, suspicious.

"Because she saved my life. She intervened for me."

"Tom!" Evanie's voice was horror-filled. "Tom, that was Margaret of Urbs, the Black Flame!" Her eyes were terrified. "Tom, she's dangerous—poisonous—deadly! You mustn't even look at her. She's driven men—I don't know how many—to suicide. She's killed men—she's tortured them. Don't ever go near her, Tom! If she saved you, it wasn't out of mercy, because she's merciless—ruthless—utterly pitiless!"

Scarcely conscious as yet, the girl was on the verge of hysteria. Her voice grew shrill, and Connor glanced apprehensively at the young doctor's face.

Evanie turned ashen pale.

"I—feel—dizzy," she choked. "I'm going—to—"

The doctor sprang forward. "You mustn't!" he snapped. "We can't let her sleep again. We must walk her! Quickly!"

Between them they dragged the collapsing girl from the bed, walking her up and down the chamber. A measure of strength returned, and she walked weakly between them, back and forth. Then, abruptly, they paused at the sound of a sharp rap on the chamber door.

The doctor called out a summons. Two Urban guards in glittering metal strode through the entrance, and stood like images on either side of it. One of them intoned slowly, deep as an anthem:

"Margarita, Urbis Regina, Sororque Domini!"

The Princess! Connor and the doctor stood frozen, and even Evanie raised weary eyes as the Princess entered, striding imperiously into the room with the scaly gold of her kirtle glittering crimson in the last rays of the sun. She swept her cold eyes over the startled group, and suddenly her exquisite features flashed into a flame of anger. The glorious lips parted.

"You fool!" she spat. "You utter fool!"

Connor flushed in sudden anger, then realized that the Princess addressed, not him, but the doctor at Evanie's left, who was fear-stricken and pallid.

"You fool!" repeated Margaret of Urbs. "Walking an electroleptic! Put her to bed—instantly. Let her sleep. Do you want to risk brain fever?"

The frightened physician moved to obey, but Connor interposed.

"Wait a moment." He shot an accusing glance at the Princess. "Do you know anything about this? Are you a doctor?"

He received a cool glance from her narrowed green eyes.

"Do you think," she drawled, "that I've learned nothing in seven hundred years?" And he alone caught the full implication of her words. She was subtly reminding him of how once before she had given him evidence of how vast was her knowledge. She turned imperiously. "Obey!" she snapped.

Connor stood aside as the doctor complied in panic.

"Where's Kringar?" the Princess demanded.

"Your Highness," babbled the medico, "he gave the girl a stimulant and left. He said—"

"All right. Get out." She nodded at the impassive guards. "You, too."

The door closed behind them. Margaret of Urbs bent over Evanie, now fully conscious, but pale as death. She placed a dainty hand on the girl's forehead.

"Sleep," she said softly.

"Leave me here alone, please," Evanie begged, trembling. "I'm afraid of you. I don't trust you, and I won't sleep. I'm afraid to sleep again."

Connor stood miserably irresolute. While he hesitated, the Princess fixed her eyes on Evanie's; they glowed emerald in the evening dusk as she repeated, "Sleep!"

He saw the fear vanish from Evanie's face, leaving her features as blank as those of an image. Then she was sleeping.

The Princess faced Tom Connor across the bed. She took a black cigarette from a box on the ebony table. It glowed magically as she removed it, and she blew a plume of perfumed smoke at him.

"Worried, aren't you?" she asked mockingly.

"You know I am."

"Well, rest your mind. I mean no harm to Evanie."

"But do you know what you're doing?"

She laughed, low laughter soft as rain in a pool.

"See here," she said, still with a taunt in her eyes, "I conceived the vitergons. Martin Sair created them, but *I* conceived them. I know what harm they can do, and I know the cure for that harm. Do you trust me?"

"Not entirely."

"Well, you have small choice." She exhaled another cloud of scented smoke. "Your little Weed is safe." She moved toward the adjoining room. "There's a bath in here," she said. "Use it, and then put on some Urban clothes. I'm inclined to dine with you this evening."

He was startled. He stared back at the mocking perfection of her face, but the green eyes carried no readable expression, as she came closer so that only Connor could hear what she said.

"Why?" he asked.

"Perhaps to recall a more pleasant meeting," she said gently. "Oh, I have not forgotten you—if that is what you are thinking. I recall every word of that day in the woods, but it may be better if you forget it, publicly. Margaret of Urbs does not care to have her private business broadcast to the city. Nor is it the affair of anyone here—or any business of yours—that I choose to get away from them all occasionally, with only the birds and the trees to bear me company. You will do well to bear that in mind, Thomas Connor!"

Suddenly her voice took on a taunting note, and the mockery in the emerald eyes was plain. "Perhaps," she said, "I have another reason for commanding you to dine with me. I may want to steal your knowledge—then kill you. I might have more than one reason for wanting to do that, but you fired a dozen shots at me on Sunday, Thomas Connor, as I stood on the balcony of the Tower. I do not fail to repay such debts."

"It will take more than you to steal what I will not give," he growled, and turned into his room, closing the door.

He stepped instantly to the hall door, opened it and gazed squarely into the impassive eyes of an Urban guard standing quietly opposite. So he was watched!

He turned back into the chamber, stripped, and entered the water of the pool, reveling in the refreshing coolness. As he bathed he could look out a window; he saw that the colossal Palace was built as a hollow square. Opposite him rose the mountainous spire of the South Tower, and far below were the wide pool and green-bordered walks of the Inner Gardens.

Drying his glowing body, he glanced distastefully at the sweat-stained pile of Weed clothing on the floor. In a closet he found Urban dress. It gave him a queer, masquerade like feeling to don the barbaric metal corselet and kirtle, but the garments were cool, and befitted his great frame. Ready at last, he flung open the door to Evanie's room.

Margaret of Urbs sat cross-legged on the bed, beside Evanie, smoking her black cigarette. Her green eyes passed appraisingly over Connor, and the glint of mockery was again in their depths.

"I always thought the ancient sculptors exaggerated their contemporaries' physiques," she said, smiling. "I was wrong . . . But you're to kneel when you enter my presence, Thomas Connor. You didn't before."

"And I don't now. As an enemy, I owe you no such respect."

"As a gentleman you do, however. But never mind—I'm hungry. Come."

"Why can't we eat here? I won't leave Evanie."

"Evanie will be dull company for a dozen hours more. I'll send a maid to undress and bathe her."

"You're very considerate, aren't you?"

She laughed maliciously.

"I have no quarrel with her. But I have with you. Come!"

The glorious green eyes swept him. Both eyes and voice—a voice that now seemed to glory in malice—were so different from those of the girl of the woods that it was hard for Tom Connor to believe they were the same. But he knew they were. And now that he and she were alone every gesture seemed to admit that.

She rose without a glance at Evanie's still, white face and Connor followed her reluctantly past the guard, whose challenge she silenced with a peremptory word, and over to the bank of elevators.

"Where to?" he asked as the cage dropped, plummet like.

"To a room of mine in the South Tower, I think. We'll have to go all the way down and walk across."

The cage came to a sickening halt. He followed her through the vast emptiness of the room of thrones, noting curiously that both her own throne and that of the Master were now occupied by cleverly executed bronze figures. He paused to examine the effigy of the Princess, wondering how long ago it had been cast.

"Third century," she said as if in answer to his thought. "Five hundred years ago. I was a child of two hundred and twenty then—and happier." Sardonic amusement was in her face and manner. "There was no Black Flame in those days. I was the madcap Princess Peggy then, reckless and daring, but sweet and noble. Or so they thought."

"I'm sure you deserved the reputation," Connor observed acidly. He meant to follow her lead in whatever she said or did. She would have no complaint that he was the first to mention their previous meeting. If she said no more about it, then it would not be mentioned at all.

She flashed her green eyes on him, eyes as icy as the green cap over Antarctica.

"I'm sure I deserve it no longer," she said in tones so cold that they startled. "Come on."

There was something fascinating, almost hypnotic, about this weirdly beautiful being.

"I'd rather dine with your image there," he remarked dryly.

16. Immortality

Margaret of Urbs laughed and led Connor through a door behind the line of thrones.

"Martin Sair's laboratory," she explained, gesturing at the chaotic confusion of glassware and microscopes. "And this"—passing into a chamber beyond—"is mine."

The place seemed more like a luxurious, sumptuously furnished library than a laboratory. There were shelves upon shelves of books, hundreds of them obviously ancient, a great vision screen, a delicately inlaid desk, and here and there bits of statuary.

"Laboratory!" he echoed. "What do you do here?"

"I think. When I want to work I use Martin's." She picked up a white carving from the desk. "See here—some of your ancient work." She added a trifle sadly, "We have no artists able to create such beauty today. It's a tragedy that the arms were broken. During the Dark Centuries, I suppose."

Connor looked at the exquisite little ivory replica of the Venus de Milo and laughed.

"Arms broken!" he scoffed. "That's a copy of an ancient Greek statue of Praxiteles. The arms were broken two thousand years before my time!"

"A copy! Where's the original? I want it!"

"It was in the Louvre, in Paris."

"Paris is in ruins. Do you know where the Louvre stood?"

"Yes."

"Then tell me! I'll have it searched for. Tell me!"

He gazed into eyes sincerely eager; the eyes now of the white-clad girl of the woods who had lolled with him on a mossy woodland bank and told him stories of the ages. That girl had loved beauty, too; had been seeking it, watching her own reflection in the black pool. It amazed him that now in her role as the frigid princess she could still be so avid for beauty.

"That's a bit of information I withhold," he said slowly, "until I can trade it for something else I may want. Evanie's safety, or my own."

The mocking light returned to her eyes. "You amuse me, Weed!" she said curtly. "But very well." She led the way to the South Tower elevators.

She was silent during the long ride to the very pinnacle of the tower. They emerged into a small chamber walled on every side in glass, and Connor stood awestruck as the city spread out before them. The palace over-topped even the colossal structures around the Park. He gazed speechless at the mighty stretch of peaks outlined in light.

The Princess turned to a black screened box.

"Send dinner to the tower," she ordered. "I want—Oh, anything. And send Sora to the room of Evanie Sair."

She flung herself carelessly on a purple couch along a glassed wall, and Connor seated himself.

"Now," she said, "what will you take for your knowledge?"

"I won't bargain with you. I don't trust you."

She laughed.

"You see me through Evanie's eyes, Tom Connor, and once—well, once I thought you were attracted to me. But no matter. We will not again speak of that time—though it does seem odd that Fate should have had me set my Triangle down where *you* were. When I was just wandering restlessly, aimlessly, seeking peace in loveliness—It's too bad you fancy yourself in love with Evanie. For I assure you she doesn't love you."

"That's not true!" he flared.

She laughed, and instantly her touch of wistfulness was gone, to be replaced by wickedness.

"Be careful," she mocked, "or I'll exact payment for that insult as well. But it was no lie."

He controlled his anger.

"Why do you say that?"

"Because when I forced her to sleep, frightened as she was, she didn't turn to you. She fought me herself. If she had loved you, she'd have instinctively called you for help."

"I don't believe you."

"Then you're a fool," she observed indifferently, and turned from him disinterestedly at the entry of two servants bearing food.

They slipped a table between the two and served a sumptuous

repast, with dishes Connor failed to recognize. He ate hungrily, but the Princess, despite her professed hunger, picked and chose and ate scarcely anything. It was a silent meal, but afterward, smoking one of the black, magically lighted cigarettes, he prepared to ask certain questions.

She forestalled him. With green eyes glowing sardonically, she looked straight at him.

"Why do you love Evanie instead of me?" she asked.

"You? Because you are not what I thought you were. Instead of being pure and sweet, you revel in evil. That is not hearsay; it is the historical record of your seven hundred years. For that I hate you, thoroughly and completely."

She narrowed her glorious eyes.

"Then you hate without reason," she said. "Am I not more powerful than Evanie, more intelligent, stronger, and even, I think, more beautiful?"

"You're outrageously, incredibly, fantastically beautiful!" he cried, as if the acknowledgement were wrenched from him against his will. "You're perhaps the most beautiful woman since Helen of Troy, and the most dangerous. And yet I hate you."

"Why?"

"Because of your lack of a little factor called character. I concede your beauty and your brilliance, but Evanie is sweet, kind, honest, and lovable. One loves character, not characteristics."

"Character!" she echoed. "You know nothing of my character. I have a hundred characters! No one can be so gentle as I—nor so cruel."

The faintest ripple of a mocking smile crossed her exquisite features, and then they were suddenly pure as an angel's. Without rising she kicked the switch of a vision screen with a dainty, sandaled toe.

"Control," she said as it glowed. A face appeared.

"A vitergon set tell to this room," she said cryptically, and then to Connor as the face vanished: "There is no scanner here. This chamber and Joaquin's in the North Tower are the only two in Urbs lacking them."

"What of it?"

"It means, Thomas Connor, that we are in utter privacy."

He frowned, puzzled. Abruptly he started back in his chair as a flash of iridescence flickered. A Messenger! And almost with his start the thing was upon him.

"Tell!" it creaked in his brain. "Tell! Tell! Tell! Tell!"

He sprang erect.

"Take it off!" he roared.

"When I have your knowledge of Venus," his tormentor said carelessly.

"Take it off, or—"

"Or what?" Her smile was guileless, sweet, innocent.

"This!" he blazed, and covered the space between them in a bound, his right hand clutching the delicate curve of her throat, his left pressing her shoulders fiercely down against the cushions.

"Take it off," he bellowed.

Suddenly there was a sound behind him, the grating of doors, and he was torn away, held by four grim-faced guards. Of course! The operator of the Messenger could hear his words. He should have remembered that.

The Black Flame pushed herself to a sitting position, and her face was no angel's but the face of a lovely demon. Green hell glittered in her eyes, but she only reached shakily for the vision switch.

"Tell Control to release," she choked huskily, and faced Tom Connor.

The Messenger tingled and vanished. The princess rose unsteadily, but her glorious eyes burned cold as she snatched a weapon from the nearest guard. "Get out, all of you!" she snapped. The men backed away. Connor faced her. "I should have killed you!" he muttered. "For humanity's sake."

"Yes, you should have, Thomas Connor." Her tones were bitterly cold. "For, then you would have died quickly and mercifully for murder, but now—now you die in the way I choose, and it will be neither quick nor merciful. I cannot"—her voice shook—"bear the touch of violence!" Her free hand rubbed her throat. "For this—you suffer!"

He shrugged. "It was worth it. I know your character now! I no longer have to guess." Mockery gleamed.

"Do you?" Her face changed suddenly, and again it was soft and pure and wistful. "Do you?" she repeated, in tones that were sad, but held that bell like quality he so well remembered. "You don't.

Do you think the Black Flame is the true Margaret of Urbs? Do you realize what immortality means?" Her exquisite face was unutterably mournful as she thrust the weapon into her belt. "You think it's a blessing, don't you? You wonder, don't you, why Joaquin has withheld it from everybody?"

"Yes, I do. I think it's tyranny. It's selfish."

"Selfish! Oh, God!" Her voice shook. "Why, he withheld it from his own mother! Blessing? It's a curse! I bear it out of my duty to Joaquin, else I'd have killed myself centuries ago. I still may, do you hear. I still may!" Her voice rose.

Appalled, he stared at her.

"Why?" he cried.

"You ask why! Seven hundred years. Seven—hundred—years! Denied love! How do I dare love a man who ages day by day, until his teeth yellow and his hair falls out, and he's decrepit, senile, old? Denied children! Immortals can't have children. Don't you think I'd trade immortality for motherhood? Don't you?"

Connor was speechless. Her voice rose to a tense pitch.

"Do you know what seven hundred years mean? I do! It means seven centuries of friendlessness. Do you wonder that I run away to the woods sometimes, seeking the companionship, the friendship, the love, that everywhere else is denied me? How can I make friends among people who vanish like ghosts? Who among the dry scientists of the Immortals is alone—and I'm bored—bored—bored!" Her green eyes were tear bright, but when he opened his lips to speak, she stopped him with an imperious gesture. "I'm sick to death of immortality! I want someone who loves me. Someone I'd love to grow old with, and children to grow up beside me. I want—I want—a friend!"

She was sobbing. Impulsively he moved toward her, taking her hand.

"My God!" he choked. "I'm sorry. I didn't understand."

"And you—will help me?" Her exquisite features were pleading, tear streaked.

"The best I can," he promised.

Her perfect lips were two rosy temptations as she drew him toward her. He bent to kiss her gently—and sprang back as if his own lips had in truth touched a flame.

Laughter! He looked into mocking eyes whose only tears were those of sardonic mirth!

"So!" she said, her red lips taunting. "There is the first taste, Thomas Connor, but there will be more before I kill you. You may go."

17. The Destiny of Man

"You—devil!" Connor choked, and then whirled at a soft click behind him. A white envelope lay in a wire basket by the elevator.

"Hand it to me," said the Flame coolly.

He snatched it and thrust it at her, in a turmoil of emotion as he watched her read it.

"Indeed!" she murmured. "My esteemed brother orders me to keep well away from you—which I shall not do—and commands you to his quarters at once." She yawned. "Take the elevator to any floor below the Tower and ask a guard. That's all."

Yet, as the cage dropped, Connor could not forget that there had been something wistful about the Princess, at his last glimpse of her. Somehow, try as he would, he couldn't hate her quite whole-heartedly, and he frowned as he found his way to the West Chambers. A guard admitted him to an inner room, and then retired quietly, leaving him facing the Master, who sat behind a paper-littered desk.

"Well, what do you think of me?" the Master greeted him abruptly.

Connor was taken aback, unprepared for the question.

"Why," he stammered, "what would I naturally think of you? You dragged me back here by torture. You nearly killed Evanie. Do you think I can easily forget or forgive such things?"

"After all, Thomas Connor, you participated in a revolt against me," the Master said suavely. "You wounded eleven of my men. Did the governments of your day deal so leniently with treason?"

"I've wondered why you are so easy on the rebels," he admitted. "Frankly, in my time, there'd have been a good many of us lined up against a wall and shot."

The Master shook his head. "Why should I do that? The Weeds are the finest of my people. *I* made the only mistake—that of giving leisure to a race not ready for it. Leisure is what has bred all these minor revolutions. But does a father kill his favorite children?"

"Does a son kill his mother?" retorted Connor.

The Master smiled bleakly.

"I see my sister has been talking to you. Yes, I refused immortality to my mother. She was an old woman—ill, infirm. Should I have condemned her to added centuries of misery? Immortality does not restore youth."

The point was incontrovertible.

"Yet you withhold it from those who have youth," Connor protested. "You keep it selfishly as a reward, to bind to yourself all men of ability. You've emasculated the rest of humanity."

"You feel that immortality is a highly desirable reward, don't you?"

"I do! In spite of what your sister says."

"You don't understand," said the Master patiently. "We'll pass the question of its desirability; it doesn't matter. But suppose I were to open it to the race, to instruct all the doctors in its secrets. Wouldn't it immediately halt all development? How can evolution function if no one dies and no children are born?"

That was a puzzler.

"You could permit it after the birth of children," Connor said.

"I could. But at the present birthrate, the land areas would provide bare standing room in just a century and a half. I could then kill off nine-tenths of the population, presumably, but what of the famines and food shortages intervening?"

Connor was silent for a long moment.

"The fault's with immortality itself!" he burst out vehemently. "Men should never have learned that secret!"

"But they have learned it. Would you have me destroy the knowledge because fools envy it—and envy it mistakenly?"

"Did you summon me here merely to justify your acts?" Tom Connor snapped in reply.

"Exactly. You possess knowledge invaluable to me. I'd like to convince you of my sincerity."

"You never will."

"See here," said the Master, still in tones of calm gravity. "Don't ever doubt that I could steal your knowledge. I know ways to encompass it, and if I failed, others would not fail."

"The Princess tried that," said Connor grimly. "She will not try it again." He fingered a small bronze bust on the desk before him. "And incidentally, what's to prevent me from flinging this bronze through your skull right now—killing you, instead of waiting for you to kill me?"

"Your word to make no move against me in the Palace," reminded the Master gently.

Connor's lips tightened. In that moment he realized suddenly what it was that had perturbed him so violently. He was beginning to believe the Master—and he didn't want to! The memory of the Messenger's torture was too recent; the picture of Evanie's helplessness was too burning. He was being won over against his will, but—

"You win," he growled, releasing the bust. "Go ahead. Tell me what all this is leading up to. You must have some objective other than the indefinite perpetuation of your own power."

The Master smiled. "I have. I plan the ultimate destiny of Mankind." He held up a hand to still Connor's quick, unbelieving protest. "Listen to me. I have bred out criminals by sterilizing, for many centuries, those with criminal tendencies. I have raised the general level of intelligence by sterilizing the feeble-minded, the incompetent. If we have fewer supreme geniuses than your people, we have at least no stupid nor insane—and genius will come.

"I try, to the best of my knowledge, to improve the race. I think I'm succeeding. At least we're far advanced over the barbarians of the Dark Centuries, and even, I believe, over the average of your mighty, ancient people. I think we're happier." He paused. "Do you?"

"In a way," Connor conceded. "But even happiness isn't always a fair exchange for—liberty!"

"Liberty? Suppose I granted liberty? Suppose I abdicated? How long do you think it would be before every sort of Weed village was at war with every other sort? Do you want the world to break up into another welter of quarreling little nations? That's what I found; out of it I've created an empire."

He drummed a finger on the desk, thoughtfully eyeing Connor.

"Moreover, I've preserved what differences I could. The yellow race was a remnant; I've bred it strong again. The red race has gone, but the black is growing. And the tag-ends of nations—I've nourished them."

"Why?" Connor demanded. "Differences are only grounds for future trouble, aren't they?"

"Civilization grows out of differences. No race can produce a high culture by itself. There must be an exchange of ideas, and that means that there must be differences."

"You're very sure, aren't you?" Connor taunted.

"I've spent centuries thinking of it. I'm confident I've found the truth. And I do the best I can."

"I wish—" Connor paused. "I wish I could believe you!"

"You can. I never lie."

"I almost feel I can. You're not the mocking devil your sister is. I rather like you."

A queer smile flickered on the Master's lips.

"I have instructed her to cease tormenting you. I assume she has been, but she'll keep away from you hereafter. . . Won't you, my dear?"

Connor spun around. Lounging carelessly in the far doorway, a half-smoked cigarette in her hand, was the exquisite form of Margaret of Urbs.

"Perhaps," she drawled slowly and advanced leisurely into the room, seating herself casually on the desk regardless of its litter of papers.

"Joaquin," she remarked, "this man neglects to kneel in my presence. In yours as well, I perceive. Shall I command him?"

"Try commanding the statue of Olin," snapped Connor.

"We could persuade him," insinuated the Princess. "After all, Evanie Sair is our hostage."

"Be still!" the Master said sharply. "You know I never impose a custom on those who reject it."

The Princess turned taunting eyes on Tom Connor and was silent. "With your permission I should like to retire," he said. "We seem to have covered the ground."

"Not entirely," said the Master.

"What more do you want of me?"

"Two things. First, your knowledge. Your understanding of the ancient mathematics, and whatever else we need."

"Granted—on condition." At the Master's inquiring look he said boldly: "On condition that any knowledge I impart be made public. You have enough secrets—though some of them are apt not to remain so!"

"I'll agree," the Master said promptly. "That was always my intention. But what secret of mine is in danger of exposure?"

Connor laughed. "What else was it you wanted of me?"

"Your blood. Your strain in the race, like an infusion of bulldog blood to give greyhounds courage. I want you to marry and have children."

"And that," said Connor bluntly, "is my personal business. I refuse to promise that."

"Well," the Master genially remarked, "we'll let Nature take its course. I'll trade you that indulgence for the revelation of what secret you suspect."

"Done! It's the Triangle rocket-blasts."

"The rocket-blasts!"

"Yes. I've heard your craft in flight. I've listened to the blasts." He turned sardonic eyes from the Master to the Princess. "The blast isn't steady. It throbs. Do you understand? It throbs!"

The Master's face was stern. "Well?"

"I know you can't control the rate of power. You've had the whole world looking for a means of controlling the rate. That's impossible. Hydrogen has its natural period like radium. You can release the energy at that single rate or all at once, as in our rifles—but you can't control it otherwise!"

There was silence.

"I know what you do in the blast. You detonate your water—a little at a time in an enormously strong firing chamber, and release the blast gradually. It's no more continuous than the power of a gasoline engine!"

"You're endangering your life!" whispered the Master. "You can't live now!"

"With her Satanic Majesty, the Goddess of Mockery, to intercede for me?" Connor jeered, staring steadily into the gray-green eyes of the Princess. In her features now was no slightest trace of a taunt, but something more like admiration. "If I'm to die, it had better be here and now, else I'll find a way to tell what I know!"

"Here and now!" said Margaret of Urbs.

"Not yet," said the Master. "Thomas Connor, long ago in my youth I knew men like you. They're dead, and it's a great loss to the world. But you're living. I don't want to kill you. I'd rather trust the fate of my empire to your word. Having heard my side, then, will you swear allegiance to me?"

"No. I'm not sure of your sincerity."

"If you were, would you?"

"Gladly. I see more with you than with the Weeds."

"Then will you swear not to oppose me until such time as you are sure? And will you swear to keep that knowledge you have to yourself?"

"Fair enough!" Connor said, and grinned. He took the bronzed hand the Master extended. "I swear it." He glanced coolly at the Princess. "And by the three kinds of metamorphs, I'm glad to swear it!"

"Two kinds," corrected the Master mildly. "Panate and amphimorph."

But Margaret of Urbs caught his meaning. A faint trace of anger glinted in her eyes.

"The Immortals," she said coldly, "do not consider themselves metamorphs."

"Then I don't consider myself Irish," said Thomas Connor. "Any freak that comes out of Martin Sair's ray is a metamorph to me."

"Enough," said the Master. "That's all, Connor."

But at the door the Princess halted Connor, and he gazed down into her upturned face.

"Do you believe," she said coldly, "that Joaquin's promise will protect you—or Evanie Sair—from me? I have my own debt to collect from you."

He glanced back at the impassive figure at the desk.

"I traded my knowledge for your word," he called to the Master. "Is it good?"

"I am the Master," said that individual calmly.

Connor gazed again at the perfect features of the Flame. Slowly he raised his hand, holding her eyes with his. And then, with a sharp gesture, he snapped his finger stingingly against her dainty nose, grinned and strode away.

At the outer door he turned. The Black Flame, her lovely face a pale mask of fury, held a beam-pistol in her hand, but she made no move as he grinned back at her. Behind her the Master smiled cryptically.

But back in his room, an amazing realization came to Connor. Under the guise of his mildness, the Master had won every single point! He had extracted from Connor the promise of his knowledge, the promise of secrecy concerning the Triangle blasts, his alienation from the Weed cause, and more than half an oath of allegiance to himself!

And all for—what? The right of Thomas Connor to bear his own children, and the same promise of safety given at their earlier meeting!

He swore softly and lay thinking of the mocking loveliness of the Black Flame.

18. The *Sky-Rat*

Connor awoke fully rested, with the ache from muscles strained by Evanie's weight almost vanished. He arose, bathed, donned his glittering Urban costume, and looked into Evanie's room.

The girl was awake at last, and apparently well on toward recovery. He breathed a deep sigh of relief. At least in one matter, then, the unpredictable Princess had been sincere.

"Evanie!" he murmured. "Are you really all right? Are you better?"

She smiled and nodded. "I feel almost myself."

"Well, we misjudged the Princess in one respect, then. I'll have to thank her for pulling you through."

Evanie's eyes widened in horror.

"Thank her! What do you mean? Tom—have you—did you see her while I—"

He was taken aback.

"Why, I had dinner with her."

"After I warned you!" she wailed. "I tell you she's like a madness that gets into your blood. A man can't even look at her without suffering—and she's cruel and utterly inhuman." She compressed her lips firmly and whispered:

"There's a scanner here—right under the light. I mustn't talk like this."

"Who cares? She won't get into my blood, Evanie. I've met only two Immortals. The Master I like. The Princess—I hate!"

"See!" she whispered. "You like the Master! Tom, he's as bad as the Princess. He's subtle, scheming, insidious! His charm is poisonous. Don't let him talk you over—please!"

He was startled at her vehemence. But the Master had his word now. Could he break it? He was more than half convinced of the great ruler's sincerity. After all, Evanie was only a sweet, impulsive country girl whose grandfather had been killed. Something of his thoughts must have shown in his expression, for her face grew suddenly hard.

"If I believed you were turning away from us to them," she said tensely, "I'd despise you, Tom. But I believe in you! Believe you're strong enough to resist the trickery of the Immortals. Don't fail me."

He could not answer her then, for the maid, Sora, came in with a tray of food. She placed it on a cleverly constructed swinging arm that held it above the bed. It was a silent meal. Sora's presence put a restraint on them, and Evanie was cold, eyeing Connor suspiciously.

He was relieved when they finished and the woman departed with the tray. He found a box of the magically self-lighting cigarettes, and puffed moodily, while Evanie watched him in silence.

A rap sounded. A Palace guard entered, bowed, and handed Connor a tiny package and an envelope sealed with the imprint of the Midgard Serpent, and departed.

Connor broke the seal and slipped a card from within, read it, and whistled. There was a queer expression on his face when he handed it to Evanie. Written on it in script as fine and precise as engraving were the two sentences:

> *We desire your presence at once in our laboratory in the East Chambers. Show our medallion to the guard at your door.*
>
> ***Margarita***
>
> *Urbis Regina, Sororque Domini.*

The royal "we." It was no invitation, but a command. Connor stared at Evanie, who stared back with narrowed eyes.

"Well?" he said at last.

"Well?"

"What can I do? Ignore it and expose both of us to her anger—if she's such a devil as you say?"

"Oh, go!" snapped Evanie. "You and your ancient strength and courage! You're like any other man before the Black Flame of Urbs—just a fool! Go!"

"And leave you?"

"I'll have Sora for company," she retorted. "Go ahead. Burn yourself at the Flame, and see if I care."

"I don't see what else I can do than go," he muttered unhappily.

He turned moodily to the door, stripping the wrapper from the tiny package. A beautifully cast golden disc lay in his hand, with the pure features of the Princess in high relief.

The guard outside challenged him at once. It gave him a grim pleasure to flash the medallion in the fellow's face, to see him salute amazedly and step aside. Connor took the elevator to the ground floor, and passed moodily into the vast cavity of the Throne Room.

He passed through Martin Sair's disorderly chamber and finally to his destination. Margaret of Urbs sat with a glass of purple wine in one hand and the inevitable cigarette in the other, her dainty sandaled feet on a soft footstool. She wore Urban dress of glistening silver, above which her black hair gleamed like metal. She gave him a sardonic smile.

"You may kiss my sandal," she said.

"Or the hem of your skirt," he retorted. "Why did you send me that note?"

She gestured at the vision screen beside her.

"Mostly to watch you and Evanie quarrel over it."

"Then you know my opinion of you."

"Yes. I was rather amused."

"Well, if you've ceased to be amused, may I go back?"

"Not immediately," said the Princess. "Don't you think I owe you a little amusement in return?"

"I'll forgive the obligation."

"But I'm very circumspect about my debts," she insisted, with that maddening twinkle of mockery in the eyes that dared him. "Isn't there anything about the Palace—or in the world—that interests you? I'll take you sightseeing."

It was an opportunity, at that. There certainly was much he would like to see in this world that had grown up a thousand years after he was born. He hesitated. The inky-haired girl gestured at a chair and he sat down. Without permission he poured himself a goblet of the wine beside her. It was quite different from the still wines of Ormon; sweet, sparkling, rich—and potent.

"I'd like to see Eartheye," he said, musingly.

"Oh, Asia's too far!" she quickly protested. "I'm only giving you an hour or so."

"Let's have something on the vision screen from Eartheye, then," he suggested. "How about Mars?"

"Well, it's night over Asia." She snapped the screen on with a negligent hand and said, "Eartheye." In a moment a bearded face appeared with a respectful salute. "Put on Mars," she drawled. "The central region of Solis Lacus."

In a moment a rosy glow suffused the screen, resolving into focus as a ruddy plain with a greenish center. Connor gazed spellbound. The planet of mystery at a distance of two miles!

Enigmatical dark spots of strangely suggestive regularity were distinguishable, a lacy tracery of cabalistic lines, the flash of something bright that might be water. A pygmy civilization? He wondered dizzily.

"I'd like to see that at first hand!" he murmured.

"So would I," said Margaret of Urbs. "I've tried to talk my esteemed brother into permission to make the attempt, without success so far."

"You?" He remembered his conversation with Evanie and Jan Orm. "But it's two and a half years there and back!"

"What's two and a half years to me?" She snapped off the screen. "Come on," she said rising.

"Where now?"

"For a little flight. I'll show you a Triangle"—she glanced at him with a mocking smile—"since you know their secret—and yet live!"

"No thanks to you!" Connor flashed at her.

"No. Were you frightened?"

"Did I seem so?"

She shook her head.

"Are you ever afraid?"

"Often. I try not to show it."

"I never am," she said, pulling a beam-pistol from a table drawer and snapping it to her waist. "Since we're leaving the Palace," she explained. "I intend to bring you back."

He laughed and followed her through the Throne Room and up to a portion of the vast Palace roof below the South Tower. A Triangle stood there on a metal flooring. He noticed the pitting and excoriations where the blast had struck. The vehicle gleamed silver, far smaller than the giant ones he had seen in flight. Connor glanced curiously at the firing chamber at the apex, then at the name *Sky-Rat* engraved on the wall.

"My *Sky-Rat*," said Margaret of Urbs. "The swiftest thing yet made by man. Your bullets are laggards beside it." She hesitated, and for a moment he could have sworn that there was a touch of shyness in her eyes. "I took one trip in this—not so long ago," she said softly, "that I will never forget. The woods of Ormon are—lovely—don't you think?"

He made no answer to that, and followed her in. The tubular chamber was luxuriously fitted, with deep cushioned seats and room enough for comfortable sleeping quarters. When they were seated she depressed a lever and the throbbing roar of the blast began.

Through the floor-port he watched the Palace drop away. Urbs Major unrolled beneath. There was a sensation of weight as the vehicle shot upward like an errant meteor.

"Frightened?" laughed the Princess.

Connor shrugged. "I've flown before," he said laconically.

"Oh—airplanes! Wait!"

19. Death Flight?

Minute by minute the Earth receded. It seemed not so much to drop as to diminish, as if the surface were condensing like a deflating balloon. Urbs Minor slipped smoothly into the square of vision and the whole panorama of the mighty city was below—Greater and Lesser Urbs with the gash of the canal between them, tiny as a toy village in the Swiss Alps.

Kaatskill slid into the square, and a dozen other previously unseen suburbs of the vast metropolis. The aspiring towers of the Palace were small as pins in a carpet, and already a little east of them, as their radial flight permitted the Earth's rotation to gain on the craft.

The Earth began to seem hazy, and off to the north a snow-white plain of clouds glistened. The vast bowl of the planet began slowly to hump in the center. It was inverting, beginning to seem spherical.

Tom Connor jumped violently as a spark crackled off his thumb. A second stung the tip of his nose. The black silken hair of the Princess rose queerly in a cloud about the perfection of her face, and sparks raced along the metal of the hull.

"The Heaviside ionization layer," she murmured. "Scared?"

"No."

Margaret of Urbs glanced at a dial.

"Thirty thousand now."

"Feet?"

She laughed. "Meters."

About twenty miles. And they were still accelerating. The surface below flowed continually inward. The sky darkened; a star appeared—another. Fifty stars; a thousand—all glistening in a black sky where the sun blazed blue-white. The Earth was decidedly globular now. The vast, inconceivable slope of the planet could be seen in all directions.

Unconsciously Connor jumped as suddenly there came a sharp patter like hail.

"Meteoric particles," said the girl, turning a knob. "Paige deflector," she explained.

"For meteors as well as bullets, eh?" he suggested.

"For the iron ones. A stone might get through."

Uncomfortable thought. Minutes passed—half an hour. Suddenly the Princess moved something. Connor was nearly lifted from his seat by the sudden lightness.

"Deceleration," she said, glancing down at the colossal convexity below. "Three hundred miles. Are you frightened?"

"Do you think so?"

She smiled a taunt. "I'll turn off the deflectors," she murmured.

There was a pattering roar. Something crashed glancingly above him and the floor tipped and spun like a juggler's platter. Margaret of Urbs laughed.

"Might I ask the object?" he queried.

"Yes," she said gently. "I'm going to commit suicide!"

As he caught his breath sharply, unbelievingly, she moved the lever before her, and the throbbing roar of the blast died suddenly. The sensation of dizziness that followed was a thousand times worse than that Connor had experienced in the swift Palace elevators.

He was utterly weightless. They were in a free fall!

The Princess was laughing at him. Deep in those lustrous, inhumanly lovely sea-green eyes of hers was the glint of mockery.

"Scared?" she whispered, as she had done repeatedly, and gave a low rippling chuckle at his silence. "Three hundred miles!" she jeered. A timeless interval. "Two hundred!"

He couldn't shift his gaze from the Satanic beauty of her face, but he grimly fought his quivering lips to firmness. There was a low whine outside that rose abruptly to a screaming shriek that went gibbering across the world. The air! They had struck the atmosphere.

The floor grew warm, almost hot—it burned. At last Connor tore his eyes from the face of the Princess and gazed down at the up-rushing planet.

They were over ocean. What matter? At that speed it might as well be concrete. How high? Two miles—a mile? Less each succeeding second. The scream was a great roaring now.

"We're going to crash," he said evenly, knowing she couldn't hear him.

Margaret of Urbs kicked a lever with a daintily casual foot. The blast roared out—too late! Or was it? Irresistible weight oppressed Connor as the sea rushed upward. So close it was now that he saw the very waters hollowed by the blast. That near!

But far enough. They were receding until the girl cut the blast again and set the rocket gently on the heaving swells of the Pacific.

Connor gulped.

"Nice flying," he said steadily. "How often can you do it?"

"I don't know," she laughed. "I've never tried before. Scared?" The reiteration of that word was getting on his nerves as greatly as had the speed of the rocket.

"Did I show it?" he asked.

"I'm afraid not." Her voice changed suddenly. She rose, whipped the beam-pistol from her side. "If I can't frighten you," she said, her eyes glittering, "I can at least kill you!" The beam flashed over him.

He took the shock without flinching. She slid her finger along the barrel until it stabbed harder, racking him. He bit his lips and gazed back into eyes, now deeply emerald. At last she laughed and returned the weapon to its place.

"Were all ancients like you, Tom?" she murmured.

Somehow he managed a calm reply.

"Some stronger, some weaker," he said carelessly.

"I think I could—love you," she whispered.

She thrust a hand suddenly toward him and involuntarily he started.

"Afraid of one thing, at least, aren't you?" she jeered. "Afraid of—me!"

Without warning he caught her arm, swept her suddenly to him. He pressed a fierce kiss on the perfection of her lips. She yielded instantly, returning the caress. For a moment her lips burned against; his like strong wine, and lights coruscated in his spinning brain. With the Black Flame of Urbs in his arms, the world seemed to fall away as it had from the rising Triangle.

He felt her lips move against his, heard her murmur: "Tom! Tom! I do love you. Say you love me!"

"Love you? Love you?" he said. But just in time he caught that familiar gleam of mockery in her eyes. "Yes," he said. "Just as I love a drink of strong liquor!"

He pushed her roughly away, grinning sardonically. Margaret of Urbs laughed, but he fancied there was a quaver in her laughter. It was the first time he had seen the diamond hardness of her poise so much as ruffled. That is, since he had seen her in her role of cruel Princess, the role she had played for seven hundred years. When he had seen her as a child of the woods she had been different.

But she quickly regained her hard control over herself. She slapped a trifle viciously at the controls, and the Sky-rat soared away from a boiling circle of ocean toward Urbs.

Arrived there, the Princess said not a word, but left Tom Connor at once. He wandered irresolutely to his room and opened Evanie's door. She sat propped against some cushions while a man in the garb of a Palace servant leaned above her. Both turned startled faces toward him. In amazement he recognized the man as Jan Orm of Ormon!

Tom Connor opened his mouth to cry an involuntary greeting to Jan Orm, but checked it at the sight of Jan's warning look and a gesture from Evanie. Of course! Jan was here in disguise, and there was the scanner with unwinking eye and attentive ear. Connor advanced to the side of Evanie's bed and bent over her.

"Don't look at Jan when you talk," she said softly.

"I won't. Lord, I'm glad to see you, Jan! I didn't know what might have happened to you."

"I'm working in the kitchen," whispered Jan, nodding at a tray on the wall-arm. He added eagerly: "Tom, you can help us! We need you."

"Help you to do what?"

"To finish—" Jan began, but Evanie interrupted.

"Help me to escape," she whispered, then shot a glance at Jan Orm. "Be careful of him, Jan," she warned. "He's been around the Black Flame."

Connor reddened. "Look here !" he muttered. "Here's exactly how I stand. For safety sake, I've sworn to the Master to make no move against him for the present, and to tell him what I know of mathematics. That can't hurt you, can it? Evanie's safety is worth more to me than that."

"What's the value of an oath to the Master?" he growled. "That needn't bind you!"

"I keep my word," Connor said, as grimly.

"But your oath doesn't keep you from helping me to escape, does it?" whispered Evanie.

"I guess not—but what's the use of it? To suffer another Messenger?"

"This time," declared Evanie, "I'll fight off any Messenger. I was worn out before, exhausted, almost helpless."

"What can I do?" asked Connor, a little reluctantly.

"Are you free to move as you will about the Palace?"

"Not entirely."

"Well, I want to see the Master. I must see him."

"Why don't you call him and ask for an interview?" Connor asked. That seemed simple enough.

"I have. All I can get is a statement from the vision room that he's busy in his quarters and can't come. I'm not supposed to leave my bed, you know." She paused. "It's probably true. Jan has heard that there's a Conclave of the Immortals of the South day after tomorrow." She glanced at Connor imploringly. "Can't you get me to him, Tom? Please—I must see him."

Connor smiled, amused, as a swift thought crossed his mind. Margaret of Urbs must indeed have been perturbed this morning. She had forgotten to reclaim her medallion. If he were to use it before she remembered—

"Perhaps I can help you reach him, Evanie," he whispered. "If you'll come at once."

20. The Conspirators

The guards passed them without question, with only a glance at the medallion.

When they reached the anteroom beyond the arch they at once saw the Master at his littered desk. Evanie dropped gracefully to one knee as they neared the ruler. But Connor stood erect and stared at Margaret of Urbs, who sat in a chair by the window, a book on her lap, a black cigarette in her fingers spiraling smoke as she stared back at him.

The Master's eyes flickered over them.

"May I ask how you two managed to arrive here?" he inquired mildly.

Connor tossed the medallion on the desk, and his lips twisted in wry amusement when he saw the quivering start that twitched the dainty lips of the Princess. She arose quickly and moved to the Master's side. She and Evanie gazed at each other across the desk. The eyes of Margaret of Urbs were faintly disdainful, but Evanie's were hostile.

It was Tom Connor's first opportunity to make a firsthand comparison of the two. He hated himself for making it, but here it was thrust upon him.

The Princess was a trifle taller, a bit more slender than Evanie, and infinitely more beautiful, lovely as Evanie was. It wasn't fair, Connor told himself bitterly—terribly unfair, in fact, to compare Evanie's beauty with the unearthly beauty of the Black Flame of Urbs. It was like contrasting the simple loveliness of a wild rose to the splendor of an orchid, or a blown milkweed butterfly to a star flying Luna moth.

The Master spoke.

"I presume you have a reason for coming."

"Yes," said Evanie. "I can't stand it—being imprisoned in a single room. I had to see you." Her lips quivered. She was a consummate actress, Connor suddenly realized. "You know I—I have—metamorphic blood in me. You know what that means. I have to move about in the open to breathe air that comes from the sky, not from Palace ventilators. So I've come to ask you for a little freedom. Just permission to walk now and then in the Inner Gardens."

Connor wondered how walking in the square of the Inner Gardens could encompass her escape, since the Palace surrounded it.

"It is my intention to release you, but not yet," the Master said. "Not until I have had what I wish from Thomas Connor."

"But I can't stand it!" the girl pleaded tremulously.

The Master turned to Connor.

"Remembering your oath," he said, "do you second this request? This is no move against me?"

"I do not break my word," Connor said.

"Well, I see no harm in it." The Master called a few syllables into the box beside him, then spoke to Evanie. "You have the liberty of the halls and the Inner Gardens—no more. As for you"—his eyes flickered over Connor—"apparently you manage without my permission. That's all."

Evanie dropped again to her knee, rose and moved toward the archway. As Connor followed, the Master called:

"Not you, Thomas Connor."

Connor turned again toward the faintly amused face of the ruler.

"I perceive," the Master said, "that my sister has disobeyed me."

The Princess laughed in that mocking way of hers.

"Do I ever obey you, Joaquin?"

"Nominally, at times." He paused, studying his sister coolly for a moment, then again turned his attention to the man before him. "As you may know," he remarked, "I have summoned a Conclave for day after tomorrow. I am completely occupied. But I do not forget your promise, Thomas Connor, nor have I lost interest in the stores of ancient knowledge. Therefore, you will accompany the Princess to the chambers behind the Throne Room and fulfill your promise by explaining to her as much as time permits of mathematics, particularly of the meaning of logarithms and of the device I have heard termed the slide-rule. She will understand you. That's all."

He met the eyes of the Princess. "I may obey you this time, Joaquin," she said, and moved out of the door.

Connor followed her. The halls betrayed the activity of the coming Conclave, and were more crowded than he had observed before. Twice grave-faced, long-haired Immortals passed them, raising respectful hands in salute to Margaret of Urbs.

She turned into the South Corridor.

"This isn't the way," he objected.

"We're going to the Tower." She glanced sideward at him. "You'll see soon why the Palace needs all of its size. There'll be twenty thousand Immortals here, and we have room for all of them—half the Immortals in the world."

"Half! Evanie said there were three million."

She gave him an inscrutable smile.

"It does no harm to let the Weeds over-estimate our strength."

"Then why tell me?"

Her smile was the unfathomable one of the Mona Lisa.

"I never do anything without reason," was her only reply.

He laughed. When once again they reached the aspiring pinnacle of the Tower, without a glance at the mighty city below, the Princess pulled pen and paper from a table, seated herself, and faced Connor.

"Well?" she queried. "Begin."

He did. It was a new Margaret of Urbs he saw now, unknown before save possibly in that brief moment when he had mentioned the Venus of Milo, or when earlier in the woods she had shown him how vast was her knowledge of and interest in history and world events.

She was eager, curious, questioning, avid for knowledge and uncannily quick to comprehend. There we're queer gaps in her learning. Often he had to stop to explain terms utterly elementary, while at other times she followed him through the most complex maze of reasoning without a question.

The afternoon waned, dusk crept over the great vista, and at length she threw down her pen.

"Enough," she said. "We must have ten-place logarithm tables worked out. They'll be priceless at Eartheye." Not until then did a trace of mockery creep into her voice. "I suppose you realize," she taunted, "that once we have your knowledge all reasons to keep you alive are gone, but the reasons to kill you remain."

He laughed.

"You'd like to frighten me, wouldn't you? Haven't you tried that often enough? The Master trusts my word. I trust his—but not yours." His lips twisted. "Had I not trusted him, I could have escaped this morning. What was to prevent me from taking your weapon away, dropping you on a deserted shore—or even kidnapping you—and escaping in the *Sky-Rat*? I never promised not to escape. What kept me here was my trust in his word, and a desire to see this game played out!"

"There is no safety anywhere in the world for you, Thomas Connor," said the Flame softly, "except in my favor. And why you still live is a mystery, so much so that I wonder at it. I have never before been so indulgent to one I hate." She flashed her glorious emerald eyes to his face. "Do I hate you?"

"You should know hatred better than I."

"Yes—and yet I wonder." She smiled slowly. "If ever I love the way I hate, not death itself could thwart me. But there is no man strong enough to conquer me."

"Or perhaps," he retorted, "that one isn't interested."

She smiled again with almost a trace of wistfulness.

"You're very strong," she admitted. "I should have loved to have lived in your ancient days. To have lived among your great fighters and great makers of beauty. At least those were men—your ancients. I could have loved one of those."

"And haven't you," he asked ironically, "ever loved a man?"

He could detect no mocking note in her voice.

"Loved? I have thought myself in love a hundred times. At least a dozen times I have gone to Joaquin to beg immortality for some man I have loved. But Joaquin swore to Martin Sair long ago to grant it only to those worthy of it, and he has kept that oath."

She smiled wryly. "It takes all a man's youth to prove himself worthy, and so the Immortals are all dry scientists—not to my taste! Joaquin refused me each time I asked for the favor, wanting to know if I were sure I'd never tire of him for whom I begged—to swear I was sure. And of course I couldn't swear." She paused thoughtfully. "He was always right, too; every time. I did tire even before old age blighted them."

"And what did you do to prove yourself worthy?" Connor mocked.

"I'm serious today," the Princess said. "I'm not teasing now. I think I could love you, Thomas Connor."

"Thank you." He grinned, suspecting the glitter in the green eyes though he did not see it. "In my time it was the custom for the man to make such declarations."

"Your time!" flared Margaret of Urbs. "What do I care for your primitive customs and prehistoric prejudices? Would you have the Black Flame as shrinking and modest as little Evanie pretends to be?"

"I'd dislike you less if you were."

"You don't dislike me. You're merely afraid of me because I represent everything you hate in a woman—and yet you can't hate me. Indeed, I rather think you love me."

He laughed, mocking now, himself.

"I'm Margaret of Urbs!" she flashed. "What do I want of you? Nothing! I don't really want you at all, Tom Connor. You'd be like all the others; you'd age. Those mighty limbs of yours will turn skinny, or else fat and bloated. Those clear eyes will be pale and watery. Your teeth will yellow and your hair fall out, and then you'll be gone!"

She pulled a cigarette from the box and blew a plume of smoke in his impassive face.

"Go brag of this—when we release you—if we do! Go tell it up and down the world that you alone of all men were strong enough to reject the love of Margaret of Urbs. Go say that the Black Flame failed to scorch you—failed even to warm you." Her voice quivered. "And go say too that no other man save you ever learned—how unhappy—she is!"

The deep eyes were tear-bright. He stared into them perplexed. Was this merely more acting? Was there nothing left of Margaret of Urbs save a lovely mask and a thousand poses—no real being within? He forced a sardonic grin to his lips, forced it, for the impossible beauty of the girl tore at him despite his will.

At his smile her face darkened.

"And then say," she said, from between tight lips, "that the Black Flame doesn't care what talk you make of her, because she burns on while you—and those you talk to—in so very few years will be dust! Dust!"

Again he laughed at her and the Flame turned suddenly away.

"I suppose you may go now," she said dully.

But Connor hardly heard her. He was caught in speculations concerning the strange black and golden soul of the Princess, baffling, hateful, fascinating to the point of deadliness, and yet—somehow wistful, almost pitiful. It was almost, he thought, as if in the glimpse he had caught of her in the freedom of the woods he had seen the true soul of the woman, and all the rest was masquerading.

He stared across at the glory of her face, now subdued to sadness as she gazed out at a million lighted windows. Then a flicker of motion caught his eye, far, far beneath him in the well of shadows in the Inner Gardens.

"Someone's in the Gardens," he observed absently.

"Oh," said the Princess listlessly, "it must be an Antarctic Immortal, enjoying a garden under the sky "She clicked the vision screen. "Garden," she ordered dully. "North bank of the pool."

A burst of choked laughter startled him. He swung about. There, shown on the screen before his eyes, was Evanie, seated on a garden bench, her head on the shoulder of Jan Orm, his arm about her waist!

"A waiter!" the Black Flame said scornfully "A Palace waiter!"

But despite her laughter and his own confusion, Connor did not fail to notice that there were still tears in her eves.

21. The Dinner at the Sleeper's

Connor awoke late next morning, and to an instant memory of the shock he had experienced at the sight of Evanie and Jan Orm. Most of the night he had spent in improvising possible excuses for the girl. Perhaps it was an innocent scene he had witnessed.

After all, she and Jan were lifelong friends, born and raised in Ormon and it might be that Evanie had turned to him in loneliness, even in pique at his, Tom Connor's own involuntary attendance on Margaret of Urbs. But the mocking suggestions of the Princess, and the memory of Evanie's contented face in the vision screen—those troubled him. And he remembered, too, Jan's confession that, he loved Evanie.

Dressing, he glimpsed her far below in the Inner Gardens, with her bronze hair glinting. She was lying at full length on the grass. He forgot breakfast and hurried into the corridor, where the guard, remembering the medallion of the Princess, merely saluted respectfully, unaware that Connor no longer possessed the disc of gold.

He descended at once to the ground level, followed an interminable passage toward the Palace's center, and flung open a door at its end. Instead of daylight, a dim-lit chamber with glowing walls lay beyond, wherein, after a moment of blinking, he descried a row of perhaps twenty men. Some stared at him, surprised, but most kept their eyes fixed steadily on the shining wall.

"I'm sorry," he said to the nearest man. "I was looking for the Gardens."

Unexpectedly, a voice spoke beside him.

"The Gardens are two stories above us, Thomas. And I see you still wander."

It was the tall, ebony-haired Master. Beside him was another Immortal, grave-eyed and sandy-haired.

"This is Thomas Connor," said the Master, "our storehouse of ancient knowledge. Thomas, this is Martin Sair, here from Austropolis." He added, "Thomas is one of those who affect not to kneel in our presence. I indulge him."

"Indulgence is a habit of yours, Urbanus," rumbled the sandy-haired man. "Does the Princess also—indulge?"

"Not willingly. Margaret is having one of her restless years, I'm afraid." He frowned. "But they pass—they pass. Look there, Thomas." He gestured toward the wall. "This is our seeing room. Here is focused every scanner in Urbs—in any of my cities, if I wish. If the Palace is the world's brain, this room is the visual center."

Connor took his eyes from a fascinated scrutiny of the legendary Martin Sair, the Giver of Life, and glanced at the walls. Millions of tiny pictures covered them, each small as a thumbnail, glowing some in colors, and some, when the distant origin was in darkness, in the dull blue-gray of the short waves. He saw flickers of movement as the pictured men and women went about their daily business.

"We can enlarge any scene there," said the Master, pointing at a row of wider screens, some even now illumined. "In this room I can follow a man's life from birth to death, so long as he remains in one of my cities." He paused musingly, then shrugged. "The Gardens are two floors above us, Thomas."

It was dismissal. Connor cast a last glance at Martin Sair, feeling as if he were gazing on a demigod. Martin Sair, the Giver of Life, greatest except the Master among all the heroic figures in the dazzling age of the Enlightenment. Then he backed away from the great Immortal and betook himself to the Gardens.

Evanie was there, lovely as a bit of the ancient statuary that dotted the square, as she lay in the barbaric costume of Urbs watching a twenty-inch column of water slip smoothly from the mouth of a giant stone lion. She gave Connor a cool glance as he approached.

"Evanie!" he said unhappily. "I've looked everywhere for you."

"Why?" she asked indifferently.

"To be with you, of course. You know that."

"I don't know it. Or has the Flame burned you at last?"

Her coolness baffled him.

"Evanie," he pleaded, "why are you so offended?"

Her mouth hardened. "You've deserted the Weeds, Tom. Do you think I could ever forgive that?"

"See here, Evanie," he said hastily. "There's one thing you seem to have forgotten. I was thrust in among the Weeds of Ormon without choice. Does that mean I have to accept your social theories blindly? Perhaps I'm too primitive for anarchy—but I think you are too!" He went on defiantly. "I don't think your theories will work, and I do think the Master's government is what this world needs. It isn't perfect, but it's better than the Weeds offer—and even for you, Evanie, I won't give up freedom of thought."

"You mean you won't think!" she blazed. "You're not fooling me, Tom! I know the way the Black Flame poisons men, and you've been with her too often! You've been burned and—" Her anger mounted. "Oh, go away!"

"Evanie," he began earnestly, and paused. Was he untouched by the devastating charm of the Princess? The dizzying warmth of her lips, his reeling brain in the hour on the Pacific—"She's the daughter of Hell!" he muttered.

"Go away!" flared Evanie. "Quitter!"

Hot words rose to his lips. But he suppressed his anger, even as the picture he had seen of Jan and Evanie flashed on his mental screen, and turned away into the Palace.

For an hour he stamped through the endless halls now crowded with arriving Immortals from Africa, Antarctica, Australia, and South America. Now and again one turned cool eyes on his forbidding countenance or smiled gravely after him. None stopped or addressed him.

He must have completed the somewhat less than a mile of circuit several times when a guard approached him. He turned a furious scowl on the fellow, but he had only a tiny black envelope inscribed in white in the precise script of the Princess. Connor ripped the missive open. A short note was inside. It read:

Come to my chambers at half after the seventh hour to escort me to dinner. Wear the black costume in your quarters, and the black cape.

Margaret of Urbs

Merely an invitation—but a royal invitation is a command. He laughed bitterly. Why not? The Black Flame could burn no more painfully than she had already, and at least he could vent his anger on her.

Although hours remained before the appointed dinner hour, he went back to his quarters, glancing indifferently at the Urban formal dress laid carefully on his bed. It was exactly like his present garb save that it shimmered black with metallic scales, and was edged with silver. Crossing to the window he sat staring down at Evanie in the Gardens, bathing her rounded limbs in sunlight, until a man in Urban dress who could only be Jan Orm joined her. He turned angrily away then, fuming.

With no breakfast or lunch, he was both short-tempered and ravenous. So when the hours had dragged by, and he finally located the Chambers on the hundred and seventh level of the South Tower, he was in no pleasant mood. Two armed guards stepped aside, and the serving woman, Sora, admitted him with a clumsy curtsy.

He passed into the anteroom, furnished, as was the Black Flame's laboratory behind the Throne Room and her place at the summit of the Tower, lavishly and ornately. But surprise leaped to his eyes as he saw the gigantic black Persian cat that gazed steadily at him, with green eyes that seemed almost a replica of those of the Princess.

"A cat!" he exclaimed. "I thought they were extinct."

"Satan is immortal," said the soft voice of Margaret of Urbs.

He whirled and faced her as she emerged from the inner chamber, and hunger and anger alike drained out of him as he stared.

She was magnificent! Garbed in a jet-black cape that dropped to her green-crystalled sandals, she seemed taller as she advanced into the room. A circlet of green gems—emeralds, he thought—bound her ebony hair, and beneath it her eyes were smoldering sea-green fire.

But he felt the thrill of surprised shock as she threw open the cape. Her brief kirtle and corselet glittered in a solid surface of green gems, and at her waist sparkled that mystic crystalline flower of many colors, glistening from red to violet, blue, and purest emerald. Then she moved toward the lamp, and in its yellow radiance her whole costume was green no longer, but the deep lavender of wine.

"Alexandrites," she laughed, answering his unspoken question. "Green by day, lavender by artificial light. Synthetic, of course. There aren't this many natural stones in the world." She turned. "Like it?"

"Exquisite!" he whispered. "You daughter of Lucifer!"

He followed her in rebellious fascination as they progressed unattended to the ground floor and into a long Palace car with stiff-backed driver and footman.

"Merimee's," she said, and the car spun silently away, mounting to the upper tier of Palace Avenue.

It was dusk, but now and then, when traffic slowed their motion, cheers sounded, and many a glance was cast at them. Margaret of Urbs ignored the glances, but smiled at the cheers.

"Who's Merimee?" Connor asked.

"A rich Sleeper in Kaatskill. Society here is largely Sleepers."

"No nobility?"

"The Immortals seldom entertain. We're a serious lot."

Kaatskill appeared, and they glided into the grounds of an imposing Grecian mansion. Lights were glowing, gay voices sounded as they entered.

There was a sudden silence as the whole assemblage knelt. Margaret of Urbs gestured and the guests arose. Merimee himself, paunchy, bald, came babbling his appreciation, his gratitude for the honor to his house.

"But the entertainment, Your Highness! On such short notice, you see—best the bureau could furnish—I know you'll forgive—"

22. Declaration

The dinner was lavish. Connor sat at the left of the Princess. Lines of servitors passed in a steady stream, bearing soups, then fish—Bombay ducks, pompano, a dozen unknown viands—and fowl—ortolan, ptarmigan, pheasant, and nameless others.

Connor was ravenous. He sampled everything, and it was the middle of the meal before he noticed the aghast looks of the crowd, and that he was almost the only one who was eating.

"Have I violated the proprieties?" he asked the Princess.

"You're supposed to eat only of the dishes I taste," she informed coolly.

"But I'm hungry. And you've eaten practically nothing."

It was true. Margaret of Urbs had taken only a little salad, though she had sipped glass after glass of wine.

"I like to tantalize these hogs," she replied in low but audible tones. "This bores me."

"Then why come?"

"A whim."

He chuckled, turning his attention to the entertainment. This, he thought, was excellent. An incredibly skillful juggler succeeded a talented magician; a low-voiced woman sang sweet and ancient tunes; a trio played tinkling melodies. A graceful pair of adagio dancers performed breathtakingly in the square surrounded by the tables, and a contortionist managed unbelievable bodily tangles. The performers came and went in silence. Not one burst of applause rewarded them.

"Unappreciative audience!" Connor growled.

"Is it?" the Princess drawled. "Watch."

The following number, he thought, was the worst of the lot. A frightened, dingy man with a half-trained dancing monkey that chattered and grimaced, but made a sad failure of the dancing. Yet at the conclusion Margaret of Urbs raised her dainty hands, and applauded.

Instantly bedlam broke loose. Applause crashed through the hall;

encores were shouted, and the astonished player stumbled once more through the ludicrous performance.

"Well, his fortune's made," observed the Princess. "N'York will want him and Ch'cago, and Singapore as well."

The master of ceremonies was presenting "Homero, the Poet of Personalities," a thin-faced Urban crowned with laurel leaves and bearing a classical harp.

He bowed and smiled.

"And who, Ladies and Lords, shall it be? Of whom do I sing?"

"Her Highness!" roared the crowd. "The Princess of Urbs!"

Homero strummed his harp, and began chanting minstrel-like :

"The Princess? Adjective and verb
Turn feeble! Glorious? Superb?
Exquisite? None of these can name
The splendor of the Urban Flame.

"Our Princess! Stars are loath to rise
Lest they be faded by her eyes,
Yet once they've risen, they will not set,
But gaze entranced on Margaret.

"The continents and oceans seven
Revolve beneath the laws of Heaven;
What limit, law, or cannon curbs
The tongue that speaks the Flame of Urbs?"

Applause, violent and enthusiastic, greeted the doggerel. Margaret of Urbs lowered her eyes and smiled.

"Who now?" Homero called. "Of whom do I sing?"

Unexpectedly, Merimee spoke. "Tom Connor!" he cried. "Tom Connor, the Ancient!"

Homero strummed his harp and sang:

"Ladies and Lords, you do me honor,
Giving the name of Thomas Connor,
That Ancient, phoenix like arisen
Out of his cold, sepulchral prison,
Thrust into life—a comet hurled
From the dead past into the world.

"What poet great enough to sing
The wonderful awakening?

Let golden Science try explain
That miracle—and try in vain;
For only Art, by Heaven inflamed.
Can dream how Death itself was tamed!"

"He'll turn this into some insipid compliment to me," whispered Margaret of Urbs. The Poet of Personalities sang on:

"Year after year the strong flesh mouldered,
Dim was the spark of life that smouldered—
Until the Princess glanced that way,
And lo! The cold and lifeless clay,
To Death and Time no longer slave,
Burst out triumphant from the grave!"

In the roar of applause Connor sat amazed at the reference to his own experience. How did Homero know? He turned to question the Princess.

"I'm tired of this," she said, and rose to depart.

The whole body of guests rose with her. She drew her cape around her and strode to the car.

"Slowly," she ordered the driver, then leaned back gazing at Connor.

"Well?" she murmured.

"Interesting. That Homero—he's clever."

"Bah! Stock verses composed beforehand."

"But—about me?"

"Don't you know you've been a newspaper and vision sensation?"

"The devil!" Connor was shocked.

"This Homero," she went on musingly. "Once, long ago, I knew Sovern, the only great poet of the Enlightenment, he who half seriously, half contemptuously, named me the Black Flame, and the only man—save you, Tom Connor, who ever flaunted me to my face. And one evening he angered me, and I exiled him from Urbs, Urbs that he loved—and too late I found that his bitterness grew out of a love for me.

"So I called him back in time to die. when not even Martin Sair could save him. And dying he said to me—I recall it—'I take my revenge in remembering that you are human, and to be human is to love and suffer. Do not forget it.'" She paused. "Nor have I."

"And was it true?" asked Connor, struck suddenly by this revelation of the fiery, imperious, untamable character beside him.

"I think, lately, that it is true," she murmured, and drew a long breath. "I have slain, I have tortured, for less violence than you have committed against me."

She flung open her cape, baring the marks of his fingers still on the exquisite curve of her throat.

"I cannot—suffer the touch of violence, and yet you have struck me twice and still live. There is a magic about you, Thomas Connor, some laughing ancient strength that has died out of the world. I have never begged anyone—but I fear you and I plead with you." She swayed against him. "Kiss me!" she whispered.

He stared down at the unearthly beauty of her face, but there was a green light in her eyes that puzzled him. Coolly he fought the fascination that was cast net-like about him. This was but another taste of the torment she had promised. He was sure of it.

"I will not," he said. "Each time I have kissed you, you have laughed at me."

"But I will not laugh now."

"You'll not trap me again by the same trick," he said. "Find another way for the torment you threatened. And when you're ready to kill me for the violence I did you, I'll die laughing at you."

"I have forgiven that," she said softly.

"Then," he said mockingly, "here's more to forgive."

He lifted her slender wrist in his mighty hand, circled it with his powerful fingers, and crushed it in a grasp like contracting steel. It gave him a grim pleasure to thus vent his turbulent emotions on her, and to see her face whiten under pain that must have been excruciating. But save for her pallor she gave no sign of agony.

He dropped her hand, ashamed of his cruelty, though it was not as if he had used his strength against a mortal woman. Margaret of Urbs seemed to him rather a female demon.

But she only said softly, "I thank you for this. It has taught me what I wanted to know, for any other than you would now be dead for it. I love you, Tom."

"Flame!" he retorted, while her eyes widened the merest trifle at the familiarity. "I don't believe you."

"But you must! After all these years upon years I am sure. I swear it, Tom! Say you love me."

"I love—Evanie." But despite his words the doubts that had been constantly creeping in on him assailed him. Evanie was still alien, somehow.

"You love me!" she murmured. "I am the Black Flame, yet I plead now. Say it, Tom!"

"I love Evanie!"

"Then will you kiss me?"

He stared down at her. "Why not?" he said savagely. "Do you think I'm afraid of you?"

He spun her against him and her lips burned against his.

"Say you love me!" she repeated in a tense whisper. "Say it!"

"I love—" he began, and the car slid to a stop before the Palace arch. The footman stood holding the car door open.

Margaret of Urbs gazed as if distraught from Connor's face to the silent attendant and back again. Abruptly she thrust herself away, her mouth quivering.

"I wish," she said tensely, "I—wish I had never seen you!"

She struck him a sharp blow across his mouth, clambered unassisted to the ground, and disappeared into the Palace, trailing her black cape behind her.

Back in his room again, Connor was in a turmoil, ashamed, perplexed, bitter.

"Caught!" he swore fiercely. "Burned! God! What a fool—what a weakling!"

For call it what he would—it was true. Fascination, infatuation, anything—the fact faced him that the Black Flame had burned Evanie from his heart. He swore viciously and battered at Evanie's door.

The blows echoed into silence. There was no response.

With a long-drawn sigh, Connor turned away from Evanie's door. Whether absent or simply ignoring him, she had failed him, and he needed her desperately now. He wanted to quench the fires of the Black Flame in her cool simplicity, to reassure himself that what he now felt was an obsession, an infatuation—anything but love.

He wanted to convince himself it was Evanie he loved by telling her so. Better never to have emerged from under the prison than to live again, loving a mask of beauty hiding a daughter of Satan.

He strode to the casement overlooking the Gardens. Dim light from the Palace windows streaked in bars across it, but he saw no sign of Evanie. But could that be Evanie—there where the bushes shadowed the pool?

23. The Amphimorphs in the Pool

Tom Connor made his way hurriedly to the Gardens. He saw Evanie crouched in the shadow of shrubbery just above the brink of the water. He dashed forward as she glanced up at him.

"Evanie!" he began. "Oh, my dear—"

"Hush!" Her voice was tense.

"But—"

"Be still. Speak softly. Do you think I want a scanner on me?" She paused. "I'd rather you'd go away," she whispered.

He seated himself stubbornly beside her, though it seemed certain she was waiting for someone. Jan Orm, probably.

"I won't go," he said in a subdued voice. "You've got to listen to me, Evanie."

"Please!" she murmured. "Be quiet, Tom. I've been waiting here six hours."

"For what?"

She made no reply. He subsided into gloomy silence, watching the great column of water that gushed from the jaws of the huge stone lion at the far end of the pool. The water, smooth as a steel pillar, fell with surprisingly little sound.

But while he gazed, it changed. The smoothness was broken. Bubbles flashed, and then the flow ceased altogether while a huge bubble glistened, billowed and broke. Something white and shining and large as a man shot with a small splash into the pool. The column of water crashed instantly back.

A webbed hand holding a silk wrapped package rose suddenly from the black water. An amphimorph!

Evanie seized the bundle, crammed it beneath an Urban cape at her side.

"Quick!" she said tensely. "Stand here beside me, Tom, so we'll block the scanner."

He obeyed wonderingly. A queer low coo came from Evanie's lips. The black waters parted again and he glimpsed the tiny round mouth and horrible face of the creature in the pool. It flopped to the bank, scuttled desperately along into the bushes. He saw it raise the lid of a manhole of a storm-sewer, and it was gone.

Pale and trembling Evanie sank down on the bank, her bronzed legs dangling toward the water. "If only we weren't seen!" she whispered. "How the devil did that thing get here?" Connor demanded.

"It rode a bubble down the water tunnel from the mountains, fifty miles. An amphimorph doesn't need much air. A big bubble will last."

"But—"

"Don't ask me how it found the maze of mains in Urbs. I don't know. I only know they have queer instinctive ways of getting where they want to go. Now it's gone into the storm-sewer. It will find its way to the Canal and so up rivers to its mountains."

"But what was that it brought, and from whom?"

"From King Orm."

"From whom?" he persisted.

"Tom," she said quietly, "I'm not going to tell you."

"What was in that package, Evanie?"

"I won't tell you that, either." She threw the cape over her arm, concealing the package. "I can't trust you, Tom. You and I are enemies."

She backed away at his anger.

"Tom, please! You promised to help me escape, didn't you?"

"All right," he yielded dully. "Evanie, I sought you out here because I wanted to end this misunderstanding. Please give me a chance to convince you I love you!"

He held out his arms to her. She backed another step.

"I won't come near you, Tom. I won't trust myself in your arms. I'm afraid of you, and I'm afraid of myself. You're strong—too strong for me physically, and perhaps too strong otherwise. You wakened my love once. I dare not chance it again."

"Oh, Evanie! Now of all times, when I need you!"

"Need me?" A queer expression flickered over her face. "So the Black Flame burns at last!" Her voice dropped to a murmur. "I'm sorry for you, Tom. I'm sorry for anyone who loves her, because she's utterly heartless. But I can't come near you. I don't dare!"

She turned and darted suddenly into the Palace, leaving him to stare hopelessly after, and then to follow slowly.

He slept little that night. Restless, tortured hours were filled with dreams of Margaret of Urbs and the sound of her laughter. He arose early and wandered dully from his room.

The halls were crowded with arriving Immortals, among whom he stalked as silent and grave as themselves. At last, tired of aimless wandering, he went into the shaded Gardens, and sat glumly down beside the pool.

Far overhead Triangles drifted with muffled, throbbing roars, and a bird sang in the bushes. Deep in his own perturbed thoughts, he was startled when he heard his name spoken softly, almost timidly.

"Tom."

He looked up. Margaret of Urbs stood beside him, garbed in the most magnificent gown he had ever seen, golden and black, and concealing her tiny feet. Instead of the circlet of the previous evening, she wore now a coronet of scintillant brilliance, and the strange flower flamed at her waist.

"Official robes," she said and smiled. "I preside this morning."

She looked a little worn, he thought. There was a pallor on her cheeks, and a subdued air about her. Her smile, almost wistful, tore at him.

"You didn't give me a chance to thank you for last night," he said.

"Did you want to thank me? For—everything?"

"No," he said stonily. "Not for everything."

She dropped listlessly to the bench beside him.

"I'm tired," she said wearily. "I didn't sleep well, and my head aches. That Grecian wine. I must see Martin Sair."

"My head aches for other reasons," he said grimly.

"I'm sorry, Tom."

"Were you laughing at me last night?" he blazed.

"No," she said gently. "No."

"I don't believe you!"

"No matter. Tom, I came here to tell you something." She paused and gazed steadily at him. "The Master will grant you immortality."

"*What*?"

She nodded. "He considers you worthy."

"Worthy! What of the children of mine he was so anxious about?"

"You're to have them first."

He laughed bitterly. "Then I'll be old and feeble by the time I'm ready for immortality. Evanie has refused me—and I refuse him! I'll live my life out in my own way."

"Think well of it first," she said slowly, and something in her voice caught him.

"Now I know I won't accept," he flashed. "You begged him for it! Do you think I'd take favors of you?"

"I didn't—" She was silent. After a moment she said, "Would you believe one statement of mine, Tom?"

"Not one."

At last his bitterness touched her. She flushed faintly. The old gleam of mockery shone for an instant.

"You're right, of course," she snapped. "There's nothing real remaining of Margaret of Urbs. She's the Black Flame that burns on illusion's altar. You must never believe a single word of hers."

"Nor do I!"

"But will you believe one sentence if I swear it by something sacred to me? One thing, Tom?"

"What's sacred to you? God? Honor? Not even yourself!"

"By the one thing I love," she said steadily, "I swear I'm speaking the truth now. Will you believe me?"

It was on his very tongue to say no. He was thoroughly surprised to hear himself mutter "Yes"—and mean it.

"Then do you remember that day in the Triangle when I said I was going to commit suicide? I swear that is the only lie I've ever told you. Do you understand? The only lie!"

She arose as he stared at her uncomprehendingly.

"I want to be alone," she whispered. "I'm going to"—a brief, wistful smile—"my thinking room."

Connor's brain was whirling. He did believe her. What of it? Evanie didn't love him. He knew that now. And he didn't love Evanie. And Margaret of Urbs—said she loved him! Could it be possible . . .

A blinding light in his brain! The Black Flame—his! The unearthly beauty of her, the wild, untamed character, his to tame—if he could. The Satanic spirit, the fiery soul, all his for life. For life? For immortality, if he chose!

An exultant shout burst from him and went echoing between the walls as he leaped to the Palace door, flung himself through.

Memory of Evanie had vanished like mist. Where was the Princess? In her thinking room? Then he remembered. The laboratory behind the Throne Room.

A speaker blared down the hall as he ran: "Conclave in thirty minutes."

The corridors were thronged; he jostled his way past crowds of guards, servants, officials, and austere Immortals. Curious eyes followed him, but no one moved to halt him.

Not, at least, until he reached the great arch of the Throne Room itself. The crystal doors were shut and a line of four impassive guards blocked the way. He moved to step between them, and a sharp challenge sounded.

He paused. "I want to see the Princess," he said firmly.

"None to pass," snapped the guard. "Master's orders."

"But is the Princess in there?"

"Her Highness," responded the guard, "entered here five minutes ago. She said nothing of anyone to follow."

24. The Atomic Bomb

Reluctantly, Tom Connor fell back. This was the only way to her laboratory; of that he was certain. He leaned against the wall and clenched his fists in a frenzy of impatience.

The glass doors opened and the Master emerged, accompanied by Martin Sair, and two other tall Immortals.

"Sir," Connor begged eagerly, "tell this fellow to pass me. I want to see the Princess."

A curious, quizzical expression flickered in the eyes of the great ruler. He shook his head.

"I'm sorry, Thomas," he said mildly. "In fifteen minutes the Princess will be needed. You can wait."

"But—I think she wants to see me!"

"Then she can wait as well." His eyes flickered again. "She has waited, not too patiently, for more than seven centuries." He moved away down the corridor, leaving Connor nonplussed.

He curbed his impatience. After all, the Master was right. Time stretched before him and Margaret of Urbs—years upon years of it. But it was hard to lose these precious moments.

He thought of the vision screens. Just behind him was the vast office opposite the Throne Room. He turned in there, bursting in upon a scene of feverish activity as the records of half the world were made ready for the Immortals of the Southern Hemisphere. Glancing about, he descried a screen on a table at the far end of the room, and twisted his way down the line of desks, ignoring a thousand staring clerks.

"The Princess," he said eagerly, snapping the switch. "In her laboratory behind the Throne Room."

On the screen flashed a girl's face, but not that of Margaret of Urbs.

"I'm sorry," she said. "No calls to any at the Conclave. Master's orders." The screen clicked blank again as he growled an angry epithet.

In the hallway he saw Evanie, staring with strange intentness at the closed glass doors. He pushed his way to her side.

"Hello," he said, and was puzzled by her sudden look of fear. But she recovered herself and glanced coolly at him.

"Oh, it's you," she said briefly.

He thought wonderingly how different was this Evanie from the timid, modest little Ormon girl of so few days ago. But he hardly cared. The Flame had burned him free of Evanie.

"Waiting for the parade of the Immortals?" he asked with a quiet smile.

"Perhaps."

"I thought you hated them so that you'd prefer not even looking at them."

Her voice changed to bitterness. "I do."

"Well, what's the answer, then?"

She glanced at a watch on her wrist.

"You'll know in a moment or two." She gave him a curiously sardonic smile. "I'm not afraid to tell you now. I'll even tell you what was in the package I took from the amphimorph. Would you like to know?"

"Of course."

Her voice quivered excitedly. "In that package was an atomic bomb!"

"An atomic bomb?"

"Yes. And do you know where it is now?" The voice rose exultant, fanatically elated. "At the wall behind the Throne of Urbs! Behind the throne where the Master's sitting this moment! My thanks for sponsoring my request for freedom, Tom. It helped."

"The Master isn't in there," he said tightly. "I saw him leave."

He saw her face whiten—and then an appalling thought struck him.

"Oh, God! But the Princess is! The Princess is!"

He dashed toward the guarded door, disregarding Evanie's cry of warning: "Tom, it's due! It's due!"

He rushed at the impassive guards, but before their challenge was uttered a thunderous roar reverberated in the vast hall like the rumbling thunder of a collapsing mountain.

A continuous screaming bellow like the clamor in hell rose in an ear-blasting crescendo, and beyond the glass doors rolled billowing clouds of steam, shot through with jagged fires.

Maddened to desperation, Tom Connor plunged against the doors. They swung inward and closed behind him, and he was in the room of the blast. Far down, behind the Master's throne, an erupting geyser of destruction appalled him—a mighty, roaring, billowing cloud of smoke-streaked steam that shrieked louder than the tortured souls of the seventh circle of hell.

Crashing discharges of stray energy etched flames through the cloud, like lightning behind a thunder-head, and the reverberations echoed above the roar of the disrupting hydrogen. The Master's throne was hidden by the bellowing fires that grounded to it.

But even that holocaust had not yet filled the vast concave of the Throne Room. The end where Connor stood, momentarily bewildered, was as yet clouded only by shreds and streamers. He lowered his head, and charged into the inferno. Margaret was caught somewhere behind that hellish blast!

Scalding steam licked at him, swirling about his body. His bare legs and shoulders stung at the touch, his face burned, but he gained the line of thrones and paused a single moment on the shielded side. What an engine of destruction! A bomb that, instead of venting its force in a single blast, kept on exploding as successive billions of atoms shattered.

No need to look for the door. The detonation, the first blast, had blown the wall open. Instantly he made a dash over the scorching debris, where the mighty girders were fantastically twisted and bent away from the roaring center, pointed up in the misty light. He launched himself at the edge of the opening, passing close to the very threshold of the trap door of Tophet.

Gamma radiations excoriated his body. The shriek of dying atoms thundered against his tortured eardrums, and he was burning—blistering. But an implacable thrust urged him on. He was responsible for this chaos, this holocaust, and Margaret of Urbs—He had violated his oath to the Master! Evanie had betrayed him into that! She had tricked him into sponsoring her plea for freedom, and because he had aided her this had happened! Jan Orm could have done no damage alone. Only Evanie, because of the inhuman blood in her, could have dealt with an amphimorph. Evanie, with whom he had thought himself in love!

And the Princess, whom he did love, was somewhere beyond.

He raged on, his mind turbulent as the blast itself, into Martin Sair's laboratory, a flaming outer region of hell clouded to invisibility. Suffocating, scorching, he crashed against its farther wall, slid along it, at last found the door.

The luxurious room of the Princess was in chaotic disorder, but only lazy wisps of steam drifted there, and the bellow of the blast was muffled. But even now the wall was cracking.

"Margaret!" he cried. "Margaret of Urbs!"

Her voice answered him. She was in a corner, crouching. Injured? No, she was searching earnestly through a pile of debris that had been swept across the room by the first concussion. He rushed toward her.

"Come on!" he shouted. "We'll break a window and get out."

She glanced coolly up.

"A window? Try it. A bullet might, but nothing less."

He snatched up a chair, spun it fiercely against the pane. The chair shattered; two tiny dents showed in the crystal, and that was all. And in the Palace, ventilated by washed air from the topmost pinnacles of the Twin Towers, no windows opened. He whirled on her.

"Then it will have to be back through the blast!" he roared. "Come on!"

She stood up, facing him. She had slipped off the gold-black robe in the steaming heat, wore now the typical revealing garb of Urbs save that the material was of black velvet instead of metallic scales.

"You can't go through in clothes like that!" he shouted.

"My Venus," she said. "It was blown somewhere here. I want it."

"You'll come now!"

"I want my ivory Venus."

The pale flash of ivory caught his eye.

"Here it is, then," he snapped, thrusting the statuette into his belt. "Now come."

Faint mockery flashed in her eyes.

"What if I don't?"

He shook a rugged fist. "You will or I'll take you."

"Why," she asked, "do you risk your life to reach me?"

"Because," he snarled in exasperation, "I was unwittingly responsible for this. I was tricked into breaking my word. Do you think I can let the Master—or you—suffer for my stupidity?"

"Oh," she said, her eyes dropping. "Well—I won't go."

"By God, you will!" He sprang to seize her but she evaded him.

But only for a moment, as again he saw the gleam of mockery in her eyes.

"Very well," she said, suddenly submissive.

He snatched the flowing robe from the floor as she turned and walked steadily toward the wall that now heaved and cracked and groaned. Before he could reach her she had flung open the door—and hell roared in upon them.

Martin Sair's laboratory was a mass of smoke and steam like the crater of Erebus that flames in the eternal ice of Antarctica. Flinging the robe over the Princess like an enshrouding blanket, Connor propelled her, muffled and stumbling, toward the evil effulgence of the screaming blast.

At the break in the wall he put his weight into a mighty thrust that sent her sliding, staggering, sprawling into the room where the fiery cloud closed, billowing, about her. Then he leaped through, his flesh writhing in the torment of the stinging rays, and blistering at the touch of scalding steam.

Margaret of Urbs was clambering to her feet, stumbling in the entangling robe, in the all but unbearable shelter of the thrones. She choked as the searing air reached her lungs.

"You hurt!" she cried. "Come on!"

Again the taunting gleam, even with blistering death staring them in the face. But she followed unresisting as he seized her arm and plunged through the blinding fog of steam and smoke that now filled the mighty room to the distant ceiling. Blind chance was their guide as they rushed ahead, staggering, coughing, teary-eyed. It seemed a long way. Were they circling in the gloom of the monstrous chamber?

The Princess dragged against Connor's arm. "No," she gasped. "This way—this way." He let her lead. They struggled through billowing masses that began to take fantastic shapes—charging monsters; heaving mountains. She staggered, stumbled, but shook off the arm he raised to support her.

"I've never needed help," she muttered proudly. "I never will."

It seemed to him that the blast roared closer. "Are we—right?" he choked.

Then, through a momentary rift he saw something that sickened him—the row of thrones, smoking and blackened in the blaze. They had circled!

Through some vagary of draught or ventilation there was a little area of almost clear air beside the throne of the Princess. Coughing and choking, they faced each other in it. He was astounded to see a flickering, taunting smile play for a single instant on her lips. Her hair singed and plastered flat by the steamy condensation, her face soot-streaked and reddened, she was yet so incredibly lovely that he forgot even their peril as her smile turned suddenly earnest, wistful.

"Dearest," she whispered, inaudibly, but he read her lips. "I'll confess now. We were safe in my room. We must have been watched in the vision screens, and men would have come to cut through the window."

He was appalled.

"Then why—"

"Listen to me, Tom. Even here I misled you, for I knew which way the door lies by the pattern on the floor. But if you will not love me, I must kill you as I promised, then both of us die! For I cannot watch you age year by year—and then perish. I cannot!"

"Flame!" he roared, his voice impassioned. "But I love you! Did you think—I love you, Flame!"

Her streaming eyes widened.

"Oh, God!" she choked. "Now it's too late!" She covered her face, then abruptly glanced up again, with a dawning hope in her eyes. "Perhaps not!" she cried. "Can they see us here? No—the steam. But men will come in moon-suits to carry away the blast—if—we can live—until then." She coughed. "But we can't." She was swaying. "You go—that way. Kiss me, Tom, and leave me. I want to die—on the throne—of Urbs. Only—a thing—like this, some accident—can kill an—Immortal!"

"Leave you?" he cried. "Not even in death!" He choked as he drew her close.

A wave of steam and fire engulfed them. "Help me to my—throne," she whispered, gasping.

Her eyes, tear-bright and sea-green in the fierce lightnings, went blank. They closed, and she slipped half through his arms. Her knees gave way as she collapsed.

25. Inferno

He held her against him. Put her on the throne? Why not? Why not hold her there until the end, die with her in his arms? Or perhaps shield her with his body until men came, or until the blast burned out. Somehow she must be saved!

Never—not even when a thousand years ago an electric current was shot through him to kill him, had his urge for life been so great as it was now. Now, when life promised so much—the love of himself and the Black Flame of Urbs, two beings who should have been dead centuries ago and in different ages—he must die!

Had Destiny kept them alive to meet and love for this brief moment before death? Madness! Better to die struggling for life. Raising the girl in his arms, he staggered away toward the wall that still shielded the room where he found the Princess.

Her weight was slight, but he had not taken ten steps when he went crashing to his knees. He struggled up dizzily. The line of diagonal black squares showed dim on the floor, yet he could not be sure that he had not changed his direction. He was suffocating; the roaring blast seemed to bellow in a gigantic throbbing, now in his very ears, now dim and faint and far away.

He battled on. Suddenly he realized that he was moving burdenless. Without even being aware of it he had dropped the Princess. He turned grimly back until he stumbled over her lying huddled with her cheek against the steaming floor. Swinging her across his shoulder, gripping her knees so tightly that his fingers bit into the silk-soft skin, he staggered back over the lost ground.

Each step was a gamble with death. If he fell now he would never rise again. He tottered on while his lungs labored in the vitiated air and the searing steam. Then behind him the blast roared fainter. Or was it simply that his senses were dulling?

It was the sharp blow of his head against the wall that brought him back from a dreamy somnolence into which he was falling, surprised to feel the weight of the unconscious girl still on his shoulder.

The wall! Which wall? In what direction was the door that meant life? He groaned and turned at random to the right, simply because his right arm clutched the limbs of Margaret of Urbs and his left hand was free to support him against the carved masonry. But an ejaculation of triumph escaped his burned, cracked lips as his hand slid over steam-clouded glass, and he saw white faces through the track it left.

He could go no further; make not one more move. The limp body of the Princess slid from his arms, and vaguely then he knew that both of them were being dragged into the safety of the corridor. He gasped in great breaths of clear air that whistled in his seared throat, and then his heart chilled as his bloodshot eyes turned on the form of the Flame.

Her face frightened him. Waxen pale, still as the image on her throne, she seemed scarcely to breathe. A grave Immortal who bent above her straightened up and said tensely:

"Get Martin Sair—and quickly!" His eyes flashed to Connor. "You're not hurt," he said. "Just rest here for some time."

There was a stir in the hallway. Two men in brown all-encompassing suits and crystal helmets were pulling something metal. It looked like a steam-shovel scoop with two fifty-foot handles. A grapple for the blast, to box it before it undermined the vast Palace.

Then Martin Sair was at hand, and the Master, his sorrowful eyes on the Princess.

"Clear the corridor," said the sandy-haired Immortal, and guards swept back the crowd.

Through the North Arch, Connor glimpsed thousands upon thousands of Urbans on the Palace lawn, and then they were hidden as the gates closed.

"He must go, too," said Martin Sair, nodding at Connor. "The fewer lungs here the better. The girl is asphyxiated."

"No!" Connor croaked, flinging an arm across the Flame.

"All right. Move aside, then."

But a roaring like all the tortured souls since creation burst from the opening doors. Out rushed the gnome-like men pulling their grapple, and Connor thrust his body between them and the Princess, taking the fierce rays on his own flesh.

The container glowed brilliant as the sun, and out beyond the North Arch a chain dropped from the sky—a Triangle to bear away the deadly thing, to drop it into the sea. And the Palace was silent now as the silence of death.

Death? Tom Connor glanced fearfully at the marble features of Margaret of Urbs. They were like death, too, and he gazed so fascinated that he was utterly surprised to look up and see Evanie and Jan Orm being herded down the corridor by half a dozen grim-faced guards.

"Trying to escape out of the South Gate," said one.

The Master turned cold, burning eyes on them, and then again looked sorrowfully down on the still perfection of the features of the Black Flame.

An Immortal placed a box at Martin Sair's side.

"Adrenalin!" snapped the Giver of Life, and took the tube the other handed him. "Amino-hyoscine! Daturamine!"

He pressed the pale flesh of the girl's arm, parted the closed lids to gaze into unseeing eyes. Finally, in the familiar manner of an ancient physician, he placed thumb and forefinger on her wrist, frowning as he felt for the faint throb of her pulse.

"Suffocated," he repeated. "Asphyxia."

In an agony of apprehension, his eyes blurred, Connor watched the slow rise and fall of her breast. Twice he fancied that the movement had ceased, and each time with an almost inaudible gasp, the labored breathing recommenced. Then it did cease; he was positive, and a great wave of despair engulfed him.

"Her heart's stopping," Martin Sair said briefly.

Dying! Tom Connor gazed wildly about the corridor. Uncomprehending, he saw the grim light of triumph in the face of Evanie Sair as she looked coldly down on the fading glory of the Black Flame.

That such beauty should perish—be thrust into the earth—turn into a heap of crumbling bones ! Unthinkable!

"Dying!" Connor croaked. "Dying!"

Martin Sair said only, "Now! Cardiacine! And get the oxygen mask ready."

"Dying!" he croaked again.

The Giver of Life glanced coldly at him.

"Dying!" He echoed impassively. "No. Dead. What of it?'"

The Master turned grimly away and passed silently into the Throne Room with a word of brief command to the guards. They thrust Evanie Sair and Jan Orm before them, but Tom Connor did not miss the backward glance of triumph which the girl flung defiantly at him.

Connor gazed desolately on the lovely clay that had been the Black Flame of Urbs, wondering dully why Martin Sair still bent so attentively above her, still kept the pale wrist in his hand.

He started when the austere Immortal moved, placed his lips close to the cold ones of the girl, and rapped out:

"Now! The mask!"

The Giver of Life jammed a cone over the still face. There was a moment's silence; nothing happened. The scientist bent closer. Abruptly he placed his hands about the waist of the Princess, shook her violently, until her head rolled from side to side. He slapped her breast, her cheeks. And then, like the faint sighing of evening wind, she breathed.

A thin, muffled gasp—no more. But life-bearing oxygen flowed into her lungs, and the suspended metabolism of her body resumed its interrupted chemistries. Her breathing strengthened to a labored, whistling, panting. "Chain-Stokes breathing," muttered Martin Sair, whose genius had recalled a spirit already treading the pathways of eternity. The Black Flame, rekindled, burned dimly and flickeringly—but burned!

It was past Connor to comprehend. The transition from the depths of desolation to the peak of hope was too vast to span in a moment. He merely gazed blankly on the mask-covered face of the Princess. When realization began to dawn, the cry of amazement and ecstasy strangled in his scarred throat and became only an inchoate gurgle. He managed a choked question.

"Will she—live?" He moved as if to clasp her in his arms.

"Don't!" snapped Martin Sair. "On your life, don't touch her yet. Give her red corpuscles time to oxygenate. The girl's asphyxiated, suffocated, strangled! Do you want it all to do over again?" His eyes perceived the anguish in Connor's face, and he softened. "Of course she'll live. Did you think Death could so easily defeat Martin Sair? He has beaten me many a time, but never in so mild a contest as this!"

The great Immortal again bent over the girl. Her breathing had eased. For a terrible instant Connor thought it was ceasing once more. Martin Sair lifted the mask from the pallid, perfect features, still quiet as marble save for the sighing of her breathing.

"Now the *elixir vitae*," he said. "That will put fire into this chilly blood."

He took a phial of ruby liquid from the hand of his silent assistant, the same potent stimulant, it appeared, that had roused Evanie from the deathlike sleep of the Messenger.

The Princess was far too deep in unconsciousness to swallow. Martin Sair poured a tiny, trickling stream between her lips, no more than a few crimson drops. It was enough. As it made its fiery way down her throat she moaned and her exquisite face twisted as if in agony. The limp hands clenched convulsively into white fists.

Martin Sair rose.

"You see," he said to his grave assistant, "there was nothing organically wrong. Oxygen-starved, that was all. The organism was undamaged. The blood had not even begun to coagulate. It was simply necessary to start the body machine working, since it was in perfect running order."

"Cardiacine is a gamble," his assistant said slowly. "I've had it rupture the hearts in some cases."

Martin Sair snorted. "Not with proper precautions. Daturamine and amino-hyoscine first. Cardiacine, is powerful, of course." He mused. "I've seen it produce pulsations in the heart of a man ten days dead."

Connor ceased to listen. Cases! As if this were a medical case, this miracle! They droned on without even a glance at the pain-racked, exquisite face. Tom Connor touched her cold cheeks, kissed the soot-streaked forehead.

"Careful!" warned Martin Sair.

"But she breathes!" Connor whispered exultantly. "You're sure—certain she'll live?"

"She'll be conscious in ten minutes. A little sick, but conscious." The scientist's tone softened again. "In two days she'll be as bright as ever. After all, her body is the body of a twenty-year-old girl. She has youth, resilience. You can stop worrying."

Someone touched Connor's shoulder; a guard, who began droning, "*Orbis Terrarum Imperator*—"

"I won't go!" Tom Connor blazed. "I'm staying here!"

"She's out of danger, I tell you," insisted Martin Sair. "If she were ever in danger—with me at hand!"

Hesitantly then, Connor followed the guard, glancing apprehensively back at Margaret of Urbs, prone on the stone floor of the corridor. Then he reluctantly went on into the Throne Room.

26. The Master Sits in Judgment

In the throne room the ventilators had drawn out the steam and smoke-poisoned air, but moisture dripped from the walls and gathered in pools on the floor. The terrific destruction of the blast was evident everywhere. No single hanging remained on walls or windows. Everything inflammable was in cinders, and the very floor was still almost blistering hot.

The far end was a mass of indescribable ruin, debris from the shattered wall, even fragments of the diorite bases of the thrones. The air, despite the humming ventilators, was stifling in the radiations from floor and walls.

The Master sat upon the half-melted wreckage of his throne, his stern eyes on Evanie and Jan Orm, who stood between guards before him.

The frightened look on Evanie's face moved Connor despite the injuries she had done him. After all, she had nursed him out of the very grave and given him, penniless and strange, a home and a place in this bizarre world. She was clinging frantically to the arm of Jan, who stood morose and impassive before the Master.

"Thomas," the ruler said, "I can get nothing from this sullen pair. Tell me what you know of this."

Connor met Evanie's terrified gaze, and it wrung pity from him. He owed much to this girl. Was it any more than right that he help her now? At least he could confuse the issue, prolong it until he could obtain the aid of Margaret of Urbs.

"I did it myself!" he said promptly.

There was no change in the Master's face.

"You?" he repeated mildly. "How?"

"I made the bomb in Martin Sair's laboratory," Connor said, with a quick warning glance at Evanie. "I made it at night, and smuggled it in here during the darkness. That's all."

"Indeed? After your oath, Thomas? And I had flattered myself that you were my friend—my esteemed friend."

There was something inscrutable in the Master's face. The grave eyes surveyed Connor sorrowfully as he fingered a beam-pistol.

"I think," said the Master, slipping out the weapon, "that I will destroy you once and for all, Connor." He leveled the gun.

"Wait!" shrieked Jan Orm. "He didn't do it—I did!" He paused as the Master's cool eyes shifted to him. "I had it made in Ormon and smuggled here to me. I hid it in the Throne Room early this morning, before anyone was about!"

"Well," said the Master slowly, "I might believe that both of you had a hand in it."

His eyes flickered over Evanie.

She drew herself erect.

"What's the use?" she said dully. "I won't have you two shielding me. I did it. I had the bomb smuggled to me by an amphimorph, who rode a bubble down the mains to the pool in the Gardens. That's the truth."

"Suppose, then," said the Master, "I destroy all three of you, and thus assure myself that the guilty one is punished."

"I don't care!" Evanie flung out defiantly. "I'm sorry I failed, but at least I've extinguished the Black Flame of Urbs—and I'm glad!"

The ruler's eyes held a curious light as he gazed over their heads. A step sounded behind them. Connor whirled to see Margaret of Urbs approaching, supported by the arm of Martin Sair. Soot-stained, the whole slim length of her right leg red and blistered by the blast, her right cheek inflamed by the contact with the steaming floor, she was yet so incredibly lovely that she was breath-taking. Tom Connor sprang to her side, slipped a steadying arm about her as she swayed willingly against him. Evanie, so pale she seemed about to faint, was leaning weakly against Jan Orm.

"What's all this, Joaquin?" asked the Princess.

"Merely an attempt to fix responsibility for the bombing, my dear."

"And have you fixed it?"

"All three claim the honor."

"I see." She paused. "Well, I can throw some light on the mystery. *I* am responsible for the bomb explosion. It was an accident. I was watching some detonol crystallize, in Martin Sair's room, and forgot to take it off the burner. I was stunned by the concussion, and

Thomas Connor rushed in and guided me out. Somewhere in the Throne Room I suppose I must have been overcome."

She paused again, staring back at the Master.

"Don't you see? Each of these three suspects the others and each is trying to shield his friends. But I did it; it was an accident."

She slipped from Connor's arm and sank wearily to the steps that led to her ruined Throne.

"I burn!" she muttered, and sipped the goblet of water that a guard held to her lips.

Quizzically, the Master gazed down at her.

"You know," he said, suddenly stern, "that to me the one unforgivable sin is the thwarting of my plans. Not even you, my sister, may stand in the way of them. While I live, I am the Master. I shall yield only when a power arises strong enough to overthrow me, for that will tell me that my work is done. When that occurs, I shall have guided humanity as far as I am able along the path of Destiny, but until then—I am the Master."

His face, austere as an image in basalt, loomed over them. For the first time Connor glimpsed dimly the colossus behind the mild mask, the diamond hardness below the silk that sheathed it. Then the ruler smiled.

"I suppose I cannot doubt my sister's word. I release all of you."

He arose and descended from the throne.

Connor followed a step or two. "I'm interested to learn," he whispered, "which of us you believe."

The Master smiled again. "Haven't I just said?" He turned away. "Of course, if I were curious, I could ask you and Jan Orm how you knew what time to set the blast. I hadn't decided on a time for the Conclave until I had it announced in the corridors, and the bomb must have been placed between that moment and the arrival of the guards."

"Or the Princess is telling the truth," suggested Tom Connor.

"Some day Margaret shall explain why detonol causes a cloud of steam," observed the Master. He continued absently, "Evanie has good blood in her. So has Jan Orm." Then he was gone, followed by Martin Sair and the guards.

Connor returned to Margaret of Urbs. Evanie's incredulous eyes were fixed on the Princess as she whispered:

"Why did you do that?"

"Because I thought it would please Tom Connor," Margaret of Urbs said frankly.

Evanie stared at her with dawning comprehension.

"The Black Flame herself burned!" she murmured wonderingly. "I see now why we can still learn from the ancients. They're miracle workers." But the next instant her brown eyes glittered vindictively. "I'm glad at least that the conquest of the Flame was during my lifetime." She bowed half in wonderment, half in mockery, before Connor. "I salute the Prince consort of Urbs!"

The Princess flushed faintly, and Connor laughed and glanced away. Something that sparkled in a pile of ashes caught his eye. He stooped to retrieve the marvelous crystalline flower, glowing brilliant and indestructible, untouched—even brightened—by the blast.

"What is this?" he asked.

"My moon-orchid," said Margaret of Urbs. "The only perfect one ever found."

He grinned and turned to Evanie.

"I promised you one. Here—our wedding present to you and Jan."

"Engagement present, rather," said the Princess. "I owe you two somewhat more than you realize." She ignored both Evanie's silence and Jan Orm's protestations of mingled embarrassment, thanks, and refusal as he held the priceless thing. "Tom," she murmured, "would you mind if we were—alone?"

It was dismissal. Jan and Evanie backed away with half-awe-struck glances at Connor. He dropped beside the weary Princess of Urbs, slipping his arm tenderly about her scorched shoulders. Even in the sultriness of that blasted chamber she shivered, her teeth chattered, so recently had the icy face of death withdrawn.

He drew her close, then halted as he heard a distant, thin clamor beyond the windows.

"What's that?" he asked sharply. "Another revolution?"

"Just the newspapers, I guess. You've been in them frequently of late." She smiled wanly. "As often as I, this past week. The Weed who sustained the ionic beams—revealed as a living ancient—proclaimed for immortality—the rescuer of Margaret of Urbs—and now—" She quoted ironically, "Margaret to Wed? Romance Rumored with Rescuer!" She nestled closer to him. "Oh, the downfall of the Black Flame will be well publicized, never fear! Let them add this to their pictures and vision broadcasts. I don't care!"

"Pictures? What pictures?" He glanced about the vast deserted chamber.

"From the seeing room, of course! Don't you suppose we were watched all during the blast, even in here, as much as the steam permitted? Don't you know we're being watched now, photographed for papers, and broadcasts? You're world news, Tom." She frowned. "They must have thought me mad to rush into that inferno with you, out of safety. Well—I was mad!"

"You can't even die in privacy here!" Connor said bluntly. "Do you suppose"—his voice dropped to a whisper—"they heard what you—what we said?"

"Above the roar of the blast? No. I thought of that when I—said it."

He smiled at that. It was so typical of the utterly strange and fascinating character of the girl. He drew her against him, and felt the pressure of something hard in his belt—the ivory Venus, still safe, still immaculate in its perfection, since it had been on the left side, shielded by his own flesh when he passed the blast.

"I know what I shall give you as a wedding present," he said slowly. "The original Venus de Milo. The most beautiful statue of the ancient world."

She smiled and a trace of the old mockery showed. "And I know what I shall give you," she said. "Life!"

"Immortality?"

"Not Immortality. Life." She turned her emerald eyes on him. "Tom, is it very hard to give up the idea of children? Men want children, don't they?"

"Most of us do—but it's a happiness well lost for you." He glanced down at her. "Listen, can't this immortality thing be undone? Wouldn't it be possible for Martin Sair to render you mortal for—a few years?"

"Of course. Further exposure to the hard rays will do it."

"And then," eagerly, "could we—"

The smile she flashed at him had in it a touch of heaven. "Yes," she said exultantly, but instantly a cloud chased away the smile. "But don't you remember what sort of children women bear who've been too long in the ray? Would you like to be father to a little amphimorph?"

He shuddered. "Thank you. We'll do as we are then."

She burst suddenly into laughter almost as mocking as her old self. Then she was as suddenly serious, tender.

"Tom," she murmured, "I won't tease you. That will be my gift to you. Martin Sair can do what you wish. There is some leeway to the process—enough, perhaps, for a single time. My permanent age is twenty now; it will be twenty-five then. But who in all the world could have anticipated that the Black Flame would assume motherhood—and like it? Tom, that's my gift to you—life! Kiss me!"

For a moment of ecstasy he felt her lips quiver against his.

"Two boys and a girl!" she murmured. "Won't we, Tom?"

"And can Martin Sair," he asked ironically, "fix that for us, too?"

"Of course. Two boys like you, Tom." She was suddenly dreamy-eyed.

"But not a girl like you."

"Why not?"

"Because," Tom Connor laughed, "I don't think society could stand a second Black Flame!"

Stories

Revolution of 1960

Steel Jeffers, president of America, was not a large man. But no one thought of size, when confronted with his fiery eyes, his thin implacable lips, and his firm jaw.

At the moment, however, as he sat at his desk in the bay window of the Blue Room of the White House, he permitted himself to relax a little, and his face lost some of its grimness. No one else was present except his athletic military aide, Lieutenant Jack Adams, in the trim black uniform of the Federal Guards; and the hawk-faced, bearded Secretary of State, James Dougherty. Two soldiers were pacing up and down on the sunlit lawn outside.

President Jeffers passed a tired hand across his eyes, then looked up inquiringly at the scowling Dougherty. 'Do you really think, Mr. Secretary, that I should sign the death warrant of those two young men?' he asked, with a touch of sadness. 'They thought they were influenced by patriotism. Isn't there some other way in which we can maintain our regime, without putting to death everyone who plots against us?'

Lieutenant Adams tensed. These men awaiting sentence had been closely associated with him—secretly, of course. For Adams was an important cog in the conspiracy to rid the country of its undemocratic President. Was there nothing he could do to save his pals?

'Excellency,' he ventured eagerly, 'would not a little mercy-'

'Nonsense!' snapped Secretary Dougherty, his red lips leering through his black beard. 'Mercy, bah! What mercy would this rabble show to us, if they ever got the upper hand? Excellency, we must be firm.'

The President sighed. 'I suppose you are right; but, even so, I hate to do it.'

A white-coated, bullet-headed man, with thick-lensed glasses, appeared in the doorway of the Blue Room, and announced with a Teutonic accent, 'Excellency, your medicine.'

'Excuse me, gentlemen,' said President Jeffers, rising with what

Adams could almost swear was a trapped expression, and stepping out into the hall.

Adams had witnessed the rubbing-out of a number of patriots in the two years during which he had served as personal aide to this autocratic President. And to think that he himself had been one of the large number of young enthusiasts who only four years ago had helped elect Steel Jeffers to the presidency, as a reaction to the autocracy of President Hanson!

The rise of Steel Jeffers had been spectacular. Elected Governor of Iowa in the same election at which John R. Hanson had been made President, Jeffers was among the first to protest against Hanson's attempted increase in executive powers. Meanwhile his astute campaign manager, State Senator Dougherty, had been building political fences. In the election of 1956, Jeffers defeated Hanson on this issue of executive usurpation, and had carried into office scores of yes-men—Senators, Congressmen, Governors, and minor officials—all carefully handpicked because of their subserviency.

Two years later, in the Congressional election of 1958, opposition candidates were intimidated or bought off, or else mysteriously disappeared. Vacancies in the judiciary, as they occurred, were filled with willing tools. The pay of the Army was raised, its size increased, and the ranks gradually padded with high grade mercenaries. The F.B.I. was disbanded; and the Intelligence Service of the Army expanded, to an extent unknown because they now went about dressed as civilians.

Yet, because of his espousal of popular causes and his ingratiating personality, Steel Jeffers had retained and increased his hold on the proletariat; for he had carefully studied his predecessors, adopting their outstanding characteristics—from the charming manner and pseudo-liberalism of Roosevelt, to the inflexible and ruthless egotism of Hanson.

After the 1958 election placed him in undisputed control of all three branches of the government, and he had arrogantly established the Roman salute and put the Army into black uniforms, there came the first rumblings against his dictator-like power. But a few ruthless blood-purges, followed by his persuasive voice on television attacking the character and loyalty of the deceased, quickly drove the opposition to cover.

Lieutenant Jack Adams, participating in some of these purges, had helplessly witnessed independent newspaper editors and statesmen lined up before machine-guns in the soundproof basement of the State War and Navy Building. And so he could now vividly picture to himself the end of his two pals. Their death would be of the clear-eyed, defiant variety. Well, if they had the courage thus to die for American freedom, he could have the courage to keep a stiff upper lip and let them die. The success of the conspiracy depended on his continuing in the good graces of President Jeffers.

Just then Jeffers strode back into the room, once more seating himself at his desk. A strange Jekyll-Hyde sort of personality, Jeffers! A few moments ago human, almost wavering, now fierce and ruthless. Briskly he scrawled his flowing signature across the foot of the death warrant. Then he turned his cold eyes toward his aide. 'Here, Adams, take this paper over to the War Department.'

'Yes, sir,' replied the Lieutenant, raising his right hand in a Roman salute. His fine features were expressionless, but he could not conceal the deep pain in his gray eyes.

'I know how you feel, Adams,' said the President. 'But you must be a good soldier—for the Cause.'

As Adams left, with the warrant clenched in his fist, he muttered to himself, 'If Steel Jeffers only knew what a good soldier I'm being—for the Cause.'

Returning to his house on P Street that evening, Adams changed from his trim black uniform into a loose gray Norfolk suit and hastened down into the cellar. The brick wall at one side was interlaced with many crisscross cracks. One irregular seam now swung open like a door. Adams felt a gust of cool musty air. A light shone dimly in the distance through the dark hole. Presently there crawled out a stocky dark young man with a serious face. Adams shook his hand.

'Well, Godfrey, no one yet seems to have discovered that we know each other, even though we do live in adjoining houses. Have the rest of the crowd arrived?'

'Here's Liam and Sim.' Two men, one tall and dark, the other short and roly-poly, crawled out through the hole.

'Had a devil of a time getting here!' the former announced. 'Black-coated soldiers everywhere, damn them! No offense to you, Adams.'

The short fat fellow chuckled. 'Never mind the black-coats, Liam,' he said. 'It's the Secret Service we ought to worry about.'

Several more men emerged from the hole in the wall.

Adams solemnly shook hands with everyone. 'Tom and Bill are dead,' be gravely announced. 'Shot against a wall. I myself carried their death-warrant over. Jeffers would have let them off with mere imprisonment, if it hadn't been for that fiendish Secretary of State of his.'

'Don't make excuses for Jeffers!' snapped Liam Lincoln, his dark eyes glittering with fanatic light. He brushed back a trailing lock of black hair. 'Jeffers is a heartless usurper, though doubtless his experience in college theatricals when he was at Princeton enables him to put on an act. Sometimes, Adams, I begin to wonder if you—'

'Well, you needn't,' the Lieutenant interrupted. 'I risk my life daily for the Cause, while you boss things in comparative safety.'

'For cripes sake!' cut in roly-poly Simeon Baldwin. 'If we can't trust each other, fellows, who can we trust?'

'You're right, Sim. I'm sorry, Jack,' Lincoln graciously apologized. 'Well, to business. Very gratifying secret reports are coming in from all over the country. Our organization is growing by leaps and bounds. The Governors of nearly half the states are either active members, or at least in sympathy. Patriotic leading citizens everywhere are waiting for the word from our little Washington group that the time has come for action. Meanwhile Sim here has completed his study of Jeffers' early life.'

'I'll skip what you already know,' said Baldwin. 'What I've lately been working on is his sister.'

'You mean the one who died on the day of Jeffers' election?' Adams asked.

'Did she?—I wonder,' Baldwin replied enigmatically.

'Did she what?'

'Did she really die? That's the angle I've been working on for the past few weeks. If she did die, old Svengali Dougherty killed her, and Steel Jeffers wouldn't have stood for that. So I believe she is hidden away somewhere to prevent her from influencing her brother.'

'But why should Dougherty fear her influence?' Asked one of the others. 'The three of them were hand-in-glove.'

Liam Lincoln laughed harshly, and tossed back his long locks of black hair. 'That was back in the days when even we were following Jeffers toward the *better economic day* for America.'

'You're right, Liam,' Adams chimed in. 'The change in the President seems to date from the death—or disappearance—of his sister. You're on the track of something, Sim. Go on.'

Baldwin continued. 'There's something fishy about the death of Helen Jeffers. The girl was in charge of her brother's campaign headquarters and apparently perfectly well, right up to election day. The coroner who signed her death-certificate hasn't been seen since. Her brother was reported prostrated by her death—went into seclusion immediately in a mountain camp—yet no doctor went with him.'

'But—weren't Southworth and Vierecke there?' Adams interrupted.

Baldwin replied, 'Southworth—now Rear Admiral and White House physician—didn't arrive at the mountain lodge until two weeks after election. Doctor Vierecke didn't land from Austria until a week after that.'

'But if Jeffers wasn't ill, why doctors at all?' asked Lincoln. 'He seemed weak and shaken when he came back from the mountains, just before inauguration.'

'That's the next point which I wish investigated,' Baldwin asserted. 'Just what is the why of Admiral Southworth and his Austrian assistant? Jack, can't you get a line on them? You're in the White House.'

'I know something about them already,' Adams diffidently replied. 'Southworth did research work in hormones, before he went into the Navy. That's how he happened to know Vierecke, for hormones was Vierecke's specialty at Goettingen.'

'Not much to go on,' said Lincoln. 'Do some spying, Jack. I understand the two of them have a fully equipped chemical and biological laboratory in the basement of the White House. Why should there be such an establishment there? We must investigate everything the least bit screwy about the President, in the hope of some day finding his weak spot. Well, go on, Sim.'

Baldwin thrust his hand into a briefcase as fat as himself, and pulled out a photograph. The others clustered around. From the picture, there looked up at them the frank sweet face of a young girl. 'Helen Jeffers,' he announced, 'just before her death—or disappearance. You'd know she was a Jeffers, wouldn't you?'

But Adams could see no resemblance to her brother. Soft wavy dark hair. Frank open eyes. Perfect features. Full alluring lips. Softly curved neck and shoulders.

Strange that such a thoroughly feminine girl had formed a compatible member of that triumvirate—with Steel Jeffers, the popular and magnetic front; and Dougherty, the practical wire pulling organizer—which had pushed Steel Jeffers up to the position of supreme power in America!

'Some baby!' murmured several of the conspirators, appraisingly.

But a stronger feeling touched Lieutenant Adams. Of course, he had seen newspaper cuts of her at the time of her brother's campaign, but this was different. He squared his shoulders with determination. His gray eyes narrowed, and a whimsical smile played on his lips.

'Gentlemen,' he announced, with mock solemnity, 'I am going to find Helen Jeffers for you.' In his mind he added: 'And for myself.'

2

The next morning, a bright sunlit June day, Lieutenant Adams swung through the streets with a determined stride on his way to his post at the White House. Mechanically he returned the Roman salutes of the black-uniformed military men whom he passed. Civilians were few on the streets of Washington these days. Washington had become a vast military establishment.

Entering the executive mansion, he passed the shrewd-faced, bushy eyebrowed old sea doctor, Admiral Southworth, going out. Adams reported to one of the Assistant Secretaries, and was informed that Steel Jeffers was not up yet. Fine! This would give him time on his own, to investigate the mysterious laboratory.

As he approached the always-locked doors in the cellar, they opened. Ducking quickly behind a pillar, he saw the bullet-headed Dr. Vierecke emerge, hat on head and without his white smock, then turn, key in hand, and lock the doors. Glancing furtively around, the doctor shoved the key into the dirt of a potted plant standing nearby, then hurried off down the corridor. Adams slipped out from behind the pillar, and followed until Vierecke left the building. Then he hastened to the office wing, and asked the appointment clerk, 'Where are Admiral Southworth and Dr. Vierecke?'

The girl consulted a memorandum book and replied, 'They've both gone to a conference over at the Public Health Service. Won't be back until after lunch.'

Grinning to himself, Adams strode back, extricated the key, from the dirt of the plant pot, unlocked the laboratory, and entered, locking the door behind him.

His gray eyes were alight with anticipation. What an opportunity! The only two men who ever entered the laboratory would be safely out of the way for the rest of the morning. And if the President wished Adams, the autocall bells throughout the White House would ring his number, and he could come running.

Most conspicuous in the room were two long workbenches with sinks, Bunsen burners, retorts, glass and rubber piping, and test tubes.

A squeaking noise in one end of the laboratory attracted his attention to dozens of caged guinea pigs. Adams strode over to the cage. On each cage was posted a sign on which each individual was identified by symbols, including some Adams had never seen. Thoughtfully he scratched his blond head, grinned, and then copied several of the charts into a little pocket notebook as samples—he could return and copy more if these few should hold any significance for the biologist among the conspirators.

He looked in the ice-chest, but found nothing there except some small unlabeled bottles.

Next he inspected a cabinet of surgical tools. The large number of hypodermic needles impressed him. His mind flashed back to the change which had come over Steel Jeffers when, wavering on the question of executing the young traitors, he had been called out of the Blue Room by Herr Doktor Vierecke, and had returned, filled with merciless determination. Could the secret of the power of the sinister cabal lie in drugs?

Adams shuddered. The brother of Helen Jeffers a drug addict? Incredible!

Nevertheless the possibility must be investigated. So, with sinking heart, Adams turned to a bank of open shelves, stacked with labeled bottles.

To his relief, he found no morphine, opium, heroin, cocaine, or any other substance the name of which he recognized as being that of a narcotic. He copied down the names of several chemicals which he did not recognize. These might be narcotics.

Then his attention was directed to several large drums, labeled *Cholesterol.* He was just jotting down the word, together with the name and address of the supply company, when a bell in the corridor outside clicked his autocall! The President wanted him.

Hurrying to the door, he was about to unlock it, when he heard voices outside. Putting his ear to the crack, he listened. In crisp tones, the old Admiral was saying, 'You fat-headed fool! Why didn't you hide the key where I told you to?'

'Ve haf two keys.'

'I left mine in my other suit. It is at the cleaners.'

'Unt I did put der key in der pot.'

'Ding! Ding—ding—ding!' insistently rang the autocall. If Adams didn't hurry, embarrassing inquiries would be made.

'Now listen, you fat-head,' said the sharp incisive voice of the old sea-dog. 'Go to the head housekeeper, and tell her to find out pronto who's been messing around that flowerpot. I'll send someone over to the tailors for my key. Report to me in the executive offices. Now vamoose!'

Footsteps of both men could be heard moving off down the corridor. Adams unlocked the door, and peered out. No one in sight; so he hastily emerged, locked the door, thrust the key in his pocket, and dog-trotted to the Blue Room.

Stopping just outside the room, he smoothed down his black uniform, and entered unconcernedly. Stepping up to the desk in the bay window, he raised his arm in a brisk Roman salute. Steel Jeffers looked up.

'Oh, yes,' Jeffers absently announced. 'Here are some papers to be taken over to the War Department.'

Adams' set jaw relaxed, and he drew a deep breath of relief. Taking the papers, he raised his arm again in salute, faced about, and strode from the room.

In the big hall outside, he ran across Admiral Southworth. The bushy-browed old sea-doctor was visibly agitated. 'Oh! Ah! Lieutenant, you going anywhere in particular?'

'War Department sir,' Adams briskly replied; and he couldn't resist adding, 'But I thought that the Admiral was at a conference.'

Southworth bent narrow eyes of scrutiny at him. 'Meeting called off. Not that it's any business of yours, you young whelp.'

'Can I do anything for the Admiral?' Adams asked innocently.

'Why, ah, yes. Step over to that tailor shop on 17th between G and F, and get a key for me. I left it in a suit. It's—it's the key to my locker at the Army and Navy Club, and I'm going to need it this noon.'

'Yes, sir,' said Adams, with expressionless face.

He took the President's papers to the War Department, and then retrieved the Admiral's laboratory key. On his way back to the White House, he racked his brains for some excuse not to deliver this key; but finally he reflected that, if he kept both keys this would merely result in Southworth having a new lock fitted.

So he handed Admiral Southworth his key.

The rest of the morning he had to attend the President; but, after that, he hurried to the stenographic office of the White House.

Seating himself at one of the desks he penned a brief note, reading: 'P.N. Investigate White House purchases of cholesterol. J.Q.A.' Then, clapping his black military cap onto his head, he strode out of the White House, and down the left-hand driveway to the corner of West Executive and Pennsylvania Avenues, where he stopped to buy a bag of peanuts from the old Italian who kept a stand there.

'Giuseppe,' said Adams, as his eye happened to light on the man's tin license plate, 'the Federal Peanut Commission wouldn't let you stay in business, if they knew what your business really was.'

'I do not understand, Signore,' solemnly replied the Italian, stroking his long gray mustaches; but there was a twinkle in his beady black eyes as he said it. 'My business is to sella da peanut, no?'

'No!' Adams replied, laughing. 'Well, here you are.' He handed over a dollar bill, folded to conceal the note which he had written.

'Grazzia, Signore,' said Giuseppe, with a bow.

Then Adams ambled back to the White House, ruminatively cracking peanuts and eating them, and wondering what Philip Nordstrom, a conspirator who held a small clerkship in the office of the Comptroller General, would be able to learn on the subject of cholesterol.

Adams was famous in White House circles for the large quantities of peanuts which he consumed; but he was fortunately not famous for the large number of notes which he left with, and received from, the grizzled old peanut-vendor.

3

That evening when the little band of patriots gathered again in Adams' cellar, Nordstrom, a tall blond youth with pale blue eyes, was ready to report.

'I got your note from Giuseppe, Jack,' he said, 'but why your sudden interest in cholesterol?'

'Why Steel Jeffers' sudden interest in it?' Adams grimly asked.

'His interest isn't sudden,' Nordstrom replied. 'The White House has been buying cholesterol in quantities ever since Jeffers first became President four years ago.'

Liam Lincoln ran one slim hand through his long black hair. 'Cabot,' he said, addressing that solemn-faced individual, 'you're a chemist of sorts. What possible use can Steel Jeffers have for so much what-you-call-it?'

Roly-poly Simeon Baldwin eagerly cut in, 'I believe we are getting somewhere!' His fat face was alight with interest. 'Maybe this cholesterol, or whatever, will furnish us the clue we're after.'

'Well,' said Cabot judicially, 'let's first hear from Jack how he got a line on this.'

Adams then related how he had explored the laboratory.

'Did you find any small bottles capped with a rubber diaphragm?' Cabot asked.

'Why-er-no,' the Lieutenant replied. 'Ought I have?'

'Well rather! All those hypodermic needles! Lots of guinea pigs, to experiment on! President getting pepped up by Dr. Vierecke every time Secretary Dougherty wants him to do something particularly diabolical'

'Come to think of it,' Adams replied, 'there were some small bottles in the ice-chest. But I didn't notice them particularly—they weren't labeled.'

'Can you get in there again?'

'Yes.'

'Then bring me one of those bottles.'

The next day at the first opportunity Adams headed for the laboratory. Admiral Southworth and his Prussian assistant were talking together just outside the door as he drew near. Their heads were close, and their manner seemed furtive.

'Now while I am in the Adirondacks,' the old sea doctor was saying in an undertone, 'are you sure that you have on hand enough—'

'Sh!' admonished the bullet-headed Vierecke, catching sight of Adams. 'Yes, ve haf plenty.' He nodded vigorously.

Southworth smiled a wind-swept smile, and held out his hand. 'Well, goodbye Franz. Take good care of everything.'

'What!' Adams exclaimed, stepping up. 'You going away Admiral?'

'Just for a couple of week's fishing.' Southworth replied.

'But look here, Sir,' Adams persisted, with the sudden hope of getting a line on Southworth's White House activities, 'you are responsible for the President's health. What if he should get sick while you're away?'

The Admiral knotted his bushy eyebrows. 'I shall be in telephonic touch with the White House at all times,' he said. 'There will be an amphibian plane on the lake, always in readiness.'

'Good,' said Adams, but not with much enthusiasm. Vierecke scowled from behind thick-lensed glasses. Southworth cast a sharp beetle-browed glance. Then the two of them moved off together down the corridor, resuming their whispered conversation.

As soon as they had turned the corner, Adams took the key from his pocket and let himself into the laboratory.

In the ice chest he found a half dozen small bottles capped with rubber diaphragms, as described by Godfrey Cabot. But only one of them had a label—a strip of adhesive tape, bearing a blurred word, of which only the first four letters remained legible: *Test* .This bottle, Adams slipped into his pocket.

Suddenly he had an idea. If he could cut off the supply of this drug even temporarily, he might get a line on its effect on Steel Jeffers. So, piercing every diaphragm with his pocket knife, he poured the contents down the sink, and threw all the emptied bottles into the incinerator chute.

The corridor was empty when he emerged. On a sudden impulse, he shoved the key back into the plant-pot in which he had originally found it. Then, as the President didn't need his immediate presence, he ambled out to the street corner and bought some peanuts. Returning some time later, he reported to the Blue Room.

What a scene of confusion he found there! The hook-nosed, black-bearded Secretary of State, pacing up and down, his face a thundercloud of wrath. Franz Vierecke, clad in his stiff white laboratory smock standing helplessly by, with a lost look on his pudgy fish-eyed face. President Jeffers seated at his desk, an expression of mingled concern and amusement on his finely chiseled features.

'Can't I do something?' Adams respectfully inquired, stepping up.

'Yes,' snapped the sinister Secretary. 'Get Admiral Southworth back here at once.'

'Oh!' said Adams, with well feigned surprise. Then wheeling around on Vierecke, 'How long has the Admiral been gone?'

'About an hour.'

'Where was he flying from?'

'*Der* Potomac Field.'

'By your leave, sir.' Stepping briskly over to the desk, Adams picked up the phone. 'Naval Base—Emergency.'

He got his number, ascertained that the plane had been gone for nearly an hour, and commanded that it be immediately recalled by radio.

A pause, during which he held the line. Then, rigidly suppressing any indication of the joy which the news gave him, he turned and reported, 'They say that the plane doesn't answer. That its radio must be out of order.'

'Ausser ordnung! Ach, mein Gott!' wailed Vierecke.

'And now,' said Adams briskly to the pacing Dougherty, 'hadn't you better tell me what this is all about?'

'Fresh young puppy!' spat the Secretary through his big black beard.

'Well, you don't seem to be being very helpful yourself, Jim,' asserted President Jeffers with some asperity. Then, turning to his aide, 'Lieutenant Adams, someone has gained access to Admiral-Southworth's private laboratory, and has stolen some small bottles containing chemicals of great value to the peace of America. The exact nature of those chemicals is known only to Southworth, Vierecke, Dougherty, and myself.'

'I can serve you without knowing, Excellency,' asserted Adams. 'Am I in charge?'

Secretary Dougherty ceased his pacing, and glared at the young officer. 'Certainly not!' he hissed.

'I happen to be the President, Jim,' Steel Jeffers interrupted incisively. 'Yes, Adams, you are in charge.'

'Good!' cried the Lieutenant. 'Excellency, will you please phone the airport, and order them to continue trying to contact the plane. Herr Doktor, come with me:'

'But—but—' spluttered Dougherty. 'Am I, or am I not, the Secretary of State?'

And, as Lieutenant Adams pushed the white-coated Vierecke from the room, he heard Steel Jeffers wearily yet firmly assert, 'Yes, Jim, you are still the Secretary of State. But it is I who am the President.'

First Adams rushed to the Executive Offices, where he summoned the entire corps of White House guards, and gave orders that no one was to leave or enter the building. Then he led the bewildered Vierecke down to the basement, and made him unlock the laboratory, and hand over a sample empty bottle.

Next Adams called the War Department for a detachment of officers from the Intelligence Service, showed them the sample bottle, and turned them loose to find the stolen ones. Then he returned to the Blue Room, to report to President Jeffers, his keen gray eyes sparkling with enjoyment of the success of his make-believe.

He was wholly unprepared for the chilling reception which was awaiting him. Steel Jeffers and his sinister pal were seated together. As Adams stepped up to the desk and gave the customary Roman salute, both men looked up, transfixing him with narrowed eyes.

Then Dougherty smiled an evil twisted smile. His rat eyes glittered. 'Where had you been, Lieutenant,' he demanded, 'just before you burst in on us and took charge of this case?'

4

From the doorway behind Adams came a smooth cold voice, 'I can answer that question, Mr. Secretary.'

Adams wheeled, and saw the clean-cut inscrutable features of

Captain Silva of the Intelligence Service. Chilling as was the sight of this notorious ace of inquisitors, yet it came as a welcome diversion. For Dougherty would have had the admission out of Adams in another moment.

Silva continued, 'Lieutenant Adams was buying peanuts at the corner in front of the White House.'

Secretary Dougherty growled, and Steel Jeffers laughed a brief cold laugh.

Captain Silva, twirling one of his pointed black mustaches, went on, 'Naturally my first step when assigned to this investigation was to check up on Mr. Adams.' Then, as Adams bristled, 'No offense, Lieutenant. One should always suspect the man who calls the police. The doorman saw you distinctly. You walked briskly to old Giuseppe's stand, bought a bag of peanuts without even stopping to chat with the Italian, as I am informed you usually do; and then returned, munching your purchase. You met no one either coming or going.'

Adams, smiling confidently now, reached inside his blouse toward his left shoulder.

'Stop him!' shrieked the Secretary.

Captain Silva leaped forward. But, before he could reach Adams, the latter had brought out a half-empty paper bag, and held it toward the Secretary, 'Have a peanut, Mr. Dougherty,' he invited.

'Bah!' spat the Secretary, knocking the bag aside with one claw-like hand. 'Peanuts! Bah!'

Steel Jeffers sniffed contemptuously. 'What did you expect? A gun? He'd have reached for his hip, not his shoulder, if he'd wanted to pot you. He's an Army officer, not a gangster. Cut out the jitters, Jim, or you'll have me jittery too.'

'Can you joke, Mr. President, when the fate of the nation is at stake? Sometimes—I wonder—' He caught himself. Then suddenly his evil eyes narrowed, as he wheeled around to Captain Silva, and pointed at Adams. 'Search him!' he commanded.

As Adams held his arms above his head, he grinned with thankful recollection of having put the laboratory key back into the plant-pot where he had found it. The search over, he asked, ignoring the discomfited Secretary, 'And now, Excellency, am I still in charge of the investigation?'

Receiving the President's nod, he swept from the room, followed by Captain Silva.

Newsboys were crying an extra on the Avenue. Adams sent one of the White House guards to buy a paper. The headlines read: *Admiral Southworth Crashes.* Adams hurriedly perused the item. It related that, on nosing down for a landing at the Adirondack lake where the Admiral had his lodge, his plane had grazed a tree. The Admiral had suffered a severe head injury and was unconscious, but was expected to live.

Adam's gray eyes flashed. It was too bad that something had to happen to the fine old sea-dog; but Southworth's incapacity would be worthwhile, if it should disclose just what part he had been playing in the life of the President!

Newspaper in hand, and with a synthetic expression of concern on his face, Adams rushed to the Blue Room. As he entered, Steel Jeffers was saying, '—which means a good long rest for me, Jim.'

'Unless that scamp Adams succeeds in finding the missing test,' added Secretary Dougherty, breaking off abruptly, as he saw the Lieutenant. 'Oh, it's you? We know the news, and are already in touch with Southworth's lodge.'

Lieutenant Adams carefully failed to find the missing bottles. He felt a bit guilty when, later in the day, Jeffers complained of a slight attack of dizziness, and retired to his bedroom. For, in spite of Adams' unquestioned loyalty to the revolutionary cause, he had developed a real affection and admiration for the chief whom he was supposed to be serving. Adams could not help believing that, if the evil influence of Secretary of State Dougherty were removed, the President would revert to the idealistic program of economic and social reform originally mapped out for him by his now-missing sister.

But, whatever good the purloined bottle of *t-e-s-t* might have done to the President, it gave very little information to the members of the conspiracy. No methods of organic chemistry of which even the expert Godfrey Cabot was capable, produced any analysis other than simple cholesterol dissolved in alcohol. The stocky young chemist was a biologist as well, and positively asserted that cholesterol could not have any bearing on Jeffers' condition.

'I looked it up in the Pharmacopoeia and in the dispensary,' he stated. 'No mention of it at all in the former. Latter merely says it is a constituent of cod liver oil. Can be isolated by first saponifying the oil, and then exhausting the resulting soap with ether. Cholesterol in cod liver oil runs about 0.46 to 1.32 per cent.'

Simeon Baldwin's chubby face beamed with a sudden idea. 'Cod liver oil!' he exclaimed. 'The very thing. I'll bet that Southworth and Vierecke have discovered what causes cod liver oil to pep people up.'

'I doubt it,' Cabot thoughtfully replied, shaking his massive head. 'I injected some into some guinea-pigs over at Public Health Service. Didn't pep 'em up a bit.'

Baldwin's face fell.

Liam Lincoln shook back his black forelock, and inquired, 'Did the label give you any clue, Godfrey?'

Cabot pursed up his lips. Nothing in either book, beginning with *t-e-s-t,*' he said, 'except, of course, the whole range of test solutions.'

'What are those?'

'Solutions of reagents.'

'And what are reagents?'

'Things used in tests.'

'Well, couldn't the *t-e-s-t* stand for that?'

'No,' judicially, 'don't think so. Cholesterol's not a reagent. Test solutions are usually kept in glass-stoppered bottles, not diaphragm-covered ones. Official abbreviation for 'test solution' is *T. S.*, not *t-e-s-t.* No. Sim's hunch is best; but the guinea-pigs don't react.'

The conspirators seemed no closer to the solution of the mystery. Nevertheless, the destruction of Dr. Vierecke's supply of little bottles, and the enforced absence of Admiral Southworth, had certainly in some unexplainable way contributed to the illness of Steel Jeffers! He remained shut up in his room, and refused to see anyone except Vierecke and Dougherty. Not even his aide, Jack Adams, or any of the servants.

Adams marveled at the speed with which, all over the country, unrest came to the surface, the moment that the iron grip of Steel Jeffers was relaxed. The Liberty League and the Civil Liberties Union staged demonstrations, of course expressing complete loyalty to President Jeffers, but disapproval of the way the country was being run during his temporary incapacity; and the dread Secret Service did not pounce upon them. Freedom of the press appeared again. Several Governors raised their voices in opposition to Federal encroachment.

A whispering campaign of rumors, as to the state of the President's health and even of his mind, swept from coast to coast. One yarn had it that Jeffers had become hopelessly insane, and that the executive orders which were being issued over his signature were forgeries perpetrated by the much-hated Secretary of State, with the collusion of that *foreigner*, Franz Vierecke.

Senator Anders of New Hampshire had the temerity to introduce a resolution declaring the Presidency vacant and calling upon Vice President Nieman to assume control.

Meanwhile Godfrey Cabot's guinea-pigs continued unaffected by the sample of the mysterious chemical which Adams had stolen from the White House laboratory. The conspirators, although still at a loss to explain the President's illness, nevertheless started a rumor, which spread and obtained a credence, to the effect that Steel Jeffers was afflicted with some obscure malady, with which only one physician in the whole world, the stricken Southworth, was capable of coping.

Admiral Southworth had finally come out of his coma, but was too weak to be moved. His assistant made a rush trip to his mountain cabin, and came back very much depressed. Rumor had it that Vierecke had gone in search of certain information, but that the Admiral had refused to talk.

At one of the secret evening meetings in the cellar of Adams' house on P Street, he and Liam Lincoln disagreed over tactics. The latter had reached the conclusion that now was the time for their movement to come out into the open and throw its forces into the scales against the national administration. Many prominent public officials throughout America, who were in touch with this Washington group, eagerly awaited Liam Lincoln's assurance that the time for rebellion had arrived.

But Adams advised further delay. 'Wait until we absolutely know just how dependent Steel Jeffers is on Admiral Southworth. Their simultaneous illnesses may be a mere coincidence.'

'Adams, I doubt your loyalty,' the fanatic Lincoln declared.

Adams leaped at him. Their pals separated them. The two apologized. But the row rankled; and it rankled especially in Liam Lincoln, for the group endorsed Adams' Fabian policy.

Leaving the White House the next evening, Adams happened to pass through the servants' entrance. His foot was on the bottom step, when the door opened behind him. He turned at the sound, and the light from within momentarily illumined a feminine figure, shrouded in a hooded cape. Dainty silver slippers and the edge of a blue evening gown protruded below the bottom of the cape, but it was the brief glimpse of the girl's face which arrested Adams' attention. Tendrils of dark hair twined beneath the edges of her hood. Her resemblance to the President was striking; but, where Steel's face was firm and masculine, hers was delicately rounded and feminine and alluring.

'Helen Jeffers!' Adams declared to himself as she passed him and dodged into the shadows.

With sudden determination, he followed her.

5

The mysterious girl from the White House hurried furtively through the trees toward the Parkway, then along its winding stretches to the Hotel Washington. Never for an instant did Lieutenant Adams let her out of his sight. He entered the hotel only a few steps behind her.

As she paused and gazed around the lobby, Adams got a better view of her face. Unquestionably it was the face of the photograph from Sim Baldwin's dossier. But where the photograph had showed a mere pretty girl, this face had the maturity and charm of a ravishingly beautiful woman—exactly the change that the four years since her supposed death could be expected to bring.

Jack Adam's heart missed several beats, and then raced madly. The girl turned full toward him. He flushed, looked away, and stepped backward stumbling over the end of a stone bench in the lobby.

'Oh, I'm so sorry!' she explained in delicious tones. 'Did I bump into you, or something?'

'Er—no,' Adams hastily replied. 'I guess it's just that I can't stand so much sheer beauty, that's all.'

'Oh,' stiffening a bit. 'Do I know you or something?'

'I guess it must have been two other fellows,' laughed Adams. And the girl laughed too.

Adams squared his broad shoulders. Here was opportunity—for the Cause, of course. He must not misplay. The twinkle in his gray eyes, and the whimsical twist of his handsome mouth, belied his fixed determination.

'After all, I do believe that we've met,' he began.

'You're making me very conspicuous,' she objected, yet she did not move away.

'I'm so sorry!' he explained. 'Let's sit down over here.' He led her to a chair in a far corner of the lobby. As she seated herself, and glanced inquiringly up at him, Adams added, 'And now that we are so well acquainted, perhaps you will tell me your name.'

He sat down beside her, and leaned across, intently studying her perfect features. She smiled back at him—provocatively. She let her cloak fall back from her shoulders, disclosing a summer evening gown of flowered blue chiffon, gently clinging, revealing.

'No,' she replied, but with the light of mischief in her violet eyes. 'I'm a stranger here—a school-teacher on a holiday. I don't pick up men—usually. I think I'm going to like you, but let's not spoil this charming interlude by knowing too much about each other. Just call me *you*.'

'Hey, you!' said Adams laughing, though his pulses were pounding madly because of her nearness. 'Are you staying at this hotel, you?'

'You sound like a detective from the Army Intelligence Service, or something, though your crossed guns indicate Coast Artillery. Perhaps you are one of the secret agents of the President?'

'Heaven forbid!' he exclaimed.

She was watching him intently. 'So you don't approve of Steel Jeffers?' she asked, innocently.

Did she know his identity? The President's sister ought to know by sight the President's aide. But was she Helen Jeffers? In fact, was Helen Jeffers even still alive?

Then suddenly a thought occurred to him. Might not her presence in Washington, rather than the theft of the missing bottles, be the cause of the slackening of Jeffers' ruthlessness? Down tumbled all the preconceived notions of the conspiracy. For a moment Adams felt depressed, then brightened again at the thought that maybe this new explanation could be turned to some use.

'A penny for your thoughts,' said the girl. 'When I asked you just now whether you approve of Steel Jeffers, you went into a blind daze. Yet that is a question which any loyal American ought to be able to answer offhand—without study.'

'Yes,' Adams replied, his eyes gazing intently into hers. 'I am a deep admirer of the President. And I am a sincere believer in the policies which elected him.' This line ought to go good with the girl who had outlined those policies, if indeed this were she. 'But I believe that he is unfortunate in the choice of some of his advisers.'

'I'm glad you like my—er—Steel Jeffers,' the girl exclaimed. 'But I am surprised that you do not approve of Secretary Dougherty.'

'I mentioned no names,' Adams hastily interposed.

'No?' She laughed her tingling silvery laugh.

'Let's not talk politics,' begged the young Lieutenant. 'Have you eaten?'

'Yes.

'Then how about a movie?'

She nodded and smiled.

At the theater, the newsreel dealt very guardedly with the President's illness, exhibiting *canned* flashes of Jeffers himself; of the sinister Dougherty; and of the flea-bitten old sea doctor, whom it reported as rapidly convalescing.

The audience greeted the picture of Jeffers with applause, at which the girl seemed to thrill. Dougherty drew hisses and some boos, at which the girl stiffened. Southworth evoked merely a rustling interest.

After the show Adams took the girl to the Washington Roof. Several of the diners turned and stared at the distinguished-looking blond young man in black uniform and his stunning dark-haired partner in blue.

The head-waiter greeted him effusively by name. Adams tried to silence the man by a glance, but the man kept on bowing and scraping and calling him 'Lieutenant Adams.'

'Oh, so you're the President's aide!' the girl announced, as the waiter seated her. 'How banal of me to have asked what you thought of him! And how dangerous of you to have revealed your disapproval of Secretary Dougherty. How do you know that I am not a Secret Service agent, or something?'

'I'd trust you anywhere,' breathed Adams.

'So?'

'Yes! And look here, Helen, why can't we—'

'Helen'? Why do you call me 'Helen'?'

Adams bit his lip. The name had come so naturally! His face took a hunted look. 'Helen of Troy, 'the face that launched a thousand ships', you know.'

Her purple eyes narrowed and her face became grave, as, ignoring the compliment, she snapped, 'That's not the truth, Adams. Why did you call me *Helen*?'

Cornered he stammered, 'I saw a picture once of the President's sister. Her name was Helen. You look so like her that I've been thinking of her all evening.'

'Well, of all the complimentary men!' she commented sarcastically.

But he was not to be laughed off. 'You are Helen Jeffers,' he insisted.

She sobered suddenly. 'Helen died four years ago. She was my sister.'

Adams gasped. 'I didn't know there were two girls in the Jeffers family.'

'There weren't. Helen was the only one.'

'But you said—'

'I said Helen was my sister. So she was.' Suddenly her voice became deep and guttural and male. 'I am Steel Jeffers.'

She paused to let that information sink in, as Adams stared in horrified silence. Then the disguised President continued, in feminine tones again, 'I played girl parts in Triangle Club shows at Princeton, and have not forgotten the art of make-up and impersonation. And so, in these hectic times, I disguise myself and go out among my subjects, like Haroun Al Raschid, to learn firsthand what they think of me. The results have been gratifying. And particularly gratifying, permit me to say, has been your own expression of loyalty to me—and to the principles which made me President.'

Adams continued to stare. Finally he found his voice, and gasped out, 'But, Excellency, you were reported too ill to leave your room. How is it safe for you to be out alone and unguarded like this?'

'I am neither alone nor unguarded, thanks to you. As to whether I am safe—Secretary Dougherty does not know that I am out,' the disguised President enigmatically replied.

6

'And now that you know who I really am,' Jeffers continued in his feminine falsetto, 'my Arabian Nights masquerade is at an end. Let us return to the White House.'

Just then the waiter bustled up. Adams handed the man a dollar bill, saying, 'I'm sorry, but the lady suddenly feels faint.'

He and his partner got up and made for the exit.

The head waiter rushed over. 'Lieutenant Adams, is there anything wrong?'

'Not at all, Pierre,' Adams assured him.

The President flashed the man a dazzling feminine smile, and murmured, 'I just feel a little faint, Pierre; but we certainly shall return some other evening.'

'I do hope so, Mademoiselle.'

Adams, still stunned, helped Jeffers on with his wrap, and escorted him to the elevator.

As they walked slowly back to the White House, Adams shuddered, sighed, and said, 'You can never know, Excellency, what a blow it was to me to find that you are not your sister. I saw a photograph of her once, and I believe that I actually fell in love with it. She must have been a wonderful girl!'

Steel Jeffers stiffened suddenly—Adams could feel it in his fingertips on the President's elbow. Then he relaxed. 'Helen and I placed the welfare of America ahead of anything else—I still do. But events—and James Dougherty—have hemmed me in. Well, anyway, I am glad that you feel as you do about Helen. Don't give up hope, Jack. Some day, perhaps—' He stopped abruptly.

'Is Helen still alive?' Adams eagerly exclaimed.

Steel Jeffers passed his hand in a tired gesture across his face, and shivered. 'I don't know just what I'm saying.' His voice broke strangely. 'In the language of the younger generation, let's skip it.'

He remained in moody silence the rest of the way to the White House, and dismissed his escort at the steps of the servants' entrance.

Lieutenant Adams stood at the foot of the steps, and gazed up at the seeming girl, until the door closed. Then he hastened to his own quarters on P Street, his mind a turmoil of emotions. All night long he tossed on his bed, longing for the girl whom he had thought he had found, only to lose again.

The next day, when Adams reported for work at the White House he learned that Admiral Southworth's condition had improved, and that a special amphibian ambulance-plane was already on its way to the Adirondacks to bring him back. Suppressed excitement pervaded the executive mansion. Secretary Dougherty smiled jeeringly through his black beard, and his eyes twinkled brightly.

He even slapped Adams jovially on the shoulder, and ejaculated, 'Well, my boy, back to normalcy, eh?' Then stiffened guiltily, as though he said too much. But Adams's thoughts were on Helen Jeffers, and he hardly noticed.

Shortly after lunch a motor-ambulance arrived at the White House from the Potomac naval air base, and two gobs with Red Cross brassards on their sleeves carried in a sheet-covered figure on a stretcher.

Secretary Dougherty bustled officiously up to the bearers, and was about to give some order, when Franz Vierecke, with unusual assertion shining in his pale blue eyes, elbowed him to one side, exclaiming, *Nein!* He moost haf rest!'

So the shrouded figure was carted off to one of the guestrooms of the White House.

But the return of Admiral Southworth did not immediately bring matters back to normalcy. The next day strikes broke out in Boston, New York and San Francisco. The police and State troops held aloof. But black-coated Federal soldiery moved in, and kept the strikers effectively in check, handling the situation with such finesse and regard for popular sympathy as to make evident that Secretary Dougherty was not in charge at the White House, and that Steel Jeffers was still running things.

Doctors and nurses were provided for Admiral Southworth, but still a black-uniformed military guard, placed in front of the door of the Presidential bedroom, denied admittance to all except Dougherty and Vierecke.

Students rioted and staged demonstrations at Harvard, Columbia, and Stanford. The ring-leaders promptly disappeared, but there were no wholesale executions.

That evening someone heaved a brick at Lieutenant Adams in the street. And all through the night he could hear sporadic popping noises throughout the city, as on the night before the Fourth. Each pop signified to his ears the elimination of one more potential enemy of the existing regime.

The next morning on his way back to work, he had to pick his way through the remains of several barricades, and once he slipped on a dark red slimy puddle. He shook his head sadly. Poor misguided individuals!

That day three things of note happened. First, an investigating committee from the Senate, headed by Senator Anders of New Hampshire, and accompanied by armed guards loaned by the State of Maryland, called at the White House, demanded to see President Jeffers, and were denied admittance. Lieutenant Adams marveled that the Marylanders were not arrested for treason. Secondly, Admiral Southworth, in a wheelchair, was pushed to the basement laboratory by Dr. Vierecke, and remained there for several hours. And that evening Liam Lincoln accused Jack Adams of disloyalty to the Cause for refusing to divulge to his fellow-conspirators the inside dope on the President's illness. Hot words again ensued, and the others narrowly averted a fight between the two of them.

The next day Senator Anders' resolution, declaring the Presidency vacant, was called-up for a vote in Congress. The leaderless yes-men of House and Senate did not know which way to turn. The few really intelligent members of the Administration forces began to wonder how to take advantage of this situation to advance their own ambition.

Then suddenly in the midst of the debate Steel Jeffers went on the air. His well-known voice boomed out of the little radio in the Senate restaurant. Instantly, the news swept up to the cloakrooms. A loudspeaker on the clerk's table was turned loose on the startled assemblage.

As the ringing appeal for peace and tranquility and loyalty resounded through the chamber, the opposition crumbled, although some die-hards still refused to believe.

'It's a trick!' cried Senator Anders. 'A tape recording of the President's voice is being used to fool us!' He rushed from the chamber, phoned the White House, and was informed that Steel Jeffers was broadcasting from his sickroom. 'But has anyone actually seen him, to know that it is he?' Anders demanded.

Over the air came the answer, in the unmistakable voice of Jeffers himself, 'You still doubt that I am back in the saddle? Then let the Senate Committee call tomorrow at 2:15. I shall receive them in person.'

The next afternoon Senator Anders and his colleagues, with their bodyguard of Maryland State troops, arrived at the White House. The doors were thrown open by the negro attendant, and they marched in.

The large hall was empty of any other persons, and had a closed-for-the-season look: shades drawn, musty smell, furniture shrouded with sheets. But, as the attendant closed—and locked—the doors, the sheets were whisked off of the supposed furniture—machine-guns, manned by black-uniformed troops.

A door opened at one side, and Secretary Dougherty emerged, grinning evilly through his black beard, his eyes snapping. Behind him there debauched into the hall a score of Federal soldiers. Rubbing his hands gleefully together, the Secretary commanded, 'Gentlemen, please reach for the ceiling.'

But the Captain of the Marylanders stepped resolutely forward. 'By whose authority?' he demanded.

'By the authority of the President!'

'It's a lie!' shouted Senator Anders. 'Steel Jeffers is dead!'

The Captain of the Marylanders snatched out his revolver, leveled it at the Secretary of State, and squeezed the trigger. A jet of flame roared forth.

7

An answering roar came from the gun of one of the black uniformed Federal soldiers, and the Maryland officer pitched forward, dead.

Secretary Dougherty staggered backward and his dark eyes rolled. He straightened. His red lips parted in an animal snarl. 'I wear a bullet-proof vest,' he snapped. 'And fortunately the Maryland militia still carry only thirty-eights, instead of forty-fives. Gentlemen, surrender.'

The entire delegation promptly raised their hands aloft, and were disarmed. The militiamen were then herded away, and the doors of the Blue Room swung open to admit the Senators.

At his desk in the bay window sat the President, pale and frail-looking, but eyes snapping with old-time vigor. At his side stood Lieutenant Adams; and banked behind him was a full squad of black-coated Federals, with automatic pistols in their hands.

'Ah!' Steel Jeffers commented, in tones appropriate to his name. 'I am highly honored. Is it true that you gentlemen have the temerity to doubt my existence?'

Senator Anders coughed embarrassedly. 'Well—er—you see, Excellency, it was quite natural—er—'

'Cannot the President of the United States take a slight rest,' snapped Jeffers, 'without a pack of jackals snarling for his corpse?' His voice broke. His eyes wavered huntedly for an instant. Then he coughed, lowered the pitch of his voice, and continued incisively, 'Kindly return to the Senate, and inform your associates that Steel Jeffers is alive—and in good health and sane! Another occurrence like this will compel me to dissolve the Congress!'

'But, Excellency,' interposed Secretary Dougherty, 'ought these traitors be permitted to leave?'

Jeffers sighed, then drew himself erect. 'Let them leave while the leaving is good!'

As Dougherty ushered out the thoroughly cowed delegation, the President turned his eyes toward his aide, and asked with a grim smile, 'Well, Jack Adams, do you approve?'

Surprised, Adams stammered, 'You—you know my views about reprisals. I am glad that you spared them.'

Jeffers smiled the ghost of a smile. 'I have set my hand to the plow, and must go on to the end of the furrow. Ah, Dr. Vierecke. You take me back to my bedroom.'

The white-coated doctor strode across the room, assisted Jeffers into his wheel-chair, and wheeled him out.

Before nightfall Governor Carter of Maryland and Senator Anders of New Hampshire had been mysteriously assassinated. America was rapidly getting back to normal.

That evening in Adams' quarters, the Lieutenant was crowing over his discomfited co-conspirator, Liam Lincoln. 'Hasn't it all turned out just as I prophesied? The time had not yet arrived for us to strike the blow for freedom. Fellows, if you'd taken Liam's advice instead of mine, where would we all be now? In a wooden box like the Governor of Maryland and the Senator from New Hampshire. As it is, both we and our conspiracy still live.'

Lincoln viciously pushed back his black forelock. His dark eyes snapped with fanaticism. 'Jack, why don't you shoot the President?' he sneered. 'You're not afraid, are you?'

Adams stared back contemptuously. 'Don't be an ass, Lincoln! If we make a martyr of Steel Jeffers, his regime will live on. And you know how much worse Secretary Dougherty would be than Jeffers.'

'But Vice President Nieman would succeed to the Presidency, wouldn't he?' asked roly-poly Simeon Baldwin.

'Not if Nieman happened to die conveniently. In that event, the Secretary of State would take over.'

'Then why doesn't Dougherty arrange both assassinations?' asked Cabot the chemist, ruminatively.

'Because, so long as Jeffers displays just the right combination of ruthlessness and proletarian appeal, Dougherty is sitting pretty. Say, that gives me something to keep in mind.' Adams' gray eyes narrowed thoughtfully. 'If Steel Jeffers should ever become permanently ill, Dougherty will bear watching.'

'You will bear watching right now,' asserted Liam Lincoln under his breath.

Adams ignored him.

In the days which followed, the President became more and more his old forceful self. Once again he took sadistic delight in the ruthless pacification of America. One by one the individuals who had raised their voices against him, either disappeared or precipitately fled the country. Those newspapers which had had the temerity to assert the freedom of the press, found their stock and bonds bought-up by the Federal Finance Corporation.

Admiral Southworth, too, recovered his health, and again devoted himself to his basement laboratory as of old.

Adams resented the growing influence of Dougherty and the resulting ever-increasing ruthlessness of the President. And he puzzled over the fact that Steel Jeffers seemed to take an amused interest in him. Formerly he had treated Adams as a mere appurtenance of the executive offices; but now, whenever he spoke to his aide, there was a twinkle in his cold eyes, with perhaps a trace of scorn and contempt in it.

At Adam's first opportunity, when Admiral Southworth and Dr. Vierecke were both absent, he hastened to the potted plant in the basement corridor. He plunged his fingers deep into the soil of the pot, he carefully sifted the earth; but the key was gone!

That night, when he reported this loss to the meeting of the conspirators, there occurred his bitterest break thus far with the fanatic Liam Lincoln, who heatedly accused him of lying—of being an admirer and a supporter of the President.

And there was just enough shadow of truth to this accusation, so that Adams could not reply very forcefully. He merely gave his usual rather lame retort about his daily risking his life in the very den of the enemy while Liam Lincoln sulked in the background.

The meeting broke up with considerable bad feeling, Lincoln's parting shot being, 'If you are really on the level, Jack, you can prove it in just one way. Get into that laboratory, and find out what is going on.'

'I will!' Adams rashly retorted.

All night he lay awake, thinking, worrying, discarding one plan after another. By morning he had evolved an idea.

So he carried a suit of overalls and a pair of telephone linemen's spurs with him to the White House, and at the first opportunity sneaked down into the subcellar, the floor below the one on which the laboratory was located. Hurriedly he donned the overalls, strapped the spurs onto his legs with the spikes outside. Noiselessly as possible, he crowded himself into the ventilator shaft and struggled up. It was tough going. The shaft was narrow and the spikes on his cleats did not bite very easily into its walls.

But finally he made it! His head reached the level of the grating of the laboratory outlet. He heard the voices of Southworth and Steel Jeffers. Peering through the grating, he almost uttered an exclamation of exultance. For Southworth held poised in one hand a hypodermic needle, and in the other a diaphragm capped bottle. By sheer luck, Adams had finally obtained sure proof of the fact that Jeffers was being inoculated regularly with the strange substance in the bottles.

Holding his breath tensely, he watched Southworth jab the needle into Jeffers' arm. The President, his coat off, and his sleeves rolled up, jerked his slim, unmuscular arm back with an exclamation, then laughed nervously.

'Guess I'll never get up enough backbone to take that needle without wincing,' he remarked a bit hoarsely.

The injection was completed in silence that remained until Jeffers had again donned his coat. Then, with an almost curt shortness, he left the laboratory, his lips tight, and his face set in an expression of stoniness and determination.

Southworth went about cleaning up the laboratory, restoring the needle and bottle to its place. Adams remained motionless in his position behind the grating.

A sound at the laboratory door attracted his attention, and he turned his gaze to see the Prussian, Vierecke, enter. Southworth turned to face him.

On Viereck's face was a triumphant grin as he closed the door carefully behind him, then drew a gun from his pocket.

Southworth stiffened. 'What does this mean, Franz?' he asked.

'It means, we haf come to der parting of der ways, Southworth. No longer are you necessary to my blans.'

In a voice level but charged with emotion, Southworth replied, 'Go ahead and kill me; but, as sure as God made little fishes, you'll lose by it. You still don't know the complete formula.'

'Don'd I? Vell, lissen to dis.' There followed a string of chemical language, quite meaningless to the man concealed in the chute.

Admiral Southworth gasped; and that gasp was a complete admission that his assistant had at last learned the whole of the secret which the Admiral had thus far so jealously guarded.

'Ha!' rang out the triumphant voice of Franz Vierecke, followed by a shot, a thud, and a gurgling groan.

8

With a sudden resolution Adams groped within his overalls with his left hand for the automatic pistol on his right hip, then shifted it to his right hand. Quietly opening the grating of the ventilator, he peered out.

The bullet-headed Franz Vierecke was standing with his back to the grille, holding a smoking thirty-eight, as he stared down at the sprawled corpse of the Admiral.

Adams reached out, leveling his automatic. Remembering Secretary Dougherty's bulletproof vest, he took careful aim at Vierecke's head: 'Hands up, Doctor!' he commanded.

The white-coated Prussian wheeled catlike, firing as he turned. But Adams fired first. Both weapons roared, and the laboratory assistant fell backward across the body of the Admiral. Adams scrambled hastily out of the shaft and thrust his gun into its holster. The two bodies still lay inert. He had to work fast! He unbuckled his climbing irons, stripped off his overalls, and thrust them all down the shaft. He took all the small bottles from the ice chest, emptied them in the laboratory sink, and threw them after his discarded equipment. He hastily wiped the dirt from his face and hands on a towel at the sink. Taking the key from the pocket of the dead Admiral, he unlocked the door, stepped out, and locked it behind him.

As he turned, and slid the key into his pocket, one of the White House guards came pattering around the corner. The man halted and raised his arm in salute. 'I thought I heard shots, Sir.'

'Correct,' Adams grimly replied. 'Vierecke and Southworth have killed each other. I go to report to the President.'

Stunned horror widened the man's eyes. Then they narrowed suspiciously, and he reached for his hip. But Adams' fist caught him on the point of the jaw. Down he went in a heap. Adams ran along the corridor toward the stairs.

In the Blue Room he found Steel Jeffers and the Secretary of State conversing together at the big desk in the bay window.

Raising his arm in salute, Adams panted, 'Things will be popping around here in a few moments, and I want to report before they pop.'

Dougherty glared at him, but Jeffers calmly said, 'Go on, Lieutenant.'

'I happened to be in the basement,' Adams replied, 'when I heard Admiral Southworth and Dr. Vierecke quarreling in the laboratory. The door was ajar, so I looked in. Vierecke was pointing a pistol at the Admiral, and the Admiral was saying, 'The injections are all gone. If you kill me, there will be no more.'

'What!' Dougherty's face went white. 'Did he—'

But Adams interrupted. 'Just a moment. I heard Vierecke retort, 'I know the formula!' He recited a lot of chemical gibberish. The Admiral nodded and admitted, 'Yes, you've got it right.'

Dougherty settled back in his chair, the color flooding his cheeks again. Steel Jeffers was watching Adams like a cat.

Adams continued, 'And then Vierecke shot the Admiral. I dashed in, but too late to save him. Of course I shot Vierecke. You'll find the two bodies lying in a heap on the floor of the laboratory. Here is the key.' He flung it down on the desk. 'And here is my gun, Sir, with one cartridge exploded.' He pulled it from its holster, laid it down beside the key, and drew himself up to attention. 'Private Jones tried to arrest me, Sir, but I thought I had better report to you.'

The two men at the desk stared at him with fascinated horror. Then suddenly Dougherty reached inside his coat, and yanked out a gun.

'The Presidency is ended!' he shouted, as he fired at Steel Jeffers.

But a split second ahead of his shot, another shot roared forth in the echoing Blue Room. Adams had snatched up his own weapon from the President's desk, and fired. The impact of its forty-five-caliber bullet smashed the forehead of the Secretary of State and hurled him backward.

There was a tinkle of glass behind the President as two black-uniformed guards crashed in through the French windows. 'Are you all right, Excellency?' they cried.

'Perfectly,' Jeffers calmly replied. 'He never touched me.'

'I—I'm glad,' breathed Adams.

'Take out the body!' the President crisply ordered. Then, as the two guards departed with their grisly burden, he turned to his aide, and said sharply, 'They do not live long, who stand in the way of Steel Jeffers. And, now, Adams, I want the truth about what happened in the laboratory. The truth, mind you!'

Suddenly, as it dawned on Adams that Dougherty's death had removed the only reason for not killing the President, he leveled his gun at Steel Jeffers. 'The truth is that I destroyed all the little bottles.'

Watching the President intently, keeping him covered with the automatic, Adams backed toward the main door of the Blue Room. He groped behind him for the knob. But suddenly the door was flung open. He was seized from behind, and his arms were pinioned to his sides. Like a flash, Jeffers dashed around the desk, and disarmed him. His captor was the guardsman whom he had slugged in the basement corridor.

The President now fired three shots in the air, and other soldiers came running.

'Take him to the War Department,' Jeffers commanded, and lock him in a cell. Don't let any harm come to him. I want him saved for public execution.'

Manacles were snapped onto Adams' wrists, and he was dragged, kicking and struggling away.

9

Adams soon saw that there was no use to struggle, and so he went peaceably. 'Let's buy some peanuts,' he proposed, as they reached the street.

'What!' exclaimed the Sergeant in charge, halting.

The old Italian on the corner shuffled up, with a couple of paper bags of nuts in his hand. 'Peanuts, Meester?' But Adams shrugged his broad shoulders, and held up his manacled hands. 'You see, Giuseppe, I can't buy. I'm a prisoner.'

'Whata for, Signore Adams?'

As they dragged him away, Adams shouted, 'For killing Southworth and Vierecke and Dougherty. They're all dead, Giuseppe! All, all dead!'

'Shut up!' shouted the Sergeant, felling him with a blow from his automatic.

Adams awoke in a windowless unlit cell. His head ached terribly. For a while he sat in darkness, and nursed his throbbing head. Then a soldier came, and brought him some food, and turned on a light. 'Well, fellow,' said the man, 'you certainly started something!'

'What do you mean?' Adams asked.

'Say!' the voluble soldier replied. 'There's hell broke-loose already, all over the country. Some crazy yap, who thinks he's Abraham Lincoln, has sent out a bunch of hooey, hollering for all patriots to rally to his standard, or some such rot. And are they rallying?'

'Well, I'll bite. Are they?'

'I'll say they are! Several Governors have seceded from the Union already, and it's funny—these were Governors who stayed loyal in the last ruckus.'

Adams chuckled. He could have named the exact Governors. For they were men who had been in touch with the Washington group of conspirators, and so had the sense to lay off until Liam Lincoln gave the word. Quite evidently Giuseppe had passed along the news of the triple killing, and the conspirators had at once sent out instructions that the time had come.

'Well, how are they making out?' Adams asked.

'Not so hot!' stoutly declared the soldier. 'You just wait until Steel Jeffers gets hold of 'em! He'll shoot 'em all against a wall! '

'How long was I unconscious?'

'You were out cold for about four hours.'

'And all this has happened in that short time?'

'Yes.'

'Phew! Lincoln certainly worked quickly!'

'Say,' asserted the soldier suspiciously, 'I'll bet you was in cahoots with that guy.' He refused to talk any further, and left.

Adams was much surprised when, later in the day, the soldier returned, all eyes, and informed him that the Dictator wanted to see him. Manacled, he was led to the White House.

As he walked with his guards the short distance from the War Department to the executive mansion, he noted a marked overnight change in the city. No street cars were running. The streets were practically deserted, except for patrolling soldiers, and an occasional marching contingent of troops. And these troops were clad in khaki service uniforms, in place of the snappy peacetime black.

In the sky above, planes circled through the cloudless blue.

Adams could hear in the distance the occasional crack of rifles, and the boom of cannons.

Sixty or so enlisted men lay on the White House lawn beside a row of neat stacks of rifles. Two armed guards marched back and forth across the front step. A khaki-clad figure on a motorcycle roared up the circular drive, delivered a dispatch to one of the sentries, and roared off again.

Indoors the White House was a strictly military headquarters. Gone were all the civilian attendants and clerks and stenographers. In their stead were khaki-clad members of the military, tense and precise.

Adams was taken direct to the Blue Room. Here again were guards. Soldiers rushed in and out with messages. And, seated at the large desk in the bay window beside the Dictator, was a leonine Army Officer with bushy gray mustaches, and four silver stars on each shoulder. The two men were busily engaged in arranging pushpins on a map.

As Adams entered under guard, Jeffers looked up. To Adams's surprise, the Dictator appeared perfectly well—in fact, younger and in better health than when Adams had been taken to prison. But, looking more closely, Adams noticed that the Dictator's cheeks had a slightly feverish tinge, and that his eyes were unduly bright.

'Sorry I can't salute, Sir,' said the prisoner. 'But, with these contraptions on my wrists, it's a bit difficult.'

Steel Jeffers laughed, but his face remained grave. 'The usually immaculate Jack Adams seems to have slept in his uniform, and to have gone without shaving. I may have to get myself a new military aide.' Then, to the Sergeant in charge of the squad, 'Unlock him, and withdraw.'

'But, Excellency-'

'Unlock him!'

'Yes, Excellency.' The Sergeant removed Adams's handcuffs, and then marched his men out of the room. Adams promptly held up his arm in salute.

'General Peters,' said Jeffers, 'would you mind receiving your dispatches in the next room for a few minutes? And please give orders that I am not to be disturbed. I wish a few words alone with the prisoner.'

The General stood up, gave a stiff Roman salute, and strode out.

As the doors closed behind him, the Dictator snapped, 'Sit down, Lieutenant!' Adams took a chair across the desk from Steel Jeffers. The latter continued, 'Did you know that your fanatical comrade Liam Lincoln has invited England and France to invade this country, to help suppress my Dictatorship?'

'I don't believe it, Sir,' Adams levelly replied.

The Dictator's eyes narrowed, and the flush left his cheeks for a moment. 'You wouldn't!' he crisply asserted. 'But it's so. Why do you tie up with an erratic ass like Liam Lincoln? He hates you. The two of you have quarreled.'

A look of startled surprise flashed into Adam's eyes.

Steel Jeffers smiled coldly. 'A mere random guess of mine, but it struck home. Lincoln would double-cross you in a minute, to further his own ambitions. So why not side with me? I have the situation well in hand. The Regular Army is concentrating in Virginia, and the loyal Navy will soon be in the Chesapeake to clear the way for me to join the Army. Adams, I can offer you—'

'I'm sorry, but nothing you could offer, would interest me.'

'No?' Watching him like a cat, the Dictator's eyes narrowed. An amused superior smile played upon his lips, as he studied his victim calculatingly. Then he purred, 'Adams, I offer you—my sister Helen.'

Adams flushed eagerly, stammered, then resolutely asserted, 'Even that wouldn't tempt me!'

'I wonder.' Jeffers seemed to be speaking to himself. 'How can you admire her, yet hate me so much?'

'She had ideals—'

'And I had those same ideals. You and the rest of your gang of young radicals were once followers of mine. Why did you desert me?'

'It was you who deserted us, Sir. Secretary Dougherty made a fascist out of you.'

Jeffers swung slowly around in his swivel chair, and stared moodily out through the big bay window. Then he turned slowly back again. 'Secretary Dougherty is dead, Adams,' he said in a low voice.

'You mean—That, if you succeed in putting down this rebellion, there will be no reprisals, no more frightfulness?' Adams felt himself weakening, hypnotized. 'What do you wish me to do?'

The Dictator leaned forward, his eyes shining eagerly. 'Give me back those bottles!' he demanded.

The spell was broken. Adams laughed grimly. 'I poured every one of them down the sink,' he explained. 'You can find the bottles themselves in the ventilator shaft, to prove it.'

The Dictator's face contorted with rage. He sprang to his feet, but instantly calmed as the door burst open, and General Peters rushed in, exclaiming, 'Excellency, all is lost! The Virginia State troops have captured Fort Monroe, and have taken over the coast defense guns and the mine fields. The Navy can't get into the Chesapeake. We're bottled up here in Washington!'

'General,' Jeffers sternly replied, 'I told you that I did not wish to be interrupted.'

Stunned and sputtering, the old war horse withdrew.

Jeffers turned back to Adams, and passed a hand across his eyes with a weary gesture. 'It's all over, Jack,' he asserted 'What would you think of my abdicating?'

'It would avoid further bloodshed.'

Steel Jeffers shook his head. 'Not if I fall into the hands of Liam Lincoln, it wouldn't. And once he tasted my blood, other heads would fall by the hundreds. No. Help me to safety. Then, with me out of the picture, let General Peters negotiate for a general amnesty.'

'Why should I do this for you?'

'You will not be doing it for me. It will be for America and for Helen.'

For Helen? Adams leaned forward eagerly. Then clamped his jaw and shook his head. 'Not for either you or Helen,' he declared levelly, 'but to put an end to the war. I may be making a terrible mistake, but—well, what are your plans?'

'I want you to communicate with your fellow conspirators, and arrange for safe conduct for yourself and a girl through their lines. Then I shall disguise myself as a girl—you have already had proof of my abilities in that line—and you will take me in your car. I have friends who will protect me until the storm blows over.'

'All right,' Adams agreed. 'I'll shave, and get my uniform pressed. Meanwhile you write me out a pass. Then I'll go to my own quarters, phone some of my pals, arrange for passes through their lines, and bring my car back here for you. Oh, and by the way, try to look less like your sister Helen than you did that time before.'

'For the sake of your peace of mind?' Jeffers taunted him.

'Please don't joke!' begged Adams seriously. 'No, it's for the sake of your own safety. The conspirators are all familiar with your sister's picture—Your name will be *Mary Calvert.*'

'Why not phone to your friends from here?'

'And have your Secret Service operatives listen in? No thanks. Besides I have to go home to get the car. I'll let you know, when everything is ready.'

He arose, extended his arm in salute, and left the room. The Dictator's eyes were filled with a strange amused light, as they followed the Lieutenant's departure.

10

A half hour later, Lieutenant Adams left the White House, all shaved, cleaned, and pressed, with a Presidential pass in his pocket. Giuseppe Albertino was at his peanut-stand at the corner, the only civilian in sight. Adams bought a bag of nuts, but left no message. If he were being watched or followed, as he half suspected, he had no intention of implicating this ally.

Steel Jeffers must have wondered why Adams should fear to be overheard if he telephoned from the executive mansion, and yet should not realize that it would be equally easy for the Secret Service to plug in on his home telephone.

Adams chuckled. He had a scheme to test the sincerity of the Dictator. He hoped—he believed—that Steel Jeffers was sincere; but the lives of all of his pals depended on Adams guessing right, and so he was determined to make no mistakes.

He was still turning his plans over in his mind as he unlocked and opened the front door of his P Street quarters. Then he halted on the threshold, and his jaw dropped.

Chairs overturned. Drawers pulled out, and their contents strewn on the floor! Books swept from the shelves! The dread Secret Service had made a thorough search; and—finding nothing, had turned spitefully devastating.

Finding nothing? There was nothing to find. Adams had carefully seen to that. And yet—With sinking heart, he rushed to the basement.

Relief flooded over him. There was no sign that the secret hole in the brick wall had been disturbed. He swung the irregular section open. Cool musty air billowed out. It felt good to his hot cheeks.

Groping on a shelf just to the left inside, he found, also undisturbed, a small electrical contraption of coils and wires and dials and switches. Then, his confidence restored, he proceeded down the tunnel to the adjoining cellar of Godfrey Cabot. Cabot's house had not been ransacked.

Adams dashed upstairs, and called Simeon Baldwin's number on the phone. Then attached his bit of electrical apparatus. 'Hello S. B.,' he said. 'This is J. Q. A.'

'Giuseppe reported that he saw you,' replied the voice of his friend. 'Say, you did a swell job bumping off Southworth and Vierecke and Dougherty! Is Liam Lincoln fit to be tied, for envy! But how come you are on the loose? We had authentic info that you were to be shot against a wall.'

'I was. But Jeffers is pretending that he thinks I was falsely accused of the three murders. He has turned me loose in the hope that I'll lead his Secret Service men to your headquarters. But I've given them the slip, and am phoning from Godfrey Cabot's house, and using the tone-invertor, as you know. You can talk freely. Are you in touch with the Allied Governors?'

'Am I?' exclaimed Baldwin's voice. 'Underground directional radio direct to Baltimore headquarters, with a tone-inverter at each end!'

'Then,' said Adams, 'you arrange with them to let me through the lines in my car—District 5656. I can put them in touch with one of the Federal Generals, who is ready and willing to throw the works.'

'Who?' exclaimed Baldwin excitedly.

'Sorry, Sim, but this has to be arranged personally. I have given my word to the old General not to breathe a word to anyone but the Allied High Command in person.'

'All right,' agreed Baldwin a bit grumpily.

'And I want a special pass signed by you, identifying me and Mary Calvert.'

'Who's she?'

'A girl friend. Lives at the Wardman Park Inn. Has relatives in Baltimore. I promised to get her out.'

'Why, you old Lothario! I thought you were in love with that dead-and-gone Helen Jeffers.'

'No time for humor,' Adams snapped. 'Mary Calvert is an old friend of the family. Send the pass over to Giuseppe, and tell him to vamoose as soon as he hands it to me. There'll be no need of his hanging around the White House any longer after I've skipped out.'

'But how'll you get through the Federal lines?'

'Forge a pass from the Dictator. I know his signature and have access to his official stationery and seal.'

'Fine. Good luck, Jack.'

'Good luck, Sim.'

Adams hung up, detached the tone-inverter, and carried it back to its niche in the secret tunnel. From his own house, he phoned Steel Jeffers, and told him that all was ready. Then he squared his broad shoulders, and smiled. 'If I've been followed and plugged in on,' he said to himself, 'Steel Jeffers will know that I've met none of my pals, and have sent out no phone calls from my house; so he won't believe that I have arranged for a pass, and he will refuse to go with me. Accordingly, if he comes along, it will be a sign that he is on the level.'

He was still smiling, as he changed into his gray Norfolk suit, thrust his forty-five into his left hand coat pocket, packed his bag, and drove his car to the White House. Parking by the servant's entrance, he entered, and made directly for the offices. Here he was handed a note from the Dictator, commanding him to report at once to the Presidential bedroom.

A totally strange girl, with curly yellow hair, let him in. She laughed at his open-mouthed amazement. Then said in the Dictator's voice, 'Well, Jack Adams, how do you like my blonde wig? Am I different enough to suit you?'

'I'll say you are, Sir! The car is waiting at the rear. And I've arranged for safe passage through the enemy lines. But what about abdication?'

'While you were telephoning from your home, I made all the necessary arrangements with General Peters. As soon as I am safe, he will contact the enemy and make the best peace possible.'

'I intimated as much to my pals, when I phoned them,' said Adams. 'But I merely told them that someone high up in your organization was willing to betray the city into Allied hands, if they would give me a pass through the lines, to arrange it.'

'Excellent!' laughed Steel Jeffers. There was a peculiar note in his laugh. Then, reaching for the phone, he called the Blue Room, and asked for General Peters. 'General, this is Steel Jeffers. If you don't hear from me by three o'clock, you know what to do.'

Returning the instrument to its cradle, the disguised Dictator said in a high-pitched feminine voice, 'Well, Jack, I am ready. Here is a Presidential pass, made out to John Q. Adams and Mary Calvert.'

'They'll never suspect you, Sir,' Adams admiringly asserted, as he picked up the bags, and led the way out to his parked car.

Circling the White House, he stopped at the peanut-stand of old Giuseppe, and bought a large supply of the nuts.

'Is the Lieutenant leaving?' asked the grizzled Italian.

'Yes,' Adams replied, 'and, if you're depending on my trade for a living, you'd better give up your stand. I shan't be back for some time.'

Driving north on 15th, to Scott Circle, Adams then cut east on Rhode Island Avenue. They hadn't gone more than a block or two, when they were halted by a squad of khaki-clad Federal soldiery. Adams flashed the pass which the Dictator had provided, and the soldiers let them through.

This was repeated every block or two. Their luck seemed too good. And gradually there came to the surface of Adam's mind a thought which had been struggling for recognition. Just why was the great Steel Jeffers cravenly fleeing for his life, disguised as a woman, and passing up the chance of using Lieutenant Adams as a decoy to trap the leaders of the conspiracy?

As Adams turned these thoughts over in his mind, the pretended girl beside him uneasily asked, 'When do we contact your friends? Here we are almost at the outskirts of the city, and you haven't yet secured the pass which is to let us through the Allied lines.'

Adams instinctively glanced up at the rear-view mirror, and saw a large black sedan following them.

'I'm going to chance it without an Allied pass,' he brusquely replied.

Just then they were halted again. But this time, as Adams was about to hand over the paper which Jeffers had given him, Jeffers himself opened his handbag and drew forth another paper. A trick? A disclosure of their identity? Probably.

'None of that!' shouted Adams, suddenly stepping on the gas, and scattering the surprised soldiery, as the car shot ahead. A few shots sounded behind them, but Adams was out of range before the soldiers could recover from their astonishment sufficiently to take good aim.

'And now, girlie, hand me over that paper,' said Adams, grabbing it with his right hand.

'Don't you call me *girlie*!' raged the deep tones of the Dictator.

'Trying to double-cross me, are you?' Adams raged back at him. 'Planning to have me lead your Secret Service to my pals? Well, I already have my pass, and am not going to my pals. You can't win, Steel Jeffers!'

He shifted the seized paper to his left hand, took the wheel with his right, and stuffed the paper into his pocket. A glance in the mirror showed him that the big black sedan had come right past the squad of soldiers without being challenged, and now was rapidly gaining on him. Adams pushed the accelerator down to the floorboard.

The Dictator reached suddenly beneath the hem of his skirt. From a knee-holster he drew a pearl-handled Luger-38. Raising the weapon, he cried, 'I can win, Jack Adams!'

Adams' left hand came up like a flash from his coat pocket, grasping his Army-45. His right elbow shot out, throwing the Dictator off balance. The little Luger exploded harmlessly. Then Adams' gun crashed down on the blonde wig. Jeffers slumped in the seat.

Adams grinned wryly, as he returned his gun to his pocket. 'I'd hate to have to hit a real girl.' Then he gave the car everything it had, and sped down the road away from the pursuing sedan.

They were almost clear of the District, when a whole company of Federal soldiers, with drawn bayonets, loomed ahead, barring the road.

11

Adams set his jaw, and his gray eyes became slits. Leaning on the horn, he stepped on the gas, and drove his car roaring and shrieking straight toward the Federal soldiers.

The soldiers parted in a mad scramble. He was through!

Adams bent low over the wheel, unhurt. Bullets splintered the rear window. One crashed through the windshield. Then came two loud explosions—both rear tires blown out. The car lurched and bumped drunkenly. It required all of Adams' strength on the wheel to hold it to its course. In a few moments the enemy sedan would overhaul him.

He glanced at the rear-view mirror, and saw the soldiers massed in the road behind him, loading and firing.

Then the big black pursuing sedan swung skiddingly around the group. Two startled soldiers stepped into its path. The sedan slid sidewise up onto the curb, ripping off two wheels, and rolled onto its side.

Adams brought his eyes back to the road just in time to see a lone soldier standing by the curb ahead, with gun raised to fire. Adams swung toward him, and sent him diving for the gutter. Then sped bumping on.

Ahead was open country. No more Federal soldiers. He was in no-man's land, between the two warring forces. Tanks lumbered about and shells crashed down all about.

Slowing down, he rearranged the Dictator's twisted blonde wig. Next he glanced through the note which Steel Jeffers had attempted to pass to the sentry. Adams smiled grimly at learning that this note identified Mary Calvert as an operative of the Secret Service, and himself as an enemy to be arrested on sight.

He tore the note into little bits and scattered them from the window of his car. 'Treacherous as usual!' he mused. 'And yet I wonder if Jeffers at the start planned to trick me. He seemed actually to weaken, to turn to me for help, when the old General burst into the room with the news that all was lost.'

Adams reached into one of the bags of peanuts which he had purchased from Giuseppe, and pulled out the pass which Baldwin had provided for him, just in time! For a dozen soldiers in the uniform of the Maryland National Guard popped out of the bushes, and held up their hands for him to stop. He stopped, and showed them his Allied pass.

'Is there a medical detachment anywhere near?' he asked. 'The last Federal who stopped us, got suspicious, and tried to stick me with his bayonet. I ducked, but the side of his rifle barrel bit Miss Calvert, and knocked her cold.'

The Dictator stirred and groaned.

'There's none closer than three miles,' said the Sergeant of the soldiers sympathetically, looking in at the crumpled feminine figure, 'and your car won't stand much more. But I tell you what. There's a State car down the road just a piece. I'll jump on the running-board and tell the guy in charge to take you.'

They bumped along for about a hundred yards to the State car.

Adams lifted the Dictator into the rear seat of the new conveyance, and got in beside him. The military chauffeur in the front seat started the car.

And now what? The Allied surgeons would instantly discover that the disguised Dictator was a man. His identity would then become known. Death for him—and probably for John Q. Adams as well.

The Dictator began to stir into life. He groaned weakly.

Adams snatched out his forty-five, and thrust the muzzle against the back of the driver's head. 'Sorry buddy,' he said. 'Draw up alongside the road.' The startled soldier did so. 'Now get out.' The soldier got out, and Adams followed him.

Quickly Adams relieved him of his gun. Then trussed him up with his belt, gagged him, and carried him a short distance into the woods.

By the time that he returned to the car, the Dictator was sitting up and staring bewilderedly around. 'Where—am—I?' he asked in a cracked voice.

'Get in front,' Adams commanded, helping him to do so. Then starting up the car, Adams continued, 'You're within the Allied lines, Jeffers. You tried to double-cross me, and I knocked you out.'

'Well, what are you going to do with me? Turn me in?'

Adams pondered for a time before answering. Finally he said, 'I suppose that I ought to, but somehow I can't. So I think I'll make you go through with your original proposal.'

They drove on in silence, both of them thinking hard. Several times they were stopped by patrols of soldiers, but their official car and the pass from Sim Baldwin got them by.

It was nearly three o'clock when they drew up before the City Hall in Baltimore. 'Miss Calvert,' said Adams pointedly, 'I can't trust you, but I'm going to give you a break. I shall have to take you into Allied Headquarters with me. But if you behave yourself, I shan't give you away.'

Steel Jeffers agreed.

General Saltonstall of Massachusetts was in charge of the Allied forces. He received Adams immediately.

Adams instinctively extended his arm in the Roman salute.

Then flushed guiltily, and brought the tips of his fingers smartly to his forehead.

General Saltonstall grinned, but otherwise ignored the mistake.

'Adams,' he said, 'I'm glad to meet on. You struck a splendid blow for liberty when you did away with those three scoundrels at the White House. Too bad you couldn't have got the usurper too.'

The pretended Mary Calvert made a wry face. Adams introduced the General to her. 'Miss Calvert was knocked unconscious by one of the Federal soldiers,' he explained, 'as we were making our escape. She's still a bit shaky. Can she sit down over in a corner, where I can keep an eye on her, while we attend to our business?'

'My Staff Surgeon is—' Saltonstall began.

But Adams interrupted, 'Our business will take only a minute, and then we'll go right to her folks. The kid's got a lot of courage. In spite of her weakness, she insisted on our coming here first.'

With a smile of courteous appreciation, General Saltonstall held out his arm to the disguised Dictator and escorted him to a seat in one corner, while Adams watched the performance with an amused twinkle in his gray eyes.

Turning back to Adams, Saltonstall asked, 'What do you propose?'

'Get me General Peters on the phone at Washington. He is expecting the call.'

'General Peters?' exclaimed Saltonstall eagerly. 'I can hardly believe it. Why, man, do you realize? If he will come over to our side, the war will be won!'

'Exactly.' Adams glanced over to note the reaction of the disguised Dictator, and saw him bite his lip.

Saltonstall barked out a command. A line was speedily put through to Washington, for communication between the two cities had not been wholly cut off, merely subjected to censorship by both sides.

'General Peters,' said Adams into the phone. 'This is Lieutenant John Q. Adams, calling from Allied Headquarters in Baltimore.'

There was a gasp on the other end of the line.

'You don't believe it?' Adams continued. 'Well, I can prove it. I was with the Dictator when he phoned you from his bedroom at half past twelve today. He instructed you to do something at three. I don't know what he meant, but I do know that he tried to double-cross me. However, he didn't succeed. He is now a prisoner in the hands of the Allies.'

'I don't believe it!' declared the voice of the old war horse; but he sounded hopeful, rather than dismayed.

'I can prove it,' asserted Adams. 'Call the White House. Ask them if they have seen Steel Jeffers since noon.'

'Is he really a prisoner?' Saltonstall interrupted, his eyes shining.

The supposed Mary Calvert sat suddenly intensely erect. Adams placed his hand over the transmitter and said, 'No! But I threw him off my trail. Evidently he hasn't yet got in touch with General Peters; and if he doesn't do so within the next few minutes, it will be too late to save the Dictatorship.' Then into the phone again, 'I give you the word of the Allied High Command that Steel Jeffers will not be harmed, if you will at once make peace.' Adams glanced at Mary Calvert, and saw her smile and relax.

'I'll call you back, as soon as I check up the White House,' said the voice of the Federal General.

While they waited for the return call, Saltonstall and his Staff conferred, and outlined the terms of peace.

Finally Peters called back, and was turned over to Saltonstall. All the Allied Generals were clustered around their Chief. Adams considered it the psychological moment to fade out of the picture, before anyone could think to ask him any embarrassing questions. So he beckoned to 'Mary Calvert,' and together they tiptoed from the room.

As he helped the disguised Dictator into the State car, he asked, 'Have you really some friends who will hide you?'

'Yes,' said Steel Jeffers in feminine tones. 'In the mountains north of here, just across the Pennsylvania border. Keep right along east on this street, and turn north on Greenmount Avenue.'

'Good!' said Adams, and soon they were speeding northward on the old York Road.

'Just think,' mused Steel Jeffers, 'I'm no longer Dictator and somehow I prefer it this way.'

He seemed younger, less careworn, than Adams had ever known him; but it was hard to tell, under his feminine disguise, how much was genuine, and how much was theatrical pose.

They drove on for a couple of hours in silence.

Suddenly Adams remarked, 'You know, we never ate those peanuts. I left them behind in my car.'

'Let's stop for a bite in this coffee shop,' suggested Jeffers, and soon they were seated at the counter.

The radio was playing a stirring march. Adams straightened his broad shoulders, and a wistful light crept into his companion's eyes.

The music hushed slightly, and a voice announced, 'This is the Federal Radio Control. The Allied troops are just marching down Pennsylvania Avenue, with Vice President—er, President now—Nieman at their head. Oh, what a day! What a day!'

Jeffers shuddered.

'Please turn it off!' snapped Adams. 'The lady would like something lighter.'

Surprised, the proprietor switched on some dance music. 'You two ain't pro-Dictator, be you?' he asked suspiciously.

Adams smiled whimsically, and shook his head.

For a while they ate in silence. Some advertising matter obtruded itself on the program, and the proprietor twirled the dials to another station. '—radio newscast. Liam Lincoln, leader of the Young Patriots, says that he now has positive proof that Lieutenant Adams, supposed hero, is a traitor; and that the supposed woman whom he brought through the Allied lines as *Mary Calvert* is really Dictator Jeffers—ex-Dictator Jeffers, we should say—in disguise.'

Without waiting to hear more, Adams hurriedly paid the bill, and piloted his companion out to their waiting car.

A gray-shirted member of the Pennsylvania constabulary, with his motorcycle drawn up on the curb, and a broad smile on his tanned face, was leaning against the front door of the car.

'Well, well!' he announced. 'Stolen car, and Mary Calvert, and little Jack Adams, and everything.'

Adams gasped, and his hunted eyes swept rapidly around for means of escape.

'Why, officer,' he said, 'I don't know what you're talking about.' His right fist suddenly flashed out squarely to the trooper's chin, knocking him back against the car. Then Adams' left fist swung, and caught the man on the ear sweeping him off the car onto the sidewalk. 'Quick!' Adams shouted.

In an instant, he and Jeffers were in the car, streaking down the road.

A sharp crack sounded behind them. Something seared the side of Adams' head. Everything went black, and his hands dropped from the wheel.

Adams, in a daze, felt strong capable hands reach across him, and seize the wheel. Nausea and unconsciousness swept over him in waves. He slumped down in a heap. Then oblivion.

12

Ages later he came half awake again. It was night. Starlight. The cool windiness of high places.

The car stopped. Voices: 'Uncle Eph.'

'Aunt Martha.'

'Steel, lad.'

'Helen.' That name cut through the fog of his delirium. 'Helen!'

Strong raw-boned male arms were carrying him. Into a house. Up some stairs. Onto a bed. Then capable feminine fingers loosened his clothing, and tucked him in. Receding footsteps. Silence.

Many days of illness, fever, delirium. Recurrent dreams of a mad flight from state troopers.

And then, one afternoon, Jack Adams awoke as from a deep sleep, and looked around him. He was lying in an old-fashioned high-post bed in a tiny room. On him was a patchwork quilt, covered by a tufted spread of homespun linen. Straw-matting on the floor. Quaint old furniture all around.

Very gingerly he pushed down the covers, and swung his long legs out of the bed. Shakily he walked to the window. Rolling tree-clad hills, bathed in sunlight, stretched away beneath his view. Where was he, anyhow? He went to the door of the room, and called down the stairs, not too loudly, 'Hi, there!'

No one answered. He opened the door to a closet, found his clothes, and put them on. Then he essayed to descend the stairs.

In the living-room he found a radio, turned it on, and sank exhausted into a chair. As the tubes warmed up, he caught, '—and if this alleged hero had been sincere, would he not have turned Steel Jeffers over to the Allied Generals? Would he have fled with the Dictator in a stolen car belonging to the State of Maryland? Would he have kept in hiding? Only traitors hide, my friends. Patriots do not fear the light of day—'

Loud handclapping. Then, in another voice, 'You have just been listening to the Federal Radio Control's debate on the subject: 'Was Lieutenant Adams a patriot or traitor?' And now for a news flash. The secret hide-out of Steel Jeffers has been found. Troops have surrounded it, and are closing in. This is the F. R. C. network.'

Adams gasped. Surrounded even now? Closing in? With sudden resolution, he forced his fever-weakened body to stand. He must find and warn Steel Jeffers!

'Why, what are you doing downstairs?' asked a sweet feminine voice, filled with concern.

Adams wheeled. A young girl in a print dress and sunbonnet stood in the doorway. Her checks were smooth and unrouged. Her figure was delicately rounded. She took off her sunbonnet, and a wealth of brown curls fell about her high forehead.

'You are Helen Jeffers?' he breathed.

'Of course!' she exclaimed. 'Who else?'

Helen! Alive and real! Helen Jeffers, as her brother Steel had promised him!

But even in his joy at finding her at last, he did not forget the ominous news which he had just heard over the air. 'Where is your brother? I just got a news flash that the troops are closing in on us.'

'My brother Steel? Steel is dead,' she replied with a touch of sadness.

Adams sobered. 'Did that State Trooper get him?'

'No, Jack.' Smiling sweetly, she stepped forward and placed her hands in his. 'Let's talk of other things, for Steel is safe from his enemies.'

'But, Helen! Here we are talking together as though we had known each other for years. And yet I've never met you. Never even seen you. Fell in love with your photograph. Did Steel tell you—'

Helen Jeffers smiled whimsically. 'We have known each other a long time, for I was the Dictator.'

'You!' Adams stared blankly.

'Yes, my brother Steel died on election-day four years ago. He and James Dougherty and I had pledged ourselves to put through our program at any cost. I closely resembled my brother. And so James Dougherty conceived the fantastic idea of turning me into a man. We reported that it was I who had died. Then I retired to a shack in the mountains; and there two biological experts, Admiral Southworth and Franz Vierecke, injected a certain derivative of the hormone testosterone into my veins—'

'So that is what the letters *t-e-s-t* meant on the little bottles!' Adams exclaimed.

The girl nodded, and continued, 'This hormone made me to all outward appearances a man, and even made me ruthless.'

'I see,' said Adams grimly, drawing away from her.

'Don't blame me too much,' she begged. 'I did it all for the Cause to which my brother had been pledged, not foreseeing where dictatorship and the unprincipled ambition of my Secretary of State would lead me. Well, anyway, Franz Vierecke had worked with the great Ruzicka, when the latter discovered how to produce testosterone synthetically out of cholesterol.'

'But, if the method was known,' Adams interrupted, 'then why all the mystery?'

'If the White House had bought large quantities of testosterone, our secret might have been suspected. Furthermore, different derivatives react differently, some even have the opposite effect from the effect which we wished. I myself discovered this to my horror, when doing some frantic experimentation on my own during Admiral Southworth's illness. So, the secret died with the Admiral and Vierecke, and my masquerade was at an end. Fortunately the sinister Dougherty did not long outlive them. Then I struggled on alone, a woman again, double-crossing even you, my only friend.' Her eyes fell.

Adams tried to hate her, but be could not. She had been no more to blame for it all than Trilby had been under the spell of Svengali.

'You poor girl!' he breathed, taking her in his arms. He kissed her as she clung close to him. Then gently he released her.

An hour or so later, after he had met Uncle Eph and Aunt Martha, and had had a shave, he and Helen sat hand in hand on the front piazza of the little farmhouse, gazing off over the beautiful rolling mountain view. And waiting, silently waiting, for what they knew was closing in on them.

Finally a cavalcade of cars drew up on the highway in front. Out of the front car leaped the fanatic Liam Lincoln, his black hair awry, his dark eyes flashing. 'There's the traitor!' Lincoln shouted, pointing a skinny finger at Adams. 'Seize him.'

State soldiers poured out of the other cars, and cautiously approached the piazza. Also roly-poly Sim Baldwin, tall Phil Nordstrom, chunky Godfrey Cabot, and others of Adams' old crowd. Even Giuseppe Albertino, the peanut man.

Studiously ignoring Lincoln's inflamed words, Adams casually remarked, 'Hello, fellows! Meet my fiancée, the girl whom I called *Mary Calvert.* Her real name is Helen Jeffers.' Adams chuckled. 'I told you fellows that I'd get her in the end. And doesn't this explain a lot of things, Liam, which were puzzling you? For example, why the Dictator gave her and me a pass out of Washington, and why I was so anxious to keep her identity a secret, until peace was concluded.'

Several of Adams' pals laughed—a nervous relieved laugh.

Lincoln angrily thrust back his black forelock. 'That's all very well, but why did you steal the State car, and assault that trooper? You threw us off the trail for days and days!'

'Well, you see, Liam, I didn't want to risk having a fanatic such as you butting in on my honeymoon.'

More laughter.

Liam Lincoln's prestige was rapidly slipping. He made one last attempt to regain it. 'Where is the Dictator?' he demanded.

Adams shrugged his broad shoulders. 'How should I know?' he replied. 'I can truthfully say that I haven't seen or heard from Steel Jeffers since his sister Helen and I left the White House together on the day the Dictatorship ended.'

Smothered Seas*

It was the year 2000. America was at war, fighting for her very life against the Asiatic Union. And yet the American people—even army officers—found time for recreation. Recreation was a necessity to take one's mind off the titanic struggle.

Lieutenant Richard Lister, clad in swimming trunks, sat on a beach rug, staring moodily out across the Pacific Ocean toward the Seal Rocks and beyond, his hands clasped across his tanned knees, his bronzed face tense.

"Let's not talk about the war; let's talk about us!" he exclaimed to Sally Amber, who sat beside him.

The girl turned her strange, dark eyes inquisitively upon him.

"You shouldn't feel that way, Dick," she said seriously. "Particularly as you're in such an important branch of the service. I'm not kidding; I mean it. Where would the country be without your Bureau of Military Biology and Bacteriology? We'd all be wiped out by the Asiatic Union's germs!"

"Sure. And if it weren't for their bacteriologists, they'd be wiped out by our germs. It's a deadlock, I tell you, like this whole war. Look at Alaska: For more than a year now the Khan has been holding that little corner from Rocky Point to Cape Epsenberg, and we haven't been able to budge his line a single inch, nor has he been able to budge ours. Each army is protected by one of those impenetrable Beckerley electrical fields.

"Alaska is the key to the whole situation, with the Khan there in person. If we could just get through his Beckerley field, and put an end to him, the whole Asiatic Union would crumble.

It's only his personality that can hold together such naturally hostile groups as the Siberian Russians, the Japs, the Chinese, the Tarters, and so forth. Without him, they'd be at each other's throats in hours!"

"Well, why doesn't somebody do something about it?" asked Sally, impishly.

---

*Written in collaboration with Ralph Milne Farley

"Lord knows we've tried!" Lister exclaimed. "Ten or a dozen brave Americans have gotten through the enemy lines, and tried to assassinate him, only to be captured, and subjected to horrible torture and death."

The girl shuddered, and pulled one corner of the beach rug up around her shoulders.

"I don't suppose I'd rate as a 'brave American'," she said.

"I'd take a chance on your bravery," Lister declared.

"Why doesn't America land troops in Asia?" Sally asked.

Lister stared at her sharply.

"You know as well as I do," he said. "Although America controls the seas ever since we annihilated the Khan's fleet off the Marianas six months ago, yet he has ten million men under arms in Asia. What good would it do us to land our five million against such odds? No, we've got to lick the mad Khan in Alaska—somehow."

"He isn't mad!" snapped Sally, unexpectedly.

"How do you know?"

"I've—I've—well, I've seen him."

"I didn't know you'd ever been in Asia."

"There are lots of things about me that you don't know," she retorted. "My father is dead, and I am quite wealthy. I've traveled a lot. Three years ago I was in the eastern capital—Harbin; and, what's more, I've been in Moscow, the western capital, too."

"So you've seen the mad Khan," mused Lister. "Did you ever see the woman they call Princess Stephanie? What's she like? She's supposed to be very beautiful."

Sally shrugged. "Oh, she's all right, if you like that type," she replied airily. "She's dark and has Khazar blood in her, and she's about my age—and anyway, why are you questioning me? Go on with your little lecture."

"About us?" he asked hopefully.

"No." She reached out one slim hand, and gently patted his knee. "About the Beckerley electrical fields. What are they? How do they operate?"

He frowned thoughtfully, trying to phrase his answer in words that a girl would understand.

"It's an application of Morelle's experiment with electrical eddy currents," he said. "I'm a botanist, not an electrical engineer, but I know that the idea involves the refraction of lines of magnetic force.

"It works like this: Over each army on the Alaskan front the scientists have created a dome of electrical tension—a magnetic field. Any shell or drop bomb passing through this magnetic field is instantly heated to white heat by the electrical eddy currents induced in it by the field, and is thus caused to explode in mid-air.

"Every city is likewise protected by a Beckerley field. You know how each auto-copter, on leaving the city limits of San Francisco, has to stop and be pushed through an iron-shielded subway until it's beyond the Beckerley field? Well, that's because the gasoline in the tank would be heated to the flash point by the walls of its container."

"How about solid shot?" asked Sally.

"That can pass through a field, of course, but what chance has solid shot of doing much damage? Our own copters could down any possible fleet of enemy planes long before they could drop enough solid missiles to do appreciable harm to a city; and as for the Alaskan front, the most that either side could do would be to chip a few rocks in the Yukon Hills.

"No, the situation's a deadlock; the Khan is swept from the sea, but his enormous army prevents our invading Asia, and neither side can advance an inch in Alaska because of the Beckerley fields. It can't even become a war of attrition, because both the Asiatic Union and the United States are entirely self-supporting, and can never be starved into submission."

"Do you think so?" asked Sally Amber in an odd voice. Suddenly she shrugged her smooth, brown shoulders as if to change the subject. "Will Admiral Allen be here Saturday?" she asked casually.

"Why, no, I don't think—" Lister caught himself abruptly. Allen had told him, in the very strictest of confidence, of a proposed attempt to cut the Asiatic supply line to Alaska by a concentrated attack of Behring Strait. The Pacific fleet, idle since the engagement near the Marianas, was to sail secretly before dawn on Saturday.

He glared. "Why do you ask such a question?" he snapped. "If I knew, I shouldn't tell, and you know it."

Sally laughed. "Silly!" she chided. "It was just that I was considering having him and you and that flying detective, Jim Cass, to a little dinner at my apartment Saturday. You see, I still haven't met Jim Cass, and you've spoken of him so often that I'm curious. After all, if he's a friend of yours, Dick—" She smiled very tenderly at him.

Lister shook his head. "Captain Cass is no friend of mine," he declared. "He's just an officer of the military intelligence who breezes into my laboratory from time to time, and pokes around looking for clues and trouble. He gives me the creeps. I never knew such a cold-blooded man! He'd turn his own mother over to a firing squad, if he thought it would help win the war."

"Well, wouldn't you or I do as much for our country?" asked Sally. "And, besides, his very coldness intrigues me. I want to meet him."

"Suit yourself," said Lister. "Have we time for another swim?"

She puckered her lips disapprovingly. "Oh, no!" she exclaimed decidedly. "The water's so full of that horrible green slime that it's no pleasure to swim. Let's start back to town."

"It is bad," he agreed. "It's just a variety of conferva—what we commonly call algae. There have been some complaints of it in the drinking water, too. It's harmless, but they ought to chlorinate the city reservoir." He rose and stretched. "Let's dress and get started, then."

It was not quite 2:00 p. m., when they landed Sally's convertible helicopter in front of the building near the Presidio that served as the office and laboratory of the local unit of the Bureau of Military Biology and Bacteriology. Lister stepped reluctantly out of the machine, and turned to Sally at the wheel.

"Tonight?" he asked hopefully.

She shook her head. "Sorry. I have to dine with some family friends."

"Tomorrow night, then?"

"I shouldn't. I—"

"But you will," he stated positively. "Heaven knows if I'll be stationed here long, and I don't want to waste a moment."

"Why?" she asked sharply. "Do you expect to be transferred?"

He bit his tongue. "No, but—"

Needed distraction came. He whirled and saluted a dark, sinister-looking army officer descending the steps of the building.

"Sally, here's Captain Cass at last. I thought he'd be in today! Sir, this is the Sally Amber you've heard me talking about so much."

Jim Cass took the hand Sally extended. "No wonder Dick's been raving," he said, staring at her appraisingly with his cold, blue eyes. "I apologize for thinking he was nuts. I didn't believe he had the good taste—"

His stare changed to a puzzled frown. "Say, haven't we met before?"

"If we had," said Sally, "I wouldn't have forgotten it." But Captain Cass stood staring, long after her copter was indistinguishable among the cross currents of traffic.

Cass was no closer to the solution when he dropped in on Lister the following day. The biologist, in laboratory smock, was busy with the war-time routine of checking water samples from half a dozen coastal cities, and had but little time to listen to his superior.

"Oakland," he muttered, "bacterial count seven per c. c; that's normal. Monterey, eleven; that's safe. Vera Cruz—say, did you ever see so much algae in the drinking water? Look at that beaker on the window sill. That's after two hours' exposure to sunlight, and it's as green as pea soup already. What's more, I saw reports from Chicago that it's just the same there. And—this is queer—from London as well."

"What's that fuzz on the trees?" asked Cass thoughtfully, looking idly out of the window. "I never saw that here before."

"Yeah, I noticed that. It's just a tree lichen, something like Spanish moss. A cryptogamous plant—that is, a spore breeder. It's related to—By the Lord! It's conferva, too, just like the algae!"

"Well? So what?"

"So nothing, except that whatever has stimulated the algae in the sea and in the drinking water, has also stimulated the lichens and the fungi. The cryptogamoids are the sort of plants that grew on earth during the carboniferous age, the age of coal."

"Maybe we're in for another age of coal, huh?"

"Hardly," said Lister, laughing. "There are several theories as to what caused the carboniferous age, such as a higher concentration of carbon dioxide in the air, or a worldwide tropical climate, or intense sunspot activity, which would induce frequent and violent electrical storms on the earth, and hence produce an abnormal amount of ozone in the air. Ozone is a particularly dense form of oxygen, and is able to filter out the death rays—"

"Death rays?" exclaimed Cass, pricking up his ears. He had been paying very little attention to Lister, but here was something in his own line—something the military intelligence ought to know about. "Death rays?"

Lister laughed again. "Not the kind of death rays the army is interested in," he said. "But there are certain invisible rays of sunlight which have a fatal effect on living creatures. Ozone filters them out.

"It's one of the remarkable instances of the balance of nature that there is normally just enough ozone in the outer layers of the atmosphere to keep out the quantity of that invisible light which would be fatal to human life, and yet let in just enough to keep the algae within reasonable bounds. Now if—Say! I wonder!"

"You wonder what?"

"Nothing! Nothing at all!"

"Lister," said Cass pointedly, "you seem to be able to be very close-mouthed about some things, and to some people. I wonder how you are with women."

"What do you mean?" asked Lister, with a guilty premonition.

"Well, for example, you didn't happen to say anything to Miss Amber about the sailing of the fleet, did you?"

Lister flushed. He hadn't, of course; and yet she might have gathered it from some of his remarks. But then, what if she had?

"Of course not," he growled. "Speaking of the fleet," he added, "I'm going over to see Admiral Allen right now."

Arrived at the admiral's quarters, Lister came directly to the point. "Sir," he said, "I've been thinking about all these algae. At the rate they are increasing, you may find your whole fleet stalled in a mass of jelly before you get to Behring Strait."

"I've thought of that," Admiral Allen replied soberly, and yet with a twinkle in his eyes which Lister couldn't quite fathom.

"But have you heard the latest reports, sir?" Lister persisted. "The Chicago River is clogged. The stuff is beginning to plug the water mains everywhere. I know it's becoming a nuisance here in San Francisco. In Texas, the Spanish moss is beginning to collect in masses heavy enough to break tree branches.

"All over the country railroad ties are turning into pulpy beds of assorted fungi, puffballs, and a hundred other varieties. The resulting decay has even caused derailings. In the moister areas, trains actually have to plow their way through vast accumulations of lichens, which have found the shaded cuts and half-decayed ties an ideal environment in which to exercise their new vitality."

"It's even worse in Asia," the admiral replied. "They say that on the tundras the lichens are growing into heaps like haystacks on the railroads, and that the algae has blocked rivers and caused floods. That's why, even at the risk of getting our entire fleet stuck in the slime, we must attack the Khan while this unexplainable growth of plants is endangering his source of supplies."

"I didn't know that," said Lister.

"Well, keep it under your hat, and don't breathe it to a soul. It is secret information that has just come in from the intelligence service. Have you any idea as to the reason for all this? I was just going to send for you, when you showed up."

"Something may have caused an abnormal increase in the ozone of the outer layers of the atmosphere, and this ozone may be filtering out those wave lengths of sunlight which ordinarily hold algae in check."

But Admiral Allen was one of those practical men who have little patience with scientific explanations of anything. So he suggested, "Might it not be some new device of Asiatic warfare?"

"I hardly think so, sir. The Khan wouldn't use this weapon which appears to be hurting him even worse than it is us."

That evening, when Dick Lister and Sally Amber were seated in a restaurant, she again broached the subject of the algae.

"I hear it's even worse in Asia than in America," she said.

"How do you happen to know that?" he asked in surprise.

"It's so then? Oh, everybody isn't so close-mouthed as you, Dick," she replied demurely. She raised her lovely dark, innocent eyes.

"Do you suppose it might be an Asiatic weapon? Or perhaps —since it seems to be even worse in Siberia than here—an American weapon?"

Embarrassed, he mumbled, "How should I know?"

"But you do know something about it, don't you?" she shot at him.

Caught off guard, he stumbled. "Eh? Oh—why, yes. The Beckerley fields—" He broke off, frowning in irritation.

"Sally," he growled, "that curiosity of yours is going to get you into trouble one of these days. This is war time, and feminine curiosity is no excuse for pumping officers. I know that you are O.K., but others might not trust you. How'd you like to stand court-martial as an Asiatic spy, just because you ask too many questions?"

"Perhaps I am one," said the girl, smiling and raising her delicately penciled brows.

"It's no joking matter, Sally. People have been shot against a wall for less than that."

"I can see," said the girl dryly, "that Captain Cass has been lecturing you."

"How—" began Lister, then bit his lip.

"How do I know? Oh, I can read men like a book—any woman can. Captain Cass doesn't like me. And I don't like men who don't like me."

She pouted prettily.

"I'm glad he doesn't," declared Lister. "It would suit me if nobody liked you, but me."

He recalled this conversation the next evening, when Cass strolled nosily into his laboratory, where he was working late over some analyses.

"Nice mess of algae," Cass observed, squinting at Lister's experimental tank. "They say the stuff is clogging the Atlantic harbors."

"You could damn near walk across the Golden Gate this morning," Lister replied, and went on to detail the latest news: train schedules disrupted in the northwest, ships stuck in harbors everywhere, even in the open seas, particularly the north Pacific.

But Captain Cass was not listening. He was leaning over Lister's glass topped desk, peering intently at something beneath the glass—a snapshot.

"What's this?" he asked sharply.

"Just a snap of Sally. Not a very good one; print's blurred."

"Um!" said Cass. His eyes narrowed. Then he said, irrelevantly, "Have you any theory about what's causing all this growth of algae?"

"Yes," Lister admitted, pursing up his lips judiciously. "But I'm not going off half-cocked. When I've verified certain points, I shall report to Washington—not to the intelligence service."

"Well, seeing as you won't tell the intelligence service anything, the intelligence service will tell you something—and for your own good. Listen carefully, and don't fly off the handle: I was attached to the Harbin legation three years ago, before the war. I got to know a lot about the Khan's eastern capital. Maybe you never heard of the woman called Princess Stephanie—or did you?"

"Yes. What about her?"

"Wait a minute. Stephanie was the daughter of Dmitri Kazarov, the Khan's chancellor. He was killed fifteen years ago in the Japanese revolution, and the Khan himself took over the raising of Stephanie. It wasn't given much publicity, but, in a town like Harbin, people talk, and they were still talking when I was there. It seemed the Khan gave her a queer education—a very queer one."

"What do you mean?"

"I mean he raised her to be the greatest spy in history. She was taught every important language, and to speak each like a native. She was taught to be at ease in every situation and every level of society. She learned military science, so as to be able to identify important information. And, when it began to be evident that she was going to be a very beautiful girl, she was even taught the knowledge of human nature! But above all—above all, I say—she learned to be cold and heartless, and immune to love. She can act the part of a woman in love, but there is no feeling in her—no feeling except the desire to serve Asia!"

"But I don't see—"

"You will. When Stephanie was sixteen—that was three years ago, when I was in Harbin—the Khan forbade her to appear in public, lest foreign residents learn her features and impair her usefulness. When she rode out-of-doors, no one was permitted within five hundred feet of her, and no one save her palace intimates really saw her face.

"But"—Cass grinned aggravatingly—"I happen to have extraordinary eyesight, as a copter observer should, and I used to watch her from the prescribed distance. Once I even turned a pair of night glasses on her. She was a beauty, all right."

"I begin to suspect, sir," said Lister grimly, "that you're about to say something you're going to be sorry for."

"Perhaps. Anyway, since the war began, there have been a lot of rumors about a brilliant feminine Asiatic spy—the Nightshade. It's my opinion that the Nightshade is the Princess Stephanie, and as for the rest, I know only this—that Sally Amber looks like Stephanie!"

"You're utterly insane!" blazed Lister. His voice rose. "It's ridiculous! Sally's no Asiatic. Does she look like an Oriental? Her skin is as white as marble—when she isn't suntanned, I mean. Her speech is thoroughly American. Her eyes—"

He stopped; suddenly he had visualized Sally Amber's eyes—dark, pure, lovely; but, beyond doubt, with the slightest possible oriental cast.

"Exactly!" declared Cass, in reply to Lister's unspoken thought.

"Lieutenant, how long have you known this girl? Are you sure that her tan is tan, and not her natural color? And isn't she about the right age? And doesn't she spend a lot of time cultivating the friendship of people like you, who possess important military knowledge? Whether she gets anything out of you is a different story, but you ought to know whether she tries, whether she ever asks leading questions, or anything like that."

"She doesn't!" snapped Lister, then groaned. He himself had chided the girl more than once on her curiosity. "Look here, captain," he said, "if Sally is an enemy spy—it's inconceivable—but if she is, I say, it's America first with me, much as I love her. Lay off of her, will you, and let me find out."

"I'm not so hard-boiled and pitiless as you think."

"How do you—"

"How do I know what you think of me? Because it's my business, as an intelligence officer, to know what people think. But, as I was saying, I'll trust you. I'll give you your chance. I'm flying tonight on a certain mission, and shall not return for two days. Until then, the case is in your hands. But, if you have not solved it by then, I shall take it over."

Lister's mental turmoil brooked no delay. Despite the fact that, if

Sally were dining out, she must already have left, he rushed across town to her apartment. She—or someone, at least—was home, for the library lights were glowing. He ignored the slow automatic elevator, and dashed up the four flights of steps to her floor.

He arrived in front of her door breathless and perspiring. There he paused, striving to calm himself.

Suddenly, he was aware of voices beyond the door. He listened, but it was impossible to distinguish words. He fancied he heard the tones of a man, but even that was not a certainty.

He rang the bell. There was a sudden silence in the room beyond; and then, after a considerable interval, the sound of footsteps. Sally herself opened the door, her face seeming strained and tense. But she smiled as she recognized Lister.

"Dick!" she exclaimed. "What's the matter? You're breathless!"

He strode past her. The room was empty of occupants, save for Sally and himself. "To whom were you talking?" he asked grimly.

"I was using the televisiphone. Why?"

"I thought I heard a man's voice in the room here."

"Dick!" she said reprovingly. "I had no idea your jealousy would lead to such imaginings." She looked up at him with her dark sober eyes. "You know you have no cause to be jealous."

"It isn't that," he replied miserably. Suddenly he burst out, "Sally, what were you doing in Harbin three years ago?"

If there was a momentary flicker in her eyes, it was almost imperceptible. "Why, I was traveling. You know I love to travel."

"You say you saw the woman Stephanie there," he pursued. "Did anyone ever tell you that you looked like her?"

Decidedly her eyes widened now. "Why—yes. Of course I've heard that. But, Dick, you don't think—" She laughed. "How absurd! You don't think that I'm the Nightshade, do you?"

"Who said anything about the Nightshade?" he snapped. "How did you know that Stephanie and the Nightshade are the same person?"

"Why, everybody hears those rumors, Dick."

"You mean that you hear everybody's rumors," he returned grimly. "Why are you so interested in everything that has to do with the war or the service—everything from fleet sailings to algae? Sally, you're not telling me the truth."

"How ridiculous!" she indignantly declared. Then, suddenly, her mood changing, she moved close to him, looking up at him out of innocent, dark eyes. "You trust me, don't you?"

"Heaven knows I want to!"

Her lovely, provocative lips smiled. "Then kiss me!" she whispered.

He obeyed, fiercely. As always, her lips burned like soft fire, but, suddenly she threw back her head, and thrust her hands against him, as though to push away from his embrace. One of her scarlet finger nails drew a sharp gash across his throat. With hurt surprise in his eyes, he released her.

"You—were hurting me," she explained, apologetically. But her eyes were watching him like a cat. "I'm sorry I scratched you."

"It's nothing," he muttered. He felt curiously dizzy—no wonder, he thought, in the grip of such violent and opposing emotions. But abruptly he found himself sitting in a chair with his head on his hands, and the room seemed to gyrate around him like the chain of a copter.

Through a haze of dizziness he heard a man's voice, and then Sally's in answer. "No, no," she said. "This was much better. If I'd called you there would have been a fight and a disturbance, and see how peacefully he sinks into stupor."

"I bow to you, Kazarovna," said the man. "There is but one Stephanie."

"I am glad that it turned out as it did," said Sally's voice.

"He is the one who knows about the algae. And now Asia shall know."

When next Lister was aware of a world about him, it was a world of a most unstable nature. Minutes passed before he realized that he was in a plane, soaring over an apparently endless expanse of brilliant white clouds. There was a further interval before he perceived that Sally Amber was sitting, calmly smoking, beside the man who piloted the machine, and that he himself was handcuffed very effectively to the aluminum arms of his seat. His head ached dully. Then, full realization dawned upon him. He was a prisoner in the hands of agents of the Khan.

His movement caught the girl's attention. She rose and made her way to the seat facing him.

"I hope you're not feeling too ill," she said gently. "I'm sorry, Dick. Drugging you was necessary."

"Then it's true!" he groaned. "You are the Nightshade—a sneaking Asiatic spy!"

"Like a sneaking American spy," she retorted. "Dick, I serve my country in the best way I can, just as you and that Cass person and the rest of the Americans serve yours."

She smiled. "He's a clever fellow, that Captain Cass. I'm afraid his suspicions will damage my value in America."

"Well, not until—" He bit his lip, and hurried on, "Of course he will. He'll get those snapshots I have of you, and turn them over to his department. You're cooked as a spy from now on, Sally."

"Oh, not that bad," she said. "You forget that every picture you have of me was taken with my camera. My camera is a very queer little mechanism; when I use it, it takes sharp, clear pictures, but when my friends use it, somehow the prints seem to come out blurred. Or hadn't you noticed that?"

He had, of course. He asked glumly, "Where are we headed for?"

"Asia," said Sally.

"Yeah, I thought so, since we're in a plane instead of a copter." Pound for pound and horse power for horse power, Lister knew that the planes were still more efficient than the copters, and the fact that Sally was using a plane meant a long flight.

"Why?" he asked, after a moment's silence.

"Don't you know? Because we have to have certain information from you. I'm sure it won't do any good to offer you safety for it, Dick; but I can promise, if it makes any difference to you."

"It doesn't," he responded grimly. "I won't sell my country for my personal safety. Anyway, I haven't the least idea what information you think I can give you. Your bacteriologists are as good as ours; our epidemics haven't been any more successful than yours."

She shook her soot-black hair. "Not bacteriology nor epidemics, Dick—algae!"

"Algae! Why?"

"Because you know the causes of this plague of slime in water, and lichens on land. It's an American weapon, and Asia needs the secret. It means everything—everything to us!"

"Indeed?" he said guardedly. "Why everything?"

"Don't act so innocent, Dick. You know quite well what the plague of lichens is doing in Siberia. It's clogging the rail lines, and the algae is blocking the rivers. You know how important it is to keep our Alaskan expeditionary force supplied with coal and oil to power the Beckerley fields, and you know that if our fields fail for lack of fuel, the war's over. We're licked.

"You Americans use Alaskan coal, but our coal has to come all the way from the Stanovoi Mountains, either by water across the Sea of Okhotsk, or by rail up through Dezhnev. And it's becoming impossible to keep the rails open; Siberia is being strangled by your accursed lichens."

"Well, what about the water route?"

"Water! Ships are stalled all over the seven seas. Look there!"

He glanced through the floor window at the Pacific, five thousand feet below, visible now through a vast opening in the clouds. The sea had a curious aspect; it was not blue, but brilliant grass-green. Peering closer, he made out two tiny vessels idle on the surface.

"As bad as that!" he muttered, wondering what was happening to Allen's mighty fleet. Would the admiral attempt to cross the choked ocean? To Sally he said, "That's fine. The more strangled Siberia gets, the better it suits me."

For the first time in their acquaintance a sign of irritation showed in her face. "It won't be for long!" she snapped angrily. "We'll get the secret out of you. Make no mistake about that Dick."

"And you," he said thoughtfully, "are sweet little Sally Amber, who said that she loved me."

Suddenly, her face was gentle. "And if I do love you?" she murmured. "If I do, would that make a difference to you, Dick?"

He laughed bitterly. "Do you think I'd believe you now? I know all about Princess Stephanie and her education. If you love anybody at all, it's the Khan!"

"Not the Khan, but Asia," she said. "The Khan is nothing to me, except for what he means to my country. For he himself, Dick, trained me from childhood to be immune to love. And yet —and yet, Dick—I have never met a man whom I—like—as I do you. You mean less to me than Asia, but more to me than any human being in the world."

"And that," he sorrowfully asserted, "is another one of your pretty lies."

For a long moment, she was silent. "No. It isn't a lie," she said at last, rising and returning to her place beside the pilot.

She addressed not another word to Lister until seven hours later, when they were soaring over Honshu and snow-tipped Fujiyama slid beneath. Then she returned to the seat facing him, smiled very gently, and said softly, "I am terribly unhappy about this, Dick."

"Humph!" he said. "You ought to be triumphant."

"But I'm not. Listen to me, Dick. The Khan's intelligence division is not gentle. A number of the operatives are Mongols, and their methods of extracting information do not include kindness. It hurts me to think of you under torture, Dick."

"You ought to have thought of that last night."

"But I can save you from it. If you'll tell me what I want to know about the plague of algae and lichens, I'll guarantee your safety. Isn't that the best way—for both of us?"

"No, Sally. I'm not saying that I have the information you want, but you can be sure that, whether I have it or not, I'll never tell Asia anything that might help."

She sighed and left him, but her glorious, dark eyes were troubled. They were still troubled when the great Khingan range loomed on the horizon, and the plane slanted down into Harbin. She even seemed to pale when at last a slant-eyed guard took the key from her, and released Lister from his seat; and she followed the grim parade, as half a dozen men herded him into the centuries-old stone fortress that served as a military prison.

She did not enter the dark stonewalled cell; but, as the door swung shut, Lister glimpsed her pale face in the corridor. Her lips formed a silent phrase; he could have sworn that it was, "I'm sorry."

Well, it was too late now for her sorrow to help him, even if he believed in its sincerity. And he smiled bitterly, as he thought of the wild mistake that had led to his abduction. The algae and the lichens! Asia strangling in the grip of a plague that arose from so simple a cause that—if he told—a schoolboy could see the remedy.

Luckily for America, the cryptogams nourished most luxuriantly in Asia; and, until he told, all advantage lay with the Western continent. Until he told! He ceased to smile, and set his jaw grimly. He was not going to tell. Torture or none, he had to be strong enough to keep silent.

Hours passed. He heard conversations in the corridor outside, but they were in some Asiatic tongue, and meant nothing to him. Then a chance colloquy in *lingua Franca* told him that the Khan was not in Harbin, but was still with the troops on the Alaskan front. At last a guard brought him a jug of water, slimy-green with algae, and a slab of coarse bread; but this man, a Mongol, spoke neither English nor *lingua Franca*, or at least refused to speak them.

It was deep night when four grim Orientals and a stolid Siberian led him from his cell to a chamber that seemed sunk far underground. A single, dim electric light illuminated it, and a dozen pairs of cold eyes surveyed him—and one pair that was not cold. Sally Amber sat at the head of the narrow table, and she met his gaze with eyes that were wide, troubled, and apprehensive.

Then she addressed him. "Dick," she said softly, "I have told the interlocutory committee that you will give them what knowledge you have concerning this plague of mosses and algae. They have promised me your safety if you tell, and I have assured Comrade Plotkin that you would."

"Then, as usual, you lied." said Lister grimly.

Plotkin spoke out of the depths of his beard. "You see, Kazarovna," he rumbled, "only one method works with these stubborn American apes. I think it best we try that method."

"Oh, no!" gasped Sally Amber. "Let me question him first. He'll tell me. I can get it from him. Please—" She broke off suddenly as Plotkin's icy eyes surveyed her curiously.

"Will you tell?" he asked Lister, and then, at the latter's stubborn silence, "Very well. The pincers under the armpits first, I think. An ounce or so of flesh from the proper places can sometimes unblock the stream of information."

Sally—or Stephanie—choked back a sob and covered her eyes. The four Mongol guards forced Lister's arm upward; for a moment, he struggled, but realized instantly that it was utterly useless. The stolid Siberian seized a glittering little instrument, and the pincers tore a ragged tatter of flesh from his armpit. He bit his lip fiercely to suppress the groan of pain that sought utterance, but there was no sound in the chamber save Sally's stifled sob.

"Why so unstrung, Kazarovna?" asked Plotkin amiably. "Surely the Princess Stephanie has witnessed more extreme measures than this."

She smiled wanly. "Of course. It's just that I haven't yet recovered from my sojourn in America—a—a horrible place!"

Plotkin nodded and turned back to Lister. "Shall we try it again?" He smiled. "Or would you prefer a variation?"

"Neither," said the biologist, "I'll tell." Impassively he met the startled, relieved, unbelieving eyes of Sally. If she was acting, he thought, it was certainly good acting!

"Good—good!" rumbled Plotkin. "You're much wiser—or at least less stubborn—than some of our countrymen whom we have found it necessary to question. Now then, let us hear the secret."

"You'd better take this down carefully," said Lister. "It's rather intricate."

He waited as Plotkin spoke in Russian to a man at his side, then began; "The plague of algae and lichens," he said slowly, "is due to the great increase in numbers of thallogens. If the conferva were checked, the trouble would disappear."

"And what," barked Plotkin, "are thallogens?"

"Thallogens are the third grand division of the cryptogamia. The group consists of the ulvae and fuci, besides the conferva."

"Can't you put that in understandable language?" snapped Plotkin.

"I can express scientific information only in the language of science," said Lister, his eyes on Sally's fascinated ones. "Your own scientists will have to translate it for you."

"Is that all?" asked the Siberian eagerly.

"That is all. Reduce the confervae, and there will be less thallogens. And when there are less thallogens, the algae and lichens will cease to trouble you. It's really very simple."

"Take him back to his cell," rumbled Plotkin. "And this had better be true, my friend, unless you crave further treatment."

"Every word of it is true," Lister asserted.

It was still deep night when, three hours later, the door of his cell opened, and a slim figure slipped stealthily in. For a moment he thought it was a boy; then he recognized Sally, wearing the shorts and rolled hose of a copterman. She closed the door quietly behind her, then rushed abruptly into his arms.

"I can't stand it!" she sobbed. "Why did you do it? Plotkin is furious—insane with rage. He'll have you rotted bit by bit with acid! He'll—he'll—Why did you trick him, Dick?"

Lister looked down into her white face. "Is this acting, too?" he asked coolly. "After all, the Princess Stephanie, the Nightshade, isn't supposed to be able to care what happens to a man."

"But I do! I love you, Dick. I care for nothing except you and Asia, but I can't bear to see you killed or tortured even for Asia." She paused, suppressing her sobs.

"Plotkin is wild," she said. "He wired a copy of your statement to the university at Tsitsihar, and back came the scornful reply that all that your words meant was that the plague of algae is due to an increase in the amount of algae."

He smiled. "Well? Isn't that true?"

"Yes, but—Oh, Dick, it's becoming horrible! They've kept the cities supplied with water by adding calcium chloride to the supply, but all through the country—all through the world, I guess—wells are choked and rivers smothered, and oceans have become heaving masses of slime. And on land the mosses spread like flames of gray fire!"

He was still suspicious, though he held the girl tightly in his arms. "Is this an attempt to play on my sympathies?" he asked. "I warn you, Sally, I'll tell you nothing."

"I don't care whether you do or not! Don't you understand, Dick? I love you!"

'If you love me, you'll help me escape from here." She pushed herself out of his arms, and stared at him with indignation at his disbelief.

"And why else do you think I came?" she asked in a very low voice. "Follow me, quickly, before Plotkin cools down enough to put his mind on the details of your torture."

She stepped to the door, rapping sharply. It opened instantly, and they passed into the dim corridor beside a young Russian guard who looked at Sally with tragic eyes. She spoke softly; the man extended his bared arm, and the girl scratched it hastily with one of her finger nails. Lister watched the man as he sank slowly into a limp sprawl on the floor.

"Thus it will seem like American trickery," she whispered. "But I am afraid he will die for treason, nonetheless."

"Why did he do it?"

"Because," she said simply, "he loves me." Lister followed her up a narrow flight of stone steps, wondering how many of the barred doors in the corridor hid American prisoners. At last, she paused. "Wait here," she whispered, and moved from his view along a passage.

He heard a low-voiced conversation in Chinese, and then Sally was at his side again. "Come on," she called softly. "I've sent this one with a fake message to Plotkin."

Lister followed her up yet another flight of steps, and emerged suddenly into starlight. They had attained the roof of the structure, and he glanced apprehensively at the lights of Harbin all around. Sally was slipping toward a copter, a tiny, single-man observer.

"Quick!" she breathed. "Get in."

"Both of us?" He frowned doubtfully at the tiny craft. "We must. For I have to show you what to do. This alone would not carry you far."

He crowded in beside her. The tiny cabin swung like a pendulum as the vertical screw whirred and whined, and bored its way heavily aloft. Sally flashed her green passage light, waiting anxiously for the reply from the ground.

"There!" she exclaimed in relief. "They've turned off this section of the Beckerley field. I have a pass, but if they had discovered your escape they might have blocked all passage—especially mine, I think; for I am sure that Plotkin has ceased to trust me."

The craft whined into darkness. The lights of the city diminished and dimmed; and, at last, Sally relaxed, leaning more comfortably against him in the close quarters of the cabin.

"We're beyond searchlights at last," she said. "Now they'll have to wait until dawn to pursue us, and by dawn we might be anywhere in this half of Asia, for all that they can tell. If this corkscrew only holds together—"

It did. When the red sunrise flashed up on the sea, they were directly over a narrow promontory that struck south into the waters. Lister gasped as he saw those waters, for surely this was the most amazing sea ever glimpsed by earthly eyes, at least since the plesiosaur looked over the oceans of the carboniferous age hundreds of millions of years ago.

It was a brilliantly smooth, green sea, seeming at first as motionless as turf. But, as the copter dropped toward the beach, Lister could distinguish motion, a slow heaving of the slime as if the vast expanse were breathing. There were no breakers, for the algae had at last tamed storm and wind, and the seas permitted the wind to slip as smoothly above them as if the waters had been covered with a film of oil. The one thing that sent a tremor of disgust through Lister was the sight of sea birds stalking dismally over a crust of slime that had dried enough to support them, gobbling up billions of flies.

Sally wasted not a glance on the scene. "The south cape of Taiwan," she said, as the copter grounded on a slimy beach, "or, as you call it, Formosa. There's a boat here—"

"A boat? How can we use a boat—in that?"

"Listen a moment. In that shed, there's one of the experimental sidewheelers, a quick adaptation by our scientists, who had foreseen this outcome, if the algae were not checked. Side-wheels can push a light hull right over the algae. They don't foul like propellers. This one has a dynoline engine, and a range of about a thousand miles."

"A thousand miles! I can't get anywhere on that!"

"You can get as far as I want you to get," she retorted with narrowed eyes. "You can reach Hong Kong—that's British—or you can make Haiphong in French Indo-China. Hong Kong is much the closer."

"But they're neutral! I'll be interned, if I go into a neutral port. I want to get back to America and my job."

"And I," said Sally softly, "want to see to it that you don't. I'm being enough of a traitor to Asia now, without letting a dangerous enemy like you return to service. All I want is to see you safe, Dick."

She turned away, and he followed her to the shed she had pointed out. There was the boat, true enough, a thirty-foot, open affair with six-foot paddle wheels like a miniature old Mississippi side-wheeler.

"Do you see this?" asked the girl, indicating a curious device of twisted glass tubing. "That's a sun-alembic. You put sea water in it, and the evaporation creates a partial vacuum in which the sea water can be distilled for drinking. The sun does it, just as it does with rain.

"Under here is concentrated food for about a month. Can you take care of a dynoline engine? If the algae clog the cooling coils, you must stop and clean them at once."

"I know all that, but what about you, Sally? Will you be safe after this?"

"I can take care of myself." Her tone was confident enough, but Lister could see that she was under a terrific strain in this struggle between duty and desire. "Oh, Dick," she said shakily, "if this war is ever over—"

"It won't be long now. As soon as the Khan's supply of fuel to Alaska fails him, he's ended."

"Ah, but he's laying—" She caught herself, flushing miserably.

"Laying a pipe line, eh?" finished Lister. "I rather thought he would. He'll power the Beckerley fields with oil, eh?"

Sally laughed bitterly. "The downfall of the Nightshade!" she declaimed. "No wonder they fear love in a spy. Dick, that is the first slip that I've ever made, and my one consolation is that long before you can get to any place from where you could send that information to America, it will be too late. The work will be completed and protected by fields. And so—goodby."

With the feel of her lips still on his, he watched the copter flutter its way into the north; then turned to the craft he was to use, whose only name was a Chinese ideograph. It slid easily into the slip and, without further hesitation, he started the engine, engaged the paddles, and was on his way.

His progress was a queer species of locomotion. The blades threw up vast lumps of green slime that fell behind with sullen, splashless *plumps*; and the light craft, thrust forward by the incredibly powerful dynoline engines, slid easily along the surface of the maggot-infested slime. It was not unduly slow; he judged that the boat made twenty-five knots.

Formosa was a receding shadow when he passed the first stalled ship. This was a Dutch freighter, and the crew—or what was left of them, since many had doubtless been put ashore by copter—

crowded the rail to watch his passage. He waved, but there was never a sign of response.

Suddenly, he realized the cause of the grim silence; his craft bore gold and purple stripes—the colors of the Khan—and the Dutch, with Borneo, Celebes, and New Guinea in the very shadow of the vast Asiatic Union, had no love for the Khan.

His coil clogged, and he paused to clean the slime from the screens. It was at this moment that the idea struck him; he sat suddenly erect, staring eastward where the China Sea met the mighty Pacific. Why did he have to go to Hong Kong or Haiphong —or any neutral port, for that matter?

What other possibilities were there? He glanced at the map of the East Indies, affixed to the cowl of the motor. There was Luzon, of course; but the Philippines, during their half century of independence, had grown far closer to Asia, in sympathy, than to the United States.

There were the Marianas, where admiral Allen had all but annihilated the Asiatic fleet, and where surely there must be an American garrison, if he could but reach them. But the Marianas lay two thousand miles out in the Pacific, close to Guam. He had fuel for half that distance, but—

He swung the craft about and set it lurching back toward the Dutch freighter. The maintenance crew watched him sullenly as he approached. He pulled close under the hull and shouted, "Any of you understand English?"

A man pushed to the rail. "Yes! What do you want?"

"Listen! I'm American, not Asian. Look!" He was not in uniform, since the biological branch did not require it, but he displayed his identification tag, with its red-white-and-blue shield plainly visible.

There was a stir. "What do you want?" asked the man above him, but in friendlier tones.

"Just some information. I want to know if there's an American or British ship stalled between here and Guam. I want to buy some fuel. You been in touch with any?"

There was a long conversation in Netherlands dialect. At last Lister's informant spoke again. "De Britisher *Resolute*—she stuck—by latitude 21' 20" and longitude 135' 60"."

Lister looked at his map, marking the position. It would do; it was almost exactly a thousand miles east of his present position, and might be a close gamble with his fuel, but it was worth the try. If he reached the Britisher and got fuel, he could then certainly make Guam or the Marianas, and give to the American army the news that the lichens had blocked the Siberian railroads, thus cutting off the fuel supply to the Khan's Alaskan Beckerley fields, but that the Khan was frantically laying a pipe line.

Between the giving out of the Khan's coal supply and the arrival of his first oil, there might be a brief gap of time, during which his Beckerley fields would be dead. If America only knew this, and could strike then, the war would be won. Lister must try to get the information to America in time!

So he set the boat lurching away into the east. Little by little, the Dutch ship faded toward the horizon, and Formosa was a dark cloud sinking ever lower. At last he was alone on a dead, green sea that barely moved, and his passage left no wake save a slightly darker green scraping, that slowly closed behind him. No fin cut the slimy surface, and but few birds soared, for their slime-bred prey was too abundant to draw them far from land.

He set his course carefully on a great circle, to conserve his fuel. The malodorous slime sickened him with its stench. The perpetual lurching of his craft added to his nausea. Day faded into a starry darkness, and darkness into day.

He made it. At the second midnight, with scarcely a pint of dynoline remaining in his tank, the lights of the *Resolute* flashed out of the darkness.

But convincing the captain was almost as difficult a job as the passage itself.

"It's deuced irregular!" that official grunted. "We're neutrals." But at last, because England had India and Papua and the Malay States, and hated Asia and all its component parts by tradition and policy, the British captain acceded to Lister's request, and Lister set out again with a full tank.

He had tried to get the captain to send a code message by radio to America for him, but to that the captain had proved adamant.

Early next morning, on glancing back, he spied a plane, winging swiftly out of the shadows that still clouded the west and the distant China Seas. Soon it arrived, and circled far above him, then slanted downward in a wide spiral. The double-headed golden eagle of the Khan's air force glittered on its wings.

The machine swung close. An arm waved vigorously, gesturing in the direction of the west. The pilot was ordering him back.

Lister stared with narrowed eyes, but permitted his boat to jog right ahead. He was not going to be turned back so easily as that. All the same, he had a feeling anything but comfortable, for he was completely at the mercy of the Asiatic aviator, should the latter choose to use bullet or bomb.

The plane circled again. Suddenly Lister realized with a start of amazement that the craft was attempting to land—to alight on that sticky mass of heaving slime! It was impossible!

But the plane seemed able to achieve the impossible. Its pontoons skipped lightly over the treacherous stuff, bounding toward him. It was all but down safely, and then—then the inevitable! Either the plane dipped or the sea heaved—Lister could not tell which—and the idling propeller struck a mass of green slime. Very gently, the plane lifted its tail and nosed over, the green corruption spewing from the spinning blades. And the pilot—for a single instant Lister had a clear view of the form that was catapulted through the air—was plunged into the impassive algae. All that remained was a quickly filling depression and the sinking plane.

But he had seen enough. Sally Amber! It was Sally who struggled somewhere in the depths of that nauseating sea. And he—he was as helpless to aid her as though he were a thousand miles away.

He spun the wheel; the boat bounced and jogged toward the spot. As near as he could bring it without disturbing the gradually closing dent in the slimy surface of the sea, he halted the craft. He seized the twenty-foot rope fastened to the bow, and tied one end of the rope firmly around his arm. Then, fixing his gaze on the spot, he plunged down into the slime.

It was like trying to swim in heavy oil. To move his arms at all required a great effort, and then he was not sure whether he was going down, or up, or sidewise, or was just churning. The stuff clogged his nose, his eyes, his ears—even his mouth, when in an unguarded moment he opened it.

His hand struck something solid. It was an instant before he realized that it was Sally's ankle. He clutched it in a grasp of desperation, and gave a yank on the rope tied to his arm. Pulling in on the rope was difficult, as he had only one free hand with which to work. Once he lost hold of the rope in the slime, and had to start all over again, groping along it from where it was tied to his arm.

He scarcely knew when he reached the surface, so thick was the coating of muck he carried with him. He thrust the girl across the gunwale, and then had to stop to clear his nose and mouth before he could even breathe. He clambered into the boat.

Sally was not unconscious, but her nausea made her almost as green as the algae she clawed out of her eyes.

"Thank you, Dick," she said, "for the rescue. I'm ashamed that I needed it."

"Why are you here, Sally?"

Her eyes hardened a bit. "Why are you here, Dick? I told you to make for Hong Kong or Haiphong."

"But I didn't promise to, Sally."

"Perhaps not, but do you think I can let you get to an American ship or port, with the information you have? It's bad enough that I let it slip, and that I helped you to escape, but I will not play traitor to Asia any further than that! Do you understand?"

"How'd you find me?"

"It occurred to me, after I left you, that you might try just what you did. I got back to Harbin before Plotkin thought of connecting me with your escape—if he's thought of it yet—so I was able to get a plane. I flew over the China Sea between Taiwan and Hong Kong, until I was sure you weren't on that route. Then I flew east.

"For two days, I've been scouring this area. You see, I anticipated that you'd head for Guam. But now, Dick, you're going where I say. We're going back to Luzon. The Philippines are neutral, but they're friendly to Asia, so I can have you interned there, and yet, with a little influence, go free myself. Start your engine."

He did. The boat took up its eastward course. "Turn about!" she snapped. When he merely smiled, she reached suddenly into the bosom of her aviator's shirt and produced a tiny Japanese automatic, one of the diminutive nine-caliber, but deadly with its high-velocity, chrome-jacketed bullets. "Put about, Dick!"

With a movement so casual that she was caught completely off guard, he kicked the weapon from her hand, and it spun off into slime. "We go my way, Sally," he said quietly.

She sobbed, "I ought to have killed you! But I couldn't, and this is the result."

Abruptly she turned her glorious eyes upon him. "Dick, do you know what will happen to me, if you take me to Guam? You know what they do to spies! Do you want me to be shot against a wall?"

"Lord!" he muttered. "I didn't think of that. Listen, Sally. The Pelew Islands are Japanese, and they're not far off my course. I'm going to land you there about midnight, and you're going to be thoroughly bound, and very tightly gagged, so you can't rouse any pursuit. After the war is over, maybe you will forgive me."

"I forgive you now, Dick," she said softly, but with a puzzling note in her voice. "The Nightshade is dead. I'm no good as a spy when you're involved. But I warn you that I shall still try to defeat you!"

Suddenly he noticed something which altered all his plans! Staring out over the horrible, slimy sea, he noticed a change. In addition to the green, there were now vast patches of brown—of dying algae!

For a moment he failed to grasp the significance of this. Then, so suddenly that Sally jumped, he shouted, "I see it all now! It has happened!"

"Wh-what?"

"The Khan's Beckerley fields are off in Alaska! His Siberian railroads are blocked at last by the fungi! He's out of fuel! It can't be our fields that are off, for our coal mines are too close behind our lines to be cut off in this way."

"How can you know that any Beckerley fields are off?" asked Sally.

"The—the—" He caught himself then proceeded, "We're not going to Pelew Island, after all. We're going to Guam. This information can't wait; for, if the American lines know it and advance at once, the war's over. Our Beckerley fields are on, and yours are off!"

"How—how do you know?"

"I'll tell you, for it can't do any harm now. You wanted to know what I knew about this plague of algae, didn't you? Well, I'll tell you, Sally. It isn't an American weapon; it's an accident!"

"An—accident?"

"Yes, or a by-product. It's the result of the Beckerley fields. I got the hunch when I learned that the center of the trouble seemed to be Alaska. Up in Alaska there are two enormous fields of force within a few hundred feet of each other, ours and yours. Between them is a hundred-mile-long zone of terrific electrical strain. What's the result? Ozone! Tons of ozone pouring up into the air, until the very envelope of air around the earth was affected.

"The normal ozone content increased, and this layer of ozone around the earth cut off the sun's death rays which had been maintaining the balance of nature. Relieved from the restraining influence of the death rays, the cryptogamia—the lichens and fungi and algae—increased to abnormal quantities.

"But it's over now. Ozone is unstable and goes rapidly back to normal. The ozone in the air is decreasing. The death rays are getting through again.

"How do I know? Because the algae are dying, and that can mean only one thing—that there are no longer two Beckerley fields opposing each other in Alaska, pouring ozone into the air. There is only one Beckerley field—ours. The Khan's shield is gone, and all we need do is advance!"

Sally was very pale now. "I wish you hadn't told me this," she whispered. "Oh, Dick, don't you see that it means that I just have to stop you? If you love me, throw me into the slime of the sea, for I'd rather die than live these next few hours trying to kill you!"

His triumphant face sobered. "Hours?" he echoed. "It will take us three days to reach Guam. Sally, when I need sleep, I'm going to tie you up. And I hope you don't resist, because Lord knows I don't want to hurt you."

But she yielded quite submissively when, a few hours later, he twisted the painter rope about her wrists and ankles. He remembered her trick of the drugged finger nail, and carefully avoided giving her another similar opportunity. Then he set and locked the gyro steering compass, and curled up on one of the seats to sleep.

When he awoke the boat was still slapping along across the slime. Sally was still securely tied and apparently in the same position, but the bottom of the boat was wet with some colorless fluid.

"What's this?" he snapped.

"It's your fuel," said Sally triumphantly. "I drained the tank."

He gasped! But in a moment he broke out in a chuckle of relief. "That isn't dynoline," he said. "That's the fresh water from the sun-alembic I was saving against a cloudy day. The water tank's air-tight, and the algae can't get in."

Sally sagged despondently in her place. "Will you untie me?" she asked dully. "I'm very cramped."

He ventured an attempt to sleep only once more, and this time lying full length against the fuel tank, while he bound Sally not only hand and foot, but lashed her to the gunwale as well. And when he awakened, she had kicked the sun-alembic to bits.

"Why'd you do that?" he asked angrily. "Although we don't need water for one more day of travel, it would be a convenience."

"I did it so that if we miss Guam we'll be dead before some scouting American plane happens to run across us."

"We won't miss Guam," he promised grimly.

As the hot, stinking day wore on, the grueling grind began to tell on Lister. All about them the algae was turning brown, and the stench was almost unbearably nauseating.

"I'm going bats," he told the girl. "A crazy poem keeps hammering at my head. I've got to pass it on, or I shall go bats. Did you ever hear the short-short-short story about Algy? All this rotting algae is what suggested it to me, I guess."

Sally turned intent catlike eyes on him, aroused from her lethargy by the possibility of his cracking.

"Go on. Tell it to me," she urged insidiously.

He laughed harshly, discordantly, gave his head a violent shake, and ran the back of his hand across his tired eyes.

"It goes like this," he said:

"Bear met Algy.
Bear et Algy.
Bear was bulgy.
Bulge was Algy."

Suddenly, he gave a wild laugh. "That's all wrong this time!" he declared. "By Heaven! The bear isn't eating Algy this time. Algae is eating the bear—the Siberian bear. We've got them licked, if we ever reach Guam."

"We never will reach Guam," the girl taunted him.

"Won't we?" he exclaimed. "Look!" A low shore line showed in the darkening east. "Guam!" he announced, sober and sane once more.

Sally was disconsolate. "I've lost, then," she whimpered. "Please, Dick, be kind to me, and—let me kiss you now, in case anything happens."

He knew what she meant. He had worried enough over the question of what would happen to the lovely Nightshade; for, despite his assurance, he knew that Captain Cass was aware of Sally's identity. The two days of grace were long since up. Cass would have reported the circumstances of Lister's disappearance.

Cass' description of Sally, together with the blurred photographs in Lister's office, would certainly identify the girl. Nothing could save her from a wall at sunrise. So he drew her into his arms with a tenderness born of despair.

Just in time he realized her intent. He caught her wrist as she struck with her drugged finger nail at his throat.

"Damn you, Sally!" he blazed. "Now I'm going to give you a dose of your own medicine. There's only one way you're safe to have around, and that is unconscious!"

But she read his purpose. Before he could seize her forefinger, she had clenched it into a stubborn little fist, and she fought him with a strength that was amazing. But at last he saw the way: disregarding her blows against his face, he slowly, inexorably, crushed her clenched fist in his hand. She cried out in pain as her own finger nails were driven into the flesh of her palm, and then, suddenly, her eyes widened, fluttered, and closed, and she sank first to her knees, then in a limp heap at his feet.

It was deep night when he carried her up the side of the U. S. cruiser *Dallas*, stalled in the algae off Agana. Thrusting her into the arms of the ship's surgeon, he rushed to report to the commanding officer his information; that he knew, from the browning of the algae, that the Khan's Alaskan Beckerley field was off. The message did not need to wait for coding, for America still held the secret of non-interceptible radio.

Scarcely an hour later came back the news that America had triumphed in Alaska.

Later in the night came the flash that the Khan was dead—his body had been positively identified. America broadcast this news to the world.

By morning, rioting and dissension had broken out all over Asia. The Asiatic Union was disintegrating. It was the beginning of the end.

There was jubilation abroad the *Dallas*, but Dick Lister could not share in it. True, yes, he had saved America. He was a great national hero. The president in person had radioed his thanks.

So Dick Lister pretended to be elated, to join in the celebration—for, of course, he had to. But, through it all, two faces haunted him: the piquant oriental features of the girl he loved, and the grim, inexorable, duty-mad features of Captain Cass. Regardless of the fact that the war was now over and won, regardless of the part which Lister had played in winning it, Cass would never rest until he had brought death to the arch-spy of the late enemy.

And so, as soon as he could, Lister broke away from the jollification, and dragged his leaden feet toward the ship's hospital. There he stood with the ship's doctor, looking down on the still unconscious Sally.

"A very beautiful girl, your fiancée," said the doctor.

"Yes. We were kidnapped together by the Khan's spies, and she was really more important than I in accomplishing our escape. This is just exhaustion—and, of course, excitement." But he knew that Captain Cass would certainly spike that story.

"Well," observed the doctor, "your coming is almost the first excitement I've had out of this war. I hope you're right about the algae being over, for it's been ungodly dull being stuck here in all this slime. One casualty is all I've seen, and that one at a distance. A young officer tried to land his plane on the algae a week ago, nosed over, and was lost. They never recovered his body."

"It's a difficult thing to do—find a body in that green muck," said Lister reminiscently. "Who was he?"

"He was—let's see—a Captain Jim Cass. We knew who it was, 'cause we'd been expecting him."

Captain Jim Cass! A week ago. Then Cass had never returned to America. He had died before the end of the two days of grace which he had granted Lister. And his knowledge of Sally's identity had died with him. Now no one would ever know!

With a sob of joyous relief, Dick Lister dropped to his knees beside the sleeping form of the girl he loved.

Shifting Seas

It developed later that Ted Welling was one of the very few eyewitnesses of the catastrophe, or rather, that among the million and a half eyewitnesses, he was among the half dozen that survived. At the time, he was completely unaware of the extent of the disaster, although it looked bad enough to him in all truth!

He was in a Colquist gyro, just north of the spot where Lake Nicaragua drains its brown overflow into the San Juan, and was bound for Managua, seventy-five miles north and west across the great inland sea. Below him, quite audible above the muffled whir of his motor, sounded the intermittent clicking of his tri-panoramic camera, adjusted delicately to his speed so that its pictures could be assembled into a beautiful relief map of the terrain over which he passed. That, in fact, was the sole purpose of his flight; he had left San Juan del Norte early that morning to traverse the route of the proposed Nicaragua Canal, flying for the Topographical branch of the U. S. Geological Survey. The United States, of course, had owned the rights to the route since early in the century—a safeguard against any other nation's aspirations to construct a competitor for the Panama Canal.

Now, however, the Nicaragua Canal was actually under consideration. The over-burdened ditch that crossed the Isthmus was groaning under vastly increased traffic, and it became a question of either cutting the vast trench another eighty-five feet to sea level or opening an alternate passage. The Nicaragua route was feasible enough; there was the San Juan emptying from the great lake into the Atlantic, and there was Lake Managua a dozen miles or so from the Pacific. It was simply a matter of choice, and Ted Welling, of the Topographical Service of the Geological Survey, was doing his part to aid the choice.

At precisely 10:40 it happened. Ted was gazing idly through a faintly misty morning toward Ometepec, its cone of a peak plumed by dusky smoke. A hundred miles away, across both Lake Nicaragua and Lake Managua, the fiery mountain was easily visible from his altitude. All week, he knew, it had been rumbling and smoking, but now, as he watched it, it burst like a mighty Roman candle.

There was a flash of white fire not less brilliant than the sun. There was a column of smoke with a red core that spouted upward like a fountain and then mushroomed out. There was a moment of utter silence in which the camera clicked methodically, and then there was a roar as if the very roof of Hell had blown away to let out the bellows of the damned!

Ted had one amazed thought—the sound had followed too quickly on the eruption! It should have taken minutes to reach him at that distance—and then his thoughts were forcibly diverted as the Colquist tossed and skittered like a leaf in a hurricane. He caught an astonished glimpse of the terrain below, of Lake Nicaragua heaving and boiling as if it were the seas that lash through the Straits of Magellan instead of a body of landlocked fresh water. On the shore to the east a colossal wave was breaking, and there in a banana grove frightened figures were scampering away. And then, exactly as if by magic, a white mist condensed about him, shutting out all view of the world below.

He fought grimly for altitude. He had had three thousand feet, but now, tossed in this wild ocean of fog, of up-drafts and down-drafts, of pockets and bumps, he had no idea at all of his position. His altimeter needle quivered and jumped in the changing pressure, his compass spun, and he had not the vaguest conception of the direction of the ground. So he struggled as best he could, listening anxiously to the changing whine of his blades as strain grew and lessened. And below, deep as thunder, came intermittent rumblings that were, unless he imagined it, accompanied by the flash of jagged fires.

Suddenly he was out of it. He burst abruptly into clear air, and for a horrible instant it seemed to him that he was actually flying inverted. Apparently below him was the white sea of mist, and above was what looked at first glance like dark ground, but a moment's scrutiny revealed it as a world-blanketing canopy of smoke or dust, through which the sun shone with a fantastic blue light. He had heard of blue suns, he recalled; they were one of the rarer phenomena of volcanic eruptions.

His altimeter showed ten thousand. The vast plain of mist heaved in gigantic ridges like rolling waves, and he fought upward away from it. At twenty thousand the air was steadier, but still infinitely above was the sullen ceiling of smoke. Ted leveled out, turning at random north-east, and relaxed.

"Whew!" he breathed. "What—what happened?"

He couldn't land, of course, in that impenetrable fog. He flew doggedly north and east, because there was an airport at Bluefields, if this heaving sea of white didn't blanket it.

But it did. He had still half a tank of fuel, and, he bored grimly north. Far away was a pillar of fire, and beyond it to the right, another and a third. The first, of course, was Ometepec, but what were the others? Fuego and Tajumulco? It seemed impossible.

Three hours later the fog was still below him, and the grim roof of smoke was dropping as if to crush him between. He was going to have to land soon; even now he must have spanned Nicaragua and be somewhere over Honduras. With a sort of desperate calm he slanted down toward the fog and plunged in. He expected to crash; curiously, the only thing he really regretted was dying without a chance to say goodbye to Kay Lovell, who was far off in Washington with her father, old Sir Joshua Lovell, Ambassador from Great Britain.

When the needle read two hundred, he leveled off—and then, like a train bursting out of a tunnel, he came clear again! But under him was wild and raging ocean, whose waves seemed almost to graze the ship. He spun along at a low level, wondering savagely how he could possibly have wandered out to sea. It must, he supposed, be the gulf of Honduras.

He turned west. Within five minutes he had raised a storm lashed coast, and then—miracle of all miracles!—a town! And a landing field. He pancaked over it, let his vanes idle, and dropped as vertically as he could in that volley of gusty winds.

It was Belize in British Honduras. He recognized the port even before the attendants had reached him.

"A Yankee!" yelled the first. "Ain't that Yankee luck for you!"

Ted grinned. "I needed it. What happened?"

"The roof over this part of Hell blew off. That's all."

"Yeah. I saw that much. I was over it."

"Then you know more'n any of us. Radio's dead and there ain't no bloomin' telegraph at all."

It began to rain suddenly, a fierce, pattering rain with drops as big as marbles. The men broke for the shelter of a hangar, where Ted's information, meager as it was, was avidly seized upon, for sensational news is rare below the Tropic of Cancer. But none of them yet realized just how sensational it was.

It was three days before Ted, and the rest of the world as well, began to understand in part what had happened. This was after hours of effort at Belize had finally raised Havana on the beam, and Ted had reported through to old Asa Gaunt, his chief at Washington. He had been agreeably surprised by the promptness of the reply ordering him instantly to the Capital; that meant a taste of the pleasant life that Washington reserved for young departmentals, and most of all, it meant a glimpse of Kay Lovell after two months of letter-writing. So he had flown the Colquist gayly across Yucatan Channel, left it at Havana, and was now comfortably settled in a huge Caribbean plane bound for Washington, boring steadily north through a queerly misty mid-October morning.

At the moment, however, his thoughts were not of Kay. He was reading a grim newspaper account of the catastrophe, and wondering what thousand-to-one shot had brought him unscathed through the very midst of it. For the disaster overshadowed into insignificance such little disturbances as the Yellow River flood in China, the eruption of Krakatoa, the holocaust of Mount Pelee, or even the great Japanese earthquake of 1923, or any other terrible visitation ever inflicted on a civilized race.

For the Ring of Fire, that vast volcanic circle that surrounds the Pacific Ocean, perhaps the last unhealed scars of the birth throes of the Moon, had burst into flame. Aniakchak in Alaska had blown its top away, Fujiyama had vomited lava, on the Atlantic side La Soufriere and the terrible Pelee had awakened again.

But these were minor. It was at the two volcanic foci, in Java and Central America, that the fire-mountains had really shown their powers. What had happened in Java was still a mystery, but on the Isthmus—that was already too plain. From Mosquito Bay to the Rio Coco, there was—ocean! Half of Panama, seven-eighths of Nicaragua—and as for Costa Rica, that country was as if it had never been. The Canal was a wreck, but Ted grinned a wry grin at the thought that it was now as unnecessary as a pyramid. North and

South America had been cut adrift, and the Isthmus, the land that had once known Atlantis, had gone to join it.

In Washington Ted reported at once to Asa Gaunt. That dry Texan questioned him closely concerning his experience, grunted disgustedly at the paucity of information, and then ordered him tersely to attend a meeting at his office in the evening. There remained a full afternoon to devote to Kay, and Ted lost little time in so devoting it.

He didn't see her alone. Washington, like the rest of the world, was full of excitement because of the earthquake, but in Washington more than elsewhere the talk was less of the million and a half deaths and more largely of the other consequences. After all, the bulk of the deaths had been among the natives, and it was a sort of remote tragedy, like the perishing of so many Chinese. It affected only those who had friends or relatives in the stricken region, and these were few in number.

But at Kay's home Ted encountered an excited group arguing physical results. Obviously, the removal of the bottleneck of the Canal strengthened the naval power of the United States enormously. No need now to guard the vulnerable Canal so intensively. The whole fleet could stream abreast through the four hundred mile gap left by the subsidence. Of course the country would lose the revenues of the toll-charges, but that was balanced by the cessation of the expense of fortifying and guarding.

Ted fumed until he managed a few moments of greeting with Kay alone. Once that was concluded to his satisfaction, he joined the discussion as eagerly as the rest. But no one even considered the one factor in the whole catastrophe that could change the entire history of the world.

At the evening meeting Ted stared around him in surprise. He recognized all those present, but the reasons for their presence were obscure. Of course there was Asa Gaunt, head of the Geological Survey, and of course there was Golsborough, Secretary of the Interior, because the Survey was one of his departments. But what was Maxwell, joint Secretary of War and the Navy, doing there? And why was silent John Parish, Secretary of State, frowning down at his shoes in the corner?

Asa Gaunt cleared his throat and began. "Do any of you like eels?" he asked soberly.

There was a murmur. "Why, I do," said Golsborough, who had once been Consul at Venice. "What about it?"

"This—that you'd better buy some and eat 'em tomorrow. There won't be any more eels."

"No more eels?"

"No more eels. You see, eels breed in the Sargasso Sea, and there won't be any Sargasso Sea."

"What is this?" growled Maxwell. "I'm a busy man. No more Sargasso Sea, huh!"

"You're likely to be busier soon," said Asa Gaunt dryly. He frowned. "Let me ask one other question. Does anyone here know what spot on the American continent is opposite London, England?"

Golsborough shifted impatiently, "I don't see the trend of this, Asa," he grunted, "but my guess is that New York City and London are nearly in the same latitude. Or maybe New York's a little to the north, since I know its climate is somewhat colder."

"Hah!" said Asa Gaunt. "Any disagreement?"

There was none. "Well," said the head of the Survey, "you're all wrong, then. London is about one thousand miles north of New York. It's in the latitude of southern Labrador!"

"Labrador! That's practically the Arctic!"

Asa Gaunt pulled down a large map on the wall behind him, a Mercator projection of the world.

"Look at it," he said. "New York's in the latitude of Rome, Italy. Washington's opposite Naples. Norfolk's level with Tunis in Africa, and Jacksonville with the Sahara Desert. And gentlemen, these facts lead to the conclusion that next summer is going to see the wildest war in the history of the world!"

Even Ted, who knew his superior well enough to swear to his sanity, could not resist a glance at the faces of the others, and met their eyes with full understanding of the suspicion in them.

Maxwell cleared his throat. "Of course, of course," he said gruffly. "So there'll be a war and no more eels. That's very easy to follow, but I believe I'll ask you gentlemen to excuse me. You see, I don't care for eels."

"Just a moment more," said Asa Gaunt. He began to speak, and little by little a grim understanding dawned on the four he faced.

Ted remained after the appalled and sobered group had departed. His mind was too chaotic as yet for other occupations, and it was already too late in the evening to find Kay, even had he dared with these oppressive revelations weighing on him.

"Are you sure?" he asked nervously. "Are you quite certain?

"Well, let's go over it again," grunted Asa Gaunt, turning to the map. He swept his hand over the white lines drawn in the Pacific Ocean. "Look here. This is the Equatorial Counter Current, sweeping east to wash the shores of Guatemala, Salvador, Honduras, Nicaragua, Costa Rica, and Panama."

"I know. I've flown over every square mile of that coast."

"Uh." The older man turned to the blue-mapped expanse of the Atlantic. "And here," he resumed, "is the North Equatorial Drift, coming west out of the Atlantic to sweep around Cuba into the Gulf, and to emerge as—the Gulf Stream. It flows at an average speed of three knots per hour, is sixty miles broad, a hundred fathoms deep, and possesses, to start with, an average temperature of 50°. And here it meets the Labrador Current and turns east to carry warmth to all of Western Europe. That's why England is habitable; that's why southern France is semi-tropical; that's why men can live even in Norway and Sweden. Look at Scandinavia, Ted; it's in the latitude of central Greenland, level with Baffin Bay. Even Eskimos have difficulty scraping a living on Baffin Island."

"I know," said Ted in a voice like a groan. "But are you certain about—the rest of this?"

"See for yourself," growled Asa Gaunt. "The barrier's down now. The Equatorial Counter Current, moving two knots per hour, will sweep right over what used to be Central America and strike the North Equatorial Drift just south of Cuba. Do you see what will happen—is happening—to the Gulf Stream? Instead of moving northeast along the Atlantic coast, it will flow almost due east, across what used to be the Sargasso Sea. Instead of bathing the shores of Northern Europe, it will strike the Spanish peninsula, just as the current, called the West Wind Drift does now, and instead of veering north it will turn south, along the coast of Africa. At three knots an hour it will take less than three months for the Gulf Stream to deliver its last gallon of warm water to Europe. That brings us to January—and after January, what?"

Ted said nothing.

"Now," resumed Asa Gaunt grimly, "the part of Europe occupied by countries dependent on the Gulf Stream consists of Norway, Sweden, Denmark, Germany, the British Isles, the Netherlands, Belgium, France, and to a lesser extent, several others. Before six months have passed, Ted, you're going to see a realignment of Europe. The Gulf Stream countries are going to be driven together; Germany and France are suddenly going to become bosom friends, and France and Russia, friendly as they are today, are going to be bitter enemies. Do you see why?"

"N—no."

"Because the countries I've named now support over two hundred million inhabitants. Two hundred million, Ted! And without the Gulf Stream, when England and Germany have the climate of Labrador, and France of Newfoundland, and Scandinavia of Baffin Land—how many people can those regions support then? Three or four million, perhaps, and that with difficulty. Where will the others go?"

"Where?"

"I can tell you where they'll try to go. England will try to unload its surplus population on its colonies. India's hopelessly overcrowded, but South Africa, Canada, Australia, and New Zealand can absorb some. About twenty-five of its fifty millions, I should estimate, because Canada's a northern country and Australia desert in a vast part of it. France has Northern Africa, already nearly as populous as it can be. The others—well, you guess, Ted."

"I will. Siberia, South America, and—the United States!"

"A good guess. That's why Russia and France will no longer be the best of friends. South America is a skeleton continent, a shell. The interior is unfit for white men, and so—it leaves Siberia and North America. What a war's in the making!"

"It's almost unbelievable!" muttered Ted. "Just when the world seemed to be settling down, too."

"Oh, it's happened before," observed Asa Gaunt. "This isn't the only climatic change that brought on war. It was decreasing rainfall in central Asia that sent the Huns scouring Europe, and probably the Goths and Vandals as well. But it's never happened to two hundred million civilized people before!" He paused. "The newspapers are all shrieking about the million and a half deaths in Central America. By this time next year they'll have forgotten that a million and a half deaths ever rated a headline!"

"But good Lord!" Ted burst out. "Isn't there anything to be done about it?"

"Sure, sure," said Asa Gaunt. "Go find a nice tame earthquake that will raise back the forty thousand square miles the last one sunk. That's all you have to do, and if you can't do that, Maxwell's suggestion is the next best: build submarines and submarines. They can't invade a country if they can't get to it."

Asa Gaunt was beyond doubt the first man in the world to realize the full implications of the Central American disaster, but he was not very much ahead of the brilliant Sir Phineas Grey of the Royal Society. Fortunately (or unfortunately, depending on which shore of the Atlantic you call home), Sir Phineas was known to the world of journalism as somewhat of a sensationalist, and his warning was treated by the English and Continental newspapers as on a par with those recurrent predictions of the end of the world. Parliament noticed the warning just once, when Lord Rathmere rose in the Upper House to complain of the unseasonably warm weather and to suggest dryly that the Gulf Stream be turned off a month early this year. But now and again some oceanographer made the inside pages by agreeing with Sir Phineas.

So Christmas approached very quietly, and Ted, happy enough to be stationed in Washington, spent his days in routine topographical work in the office and his evenings, as many as she permitted, with Kay Lovell. And she did permit an increasing number, so that the round of gaiety during the holidays found them on the verge of engagement. They were engaged so far as the two of them were concerned, and only awaited a propitious moment to inform Sir Joshua, whose approval Kay felt, with true English conservatism, was a necessity.

Ted worried often enough about the dark picture Asa Gaunt had drawn, but an oath of secrecy kept him from ever mentioning it to Kay. Once, when she had casually brought up the subject of Sir Phineas Grey and his warning, Ted had stammered some inanity and hastily switched the subject. But with the turn of the year and January, things began to change.

It was on the fourteenth that the first taste of cold struck Europe. London shivered for twenty-four hours in the unheard-of temperature of twenty below zero, and Paris argued and gesticulated about its *grands froids*. Then the high pressure area moved eastward and normal temperatures returned.

But not for long. On the twenty-first another zone of frigid temperature came drifting in on the westerlies, and the English and Continental papers, carefully filed at the Congressional Library, began to betray a note of panic. Ted read the editorial comments avidly: of course Sir Phineas Grey was crazy; of course he was—but just suppose he were right. Just suppose he were. Wasn't it unthinkable that the safety and majesty of Germany (or France or England or Belgium, depending on the particular capital whence the paper came) was subject to the disturbances of a little strip of land seven thousand miles away? Germany (or France, *et al*) must control its own destiny.

With the third wave of Arctic cold, the tone became openly fearful. Perhaps Sir Phineas was right. What then? What was to be done? There were rumblings and mutterings in Paris and Berlin, and even staid Oslo witnessed a riot, and conservative London as well. Ted began to realize that Asa Gaunt's predictions were founded on keen judgment; the German government made an openly friendly gesture toward France in a delicate border matter, and France reciprocated with an equally indulgent note. Russia protested and was politely ignored; Europe was definitely realigning itself, and in desperate haste.

But America, save for a harassed group in Washington, had only casual interest in the matter. When reports of suffering among the poor began to come during the first week in February, a drive was launched to provide relief funds, but it met with only nominal success. People just weren't interested; a cold winter lacked the dramatic power of a flood, a fire, or an earthquake. But the papers reported in increasing anxiety that the immigration quotas, unapproached for a half a dozen years, were full again; there was the beginning of an exodus from the Gulf Stream countries.

By the second week in February stark panic had gripped Europe, and echoes of it began to penetrate even self-sufficient America. The realignment of the Powers was definite and open now, and Spain,

Italy, the Balkans, and Russia found themselves herded together, facing an ominous thunderhead on the north and west. Russia instantly forgot her longstanding quarrel with Japan, and Japan, oddly, was willing enough to forget her own grievances. There was a strange shifting of sympathies; the nations which possessed large and thinly populated areas—Russia, the United States, Mexico, and all of South America—were glaring back at a frantic Europe that awaited only the release of summer to launch a greater invasion than any history had recorded. Attila and his horde of Huns—the Mongol waves that beat down on China—even the vast movements of the white race into North and South America—all these were but minor migrations to that which threatened now. Two hundred million people, backed by colossal fighting power, glaring panic-stricken at the empty places of the world. No one knew where the thunderbolt would strike first, but that it would strike was beyond doubt.

While Europe shivered in the grip of an incredible winter, Ted shivered at the thought of certain personal problems of his own. The frantic world found an echo in his own situation, for here was he, America in miniature, and there was Kay Lovell, a small edition of Britannia. Their sympathies clashed like those of their respective nations.

The time for secrecy was over. Ted faced Kay before the fireplace in her home and stared from her face to the cheery fire, whose brightness merely accentuated his gloom.

"Yeah," he admitted. "I knew about it. I've known it since a couple of days after the Isthmus earthquake."

"Then why didn't you tell me? You should have."

"Couldn't. I swore not to tell."

"It isn't fair!" blazed Kay. "Why should it fall on England? I tell you it sickens me even to think of Merecroft standing there in snow, like some old Norse tower. I was born in Warwickshire, Ted, and so was my father, and his father, and his, and all of us back to the time of William the Conqueror. Do you think it's a pleasant thing to think of my mother's rose garden as barren as—as a tundra?"

"I'm sorry," said Ted gently, "but what can I—or anyone—do about it? I'm just glad you're here on this side of the Atlantic, where you're safe."

"Safe!" she flashed. "Yes, I'm safe, but what about my people? I'm safe because I'm in America, the lucky country, the chosen land!

Why did this have to happen to England? The Gulf Stream washes your shores too. Why aren't Americans shivering and freezing and frightened and hopeless, instead of being warm and comfortable and indifferent? Is that fair?"

"The Gulf Stream," he explained miserably, "doesn't affect our climate so definitely because in the first place we're much farther south than Europe and in the second place our prevailing winds are from the west, just as England's. But our winds blow from the land to the Gulf Stream, and England's from the Gulf Stream to the land."

"But it's not fair! It's not fair!"

"Can I help it, Kay?"

"Oh, I suppose not," she agreed in suddenly weary tones, and then, with a resurgence of anger, "But you people can do something about it! Look here! Listen to this!"

She spied a week-old copy of the London Times, fingered rapidly through it, and turned on Ted. "Listen—just listen! *'And in the name of humanity it is not asking too much to insist that our sister nation open her gates to us. Let us settle the vast areas where now only Indian tribes hunt and buffalo range. We would not be the, only ones to gain by such a settlement, for we would bring to the new country a sane, industrious, law-abiding citizenry, no harborers of highwaymen and gangsters—a point well worth considering. We would bring a great new purchasing public for American manufacturers, carrying with us all our portable wealth. And finally, we would provide a host of eager defenders in the war for territory, a war that now seems inevitable. Our language is one with theirs; surely this is the logical solution, especially when one remembers that the state of Texas alone contains land enough to supply two acres to every man, woman, and child on earth!'*" She paused and stared defiantly at Ted. "Well?"

He snorted. "Indians and buffalo!" he snapped. "Have you seen either one in the United States?"

"No, but—"

"And as for Texas, sure there's enough land there for two acres to everybody in the world, but why didn't your editor mention that two acres won't even support a cow over much of it? The Llano Estacado's nothing but an alkali desert, and there's a scarcity of water in lots of the rest of it. On that argument, you ought to move to Greenland; I'll bet there's land enough there for six acres per person!"

"That may be true, but—"

"And as for a great new purchasing public, your portable wealth is gold and paper money, isn't it? The gold's all right, but what good is a pound if there's no British credit to back it? Your great new public would simply swell the ranks of the unemployed until American industry could absorb them, which might take years! And meanwhile wages would go down to nothing because of an enormous surplus of labor, and food and rent would go sky high because of millions of extra stomachs to feed and bodies to shelter."

"All right!" said Kay bleakly. "Argue all you wish. I'll even concede that your arguments are right, but there's one thing I know is wrong, and that's leaving fifty million English people to starve and freeze and suffer in a country that's been moved, as far as climate goes, to the North Pole. Why, you even get excited over a newspaper story about one poor family in an unheated hovel! Then what about a whole nation whose furnace has gone out?"

"What," countered Ted grimly, "about the seven or eight other nations whose furnaces have also gone out?"

"But England deserves priority!" she blazed. "You took your language from us, your literature, your laws, your whole civilization. Why, even now you ought to be nothing but an English colony! That's all you are, if you want the truth!"

"We think differently. Anyway, you know as well as I that the United States can't open the door to one nation and exclude the others. It must be all or none, and that means—none!"

"And that means war," she said bitterly. "Oh, Ted! I can't help the way I feel. I have people over there—aunts, cousins, friends. Do you think I can stand indifferently aside while they're ruined? Although they're ruined already, as far as that goes. Land's already dropped to nothing there. You can't sell it at any price now."

"I know. I'm sorry, Kay, but it's no one's fault. No one's to blame."

"And so no one needs to do anything about it, I suppose. Is that your nice American theory?"

"You know that isn't fair! What can we do?"

"You could let us in! As it is we'll have to fight our way in, and you can't blame us!"

"Kay, no nation and no group of nations can invade this country. Even if our navy were utterly destroyed, how far from the sea do you think a hostile army could march? It would be Napoleon in Russia all over again; your army marches in and is swallowed up. And where is Europe going to find the food to support an invading army? Do you think it could live on the land as it moved? I tell you no sane nation would try that!"

"No sane nation, perhaps!" she retorted fiercely. "Do you think you're dealing with sane nations?"

He shrugged gloomily.

"They're desperate!" she went on. "I don't blame them. Whatever they do, you've brought it on yourselves. Now you'll be fighting all of Europe, when you could have the British navy on your side. It's stupid. It's worse than stupid; it's selfish!"

"Kay," he said miserably, "I can't argue with you. I know how you feel, and I know it's a hell of a situation. But even if I agreed with everything you've said—which I don't—what could I do about it? I'm not the President and I'm not Congress. Let's drop the argument for this evening, honey; it's just making you unhappy."

"Unhappy! As if I could ever be anything else when everything I value, everything I love, is doomed to be buried under Arctic snow."

"Everything, Kay?" he asked gently. "Haven't you forgotten that there's something for you on this side of the Atlantic as well?"

"I haven't forgotten anything," she said coldly. "I said everything, and I mean it. America! I hate America. Yes, and I hate Americans too!"

"Kay!"

"And what's more," she blazed, "I wouldn't marry an American if he—if he could rebuild the Isthmus! If England's to freeze, I'll freeze with her, and if England's to fight, her enemies are mine!"

She rose suddenly to her feet, deliberately averted her eyes from his troubled face, and stalked out of the room.

Sometimes, during those hectic weeks in February, Ted wormed his way into the Visitor's Gallery in one or the other Congressional house. The out-going Congress, due to stand for re-election in the fall, was the focal point of the dawning hysteria in the nation, and was battling sensationally through its closing session. Routine matters were ignored, and day after day found both houses considering the unprecedented emergency with a sort of appalled inability to act in any effective unison. Freak bills of all description were read, considered, tabled, reconsidered, put to a second reading, and tabled again. The hard-money boom of a year earlier had swept in a Conservative majority in the off-year elections, but they had no real policy to offer, and the proposals of the minority group of Laborites and Leftists were voted down without substitutes being suggested.

Some of the weirdest bills in all the weird annals of Congress appeared at this time. Ted listened in fascination to the Leftist proposal that each American family adopt two Europeans, splitting its income into thirds; to a suggestion that Continentals be advised to undergo voluntary sterilization, thus restraining the emergency to the time of one generation; to a fantastic paper money scheme of the Senator from the new state of Alaska, that was to provide a magic formula to permit Europe to purchase its livelihood without impoverishing the rest of the world. There were suggestions of outright relief, but the problem of charity to two hundred million people was so obviously staggering that this proposal at least received little attention. But there were certain bills that passed both houses without debate, gaining the votes of Leftists, Laborites, and Conservatives alike; these were the grim appropriations for submarines, super-bombers and interceptors, and aircraft-carriers.

Those were strange, hectic days in Washington. Outwardly there was still the same gay society that gathers like froth around all great capitals, and Ted, of course, being young and decidedly not unattractive, received his full share of invitations. But not even the least sensitive could have overlooked the dark undercurrents of hysteria that flowed just beneath the surface. There was dancing, there was gay dinner conversation, there was laughter, but beneath all of it was fear. Ted was not the only one to notice that the diplomatic representatives of the Gulf Stream countries were conspicuous by their absence from all affairs save those of such importance that their presence was a matter of policy. And even then, incidents occurred; he was present when the Minister from France stalked angrily from the room because some hostess had betrayed the poor taste of permitting her dance orchestra to play a certain popular number called "The Gulf Stream Blues." Newspapers carefully refrained from mentioning the occurrence, but Washington buzzed with it for days.

Ted looked in vain for Kay. Her father appeared when appearance was necessary, but Ted had not seen the girl since her abrupt dismissal of him, and in reply to his inquiries, Sir Joshua granted only the gruff and double-edged explanation that she was "indisposed." So Ted worried and fumed about her in vain, until he scarcely knew whether his own situation or that of the world was more important. In the last analysis, of course, the two were one and the same.

The world was like a crystal of nitrogen iodide, waiting only the drying-out of summer to explode. Under its frozen surface Europe was seething like Mounts Erebus and Terror that blaze in the ice of Antarctica. Little Hungary had massed its army on the west, beyond doubt to oppose a similar massing on the part of the Anschlus. Of this particular report, Ted heard Maxwell say with an air of relief that it indicated that Germany had turned her face inland; it meant one less potential enemy for America. But the maritime nations were another story, and especially mighty Britain, whose world-girdling fleet was gathering day by day in the Atlantic. That was a crowded ocean indeed, for on its westward shore was massed the American battle fleet, built at last to treaty strength, and building far beyond it, while north and south piled every vessel that could raise a pound of steam, bearing those fortunates who could leave their European homes to whatever lands hope called them. Africa and Australia, wherever Europe had colonies, were receiving an unheard of stream of immigrants. But this stream was actually only the merest trickle, composed of those who possessed sufficient liquid wealth to encompass the journey. Untold millions remained chained to their homes, bound by the possession of unsalable lands, or by investments in business, or by sentiment, or by the simple lack of sufficient funds to buy passage for families. And throughout all of the afflicted countries were those who clung stubbornly to hope, who believed even in the grip of that unbelievable winter that the danger would pass, and that things would come right in the end.

Blunt, straightforward little Holland was the first nation to propose openly a wholesale transfer of population. Ted read the note, or at least the version of it given the press on February 21st. In substance it simply repeated the arguments Kay had read from the London paper—the plea to humanity, the affirmation of an honest and industrious citizenry, and the appeal to the friendship that had always existed between the two nations; and the communication closed with a request for an immediate reply because of "the urgency of the situation." And an immediate reply was forthcoming.

This was also given to the press. In suave and very polished diplomatic language it pointed out that the United States could hardly admit nationals of one country while excluding those of others. Under the terms of the National Origins Act, Dutch immigrants would be welcomed to the full extent of their quota. It was even possible that the quota might be increased, but it was not conceivable that it could be removed entirely. The note was in effect a suave, dignified, diplomatic 'No.'

March drifted in on a southwest wind. In the Southern states it brought spring, and in Washington a faint forerunner of balmy weather to come, but to the Gulf Stream countries it brought no release from the Arctic winter that had fallen on them with its icy mantle. Only in the Basque country of Southern France, where vagrant winds slipped at intervals across the Pyrenees with the warm breath of the deflected Stream, was there any sign of the relaxing of that frigid clutch. But that was a promise; April would come, and May—and the world flexed its steel muscles for war.

Everyone knew now that war threatened. After the first few notes and replies, no more were released to the press, but everyone knew that notes, representatives, and communiqués were flying between the powers like a flurry of white doves, and everyone knew, at least in Washington, that the tenor of those notes was no longer dove-like. Now they carried brusque demands and blunt refusals.

Ted knew as much of the situation as any alert observer, but no more. He and Asa Gaunt discussed it endlessly, but the dry Texan, having made his predictions and seen them verified, was no longer in the middle of the turmoil, for his bureau had, of course, nothing to do with the affair now. So the Geological Survey staggered on under a woefully reduced appropriation, a handicap shared by every other governmental function that had no direct bearing on defense.

All the American countries, and for that matter, every nation save those in Western Europe, were enjoying a feverish, abnormal, hectic boom. The flight of capital from Europe, and the frantic cry for food, had created a rush of business, incessant, avid, and exports mounted unbelievably. In this emergency, France and the nations under her hegemony, those who had clung so stubbornly, to gold ever since the second revaluation of the franc, were now at a marked advantage, since their money would buy more wheat, more cattle, and more coal. But the paper countries, especially Britain, shivered and froze in stone cottage and draughty manor alike.

On the eleventh of March, that memorable Tuesday when the thermometer touched twenty-eight below in London, Ted reached a decision toward which he had been struggling for six weeks. He was going to swallow his pride and see Kay again. Washington was buzzing with rumors that Sir Joshua was to be recalled, that diplomatic relations with England were to be broken as they had already been broken with France. The entire nation moved about its daily business in an air of tense expectancy, for the break with France meant little in view of that country's negligible sea power, but now, if the colossus of the British navy were to align itself with the French army—.

But what troubled Ted was a much more personal problem. If Sir Joshua Lovell were recalled to London, that meant that Kay would accompany him, and once she were caught in the frozen Hell of Europe, he had a panicky feeling that she was lost to him forever. When war broke, as it surely must, there would go his last hope of ever seeing her again. Europe, apparently, was doomed, for it seemed impossible that any successful invasion could be carried on over thousands of miles of ocean, but if he could save the one fragment of Europe that meant everything to him, if he could somehow save Kay Lovell, it was worth the sacrifice of pride or of anything else. So he called one final time on the telephone, received the same response from an unfriendly maid, and then left the almost idle office and drove directly to her home.

The same maid answered his ring. "Miss Lovell is not in," she said coldly. "I told you that when you telephoned."

"I'll wait," returned Ted grimly, and thrust himself through the door. He seated himself stolidly in the hall, glared back at the maid, and waited. It was no more than five minutes before Kay herself appeared, coming wearily down the steps.

"I wish you'd leave," she said. She was pallid and troubled, and he felt a great surge of sympathy.

"I won't leave."

"What do I have to do to make you go away? I don't want to see you, Ted."

"If you'll talk to me just half an hour, I'll go." She yielded listlessly, leading the way into the living room where a fire still crackled in cheerful irony. "Well?" she asked.

"Kay, do you love me?"

"I—No, I don't!"

"Kay," he persisted gently, "do you love me enough to marry me and stay here where you're safe?"

Tears glistened suddenly in her brown eves. "I hate you," she said. "I hate all of you. You're a nation of murderers. You're like the East Indian Thugs, only they call murder religion and you call it patriotism."

"I won't even argue with you, Kay. I can't blame you for your viewpoint, and I can't blame you for not understanding mine. But—do you love me?"

"All right," she said in sudden weariness. "I do."

"And will you marry me?"

"No. No, I won't marry you, Ted. I'm going back to England."

"Then will you marry me first? I'll let you go back, Kay, but afterwards—if there's any world left after what's coming—I could bring you back here. I'll have to fight for what I believe in, and I won't ask you to stay with me during the time our nations are enemies, but afterwards, Kay—if you're my wife I could bring you here. Don't you see?"

"I see, but—no."

"Why, Kay? You said you loved me."

"I do," she said almost bitterly. "I wish I didn't, because I can't marry you hating your people the way I do. If you were on my side, Ted, I swear I'd marry you tomorrow, or today, or five minutes from now—but as it is, I can't. It just wouldn't be fair."

"You'd not want me to turn traitor," he responded gloomily. "One thing I'm sure of, Kay, is that you couldn't love a traitor." He paused. "Is it goodbye, then?"

"Yes." There were tears in her eyes again. "It isn't public yet, but father has been recalled. Tomorrow he presents his recall to the Secretary of State, and the day after we leave for England. This is goodbye."

"That does mean war!" he muttered. "I've been hoping that in spite of everything—God knows I'm sorry, Kay. I don't blame you for the way you feel. You couldn't feel differently and still be Kay Lovell, but—it's damned hard. It's damned hard!"

She agreed silently. After a moment she said, "Think of my part of it, Ted—going back to a home that's like—well, the Rockefeller Mountains in Antarctica. I tell you, I'd rather it had been England that sunk into the sea! That would have been easier, much easier than this. If it had sunk until the waves rolled over the very peak of Ben Macduhl—" She broke off.

"The waves are rolling over higher peaks than Ben Macduhl," he responded drearily. "They're—" Suddenly he paused, staring at Kay with his jaw dropping and a wild light in his eyes!

"The Sierra Madre!" he bellowed, in such a roaring voice that the girl shrank away. "The Mother range! The Sierra Madre! The Sierra Madre!"

"Wh—what?" she gasped.

"The Sierra—! Listen to me, Kay! Listen to me! Do you trust me! Will you do something—something for both of us? Us? I mean for the world! Will you?"

"I—I—."

"I know you will! Kay, keep your father from presenting his recall! Keep him here another ten days—even another week. Can you?"

"How? How can I?"

"I don't know. Any way at all. Get sick. Get too sick to travel, and beg him not to present his papers until you can leave. Or—or tell him that the United States will make his country an alternate proposal in a few days. That's the truth. I swear that's true, Kay."

"But—but he won't believe me!"

"He's got to! I don't care how you do it, but keep him here! And have him report to the Foreign Office that new developments—vastly important developments—have come up. That's true, Kay."

"True? Then what are they?"

"There isn't time to explain. Will you do what I ask?"

"I'll try!"

"You're—well you're marvelous!" he said huskily. He stared into her tragic brown eyes, kissed her lightly, and rushed away.

Asa Gaunt was scowling down at a map of the dead Salton Sea when Ted dashed unannounced into the office. The rangy Texan looked up with a dry smile at the unceremonious entry.

"I've got it!" yelled Ted.

"A bad case of it," agreed Asa Gaunt. "What's the diagnosis?"

"No, I mean—Say, has the Survey taken soundings over the Isthmus?"

"The *Dolphin's* been there for weeks," said the older man. "You know you can't map forty thousand square miles of ocean bed during the lunch hour."

"Where," shouted Ted, "are they sounding?"

"Over Pearl Cay Point, Bluefields, Monkey Point, and San Juan del Norte, of course. Naturally they'll sound the places where there were cities first of all."

"Oh, naturally!" said Ted, suppressing his voice to a tense quiver. "And where is the *Marlin*?"

"Idle at Newport News. We can't operate both of them under this year's budget."

"To hell with the budget!" flared Ted. "Get the *Marlin* there too, and any other vessel that can carry an electric plumb!"

"Yes, sir—right away, sir," said Asa Gaunt dryly. "When did you relieve Golsborough as Secretary of the Interior, Mr. Welling?"

"I'm sorry," replied Ted. "I'm not giving orders, but I've thought of something. Something that may get all of us out of this mess we're in."

"Indeed? Sounds mildly interesting. Is it another of these international fiat-money schemes?"

"No!" blazed Ted. "It's the Sierra Madre! Don't you see?"

"In words of one syllable, no."

"Then listen! I've flown over every square mile of the sunken territory. I've mapped and photographed it, and I've laid out the geodetics. I know that buried strip of land as well as I know the humps and hollows in my own bed."

"Congratulations, but what of it?"

"This!" snapped Ted. He turned to the wall, pulled down the topographical map of Central America, and began to speak. After a while Asa Gaunt leaned forward in his chair and a queer light gathered in his pale blue eyes.

What follows has been recorded and interpreted in a hundred

ways by numberless historians. The story of the *Dolphin* and the *Marlin*, sounding in frantic haste the course of the submerged Cordilleras, is in itself romance of the first order. The secret story of diplomacy, the holding of Britain's neutrality so that the lesser sea powers dared not declare war across three thousand miles of ocean, is another romance that will never be told openly. But the most fascinating story of all, the building of the Cordilleran Inter-continental Wall, has been told so often that it needs little comment.

The soundings traced the irregular course of the sunken Sierra Madre mountains. Ted's guess was justified; the peaks of the range were not inaccessibly far below the surface. A route was found where the Equatorial Counter Current swept over them with a depth at no point greater than forty fathoms, and the building of the Wall began on March the 31st, began in frantic haste, for the task utterly dwarfed the digging of the abandoned Canal itself. By the end of September some two hundred miles had been raised to sea-level, a mighty rampart seventy-five feet broad at its narrowest point, and with an extreme height of two hundred and forty feet and an average of ninety.

There was still almost half to be completed when winter swept out of the north over a frightened Europe, but the half that had been built was the critical sector. On one side washed the Counter Current, on the other the Equatorial Drift, bound to join the Gulf Stream in its slow march toward Europe, And the mighty Stream, traced by a hundred oceanographic vessels, veered slowly northward again, and bathed first the shores of France, then of England, and finally of the high northern Scandinavian Peninsula. Winter came drifting in as mildly as of old, and a sigh of relief went up from every nation in the world.

Ostensibly the Cordilleran Inter-continental Wall was constructed by the United States. A good many of the more chauvinistic newspapers bewailed the appearance of Uncle Sam as a sucker again, paying for the five hundred million dollar project for the benefit of Europe. No one noticed that there was no Congressional appropriation for the purpose, nor has anyone since wondered why the British naval bases on Trinidad, Jamaica, and at Belize have harbored so large a portion of His Majesty's Atlantic Fleet. Nor, for that matter, has anyone inquired why the dead war debts were so suddenly exhumed and settled so cheerfully by the European powers.

A few historians and economists may suspect. The truth is that the Cordilleran Inter-continental Wall has given the United States a world hegemony, in fact almost a world empire. From the south tip of Texas, from Florida, from Puerto Rico, and from the otherwise useless Canal Zone, a thousand American planes could bomb the Wall into ruin. No European nation dares risk that.

Moreover, no nation in the world, not even in the orient where the Gulf Stream has no climatic influence, dares threaten war on America. If Japan, for instance, should so much as speak a hostile word, the whole military might of Europe would turn against her. Europe simply cannot risk an attack on the Wall, and certainly the first effort of a nation at war with the United States would be to force a passage through the Wall.

In effect the United States can command the armies of Europe with a few bombing planes, though not even the most ardent pacifists have yet suggested that experiment. But such are the results of the barrier officially known as the Cordilleran Intercontinental Wall, but called by every newspaper after its originator, the Welling Wall.

It was mid-summer before Ted had time enough to consider marriage and a honeymoon. He and Kay spent the latter on the Caribbean, cruising that treacherous sea in a sturdy fifty-foot sloop lent for the occasion by Asa Gaunt and the Geological Survey. They spent a good share of the time watching the great dredges and construction vessels working desperately at the task of adding millions of cubic yards to the peaks of the submarine range that was once the Sierra Madre. And one day as they lay on the deck in swimming suits, bent on acquiring a tropical tan, Ted asked her a question.

"By the way," he began, "you've never told me how you managed to keep Sir Joshua in the States. That stalled off war just long enough for this thing to be worked out and presented. How'd you do it?"

Kay dimpled. "Oh, first I tried to tell him I was sick. I got desperately sick."

"I knew he'd fall for that."

"But he didn't. He said a sea voyage would help me."

"Then—what did you do?"

"Well, you see be has a sort of idiosyncrasy toward quinine. Ever since his service in India, where he had to take it day after day, he develops what doctors call a quinine rash, and he hasn't taken any for years."

"Well?"

"Don't you see? His before-dinner cocktail had a little quinine in it, and so did his wine, and so did his tea, and the sugar and the salt. He kept complaining that everything he ate tasted bitter to him, and I convinced him that it was due to his indigestion."

"And then?"

"Why, then I brought him one of his indigestion capsules, only it didn't have his medicine in it. It had a nice dose of quinine, and in two hours he was pink as a salmon, and so itchy he couldn't sit still!"

Ted began to laugh. "Don't tell me that kept him there!"

"Not that alone," said Kay demurely. "I made him call in a doctor, a friend of mine who—well, who kept asking me to marry him—and I sort of bribed him to tell father he had—I think it was erysipelas he called it. Something violently contagious, anyway.

"And so—?"

"And so we were quarantined for two weeks! And I kept feeding father quinine to keep up the bluff, and—well, we were very strictly quarantined. He just couldn't present his recall!"

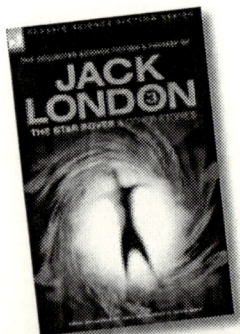

Printed in the United Kingdom
by Lightning Source UK Ltd.
124680UK00001B/205/A

9 781846 770623